the Caravaggio Conspiracy

the Caravaggio Conspiracy

WALTER ELLIS

The Lilliput Press * Dublin

First published 2012 by
THE LILLIPUT PRESS
62–63 Sitric Road, Arbour Hill,
Dublin 7, Ireland
www.lilliputpress.ie

A CIP record for this title is available from
The British Library.

10 9 8 7 6 5 4 3 2 1

ISBN 978 1 84351 198 4

Set in 10.5 on 14 pt Minion by Marsha Swan
Printed in the UK by MPG Books, Bodmin, Cornwall

1*
The future: Rome

The Prophet – peace and blessings be upon Him – was asked, which would fall first, Constantinople or Rome? He replied: 'The city of Heracles [Constantinople] will be conquered first; then Rome' ... The conquest of Rome means that Islam will return to Europe and, insh'Allah, Europeans will convert to the true faith and proclaim Islam in the world.

—Sheikh Yousuf al-Qaradawi,
spiritual leader of the Muslim Brotherhood

The death was expected but the world still wept. The 266th occupant of the Throne of Peter died peacefully in his sleep in the early hours of a Monday morning in June. In his last days, propped up by pillows, unable to greet the crowds from his balcony, he lamented the fact that he had left so much undone. But as his obituaries pointed out, in advance of the Second Coming and the Judgment, no pope's work was ever finished.

The state funeral, conducted in sweltering heat, was a global media event as well as a sacred ritual. The presidents of the United States, Russia and the European Union travelled to Rome to pay their respects and consult on the Islamist violence now sweeping the world. Leaders from Latin America, Africa, the Philippines, Canada, Australia and New Zealand were there, as well as the Secretary General of the United Nations and several reigning monarchs, including those of the United Kingdom and Spain.

Throughout the rites, while police and security cameras scanned the congregation, the officers and men of the Swiss Guard, under the command of Colonel

Otto Studer, stood watch. Alarmists had warned of an Islamist protest of some kind – perhaps even an act of terrorism directed against the Church or visiting world leaders. In fact, the only episode recorded during the mourning period was a small explosion in the thirteenth-century cloisters of San Giovanni in Laterano, the Pope's own cathedral, which injured a gardener and damaged two of the famous twisted columns. The bomb, a makeshift device that had apparently been thrown over the cloister wall, was soon forgotten. Instead, what journalists and visitors commented on was the extent and efficiency of the Vatican machine.

The interment that followed the three-hour-long Requiem Mass was a private ceremony, attended only by close family members and senior Church dignitaries, headed by Bosani. The body was taken from the basilica, via the Door of Death, to the grottoes beneath, where it was transferred to a coffin of cypress wood containing several gold, silver and copper coins equivalent to the years of his reign. The *Rogito*, an official eulogy, signed by leading members of the Curia, was also enclosed. The cypress coffin was set into a second casket, made of zinc. Finally, the two coffins together were placed inside a third, fashioned from elm, which was hammered shut with nails of pure gold. As prayers were said and a single bell tolled, the resulting container, weighing close to half a tonne, was slowly eased into its waiting sarcophagus.

The regret felt at the Pope's passing was compounded for the faithful by the insignificance of his pontificate. It had been hoped that the Holy Father, chosen in succession to Benedict XVI, would inaugurate a period of positive change in the Church, starting with an *ex-cathedra* denunciation of paedophile priests and a review of the rules on clerical celibacy. Instead, he had left it in confusion and disarray. The one undoubted bright spot, observed more keenly than many cared to admit, even within the Curia, was that he had proved not to be the Antichrist, Peter the Roman, as set out in the disputed prophecies of the twelfth-century Irish mystic, St Malachy.

For that, if nothing else, the Church was profoundly grateful.

The funeral bell had ceased to toll. Since prising the Fisherman's Ring from the late Pope's dead finger, Cardinal Lamberto Bosani, Camerlengo, or High Chamberlain, of the Holy Roman Church, was *primus inter pares* within the Sacred College, charged with administering Church business and organizing the papal election. For several minutes, as the Pope's grieving family returned to the basilica, Bosani remained behind, observing with quiet satisfaction as a team of Vatican workmen levered the heavy marble tombstone into place. Then he left quickly. There was work to be done and no time to waste.

2*
April 1602: Rome

Michelangelo Merisi, known as Caravaggio after his home town east of Milan, looked up from his most recent commission, *Death of the Virgin*, intended for the church of Santa Maria della Scala in Trastevere. His model, 23-year-old Anna Bianchini, a striking red-haired courtesan often used by the city's artists, was lying full-length on a kitchen table, with one hand resting on her stomach, the other stretched out on a cushion.

She looked ravishing, but Caravaggio's mind was elsewhere. Earlier in the day he had been insulted by one of the most influential men in Rome. Father Claudio Acquaviva, Superior General of the Society of Jesus, had turned up a little after midday at the home of the banker Ciriaco Mattei and demanded to view his *Supper at Emmaus*, newly completed and still awaiting its final coat of varnish.

The moment when the resurrected Christ revealed himself to two of his disciples in Emmaus was a familiar theme. Of the two versions seen by Mattei, one, by Titian, had struck him as bloodless and stylized, while the other, a Veronese, was almost comically overcrowded, with Christ barely visible among a host of the patron's family seeking his blessing.

But the Caravaggio was breathtaking – worth every baiocco of the 150 scudi Mattei had paid for it. It was, he told its creator, as inspired and brilliant in its execution as anything produced in the last hundred years.

Acquaviva didn't share the banker's judgment. Instead of admiring the canvas, set on an easel next to a window, the black-clad divine had recoiled, claiming it was 'sinful and quite possibly heretical'. The fact that Christ, just prior to his

Ascension, had been portrayed without a beard caused him literally to splutter with indignation.

Caravaggio's nature had once been judged by a Jewish apothecary – a man whose skill extended beyond leeches and potions to the science of the four humours – to be a dangerous mix of choleric and melancholic. On this occasion, as he recalled Acquaviva's splenetic response to his art, the dominant emotion was rage.

'Bloody Jesuits!' he began, causing Anna to roll her eyes. 'I said to him, after he was resurrected, not as a man but as the Saviour of the world, Jesus probably wouldn't have a beard. When you think about it, it was probably the fact he was clean-shaven that made it so difficult for the disciples to recognize him. They'd spent most of the previous three years in his company, yet it was only halfway through the meal that it hit them who he *was*. But Mattei stopped me. Said I'd only make matters worse.'

'Wise man,' said Anna.

'Scared of getting on the wrong side of the Jesuits more like. Do you know what Rubens said about my *Emmaus*? He said it was a work of genius. It humbled him, he said. Not Acquaviva. Christ, no! Treated me like a serving boy. He's supposed to be a humble man – a learned friar, simple in his tastes. Yet the moment I opened my mouth, it was obvious he thought I was lucky to be in the same room as him, breathing the same air. My clothes were a disgrace, he said. My hair was a mess. Who does he think he is? Fucking bigot.'

Anna's eyes widened. 'You want to watch what you say, Michelangelo. The Church runs Rome. For God's sake, it *is* Rome. You'll get yourself into trouble if you go on saying stuff like that about them.'

'Are you saying I'm wrong?'

'I'm not saying nothing. I'm just pointing out that if the *sbirri* come calling, it's no good you telling them the Jesuits are a load of hypocrites.'

The *sbirri*, Rome's corrupt, ineffectual police force, were no friends of the city's artists. Unable, or unwilling, to do much about real crime – murder, burglary, footpads, the ill-treatment of the poor by the Church and nobility – they preferred to concentrate on the crimes that they *could* solve, mainly prostitution, sodomy and drunkenness. Just a week before, the artist had spent a night in the cells of the Tor di Nona, a notorious interrogation centre, after getting into a fight in the Turk's Head tavern. If it hadn't been for the intervention of Cardinal Del Monte, his erstwhile patron, who had known him for years, he could have gone to jail for three months, or even been sent to the galleys.

'I suppose you're right,' he said.

Anna brightened. 'Course I am. And, by the way, Acquaviva wasn't wrong about the way you dress. You're making good money these days, you're one of the most famous painters in Rome. And you're really quite good looking, with those thick lips and ebony eyes. So why not smarten yourself up and buy some decent clothes?' She raised her hand to scratch her nose, causing Caravaggio to look sternly at her.

'Stay still,' he said.

'What? You mean if I don't put my hand back in exactly the same position, you'd paint two of them?'

'*Anna!*'

'Anyway, it's funny what you were saying. 'Cos there was this Dominican, from Venice, came to see me the other day – in town to discuss legal business. He says Rome's an abomination, full of whores and thieves and the worst kinds of priests.'

'Keep still. And he told you this while he was fucking you, did he?'

'Afterwards, matter of fact, while he was picking at some olives and enjoying a glass of wine.'

'Typical. What was his name?'

'I can't tell you that.'

'Why not?'

Anna looked at him with an expression of perfect mock seriousness. 'Priests aren't the only ones with secrets, you know.'

'Oh … right. I forgot about the Knocking Shop Code of Conduct. So what did he say about the clergy?'

'He said there wasn't a sin in Christendom that the priests and bishops of Rome don't commit on a daily basis. Cardinals too. Said it wouldn't surprise him if some of them didn't even believe in Our Lord.'

'That's going a bit far, don't you think?'

'That's what I said.'

'And how did he reply?'

'He stuck his hand between my legs.'

'I'll bet he did.'

'What?'

'Never mind. Stop fidgeting. Remember, you're not only a virgin, you're the Mother of God. You're not supposed to look as if you were born in a bawdy house.'

'You didn't mind last time.'

'When was that?'

'*The Flight into Egypt*. One of my best, if you ask me.'

'Very true,' said Caravaggio. 'But you were younger then.'

Anna glared at him. 'You saying I'm past it?'

A tricky one. After all, she was past twenty now. He remembered how she looked when she posed for the Egyptian painting, holding the baby Jesus to her breast. She had just learned she was pregnant – not by him, as it happened – and the news had filled her with a kind of ... holiness. But then she'd had a miscarriage, all too common in her line of work, which, as it happened, made her perfect for his next commission, the *Penitent Magdalene*. The composition, though more narrowly focused, was practically the same: crouched over, shoulders bent, hands clasped on her lap, her long red hair streaming down her right shoulder. The difference this time was that she was consumed with grief. There was a hole in her life – an emptiness at the heart of her. The awareness she had shown of her loss was not only genuine, it had moved him to tears.

'Well?' she said, holding her pose with obvious difficulty. 'I'm waiting.'

Caravaggio rubbed his nose violently with the knuckles of his left hand. 'Don't be daft, Anna,' he said. 'If anything, you're more beautiful now than you were then. It's just that, these days you ... you know more – and it shows.'

'I should bloody well hope so. In this town, you need a good head on your shoulders, and a long memory, just to survive. Why do you suppose I keep a list of my clients hidden away, along with all their hidden bits – identity marks, if you know what I mean? It's because I don't want no one doing me harm and thinking they can get away with it. The way things are, if you've not got the pox, you've got the plague, and even if you haven't, the *sbirri* want to cut your nose off, or your ears, just 'cos you try to earn a decent living with the gifts God gave you. That's Christian charity for you.'

This made Caravaggio smile. He had always liked Anna. She stood up for herself – didn't let men walk all over her. 'So what about your Dominican?' he asked her. 'The one from Venice. He mention anything about the Turks? Longhi thinks they're getting ready for war.'

Onorio Longhi, from Lombardy, was an architect and a loudmouth and one of Caravaggio's close circle of drinking companions. War and fighting were in his blood.

Anna's eyes widened at the mention of Longhi's name. 'No surprise there,' she said. 'You know what they say about Onorio ... if he's not wearing a sword, it's because he's got a dagger down his tights.'

Caravaggio grinned at the aptness of the observation. 'That's as maybe,' he said. 'But what did the Good Father have to say about it?'

'He said the Turks were building up their navy and he wouldn't be surprised if they sailed on Crete. In that case, he said, it would be up to the Venetians to save the day – as usual. The Pope would just celebrate High Mass and call on divine aid.'

'Sounds about right.' He mixed a little more red for the Virgin's dress. 'Has it ever occurred to you, Anna, that we're only Christians for as long as we keep the Ottomans at bay?'

'Speak for yourself. I was born a Catholic and I'll die a Catholic.'

Caravaggio winked at her. 'Hopefully in your bed,' he said.

She sniffed loudly. 'Can I have a glass of wine?'

'I told you – keep still!'

But she was tired of suffering for his art. She rolled her eyes and let out a sigh. Surreptitiously, while Caravaggio concentrated on his canvas, she moved her right arm away from her abdomen, unlaced her bodice and placed her hand on her newly exposed left breast so that her nipple stood up between her fingers. The painter looked round, exasperated. Then he threw down his brush and leapt on her. She laughed and reminded him that this would cost him extra.

3*
The future: conclave minus 18

Cardinal Bosani swirled the glass of San Felice beneath his nose and breathed in the wine's sensuous perfume. He drew it to his lips but didn't drink. For several seconds he closed his eyes, luxuriating in the headiness of the vintage before resuming his steady scrutiny of the assembled guests. A chill ran round the table as he shifted his gaze from one black-clad archbishop to the next. It was said that when the Camerlengo entered a room, even a crypt, the temperature fell by one degree. A second lengthy pause ensued before he nodded to the grave-faced major-domo standing next to him awaiting his verdict. The flunky bowed, then signalled to the under-waiter at the opposite end that he should begin to pour. Bosani smiled thinly, pleased as always that so small an act of judgment on his part as his assessment of a moderately expensive Tuscan red should be invested by his colleagues with so much … *hope*.

He waited until everyone's glass was full before raising the main business of the day. 'Eminences, we have discussed recent events and reviewed the position of the European Church. It is time to move on. The Holy Father is dead, God rest his soul, and during the *sede vacante* in which the Throne of Peter sits empty, it is our solemn duty to prepare the way for his successor. Naturally, we pray to our father in heaven to guide us to the correct decision. But in advance of the conclave, it will assist us if we can reach a consensus on the manner of man that is needed to carry out the tasks ahead.'

The twelve primates, all European, looked lost in thought.

'We do not live in normal times,' Bosani continued, his baritone voice caressing the ears of his audience as much as the San Felice caressed their throats. 'The world is in crisis, and with the United States once more withdrawn into itself following its withdrawal from Iraq and Afghanistan, and with Pakistan and Iran now in possession of the "Islamic bomb", it is left to us in Europe to give a lead.'

A murmur of approval rose from the lips of most of those present. But not all. Bosani took careful note of the dissenters. 'By Europe, I mean, of course, Christian Europe – Catholic Europe. For two thousand years, the Church has been at the heart of this continent's history. It was the papacy, assisted by the Curia and the College of Cardinals, that made Europe pre-eminent in world affairs.

'This is our legacy. As leaders of the universal Church, we must always be mindful of the needs and contributions of others. We offer grateful thanks for the work of cardinals, bishops and priests of all nations, as well as the Religious of both sexes. These have helped guide our conscience for centuries. Yet it is we, here in Rome, and you as the most senior princes of the European Church, who today must usher our beleagured continent into a new age.'

Halfway around the table on the left-hand side, someone cleared his throat. It was Cardinal Horst Rüttgers, the German primate, appointed by the late pontiff.

Bosani paused in his discourse, twisting his signet ring as he did so. 'Cardinal Rüttgers, is there a matter you wish to raise?'

'Indeed, Camerlengo. It is simply that the conclave is not intended, surely, as an instrument of earthly power. It is true, of course, that our world is troubled, Europe especially so. Our birth rate has fallen alarmingly in recent decades – though not so alarmingly as our attendance at Mass. It is only by virtue of high immigration that our economies are not shrinking. And yet, undeniably, the very immigrants who keep our schools open are neither European nor Christian, but Muslim. Soon, it is said, there will be more worshippers in mosques than in churches.'

Bosani toyed once more with his ring. 'And what is your point, Eminence?'

The German, a clean-cut, elegant figure from the Black Forest, had once been a campaigning bishop in southern Brazil. Since returning to his homeland as Archbishop of Freiburg, he was best known for his pioneering work among car workers in Baden-Württemberg. 'My point,' he said, 'is that in the twenty-first century we in the Church are no longer the arbiters of history. It might even be said that our institutional cover-up of decades of paedophilia within the clergy has rendered us morally bankrupt. It is not for us, as Catholics, to determine which set of beliefs shall be uppermost and which derided and scorned. Today, in a multicultural society, bequeathed to us by fifty years of change, our goal should be to improve the lives and spiritual welfare of all our people. At no stage are we justified in setting white against black or Christian against Muslim.'

A Spanish cardinal from Andalusia opened his mouth to intervene, but Bosani motioned him silent. 'Do you mean, Cardinal Rüttgers, that we should confine ourselves to increasing the numbers attending Mass?'

'The numbers and their welfare,' Rüttgers responded. 'Yes. That would be a start. And it would be appropriate to our calling. We are servants of God, not servants of the state.'

Bosani stared at the faces turned in his direction, then slowly shook his head. A week earlier, he had been Secretary of State and president of the civil administration of the Holy See: the second-most powerful man in the Church. But then the Pope had died and all executive appointments had lapsed – all save one. The Camerlengo, uniquely, remained in place to oversee the election. It was for this reason that Bosani had persuaded His Holiness to grant him the secondary title alongside that of Secretary of State, arguing that it removed one more layer of redundant bureaucracy. He nodded at the memory. That had been especially prescient of him. But time was pressing. The *Novemdiales*, the nine days of mourning, would soon be up. It was time to strike down the idea that the Church was a democracy. He had not, even when he was young, been a patient man. At the age of seventy, he found it next to impossible to tolerate dissent.

'Eminence,' he began, focusing on the German, 'as the naivety of your comment on the deplorable practice of paedophilia reveals, you are new to the workings of the Curia. So I ought not to be surprised to discover that you do not as yet fully appreciate how the work of the Church, as seen from the Holy See, reaches into every area of human activity.'

At this, the German stood up. The sound of his chair scraping on the polished floor caused several to wince. 'That,' he said, 'is a very condescending remark, which I must ask you to withdraw.'

The Italian pursed his lips. 'I was perhaps a little indelicate,' he said. 'But not inaccurate. However, if you are offended, I apologize. Now please resume your chair.'

Rüttgers looked for a second as if he would continue his defiance, then appeared to think better of it. The Camerlengo was, by all accounts, vindictive and unforgiving. To oppose him once his mind was made up was to risk marginalization, usually in the form of an offer from the Vatican that one could not possibly accept.

As soon as Rüttgers sat down, Bosani resumed. 'We live in desperate times, gentlemen. The Church is in turmoil, assailed from within and without. Only last week, a playwright in Rotterdam was seriously injured by a group of thugs after he wrote an article about the growing Islamicization of the Netherlands – where, as I may remind you, nearly a quarter of the population under the age of twenty is now Muslim. A demonstration by the Khilafah Salvation Front outside the European

Parliament in Strasbourg ended in a riot in which a dozen or more police officers were hurt, two of them seriously …'

'As were scores of the demonstrators.' Again, the intervention was from Rüttgers.

Bosani refused to be drawn. 'It is obvious that we must tread carefully and search deeply before making a decision about whom to place on the Throne of Peter. Yet I call upon each of you to use what influence you possess to ensure the election of the candidate who will see the world for what it is – weak, dysfunctional, morally corrupt – and bring order to the chaos that threatens our very existence. Above all, Eminences, Rome must be led by a pope who is ready to confront Islam and establish a limit on the tolerance with which we regard its present incursions into our heartland.'

This last remark, which caused several audible intakes of breath, produced a second intervention, this time from the Archbishop of Dublin, Cardinal Henry McCarthy, a thickset man in his late seventies, with alarming eyebrows and a shock of white hair, for whom the upcoming conclave would be his last. 'What are you saying, Eminence? No one knows better than I the issues that confront our Mother Church in relation to Islam. In the last fifteen years, Catholic Ireland has taken in a huge influx of Muslims and I have become better used than I would wish to interfaith meetings and taking my shoes off before entering a mosque. But to suggest that we in Europe, without sanction from the greater universal Church, should in some sense declare war on the Muslim world has to be asking for trouble.'

'My dear old friend,' said Bosani, throwing up both hands in a gesture of mock surrender. 'Of course not. I am suggesting no such thing.'

'What, then?'

'What I am suggesting is that we need a new pope for a new era, one who is not afraid to speak in particularities and is not a prisoner of political correctness. We need a pope who will speak up for the Catholic and European position, who recognizes the extent of demographic change and the undeniable fact that Islam in the twenty-first century is not going to be wished away. We need a Holy Father who stands up for the Christian heritage and civilization that has been built in Europe over two thousand years of history.'

'You mean a pope ready to call for a crusade?'

Bosani paused before responding. 'Crusade is not a word to be used lightly. It has too many connotations of blood and chaos … to say nothing of failure. But if by crusade you mean steadfast purpose and resolve, directed without pity and without fear at the achievement of Christ's kingdom on Earth, then crusade it is.'

Rüttgers, clad like the others in a black soutane, signifying mourning, shifted uncomfortably in his chair. The Irishman stared out the mullioned window of

Bosani's conference room and began to recite. 'I summon today all these powers between me and those evils; against every cruel merciless power that may oppose my body and soul; against incantations of false prophets; against black laws of pagandom; against false laws of heretics; against craft of idolatry; against spells of witches and smiths and wizards; against every knowledge that corrupts man's body and soul.' He halted and looked at the sea of bewildered faces around the table. 'St Patrick's Breastplate,' he said, by way of explanation. 'Best understood in Irish.' Then he turned to their host. 'It might help, Camerlengo, if we knew who you had in mind.'

Bosani smiled, exposing the tips of his incisors. 'What matters, Eminence, is not who I may have in mind, but who is best suited to do the Lord's work. For guidance on that, I can only recommend that you pray each morning and evening from this day forth, then vote according to your conscience.'

'Amen to that,' said Rüttgers.

As the cardinals dispersed, Bosani's secretary, Father Cesare Visco, tall and thin, from Messina in Sicily, approached his boss. 'Eminence, what are we going to do about Rüttgers? I fear he could spell trouble.'

Bosani eyed his young companion. 'I am aware of it, Cesare. The conclave will take place eighteen days from today. Eighteen days! Up until now we could hope to *persuade* individuals to join us, or at least to give us a hearing. Those who opposed us could gradually be isolated. We no longer have that luxury. There may only be four German cardinals, but Rüttgers is the primate and he could damage us. The Austrian and Swiss churches may also take their lead from him. He is that sort of man, unfortunately. Even more important than his standing in Europe is his following in Latin America. That is what I really worry about. Remind me: how long was it he worked in Porto Alegre?'

Visco carried the histories and voting records of every cardinal elector in his head. 'Seven years,' he said after only a brief reflection. 'He went originally as a pastor to the German-speaking minority, but ended up as a champion of the poor of every ethnic group, with a reputation that spread throughout South America.'

'With its twenty-two cardinal electors. Yes. Just yesterday, the dean said to me that if Rüttgers hadn't gone back to Germany he could easily have been head of the Church in Brazil. He could rally many to his cause.'

'– Who already feel that a Third-World Pope is vital for the Church's future.'

'Precisely.' Bosani paused for several seconds, examining his fingernails. 'I fear that it may be time to provide a small demonstration of the nature of the threat we face.'

'How small?'

'Something that will make headlines. Something to concentrate minds. But nothing too obviously … *horrific*. I don't want the mob rising in the streets. That would be counter-productive. What I have in mind is something more … focused.'

The priest thought for a moment. 'There is always the appeal case in Bologna.'

'Is that still going on?'

'A ruling is expected tomorrow.'

'And the judge?'

'Carlo Minghetti. An Opus Dei member all his adult life. He will uphold the sentences. He may even increase them.'

'I don't doubt it. Men like Minghetti feel they embody both God and the law. But His Honour may yet serve our purpose. Do you follow me?'

'A warning.'

'A sign of the times. Something for Their Eminences to think about as they prepare for the conclave.'

'I shall see to it.'

'Very well. In the meantime, send Franco to me.'

'Franco? Are you sure?'

The Cardinal took off his skullcap and ran his elegant fingers through his thinning crop of black hair. 'Ask him to meet me at the residence after prayers. And one more thing: bring me the files on Cardinals Salgado and Delacroix. Their silence today spoke volumes. It is time they were reminded of their Christian duty. For there is much to be done and they too have their part to play.'

4*
July 1603

Caravaggio called out in the night but nobody heard. Three, sometimes four times a week for the last four years he had dreamed the same terrible dream. It began a little before noon on the morning of 11 September 1599. He was on the Ponte Sant'Angelo to witness the execution of Lucrezia Cenci, her daughter Beatrice and her elder son Giacomo. Following the most intense interrogation and a trial that lasted months, the three adult Cenci had been condemned to death by the Pope for the murder of Lucrezia's villainous husband, Count Francesco. It was a decision that had aroused enromous controversy. Everybody, it seemed, had an opinion. Seated beneath the scaffold on one of the hottest days of a long, hot summer, Caravaggio was sweating profusely. He wished he hadn't come. He need not have done so. He could have stayed away and none would have blamed him. But he had been drawn to the occasion as if by Death himself.

Directly ahead, blotting out the sky, lay the bulk of the Castel Sant'Angelo, dating back to the time of the Emperor Hadrian. If the Muslims ever conquered Rome, it would be here that the last Pope would take his stand. The sun, directly overhead, bore down on a huge crowd made up of city dwellers of every class, as well as foreign observers come to witness the reality of papal justice. One of the two executioners, a giant of a man wearing a leather mask and apron, nudged the other with his elbow and whispered something. The second man, smaller with a scar down one cheek, turned his head and grinned at Caravaggio as if to say, 'Don't forget to put us in the picture.' Next to them on the scaffold, erected on the bridge, stood the instruments of their trade: a long-handled axe, its scythe-like blade glinting dully in the sunlight; a heavy bludgeon inlaid with metal studs; and a set of iron tongs in a chafing dish filled with hot coals. He tried not to look at these, but he was transfixed. To his right, several members of a well-known noble family were being shown to their reserved seats by a young priest. Nuns offered them iced water with lemon juice, and sweetmeats.

Caravaggio tried to avert his eyes from the axe but could not. Moments later, a ripple of excitement ran through the crowd. Twisting round, he was able to make out the tumbril bearing the Cenci to their doom. The cart, drawn by two farm horses, was flanked by armed men, led by a bishop and two hooded members of the Confraternity of St John the Beheaded, known as the Decollati. But it was the small family group that inevitably held Caravaggio's attention. Lucrezia, the mother, who had devised the plot that ended in the murder of her husband, stood between Giacomo and Beatrice. Bernardo, the youngest boy, just twelve years old, forced by papal decree to witness the excecutions, buried his head in his mother's skirts.

Attempting to escape his dream, Caravaggio tried to rise out of his seat. He knew what was going to happen: he had seen it in his dream many times before. But he couldn't move. His legs were paralyzed. The Cenci, hand in hand, were being led past him towards the steps leading up to the scaffold. Behind, in the piazza, the crowd fell silent, as if struck dumb in contemplation of the horror to come.

Everyone in Rome was familiar with the story. The Cenci were one of the greatest noble families of Italy. But Don Francesco was a monster. No woman, nor any girl approaching puberty, was safe from his predations. As well as a rapist, he was a murderer three times over, and a thief whose brutality and greed had landed him in prison several times. In the past, he had always bought his freedom with 'generous' donations to the Church. It was his rape of Beatrice, his step-daughter, in front of her mother that convinced the family that it was time to act. Giacomo, with the support of one of his servants, confronted his father and in the midst of a violent argument stabbed him to death, throwing his body into the street from an upstairs window. Everybody in Rome knew the circumstances of the murder. Nobody doubted the righteousness of the act. What Giacomo and his family failed to take into account was the extreme rapaciousness of Pope Clement VIII, the former Ippolito Aldobrandini.

The Aldobrandini, with their roots in Florence, had profited hugely from their Vatican connections. The Pope's younger cousins, pushed forward by their uncle, had married into the Pamphilj and Farnese families, becoming at a stroke key members of the ruling class. But no one joined the nobility without bringing something to the table. Power and influence were commodities like anything else, traded on the open market. Thus it was that Clement, dismissing pleas for mercy from every corner of Europe, pronounced that the Cenci must pay with their lives for the death of Don Francesco. Their estates, according to a codicil buried in the text, would be forfeit to the Aldobrandini.

No one was surprised by such a display of greed. That was how things were done in the Eternal City. It was the way they had always been done. To the victor the spoils. But the executions themselves were regarded as exceptional. Not since classical times had one entire family been sacrificed in cold blood to serve the interests of another.

By a convention dating back to the time of Leonardo, artists, including the 28-year-old Michelangelo Merissi, had been invited to record the final minutes of the condemned. Meanwhile, from the ramparts of Castel Sant'Angelo, raised above the multitude, the Pope would have an uninterrupted view of the proceedings.

Looking up at the scaffold, locked into his nightmare, Caravaggio watched, appalled, as Beatrice, her hands tied in front of her, halted next to his chair. He had been sketching the headsman and she glanced down, then caught his eye. He turned away. 'Will you sketch me, too?' she asked him. But he didn't – couldn't – reply. One of the Decollati took her gently by the elbow and urged her forward. She mounted the steps behind her mother and older brother. Young Bernardo was held back for a moment, then compelled to follow.

What ensued would never leave the artist, not even for a single day. It haunted his nights. It infused his art. Now, as he turned over and over in his sleep, he saw it all again, as red and bloody as the morning on which it happened.

The mother, Lucrezia, was first to be led to the block. She fainted, and was revived with cold water. Afterwards, she stood tall and unwavering, saying the rosary along with her assigned *Decollato* while unfastening the top of her bodice so that the axe would not become entangled with her clothing. As she knelt down and forward, the executioner looked up towards the distant figure of the Pope, poised like an emperor in his box at the Colosseum. At the same time, the masked *Decollato* placed a wooden board, on which was painted a representation of the martyrdom of St John, in front of the condemned woman's face so that it was the last thing she saw. The Pope nodded. The axe fell and the head of Lucrezia Cenci rolled forward, spurting blood from the neck.

At the same moment, the crowd let out its breath.

The *Decollato* set down his board and from one of his pockets drew out a black silk cloth, in which he wrapped the severed head before carrying it over to a rough coffin in which the second headsman was already depositing the body.

Caravaggio paled and realized that he was trembling. But he couldn't stop staring. Next to die was Beatrice, a famous beauty, her blonde hair tied back, her neck long and inviting, like a swan's. She said her prayers, murmured some words to her younger brother, which the artist couldn't hear, and took her place on the block, so that her throat reddened with her mother's blood. Few of those watching believed she deserved her fate, and her courage in the face of death had a serenity about it that caused a hush to fall over the crowd. Someone called out, 'Spare her! For pity's sake!' But to no avail. Once more, the Pope nodded. Once again the axe fell.

There was a sound of shattered bone and the thud of the axe biting into the wood. As the axeman wrenched his blade free, Beatrice's head shot off the block and skittered towards Caravaggio, rolling over and over until it came to a halt on the edge of the scaffold above where he sat so that her eyes, frozen in shock, appeared to be staring at him. Blood ran in rich red streams from her neck. He cried out and was sick.

Now Giacomo was hauled forward. Not for him the swift end offered by the axe. For him, as the one adjudged by the Inquisition to be most culpable, the penalty would be particularly awful. With his hands already tied behind his back and his legs in shackles, he was bound by his neck and ankles to a stake and his tunic ripped from his torso so that his breast was bare. As the bishop from the Holy Office read out the details of his crime and the sentence imposed, the second executioner lifted the heavy tongs from the chafing dish and showed the red-hot ends to the multitude. A sigh went up. Giacomo, after weeks of torture, had prayed he was immune to further pain, but to Caravaggio, just twenty feet away, his eyes told a different story. The masked executioner advanced on him, baring his teeth, then, with a grunt, clamped the glowing ends of the tongs, like pincers, onto the skin and muscle of his victim's chest. Next, he twisted the steel jaws, first one way, then the other, and jerked back, ripping off a section of flesh. The resulting scream rang out across the Tiber, scattering a group of hooded crows perched on the statues on either side of the bridge.

'Do you repent of your wickedness?' the bishop called out. Giacomo could not answer. He could only scream.

Unsheathing a knife at his belt, the executioner peeled off the seared flesh, threw it into the corner, then advanced again, repeating the vicious act of torture three times as the thousands looking on either urged him to greater efforts or else averted their eyes.

Caravaggio felt his stomach heave again. But he had to watch. He had to know what was being done in God's name.

By now the planks beneath the squirming figure of Giacomo Cenci had turned scarlet and the stench of burnt flesh filled the air. It was time for the final act. Releasing the condemned man from the stake, the chief executioner grabbed him by the hair and bundled him four paces across the scaffold to the waiting block. Giacomo, delirious with pain, called out to God and all the saints to save him and show him mercy. Perceiving this to be moment of truth, the *Decollato* holding on to Bernardo jammed the boy's eyes open, forcing him to watch his brother's last moments. It was almost done. The headsman directed a savage kick at the back of Giacomo's legs, forcing him onto his knees, and pushed him forward as if he were a pig in an abattoir. Then, stretching out his hand, like a surgeon, he took hold of the bludgeon. Pope Clement inclined his head almost imperceptibly, as if unwilling to take on such a terrible burden of responsibility. But the executioner did not need further instruction. Raising the bludgeon, with its metal studs, he held it high for a second, then brought it down with all the force at his command. Giacomo's skull shattered into pieces, splattering everyone with blood and brains. His body shook for a second, and was still.

The Pope rose and turned away. It was time for His Holiness to pray for the souls of the departed.

On the scaffold, Bernardo fainted. As the executioners flayed his brother's body and hacked it into pieces, which they hung on hooks, he was led away into a lifetime of captivity as a galley slave. The boy had done no wrong, but was condemned as a member of a wicked family, guilty by association of the crime of patricide.

In his dream, as in life, Caravaggio looked down at his sketch of Beatrice and noticed that it was streaked with real blood. His hands shook and he wept.

When he woke seconds later, still uttering small cries, he wiped the tears from his face and sat up in his bed, which as usual was soaked with sweat. His mouth was dry; he reached for a cup of water on an adjacent table and drank it down. The executions had taken place more than three and a half years before under a different Pope. But to the artist, Beatrice Cenci's eyes still stared at him as her life's blood spilled from her neck onto the scaffold on the Ponte Sant'Angelo. It was as if the events of September 1599 had occurred just minutes before. They would be the key to his art and the keenest point of entry into the state of his mind.

5*
The future: conclave minus 17

Judge Carlo Minghetti was not one of those Italian jurists who pretended indifference to the media. As his cases progressed, particularly those involving terrorism, he found it helped him make sense of the previous day's proceedings to read a crisp, 400-word summary in La *Stampa* or the *Corriere della Serra*. It amused him to compare the commentaries by so-called legal experts and pundits of left and right who presumed to read his thought processes and anticipate his judgments.

As one of Italy's top anti-terrorist judges, Minghetti had earned a reputation for upholding the rule of law even in the most difficult of cases. It was well-known that he was a conservative. He had been a member of Opus Dei, the most reactionary religious movement in the Catholic Church, since the year he graduated from the University of Ferrara. But not even his worst enemies – among whom he counted the Jesuits, the Muslim Brotherhood and the Green Party – had ever accused him of bigotry.

The case on which he was due to rule today was a particularly interesting one. Two men, a Moroccan and a Bosnian, charged with bombing an immigration office in Bologna, had been convicted by a lower court and sentenced to seven years' imprisonment, to be followed by deportation. Had anyone died as a result of their actions, they would have faced a life sentence, but the blast had occurred at two o'clock in the morning and the only victim, a passing drunk, had merely required treatment for cuts and brusies. The defendants' lawyers had appealed on the grounds that their clients, allegedly, confessed under duress – which was perfectly possible. Hearing the appeal had meant reviewing much of the original evidence and then questioning both city detectives and agents of the anti-terrorist police, DIGOS.

Speculation in the morning's media, including no doubt the internet – on which his career received detailed, almost line-by-line scrutiny – centred not on the guilt or innocence of the accused but on the extent to which Minghetti would extend the sentence imposed by the lower court.

How little they knew him.

His front-door buzzer sounded three times. It was the signal that his official car had arrived to take him to court. The judge downed his second cup of espresso, kissed his wife and picked up his briefcase.

'I'll be back at three o'clock,' he said.

'Don't worry,' his wife replied, running her right hand through his silver hair while with her left patting his jacket pocket to make sure he hadn't forgotten his mobile phone. 'Everything is packed and ready. We'll be on the road to Rimini five minutes after you come out of the shower.'

Her husband nodded, checked his watch and disappeared in the direction of the front door, where the police officer in charge of his personal security was waiting.

'*Buon giorno, Giudice.*'

'Good morning, Emilio. Looks like another fine day.'

The officer smiled. The temperature in Bologna had been in the mid-thirties for six weeks. It hadn't rained since the second week of March. Eyeing the villas opposite and the street as far as the next corner, he leaned forward to open the car door.

It was at that moment that the shots rang out.

There were four in all, fired so quickly, one after the other, that it seemed impossible they could have been individually aimed. The police forensic team would later record that they struck the brick wall behind which Minghetti was standing no more than ten centimetres above his head, forming a shallow ellipse, or crescent. Whoever was responsible was obviously an expert and the intention, apparently, was not to kill, but to make a point.

The police officer, who had spun round with commendable speed and self-control to pull the judge forward and down, drew his sidearm and slithered forward, waiting for a target to present itself. At the same time, the official driver got on his car radio and called for backup.

Two carloads of Carabinieri were on the scene within minutes, closely followed by an ambulance. But the incident had concluded. Whoever had fired the shots had done so from a considerable distance, using a high-powered rifle with a telescopic sight. By now there would be no trace of him. He would simply have melted into the heavy morning traffic.

Two hours later, appellate court number two of Bologna's Palace of Justice, in the Piazza Tribunali, opened for business, Judge Carlo Minghetti presiding. A crowd had gathered outside and the public gallery was filled.

Judge Minghetti, dressed in black robes and white cravat, signalled to the clerk of the court to shut the doors.

'This morning,' he began, 'an attack was made not simply against my person but against Italian justice. That attack is now being investigated by the Carabinieri and the anti-terrorist police. If the intention was to intimidate this judge, then it has failed.'

At this, everyone in the courtroom, other than the defendants and their supporters, broke into wild applause.

Minghetti brought down his gavel sharply and called for order. '*Silenzio!*' he said. 'Silence in court.'

The applause died down. Minghetti resumed. 'The accused, here today to hear my ruling on the sentence imposed against them by a lower court, should know that the verdict I am about to deliver will not differ in any respect from the one I had intended to deliver before the incident outside my home.'

Reporters in the press box smiled and shook their heads. Two young men in the public gallery rolled their eyes. The wife of the injured drunk looked for a moment as if she was about to utter a comment, but was silenced by a glower from the bench. Once again the gavel came down hard.

Minghetti's assertion that he had been unaffected by the shooting was not entirely accurate. Having considered the case against the accused, taking into account their claims of intimidation by investigating officers, he had decided the previous night, over a glass of grappa, to increase their sentences from seven years to eight. Now he added a further twelve months. He felt he owed it to himself and his wife as much as to the *amour propre* of civil society. And if it shocked those two bastards in the dock, and those who supported them, so much the better.

'Be grateful,' he told the prisoners, 'that your case has been heard in a country where the rule of law is not influenced by the violence and intolerance which each of you represents and which will never, I trust, be tolerated in a Christian society.'

Again, the court burst into applause. This time, Minghella did not intervene.

Three hundred kilometres south, far from the clamour of events, Cardinal Bosani and Father Visco watched the evening news on Italian state television. They were relaxing in the Camerlengo's private sitting room in the Governorate.

'Whose idea was it that the bullet holes should form a crescent?' Bosani wanted to know. 'That was a nice touch.'

'Not mine, Eminence,' Visco replied. 'I regret to say that it would never have occurred to me. But I trust that the incident overall met with your approval.'

Bosani patted his secretary's hand reassuringly. 'You did well, Cesare. The righteous anger of a Christian people was on display in that court today. Minghetti came across as an avenging angel, yet one acting within the law, guided by high Catholic principle. The cardinal electors will have taken note. It will be their duty to elect a pope whom those who praise Minghetti as a man of principle – and an officer of Opus Dei – can equally well respect.'

6*
Conclave minus 16

*'I have yet many things to say unto you, but you cannot bear them now.
Howbeit when He, the Spirit of Truth, is come, He will guide you into all
truth: for He shall not speak of himself; but whatsoever He shall hear, that
shall He speak: and He will show you the things to come.'*

—John 16: 12-13

The fourth-floor office of Father Declan O'Malley, Superior General of the Jesuits,
overlooked the Borgo Santo Spirito, just a hundred metres from St Peter's Square.
Strictly speaking, the Curia Generalizia of the Company of Jesus was part of Rome,
and Italy. But as a concession to the Vatican, it was designated *zona extraterrito-
riale*, giving O'Malley the *de facto* status of an ambassador.

The Irishman, the first of his race to head the institution created in 1540 by St
Ignatius Loyola, looked frail at first glance. His hair was snow-white and his dark
eyes were sunk deep into his head. In fact, though into his seventies, he was fit and
wiry, still able to get through Mass in thirty minutes flat, with or without an altar boy.

Today was a special day for him. His nephew Liam, in Rome for the summer,
had called to tell him that he was on his way over to say hello. It wasn't, in fact,
their first meeting. O'Malley had previously arranged for his nephew to attend the
annual summer party at the Irish College two days after he flew in from Dublin. But
it was the first time in ten years at least that he had visited him on his home turf.

With his old-fashioned looks, set off by a thick head of reddish-blonde hair,
Liam Dempsey reminded his uncle these days of the young Robert Donat, from
The Thirty-Nine Steps. He had had a hard upbringing – harder even than he knew.

Kitty – O'Malley's sister – had died giving birth to him. Her husband, because of the intensity of his belief, gave priority to the child. O'Malley, keenly aware of the enormity of his brother-in-law's dilemma, had not presumed to instruct him on the Church's teaching, confining himself to expressions of sympathy and support that he now saw as hollow and inadequate. Pat Dempsey's decision to sacrifice his wife was the cross he would bear, alone, for the rest of his days.

In the years that followed, O'Malley watched intermittently as Dempsey's faith calcified, becoming harsh and brittle, robbed of all outward show of affection. He remembered how he had looked on, dismayed, as his nephew grew up an only child in a home lacking a mother and with a bereaved father who saw in him the origin of his loss.

Liam, now aged twenty-eight, was never told of the choice that was made. His father felt that the weight of the knowledge of what he had done was for him alone, and O'Malley respected his decision. Later, as he pursued his vocation in a variety of locations across the globe, he often thought about the brother-in-law he had left behind. It seemed to him that with Kitty gone, it was his brother-in-law who had pursued a monastic life, not him. While he travelled the world, writing his books and moving up in the Company of Jesus, it was Pat who laboured alone, getting up each morning at five, saying his prayers, attending to his cattle, seeing to it that his son was fed and educated. Which of them had better answered Christ's call? He didn't have the answer.

It wasn't easy for the son either. Every day, in all weathers, Liam had trudged two miles from the farm in Bearna, overlooking Galway Bay, to the local national school, returning home each evening to help with the milking. His father, in permanent mourning, was both taciturn and a strict disciplinarian, showing his emotion only when drunk. How Liam had emerged mentally intact was a mystery. In fact, while playing rugby enthusiastically and developing an eye for the girls, he did well, taking a history degree at Trinity College, Dublin, then winning a place at the Irish army officer training college.

It was two years after he was commissioned into the Western Brigade that a second calamity befell him. His battalion was posted to Iraq to serve under the UN flag, keeping the peace beween Arabs, Turks and Kurds. A bomb, detonated as his patrol passed a water trough, killed five of his soldiers and left Liam, at the head of the column, grievously wounded. His recovery, in a specialized burns unit in Marseille, was long and agonizing. He had spent months in virtual isolation, barely able to move, with some saying privately that he'd be better off dead.

It was O'Malley, speaking from behind a surgical mask, who brought the young lieutenant the news that in the meantime his father had died from a stroke. Unable to offer the consolation of prayer, he had just stood there, watching. The loss, on top of everything else, was wretched. Father and son hadn't spoken for more than two years, ever since Liam announced that he had lost his faith. Now they could never be reconciled.

But nothing stood still. Eighteen months on, he was about to start his PhD at University College, Galway. His thesis, examining the relationship between Garibaldi and Pope Pius IX during the *Risorgimento*, meant learning Italian, and to this end, having acquired the basics in Dublin, he had taken a three-month lease on a spacious apartment next to the Tiber. The young man's resilience both astonished and humbled O'Malley. How he had emerged sane and well from a life so steeped in misfortune was to him nothing short of a miracle – but one in which God apparently played no part.

O'Malley prayed regularly for Liam and his father, as well as for the soul of his departed sister, who had sacrificed her own life for the sake of her son. But their blighted lives, bound together in tragedy, had made him wonder about the nature of his calling. Had he truly given up everything in order to follow Jesus? He had not ministered to the poor or the sick. Worse, he had spoken out only in private against the Holy Father's decision to address the growing paedophile scandal not as a mortal sin but as if it were a mere misdemeanour – an embarrassment to be swept beneath the carpet. The fact of the matter was that he had made no difference in the world, and that troubled him. He had risen in the Church as a favoured son, comfortably housed, respected by the media, a confidant of popes. It was undeniable that he had always worked hard. But that had been his pleasure. As a young priest, he had left Ireland as soon as he could. His doctoral thesis, written while a graduate student in Louvain, examined the legal code of the great Byzantine Emperor Justinian against that of his future Ottoman counterpart, Suleiman the Magnificent. The resulting paper, published in several languages, was acclaimed as a model of its kind and his reward was a five-year appointment as special advisor to the Papal Nuncio in Istanbul.

Success in this demanding role led to speculation in Rome that he would be offered a professorship at the city's Pontifical Institute for Arab and Islamic Studies. To his considerable annoyance, the job went instead to a member of the Society of Missionaries of Africa, the White Fathers. An intellectual with no pastoral experience, O'Malley was told he must spend four years as spiritual director of a retreat house in Milwaukee – a move likened by colleagues to the State Department in Washington selecting a high-flyer to be consul-general in Cardiff. Yet even this apparent setback turned out to his advantage. Those who expected him to chafe against his exile in the Midwest were surprised when his next publication, *Between Heaven and Earth*, turned out to be a celebration of inter-faith encounters with the Lakota Indians. The book, which reached number thirty-eight in the *New York Times* bestsellers' list, did not go unnoticed in high places. Its author's return to the mainstream followed within three months of its publication. He was appointed *socius*, or deputy head, of the sprawling Chicago Province, where he served for three incident-packed years before being posted to Rome as vice-rector of the Irish College.

The sun streamed in through the open window in the Borgo Santo Spirito. For a moment, O'Malley felt a chill of loneliness pass through him. Then it passed. There was a knock at the door – not as polite as he might have wished. It was Father Giovanni, his private secretary.

'Your nephew, Father General,' he said. 'Could I point out to you that you have a busy schedule today?'

'You have already done so, Giovanni.'

A scowl passed over the young priest's face as he withdrew. Behind him stood the tall, languid figure of Liam Dempsey.

O'Malley stood up and threw open his arms. 'Liam! Come in, come in. I can't tell you how good it is to see you.'

Dempsey beamed as he advanced across the floor to his uncle. Their embrace was more than a greeting, it was a reconnection. O'Malley did his best to hide the awkwardness he felt. He stood back, his hands still on his nephew's shoulders. 'You look good,' he said.

'I feel good.'

The Jesuit smiled, perhaps a little ambiguously, and indicated an ancient leather armchair. 'Take the weight off your feet,' he said.

Dempsey sat down.

'So what's been happening?'

'In Rome, you mean? Or back home?'

'Let's start with home. Did you ever get that money you were owed?'

Dempsey had recently sold the family farm. A Swedish home furnishings company had bought it, but the size of the final payment depended on the success of a planning application aimed at transforming the land into a retail park, complete with space for a thousand cars.

'Yes,' said Dempsey. 'The cheque turned up in my bank three days ago.'

'Was it what you were expecting?'

'Absolutely.' Dempsey told him the amount, which made O'Malley draw in his breath.

'Sounds like you'll not be needing a student loan, then. But sure who could begrudge you it after all you've been through? What else?'

There was news of a cousin from Athenry who was getting married in the autumn. O'Malley remembered the young fellow as a gawky teenager with a gap-toothed smile. He hadn't seen him in years. Another cousin, a computer technician, whose daughter had just received her First Communion, was about to be made redundant following a decision by his American employers to transfer production back to Seattle.

The priest registered his sympathy. He knew all about the ravages that had resulted from the recession that began in 2008. First the property market had collapsed, taking the construction industry with it, and then the banks had gone belly-up. It was hard to believe the extent of the greed, incompetence and fraud that had masqueraded as the Celtic Tiger. The recovery, aided – hindered, some said – by the EU, still had a long way to go. But he was heartened when Dempsey announced he had paid off his cousin's car loan. That had been generous of him. 'So what about the place itself?' he asked. 'Galway, I mean. It's been a while.'

His nephew blew out his cheeks. 'You'd hardly recognize it. Bearna's virtually gone now. It's become a suburb. There's estates and apartment blocks that reach almost to the water's edge, even if half of them are still waiting for buyers or tenants. Did you know the city population is expected to hit a hundred thousand in the next five years, a quarter of them either foreign-born or else descended from immigrants? De Valera wouldn't know what to make of it – and he was from Puerto Rico.'

O'Malley smiled. He hadn't been back to Galway in years.

Dempsey glanced out the window in the direction of St Peter's. 'You remember the talk there was when the old riverside mosque opened? Well, you should see the new place, complete with minaret. It's part of an Islamic study centre – one of the largest in Ireland. It's hard to take it in. When I started school, you were a foreigner if you came from anywhere east of Castlebar. Now there's women in Merchants Road wearing burkhas, and halal butchers in all the main shopping centres. Some of the kids even speak Irish. I read somewhere that Muhammad's now the ninth-most common boy's name in the country.'

'Changed times,' O'Malley said. He had listened as patiently as he could, realizing to his shame that he had completely lost touch with his birthplace and that, so far as his family was concerned, the only one he felt close to these days was Liam. His own parents were long dead. Their house had been bought by a Lithuanian plumber and his wife. His sole remaining sibling, Eamonn, was in San Diego, married to a woman from Panama.

'But how are *you*, Liam?' he interjected, surprising himself with the peremptory tone of his voice. 'In yourself, I mean. Tell me the truth. Don't hold back because of' – he ran his hands down the length of his cassock, symbol of his priestly separation from the world – 'because of *this*!'

Dempsey sat back in the armchair, only his eyes registering the tension that these days was part and parcel of his life. 'I'm grand, Uncle Declan. You can stop worrying about me. Life's looking up. Rome is great. I've got this terrific apartment across the river and my Italian is coming on a treat. I'm even seeing someone – a girl, I mean. Someone I met at the Irish College bash.'

'Is that a fact? And who would that be – if you don't mind my asking?'

'Her name's Maya – Maya Studer ... the daughter of Colonel Otto Studer. You'd know him, I'd imagine.'

'The Commandant of the Swiss Guard? But that's extraordinary.' O'Malley looked quizzically at his nephew. 'It's not serious, though – is it?'

'Not yet,' said Dempsey. 'A bit too early to say. But we're having lunch today, so you never know.'

'You never cease to surprise me. But I'm happy for you ... truly.'

Dempsey nodded. He was fond of his uncle, but wary of the tradition he represented. 'That's enough about me, though,' he said. 'The real question is, who's going to win the big election?'

O'Malley leaned back in his chair, relieved to be back on home turf. 'Well,' he said, 'it turns out not everyone in the Church is as relaxed about the Muslim issue as the citizens of Galway. There are even those – and I'm talking about people at the very summit of Church government – who think that the next pope's first priority should be the instigation of open conflict with Islam.'

'You're kidding me. And who do they imagine is going to take that on?'

'I wish I knew. Whoever fills the bill. There's no shortage of bigots in the Sacred College.'

'I suppose. But what would they be looking for?'

'For starters, a halt to immigration; the ruthless repatriation of "illegals"; a rejection of Muslim schools; the banning of the hijab and headscarves; basically, an end to any notion of equality or parity of esteem. Whatever it takes to underline that Europe is a Christian continent.'

'Right. Well, I'm sorry to hear it, but not surprised.'

'What do you mean?'

Dempsey ran a hand through his hair. 'Face it, Uncle, after football and the economy, immigration, especially Muslim immigration, is the single-biggest talking point in Europe. There's whole swathes of our major cities that have been taken over by new arrivals from North Africa, Pakistan and Turkey. We've had protests and counter-protests. And the legislation designed to protect us from terrorism has turned Europe into an armed camp. Not that it's made us any safer. Only the other day there was that bomb at the Lateran Palace. Yesterday there was the business in Bologna. Muslims may feel the suspects were hard done by, but most Italians, I can tell you, are on the side of the judge.'

O'Malley shrugged. 'Understandable, I suppose. It'd be hard not to sympathize with a man who's been shot at just for trying to do his job.'

'Exactly. But there's a lot of hate out there – on both sides. The average European, having more or less given up on God, now finds himself facing growing demands from Islamists and Imams who seem to want to build a mosque in every high street and generally put the clock back four hundred years. If that's progress, give me Karl Marx every time. The way I look at it, the history of Europe over that same period has been characterized, as much as anything, by our gradual giving up of religious obligation. No offence, but we've grown up. When I went to Sunday school, I couldn't wait to get out. I'd be bored rigid. But for young Muslims, decades into the twenty-first century, Islam is everything. It's what they live for. It's what *defines* them.'

Now the priest raised a critical eyebrow. 'You should be careful what you say, Liam. They're not all suicide bombers. Most of them are good people, working hard to provide for their families. As to their devotion, maybe it's the nature of the beast.'

'Meaning what?'

'Well, you only have to contrast the clarity of the Qu'ran – inextricably linked to lifestyle and conquest – with the ad-hoc nature of Christian belief.'

Dempsey was immediately on his guard. He had no time for either side in this particular debate. The way he saw it, the two faiths were opposite sides of the same counterfeit coin. But there was an argumentative side to his nature and he couldn't resist the opportunity to make a point. 'What are you telling me? That the Qu'ran hasn't changed for fifteen hundred years? You must be kidding.'

'I'm serious,' O'Malley replied, raising his voice against the noise of a Vespa scooter drifting up from the street below. 'At least, not since the earliest times. Tradition has it that it was revealed to Muhammad by the Archangel Gabriel – Jibra'il in Arabic – who required him, over a period of twenty-two years, to learn it *sura* by *sura*, verse by verse, and to teach it to others by the same method.'

'And I thought remembering my Catechism was hard.'

O'Malley ignored the crack. 'Matter of fact, the word Qu'ran means "recital". Only after Mohammad's death in 632 were scribes recruited to take it down verbatim from the Prophet's close companion and disciple, Zaid bin Thabit, who, like his master, had committed it to memory. Some years later, at the time of the third Caliph, Uthman bin Affan, war interrupted the process and different versions started to appear. When peace was restored, Uthman had all copies recalled and burned, to be replaced by a new, authorized version – essentially the one we have today.'

'Not like the Bible, then,' Dempsey said. 'In scriptural terms, isn't that a horse designed by a committee?'

O'Malley checked to see that the door to his office was shut. 'If you mean it's like a camel, they both came out of the desert and they've both been around a long time. But it's a mess, no question about that. It wasn't until the second century that St Irenaeus, a French bishop born in Anatolia, gathered the oral tradition and existing texts into a single construct.'

Dempsey could see what was coming. 'Except that not all of his fellow scholars agreed ...'

'Too right, they didn't. The "final" version turned out to be anything but and the process of selection continues to this day. There's any number of books – the Gospel of Barnabas is a case in point – whose claim for inclusion in the Bible is not without foundation. Barnabas, you may recall, spent several years as right-hand man to St Paul during his missions to Asia Minor. He's mentioned in Luke's Gospel ahead of the Apostle. Well, according to Barnabas, not only was Judas crucified in Christ's place, allowing Jesus to go straight to heaven, but a greater prophet, named in some translations as God's Messenger, in others as Muhammad, would eventually emerge and bring the true faith to a waiting world.'

Dempsey sat up and stretched his shoulders. 'So what do *you* think?'

O'Malley's face gave nothing away. 'There's a verse in St John's Gospel that speaks of a mysterious someone who in the future will hear the "spirit of truth" and speak what he has heard, showing us the shape of things to come. The Church has generally preferred to withhold comment on this – which is why you won't hear it quoted from the pulpit.'

'What's the Muslim view?'

'Oh, they're all for Barnabas. No surprise there.'

'But not the Vatican?'

'Hardly. To Catholic theologians Barnabas offers a rope to hang fools and knaves. Never forget, Liam, the Catholic Church and Islam regard each other as inhabiting essentially the same universe. Each accuses the other of serious doctrinal error, but this doesn't mean they don't see aspects of the truth in each other's beliefs. They're like sibling rivals – they're *connected*.'

'Which brings us back to Muhammad. How do you rate him? If I remember rightly, Pope Benedict seemed to think he was steeped in violence.'

'Oh he was, he was – even if that wasn't quite the message His Holiness was trying to get across. But then so were many of the popes, some of whom wore armour and commanded their armies from the front. Urban II gave us the crusades. Julius II was almost welded to his warhorse. Gregory XVI suppressed insurrections in the papal states with unbelievable cruelty well into the 1840s. So if you're talking Us and Them, it's good to remember sometimes who "we" are and where we came from.'

'But what about all those stories dad used to read me from the Bible when I was a kid? The miracles, the Virgin birth, the empty tomb? Were half of them made up? Is there any truth to any of it?'

O'Malley could sense the mischief in his nephew's voice. He ran a finger round the inside of his Roman collar as if trying to free himself from its constraints. 'Truth? T.S. Eliot was right when he said, "Oh do not ask, 'What is it?'" We like to believe that faith is supported by scholarship and scholarship by faith. But the "facts" of almost any case can be disassembled and reconstructed to fit whatever seems most important to us at the time. In the end, we believe whatever makes us feel most comfortable.'

'Which means that you believe Christ rose again on the third day and ascended into heaven …'

'… "And sits on the right hand of God the Father Almighty; from thence he shall come to judge the quick and the dead." Yes, Liam, I believe that. How could I not?'

Looking at his uncle, dressed in his cassock, with a silver cross around his neck, Dempsey wondered what his father would have made of all the questioning that fuelled theology at the higher level. Theirs was a house in which the Sacred Heart of Jesus glowed in the dark from its position on top of the mantlepiece. The first thing you saw when you walked in the front door was the Child of Prague – a statue of the infant Jesus, wearing a crown and golden robes. Not divine? Not risen from the dead? Dad would be spinning in his grave just at the thought of it.

A knock at the door interrupted his musings. It was Father Giovanni, holding a clipboard. 'I hope you haven't forgotten, Father General,' he said, 'but you have a busy schedule of appointments today, including lunch with the Spanish Provincial General and a three o'clock with the dean.' He tapped the clipboard. 'And I've got at least twenty letters here awaiting your signature.'

O'Malley toyed with a paper knife. 'Okay, Giovanni, I'll be five minutes.'

The priest withdrew reluctantly, giving Dempsey a dirty look.

'Don't mind Father Giovanni,' O'Malley said, replacing the paper knife. 'He's the sort of young man, increasingly common in the order, who thinks the suffix SJ should be followed by MBA.'

'I should go all the same. You're obviously busy.'

'And you're due to have lunch with Fräulein Studer – more entertaining company, I should imagine, than the Spanish Provincial. But thanks for dropping in. I appreciate it. It's not often these days that I get the chance to discuss religion.'

'I won't even comment on that,' Dempsey said.

O'Malley stood up and walked round his desk to embrace his nephew. 'Next time let's meet over a pint.'

'Good idea. Just give me a call.'

Dempsey turned to go. Just as he reached the door, his uncle called out to him: 'Oh, and give my regards to Maya. Tell her it's been a while since I saw her at Mass.'

As he walked down the four flights of stairs towards the front hall, past endless photographs and lithographs of leading Jesuits from the previous two hundred years, Dempsey felt the walls closing in on him. He had never had much time for organized religion. It was one thing to talk theology with his uncle, who had a knack of combining faith and scholarship. But these days he could no more genuflect in front of the altar than he could kiss a bishop's ring. At the bottom of the stairs, he found himself confronted by a portrait of St Ignatius Loyola, the Jesuits' founder, looking both ascetic and scheming, as if there were no lengths to which he wouldn't go to promote the power and privilege of God. The eyes, he noted, did not follow him, the way they did in some paintings he had seen. Instead, they stared behind him, almost through him, towards some higher truth to which he would never be privy. He shivered and turned away. Outside, in the real world, the sun was shining.

7*
August 1603

Caravaggio had just drawn his shirt over his head – the same one he had worn for the past three days – when he heard his front door open and footsteps on the stairs. He groaned. His lodgings, on the Vicolo dei Santi Cecilia e Baggio, in the heart of the Artists' Quarter, were an open house for rebels of all kinds. Painters and poets, out-of-work soldiers, pimps and whores, popped in and out just to pass the time of day or to catch up on the latest gossip. But this time it was his pupil and sometime manservant Bartolomeo Manfredi, who in return for lessons on the art and science of chiaroscuro ran errands for him and, when it suited him, prepared his meals.

'Bad news, master!' the Lombard called out, pushing open the door of the bedchamber without knocking. '*The Death of the Virgin* has been turned down. They say you used a whore as your model and have scandalized the Church.'

'What?'

'They say you used a whore …'

'I heard you the first time, Bortolomeo. What do you mean, they *rejected* it? *Who* rejected it?'

Manfredi, a swarthy figure whose leg muscles showed through his tights, sniffed loudly. 'The Discalced Carmelites.'

'The Discalced Carmelites? What the fuck do they know about art? What do they know about anything, come to that? They're a charitable order – when they're not buggering young boys, that is.'

Manfredi picked up a camel-hair brush and tested the bristles between finger and thumb. 'But it's their church. And it's their altar it's supposed to hang in. Perhaps if you'd read Cherubini's instructions ...'

Caravaggio looked blank. Laerzio Cherubini, a morbidly pious lawyer, with close links to the Curia, was the one who had commissioned the painting, intended as an alterpiece for the newly completed church of Santa Maria della Scala in Trastevere.

'You must remember, Master. He wrote them out for you. Very explicit, as I recall – straight from the Council of Trent.'

The Council of Trent! Caravaggio was sick to the back teeth of hearing about the Council of Trent. It was like an albatross around the neck of thinking artists, laying out acceptable iconography and protocols while strangling genuine creativity. Caravaggio had flipped through Cherubini's list and promptly stuck it under a candlestick, where it still lay.

By now, he had reached the stage of his toilette where he was rooting around for his shoes. He was down on his knees, extending his left hand beneath the bed as far as it would go. There was a lot of dust there, he soon discovered, and the remains of at least one dead mouse.

'And I was supposed to tailor my vision according to his whims?' he called out, mockingly. 'Is that what what we've come to?'

'I should have thought it was obvious. Cherubini's one of the most devout bastards in Rome. Known for it. And he made it plain he wanted a Virgin he could live with, so to speak.'

'Aaah! Gotcha!' said Caravaggio, coming up triumphantly with the missing shoe and blowing off a thick film of dust. 'So what is it about my Virgin that he can't live with? – bearing in mind that I am your master and I *do* employ you.'

'Simple. She's a whore. *Zoccola* was the word I heard. Not only that, her legs and feet are bare. You'd never guess she was about to be raised up into heaven. Take one look at your Madonna and all you can say is, she's dead, time to call in the mortician.'

'But she *is* dead, Bortolomeo. That's why it's called *Death of the Virgin.*'

The manservant – he preferred to think of himself as an apprentice – was not to be moved. He had already placed the camel-hair brush in his pocket and was looking through a box of colours. 'Yes, but in the contract you signed, "death" was intended to mean "dormition" or "transition". The idea, as you must know, was that the Virgin would be seen on the cusp of her assumption. I don't think she was meant to look as if she had just succumbed to the plague.'

Caravaggio pulled on his shoe, noting with dismay that his big toe peeked out the end. 'Don't be a cretin, Bortolomeo,' he said. 'You can search the Bible all you like and you won't find any mention of the Assumption. I might as well do a painting of five hundred angels dancing on the head of a pin – come to think of it, that would probably sell. I asked a priest a couple of months back – a Jesuit, no less – where was the evidence that the Mother of God "transitioned" into heaven while half the characters in the New Testament looked on. And guess what?' Manfredi shrugged. 'He said there wasn't any. There's actually no mention of Mary after Pentecost. One minute the Church is telling us that the only biblical truths we can rely on are in the authorized version, the *Vulgate*, approved by the Pope, and the next they're saying we should stick to myth when myth is better. Well, which is it?'

'Don't ask me,' Manfredi said. 'Not my department. I just know which side of my bread soaks up the olive oil.'

But Caravaggio was not to be mollified. 'I'll tell you what else I bloody did. I went to see Cardinal Baronio. He's as orthodox as they come. For Christ's sake, he's the one writing the official history of the Church. And *he* says the Madonna had a fully human nature and, of necessity, underwent the same experience of death as everybody else.'

'Yes, Master, I don't doubt it. But was she a whore?'

'What's that go to do with it?'

'Well, it's obvious who your model was.'

Caravaggio pulled a scrap of cheese from his beard and swallowed it. 'Anna Bianchini is a very beautiful young woman.'

'Very true. And she charges five scudi for a screw.'

'So?'

'So she's a prostitute.'

'When do we ever get to meet a woman who isn't? Fathers protect their daughters' virginity like Cerberus guarding the gates of Hell.'

'Yes … but that's not the point, is it?'

'It's the truth. Come to that, I used Fillide Melandroni as Saint Catherine for Cardinal Del Monte. And she's a whore … mind you, Del Monte would rather she'd been a boy. I used Fillide again as Mary of Cleophas in the *Deposition of Christ*. You remember that? Everyone from the Pope down described it as a masterpiece. So what is it they want from me? 'Cos I'm fucked if I know.'

Manfredi crossed the room to a small table and poured some water from a jug into a shallow basin. 'Don't ask me,' he said. 'But if you're thinking of arguing the toss with Cherubini, I'd freshen up first. You know what a stickler he is for cleanliness. Next to godliness, he says.'

'Like a fucking Lutheran.'

Manfredi snorted. 'Just make sure you don't tell him that.'

Twenty minutes later, after rinsing his face and hands and dragging a comb through his hair, Caravaggio set out for the Palazzo Cherubini on the Via di

Giustiniani. His own lodgings were cramped and dark, but he had no need of light. Soon, though, as he turned the corner onto the Via della Scrofa, he could feel the world open up and the sun bore down on him from a sky the colour of stem irises. There were a lot of pilgrims out today – many of them from Genoa, by the sound of them. Must be a feast day or something. But then, when wasn't it? Head down, he raced past the church of Sant'Agostino, averting his gaze from a group of whores on their way into Mass, led by the haughty figure of Fillide Melandroni, who, he remembered, had recently got herself arrested after cutting the face of one of her rivals. Someone else he avoided was the barber, Lucca, who called out to him from the doorway of his shop, snipping in the air with an outsized pair of shears.

'Master Caravaggio! Long time no see. Just five minutes in my chair and you'd be a new man.'

'Some other time, Lucca!'

He almost stopped at a colour seller's next to the Albergo della Scrofa. He could do with some more reds. He'd rather taken a fancy to red of late and wanted to expand his range. Problem was, he owed him money – quite a lot of money, as a matter of fact. Then he heard a clock strike in the Piazza Navona and hurried on, stepping over a pile of ordure recently arrived, from the smell of it, from a window overhead.

The cobbles outside the larger houses were slick with shit and piss, except for a path outside each front door. Where did it all go? he wondered. Couldn't be healthy. In classical times, they had drains. Not any more. If someone could come up with a proper sewage system, some wag had written, they'd clean up. Too true! By now he'd reached the church of San Luigi dei Francesi – the French church. He paused for a second, debating whether or not to go in. The church, run by a group of canons acting for the French ambassador to the Holy See, had recently installed the last of three of his paintings in the church's Cantarelli chapel, depicting key moments in the life of St Matthew, and he wanted to check they'd got the lighting right. But there wasn't time. After he'd settled with Cherubini, he was due to meet his friends, Onorio and Prospero, at the Turk's Head. They'd drink some wine, set the world to rights, then slip off and play a game of racquetball or maybe just pass the time in the brothel. It depended. Either way, it would beat half an hour of pietistic talk with the priests of San Luigi. Previously, he had only dabbled in religious art as a kind of sideline, to give him respectability and up his fees. Rome was, after all, the centre of the Christian world. Now he knew why. His three renderings of the Apostle had taken him an age to complete – when he was working on them, that is, for he had other customers as well, looking for their card-players, or baskets of fruit or lewd depictions of boys and young men. 'The dirtier, the better,' one banker had said, commissioning a study of Bacchus. 'Only don't make him too well hung – wouldn't want to give the wife ideas.' As if they didn't have ideas already! God preserve him from half-wits. One thing about ordinary people, though: they tended not to quibble. Very respectful, most of them. Not like the French bloody canons! They'd rejected his first version of St Matthew and the Angel, and if it hadn't been for the banker Vicenzo Giustiniani, who snapped it up without batting an eyelid, then paid for its replacement, he would have been seriously out of pocket. According to the canons, the original was irreverent and ignoble. They didn't like it that he had shown the saint with his bare legs and feet sticking out. A more 'magisterial' rendition was what they required, with Matthew robed as a senator, busy with his Gospel, his legs and feet lost in shadow. What was it about bare feet anyway? Did they think the Apostles didn't have feet – or legs for that matter? Did they imagine they floated along, trailing decorous robes, never making actual contact with the ground? In the old days, he could paint what he liked and how he liked. But that was when he was new to Rome and worked without commissions. Now that he was 'celebrated', all such freedom was lost. Christ! Here he was, on his way to plead with Laerzio Cherubini, one of the most infuriating men in Rome, so hypocritical he'd come to believe his own lies. Onorio said he'd been born with a poker up his arse – and he wasn't far wrong. It was just as well they both spoke Italian, for other than that they had no language in common.

Not far now. Which was just as well, for he was breaking into another of his sweats. Weaving in and out of the pilgrims and beggars and street traders and lines of nuns, he ignored the beckoning fingers of an ageing and decidedly ugly whore (while noting to himself that she might do for a St Anne he had in mind). He also put some distance between himself and Paolo Leone, his wine merchant, who called out to him, in the name of God and all his blessed saints, to settle his bloody bill. 'Yes, yes, Paolo, this afternoon for sure! Don't worry about it.'

Another he avoided on his journey was Ranuccio Tomassoni, whose family controlled the Campo Marzio. Ranuccio was a young *bravo* in search of a big reputation. He liked to take on Caravaggio at cards or racquetball, at which he hardly ever won, and failing that would outbid him in the brothel, using family money. If he'd had the time, he'd have given him a clip around the ear – or maybe run him through. But he was in a hurry.

And then, all at once, he had arrived. The Palazzo Cherubini, four storeys high, pink as a cherub's arse, was new and still smelled of wet plaster. Its owner, once a common soldier, grown rich as a Church litigant, was impossibly tall, with a hook nose and bushy eyebrows. Why he hadn't opted for a career in the Church was a mystery. In a city in which religious devotion was measured by the hundredweight, Cherubini attended Mass every day of his life, twice on Sundays, and, when he wasn't defrauding his clients, could usually be found in an attitude of prayer.

Cynics pointed out that he had tried to shorten his time in Purgatory by forcing most of his children to join religious orders, which was probably true. Caravaggio didn't give a toss either way.

He banged on the large, double-fronted door, embossed with the owner's newly acquired coat of arms, which looked like three funeral urns against a sea of troubles. Eventually, a wizened maidservant drew back the bolt and peered out, suspiciously. With her warty nose and blackened teeth, she looked like she belonged in a portrait he'd once seen by Ghirlandaio.

'Oh,' she said, sensing trouble. 'Master Caravaggio – it's you.'

'Is your master in?'

'He's busy.'

'Don't give me that.'

'He's talking to a bishop.'

'All the better, then.' And with that he pushed his way past the startled woman, who waddled after him flapping her arms, and strode straight into the main reception room at the end of the corridor.

Cherubini, wearing a burgundy-coloured doublet and hose, with a preposterous fur-lined hat on his head and two sticks for legs, was examining a technical drawing of a proposed addition to Santa Maria della Scala laid out for his approval on a brightly polished table. Next to him stood a short, fat bishop, as bald as a tennis ball, who looked as if he was no stranger to a good table.

Caravaggio bowed to the bishop, then got straight to the point. 'What's this about you turning down my Virgin?'

Cherubini turned around slowly. He had a long, thin neck and, with his skinny legs and bulbous clothing, put the artist in mind of a brochette on a chef's spit. A lugubrious, world-weary expression clung to his face, which could have belonged to a mask from the commedia dell'arte. Realizing the source of the interruption, Cherubini groaned theatrically and clasped his hand to his forehead. 'Master Caravaggio ...'

'The very same. You haven't forgotten my name, apparently, but you do seem to have let it slip your mind that you still owe me the small matter of 230 scudi.'

The lawyer grimaced, but stood his ground. 'Look,' he said, 'this is not a convenient moment. As you can see, I am busy discussing church matters with His Grace. Do you mind calling back later?'

'Busy? *Busy*? What do you think I've been these last three months? I've produced a painting for you that, in the opinion of many, is a masterpiece, fit to be compared to anything by Titian or Raphael. And now I hear that it's been turned down by you and the canons because the Virgin has bare feet!'

'I assure you ...'

'And by the Discalced Carmelites, no less. Master Cherubini, may I ask you what "discalced" means?'

'Why, it is Latin, of course. *Dis calceus* ... without shoes.'

'*Without shoes*! Exactly! They go about Rome without any shoes on, even in the dead of winter, just to show how bloody *holy* they are. But now, when I show the Virgin lying on her deathbed, they complain that I'm a blasphemer because she isn't wearing shoes. Well, since when does anyone ever wear shoes in bed? For a quick five minutes in the local knocking shop maybe, but not, I suspect, if you're about to meet your Maker.'

At this, the bishop couldn't help laughing, which only added to Cherubini's sense of insult. Drawing himself up to his full height, he narrowed his eyes and bared his teeth, which were a bright yellow. 'Good God!' he said. 'This is *unconscionable*. They were right about you, Merisi. You *are* a blasphemer!'

'In fact, Master Cherubini, I'm a Milanese. But let that pass. I did what was asked of me. I produced a finished canvas, on time, to specifications, and all I've got to show for it is a miserable advance of fifty scudi.'

Cherubini ran a veiny hand down the full length of his face, as if conjuring up a new expression fresh from the wreckage of the old. The truth was, he planned to sell the painting in the commercial market. Several experts, among them Vincenzo Giustiniani and the Flemish master, Rubens, had pronounced it first-rate, worth twice at least what Cherubini was paying for it. So it was just a matter of allowing a discreet interval to pass between saying no to it and realizing a handsome profit.

'And you *shall* be paid,' he announced, a new orotundity entering his delivery. 'For I am a man of my word. Indeed, you shall be paid this very week. But as for the painting being installed in Santa Maria della Scala, well, I'm afraid that is quite out of the question. Quite aside from the matter of the bare feet, your model for the Virgin turns out to have been be a dirty whore from Ortaccio ... a slut whose favours you have no doubt enjoyed many times. More than that – more than that, even – you have depicted Our Lady as ... *dead*, when, quite explicitly, she was to have been shown on the point of her dormition into heaven.'

Caravaggio adopted a defiant pose, with his hands on his hips. The bishop, a Spaniard, who knew well the artist's high standing at the papal court, was enjoying this unexpected diversion and stared at the artist with a grin on his face, waiting for the next outburst.

'Have you ever actually read the Bible, Master Cherubini?' Caravaggio asked.

'What? How dare you!'

'Because, if you have, perhaps you would be so kind as to point out to me where it says that Mary, the Mother of Jesus, did not die like the rest of us, but "dormissioned" into heaven, leaving no trace of her earthly body behind.'

'It is set out quite clearly in the *Golden Legend*.'

'The what?'

'The *Golden Legend* … the Lives of the Saints. You know very well …'

'– I know very well, Signor, that The Golden Legend is a story book and no substitute for the word of God.'

This was too much for Cherubini, who by now was smouldering with rage. 'Happily for the Church,' he boomed, 'not all artists take so lofty a view. You should know that a new work has been commissioned, showing the dormition of Our Lady, by the esteemed artist Carlo Sarasceni, and it is this, rather than your own sacrilegious daub, that will occupy the altarpiece in Santa Maria della Scala.'

This news stung Caravaggio. Sarasceni, a Venetian who had lived in Rome for the last five years, was a friend and one of his most devoted admirers. It was hard to believe that he would accept a commission in such circumstances. But then, he reflected, times were hard, business was business and everyone was out to make as much as they could before they were thought old hat or the plague got them.

'Daub it might be to you, Signor Cherubini,' he retorted. 'We shall see how history judges your action. I wonder which of us will be remembered a hundred years from now, the artist or the … *lawyer*.'

For a moment, Cherubini was speechless. Caravaggio could have chosen no more personal line of attack. Then he recovered his voice. 'Get out!' he said. 'Leave my house. You shall be paid your thirty pieces of silver. Do not, however, on pain of arrest for trespass, dare to darken my door again.'

But before he had finished speaking, Caravaggio had already gone.

That afternoon, in the Turk's Head, Prospero Orsi and Onorio Longhi, Caravaggio's two closest companions in Rome, listened indulgently as the monstrous tale unfolded of how Cherubini – a buffoon as well as a rogue, and quite possibly a child molester – had rejected *Death of the Virgin* and given a fresh commission in its stead to Carlo Sarasceni.

'I'm not surprised, to tell you the truth,' Longhi said, as soon as he could get a word in edgeways. 'The wonder is that Carlo didn't get in before you at the French church. I mean, he speaks French half the time and gets all his clothes sent from Marseille. I don't know why he doesn't just go and live there.'

'But you're not saying he'd have stolen the commission, are you?' Caravaggio asked. This was a question of honour and he was not ready to concede the point.

Longhi flicked a lock of his blonde hair away from his face. 'No – probably not. But he wanted it. He thought he was the obvious choice, even if he does call himself a Caravaggista.'

'Remind me to give him a kick up the arse next time I see him.'

'By all means.'

'And I'll hold him down while you do it,' Orsi added. He was a small man, known generally as Prosperini, but was always there at the first hint of trouble, ready to lay in with with either fists or rapier. 'Mind you,' he continued, 'it's not Carlo's fault that Cherubini's a prick.'

'No,' Caravaggio agreed. 'And I can't blame him for picking up on the job after I'd already had my go. But he'd better bloody well wait until I've been paid before starting. Otherwise, he and I will have a serious falling out.'

'Funny he should come up like this,' Orsi said. 'I ran into him the other day. He'd just come back from Venice. His father's ill, apparently. He says the Doge and his advisers are scared the Ottomans are going to attack the city. Turns out the Sultan has re-built his fleet, and his generals and admirals are looking for any excuse they can find to go to war.'

'So Anna was right, then.'

'What do you mean?'

'She told me a while back that one of her clients – a Dominican from Venice – was worried the Turks were getting ready for war. He said all the Pope would do was celebrate High Mass and pray for God's intervention.'

Longhi was picking at his teeth with a sliver of wood he'd peeled from the edge of the table. 'If you ask me,' he said, 'a proper war would do us all a world of good. I haven't had my sword out of its scabbard in months.'

'Bollocks!' said Orsi. 'You were arrested just last month. You hit a baker over the head with the hilt of your sword after he overcharged you 10 baiocci for a loaf of bread. I was there, remember.'

'Yes, well that doesn't count, does it? He wasn't a gentleman and I didn't cut him, did I? Get your facts straight.'

'Do you really think the Turks will have another go?' Caravaggio asked. 'You'd think after Lepanto …'

The Battle of Lepanto, the greatest naval confrontation for a hundred years, had been fought in 1571, off the west coast of Greece, between the Holy League, led by the Pope, and the Ottomans, resulting in a famous Christian victory. But Cyprus had still been wrested from the Venetians and there were endless rumours of fresh incursions into Hungary and Austria, even of an upcoming assault on Vienna itself.

'Lepanto was thirty years ago,' Longhi said. 'The Turks have learned a lot since then. They've got new guns and new tactics. There's even talk they've built a squadron of galleasses, high as houses. If you ask me, another war is only a matter of time.'

Orisi looked thoughtful. 'I spoke to this Monsignor from the Apostolic Palace the other day, after Mass. He'd seen me at Cardinal Orlandi's. I'm still working on that fresco about Lepanto and he came over to see how I was doing. Anyway, we got to talking about the Ottomans. Turns out he'd been to Isfahan recently as part of a delegation from the Holy See. He told me that Shah Abbas of the Persians had called on the Pope to agree an alliance against the Turks, who he said were our common enemy. The Pope was interested. Very interested, apparently. I mean, he's got enough to do with the Protestants on the one hand and stuck-up Venetians on the other. But Cardinal Battista – our esteemed Camerlengo – was dead against it. A plague on both their houses, he said. The pair of them, Persians as well as Turks, were Muslim and therefore our sworn enemies, and we'd be better off striking a pact with the devil himself. Some Hospitaller or other, over on business from Malta, backed him up. It did the trick. Now it looks as if the Pope's gone cold on the idea and we're all back where we started.'

Orazio Battista, a member of the Sacred College since the time of Pope Sixtus V, was easily the most powerful Cardinal in Rome, to whom even the cardinal-nephews deferred. As Camerlengo of the Apostolic Camera, the Vatican treasury, he controlled the finances of the Holy See and the Papal States. He knew the wealth of every member of the Curia and how that wealth had been acquired.

'A hard man to fathom,' Caravaggio said. 'He knows where the bodies are buried.'

'Yes,' said Longhi. 'But that's mainly because he dug the graves.'

'Exactly. And popes depend on bastards like that. They may talk about the power of prayer, but it's the Inquisition and the army they rely on in a crisis.'

Orsi dispensed another round of drinks. 'You know what they say about Battista. Get on his wrong side and the next thing you know you're strung up by the arms in the Tor di Nona, begging for mercy … either that or crawling around the scaffold looking for your head.'

At that thought, Caravaggio shivered.

'Well,' said Longhi, 'hold on a moment. Maybe we're looking at this the wrong way round. See it from Battista's perspective, perched up there in the Vatican. Christian Europe must seem pretty well invincible to him right now. As far as he's concerned, it's not the Turks that are the problem, but the English and the Dutch – and they're a long way from Rome. Look at our monuments, our churches, our city walls, the cardinals and princes in their finery. The Swiss Guard, too, of course, and the Knights Hospitaller out there in Malta. And, please, let's not forget the *sbirri*. The moment the Turks appear on the top of the Quirinal Hill, they'll be arrested for carrying scimitars without a permit.'

The other two grinned at this. But Longhi wasn't finished.

'The point is – and this is what they all forget – the Muslims don't give up that easily. They're hard bastards, fighting for a cause they believe in. They think history's on their side, no matter how long it takes. And from what I hear, if they die in battle they go straight to heaven, with seventy virgins each to attend to their needs.'

'Is that a fact?' Orsi asked. 'Well, they wouldn't stay virgins for long if it was me.'

This prompted Caravaggio to yawn expansively. 'Listen to him, Onorio. You'd never guess he had the smallest prick in Ortaccio.'

'All the same,' said Longhi, 'you watch. Before we're too old we'll be out there on the Hungarian plains, fighting for Christian survival.'

'We can only hope,' said Caravaggio.

8*
Conclave minus 15

Maya Studer had been looking for a way of escape when she first met Liam Dempsey. The reception at the Irish College on the Via dei Santo Quattro had been dull even by the standards of ecclesiastical hospitality in Rome. An elderly Italian bishop was shamelessly flirting with her by the drinks table, seeking to impress her with the extent of his connections. Several times he patted her hand; once he even stroked her arm. She had smiled politely, then, when Dempsey drifted past on his way to the college garden, she had hooked her arm under his and announced in impeccable Italian: 'I'm sorry, Your Grace, but my fiancé and I really have to go. We're trying for a baby, and the way my cycle works this afternoon may be our best hope.'

Frustratingly for Dempsey, that had been the high point so far. He hadn't even kissed Maya yet, let alone slept with her. She wasn't that kind of girl – or so it seemed. But she was happy enough to spend time in his company. This was their second lunch date and the next step, apparently, was to go to a movie.

They had met in front of the Fontana del Moro, at the southern end of the Piazza Navona. Now, as they made their way past jugglers, human statues and several prostrate beggars to the Tre Scalini restaurant, she again hooked her arm under his so that he thought they must look like two young lovers. It felt good. Maya, like nearly all upper-class Swiss, was an accomplished linguist, born and raised in the German-speaking canton of Schaffhausen, near the border with Baden-Württemberg. Twenty-six years old, she had the most startling green eyes and thick black hair. Her designer clothes were from the Milan fashion houses and her shoes from Bologna. Today, she wore a high-waisted, pale-lemon skirt that ended some three inches above her knees and a white, ruffled blouse, the top three buttons of which were undone, exposing a deep and well-defined cleavage. She made Dempsey, in his jeans, blue shirt and sneakers, feel like a peasant. But it wasn't just her clothes. A lawyer by training, she had recently returned to Europe from the United States, where she had earned an MBA at the Harvard Business School. In the meantime, she had been recruited to a job in the legal department of UBS Bank in Zurich and was due to start work in September. So even if they ended up having a summer romance, Dempsey doubted that he'd ever see her again much past the autumn. Still, that still left a good eight weeks and he was determined to make the most of it.

He didn't like to admit it, but he was nervous. It was almost two years since he'd been with a woman. He felt like a born-again virgin.

When they reached the Tre Scalini, with its unrivalled view of Bernini's Fontana dei Quattro Fiumi he realized, too late, that he should have booked. The day was hot and sticky and the tables beneath the big umbrellas were hopelessly crowded.

But then Maya smiled at the major-domo in his crisp linen jacket, and seconds later a table appeared, as if by magic, followed by a waiter bearing a complimentary bottle of Pellegrino. The grateful diners ran their eyes quickly down the lunch menu and ordered pasta and a bottle of Frascati.

Though Dempsey imagined Maya to be somewhat 'proper' in her attitude to men – a product, perhaps, of her Swiss upbringing – the reality was very different. There had been a string of lovers during her student days, in all of whom she lost interest as soon as the thrill of conquest faded. At Harvard, a little older and wiser, she had slept with three of her fellow graduate students and conducted a protracted, on-off affair with her director of studies. The fact of the matter is, she was waiting for the young Irishman to make the first move. She knew that he had been through hard times since his trauma in Iraq and probably hadn't been with a woman for at least a year. She wouldn't blame him if he lacked confidence. Who wouldn't, she told herself, after spending twelve months in reconstructive surgery? But so far as she was concerned, he was quite exceptionally attractive. In one sense, he was conventionally handsome, with strong, regular features and a thick mane of hair. But it was his eyes that had really drawn her attention. They looked haunted, as if they had seen too much of the world's horror. She could imagine him playing a brilliant, but vulnerable young doctor in an afternoon TV drama, or maybe a soldier – which, of course, was what he had been. She didn't doubt that sooner or later – preferably sooner – they would go to bed together. What happened after that was anybody's guess.

The Frascati had arrived and Dempsey poured each of them a glass.

'*Sláinte!*' he said.

'*Sláinte chugat* – good health to you.'

'Jesus Christ! Do you speak Irish as well?'

This made her laugh. 'No,' she said. 'It was something the rector of the Irish College said to me the other night.'

'The rector? So he was hitting on you as well.'

'Why, are you jealous?'

'I just remember the bishop with his hand on your arm.'

'Even men of God have eyes,' she said, staring at him across the top of her glass. 'And desires.'

'Don't we all?' he said.

They sipped at their wine.

'What would you be doing if you were back in Galway?' she asked.

He thought for a second. 'Probably looking out at the rain through a pub window.'

The thought pleased her. 'Maybe you'll take me there some day,' she said.

'You never know,' he replied. He wondered if he should make the first move.

The waiter brought their order.

Dempsey raised a forkful of lightly grilled zucchini. 'Let's talk about you for a change. You must have had a strong Catholic upbringing to have a father who ended up as commandant of the Swiss Guard. You don't get much more faithful than that.'

'Hold on,' she replied, laughing. 'Didn't you tell me your childhood home was full of religious statues?'

'That's true. My father said the rosary a dozen times a day. Sometimes when he was on the phone he'd pass the old-fashioned flex through his fingers like it was a set of beads.'

Maya tried to picture Mr Dempsey, his mouth moving in silent prayer as he listened to his bank manager recommending a new vehicle for his savings.

'Do you miss him?'

The blue in his eyes turned to ice as he considered his reply. 'He wasn't an easy man,' was all he said.

'Perhaps he would have said the same about you.'

'Perhaps.'

She reached for the bottle of Frascati and refilled their glasses. 'But tell me more about your uncle. If you think my father is a leading Catholic, what about him? He must be the first ever Irish Superior General. Is that right?'

Dempsey responded gratefully to the change of subject. 'He's the first all right. A pioneer. Not quite the same thing, though, is it? While my uncle gets to dress in black from head to foot, your father is a one-man sartorial riot, with scarlet tunic and knee-britches, buckled shoes, a ruff and a silver helmet with an ostrich feather in it.'

'He looks good, don't you think?'

'I'd certainly pick him out in a police line-up.'

'Except,' said Maya, 'that he's the head of the police.'

Now Dempsey was grinning. 'Seriously,' he said, 'what made him go for the job? He and your mother get a pretty cool apartment, I'll grant you that. But it's still a bit of an odd thing to do. Like being colonel-in-charge of the Beefeaters.'

'For a start,' said Maya, twisting a mouthful of pasta onto her fork, 'he didn't go for the job. He was asked. You have to be invited. And for another thing, he'd been a top business executive for twenty years and an army officer for seven years before that, with five more years in the Reserve. So it was time for a change. As for being a good Catholic, I'd say he's above average, nothing more. But he believes in it and his loyalty to the Pope is absolute.'

Dempsey put his fork down and raised his glass to his lips. 'So if he heard there were shenanigans afoot in the conclave, he'd be concerned?'

'Shenanigans? I don't understand.'

'Goings-on. Things that shouldn't be happening.'

'What are you suggesting?'

'Just thinking aloud. If he heard there were people in high places putting undue pressure on certain cardinals to give their vote to a certain hardline candidate, would that be something your father would take notice of?'

She looked at him hard. It was obvious to him that she didn't like the direction in which their conversation was going. 'Of course he'd take notice,' she said. 'But there'd be nothing he could do … not unless there was murder involved, or blackmail – something of that order. You have to realize that in the interregnum between two papacies my father's primary, indeed sole loyalty, is to the College of Cardinals.'

'But there are hundreds of cardinals, from all over the world, most of whom he's never met. How can he be loyal to all of them?'

'It's an institutional loyalty, stupid. It works through the Camerlengo.'

'Cardinal Bosani?'

'Yes, but …'

'And what if the Camerlengo is pursuing his own agenda?'

Maya bristled. 'Don't be ridiculous!'

Dempsey's eyes darted round the tables next to them, where various combinations of Italians and lesser races were enjoying their lunch. 'Keep your voice down,' he said. 'Don't you know, the Curia's agents are everywhere?'

This stopped her in her tracks. Then she caught the look in his eyes and the tension dissolved in a flash. 'Oh!' she said. 'I get it. You are making fun of me.'

'Maybe I am and maybe I'm not,' he said. 'It's just that my uncle has got the crazy idea that Cardinal Bosani wants a pro-European, anti-Muslim Pope. He thinks there's a faction in the Curia out to provoke a confrontation with Islam.'

'What on earth for?' She looked dubious.

'A Catholic revival, I suppose. Just what we need in these troubled times.'

Maya leaned in, sensing the antipathy. 'Bosani is not my favourite cardinal. He's a smooth-talking bully with an over-inflated sense of his own importance. But he's not a madman. No one who wanted war in Europe could ever earn the confidence of two popes. The idea that he could rig the vote in favour of his own candidate is preposterous. For a start, it ignores the fact that most of the cardinals due here next week have all sorts of ideas about who would do the best job. Take it from me, all Cardinal Bosani wants is a pope who stands up for the faith in troubled times. Is that so too much to ask?'

'I suppose not,' said Dempsey, appearing to accept the logic of her argument. 'I think maybe my uncle's just a bit on edge because there aren't any Jesuits in the race. Even so, if you hear anything, you might let me know ... just to put his mind at rest.'

'He sounds a bit paranoid, if you don't mind my saying so.'

'Aren't they all?' he said. 'More to the point, are you still on for a film tonight? Only, Rome's full of tourists and I'd need to book in advance.'

She looked at him and her face softened. He was a hard man to say no to. 'I'm not sure if the Irish and the Swiss were ever made to get along,' she said. 'But I'll give it a go ... for now. Call it an experiment.'

'Excellent,' he said. 'I'll pick you up at seven-thirty. Dress informal.'

9*
Conclave·minus 14

Dempsey had never even heard of the Galleria Doria Pamphilj until his uncle gave him a free ticket courtesy of the Rome tourist office.

'Take my word for it,' O'Malley said. 'There's no finer gallery in Rome. What's more, this is no ordinary ticket. It grants you admission for an hour after the gallery has officially closed, so you should have the place almost to yourself. A rare privilege.'

'Do you get upgraded on flights home as well?' Dempsey asked, impressed despite himself.

'Matter of fact, I do,' the Father General replied. 'But don't tell anyone.'

Next day, Dempsey spent eight straight hours in the National Library on the Viale Castro Pretorio, researching material for his PhD. It turned out to be a rather one-sided quest. While there were hundreds of letters and documents relating to Garibaldi and King Victor Emmanuel, the papers of Pope Pius IX were mostly locked away in the Vatican Library. He did, though, find one quotation from Pius – the last pontiff to reign as sovereign of the Papal States – that struck him as relevant to present-day tensions in Italy. The Jews, His Holiness said in a speech in 1871, were 'dogs', and there were too many of these 'dogs' in Rome. 'We hear them howling in the streets. They disturb us everywhere we go.' Substitute Muslims for Jews and it was the same situation today. Now *there* was a pope Bosani could respect.

It was after four o'clock before he started out for the Pamphilj gallery. It was rush hour – what the Italians called *l'ora di punta*. The pavements were packed with commuters heading to the Metro or making their way to the main railway station a little further west. Dempsey drew a deep breath as he left the cool seclusion of the library. It was yet another sticky summer's evening. The air-conditioning units, turned up to high despite the latest government regulations, droned overhead, dripping water steadily onto the ground. He considered taking a bus, but Roman bus routes were incredibly complicated. It was said you had to be born in the city to have any hope of understanding them. Better to take a little longer on foot than end up a kilometre or more in the wrong direction.

It was when he stopped for a cold beer off the Via della Gatta that he learned from RaiNews 24 that the gardener injured by the bomb in the cloisters of the Lateran cathedral had died two hours earlier in the San Giovanni Hospital. Few of the tourists in the crowded bar understood the bulletin, but a definite murmur of hostility rose from the Romans present.

'Bloody Arabs!' one man with a leather jacket and a comb-over said beneath his breath. 'One minute they're shooting at a judge, the next they're blowing the legs off one of the Pope's gardeners.'

'Poor bastard,' someone said. 'Didn't even know what hit him.'

The barman nodded. 'But when's the government going to bloody well do something? Pity we can't have Berlusconi back. They'll be bombing my mother when she comes out of Mass before anyone sits up and takes notice.'

Dempsey finished his beer and headed back into the evening sunshine. He understood the sentiment. After his own experience, he had no time for Islamic terrorists. But he still found this kind of talk wearing.

Two minutes later, he arrived at the Palazzo Pamphilj, next to the old Collegio Romano. He showed his invitation to a uniformed guard and was directed towards a set of marble stairs. The sculpture room, the first stop on the tour, didn't interest him. He'd never cared much for sculpture, which always reminded him of public parks filled with bronze aldermen in frock coats, or 'martyrs' calling on others to follow their example. Hurrying past a lubricious centaur and a tiny figure of Socrates reclining in the fireplace, he followed the signs up another set of stairs to the first of the picture galleries.

The initial impact was of a saleroom he had once visited in Dublin. There were paintings – hundreds of them – stacked all the way up to the ceiling. Some were so jammed together that it was hard to make them out. It was the painterly equivalent of *l'ora di punta*.

There was, of course, one exception. The celebrated portrait of Innocent X by Velàsquez was displayed in its own secluded *gabinetto*, next to a bust of the pontiff by Bernini. The decision to keep the Velàsquez separate from the rest of the collection was nothing new. Isolation was a fact of life for those who sat on the Throne of St Peter's. It was central to their role. And it was appropriate that the only face Innocent had to gaze upon when the public took their leave each evening was his own – which was almost certainly the case in real life.

Dempsey sympathized. For the first four weeks of his burns treatment, smeared with antibiotic cream, he had been secured inside a pressurized steel chamber filled with oxygen. The sensation was disorientating. He had felt like an astronaut lost in space. Every day he went to sleep and wakened in the same position, face down, arms and legs outstretched, as if he were crucified – except that he had never felt further from God. The longer-term treatment was only marginally more bearable. His extreme susceptibility to infection meant that for the next three months doctors and nurses, wearing masks and speaking to him in French, were his only contact with the world. Each morning, to a background of Mozart, Berlioz and Strauss, specialist technicians would scrape away the dead tissue from his back, buttocks and thighs – an excruciating procedure known as debridement. In a bid to promote the generation of healthy tissue beneath, whole layers of scabs were removed. But the worst part came when grafts from a specially bred pig were attached to the still-forming sub-cutaneous layers of his skin. It was as if he were being robbed of the last remaining vestige of his humanity and turned into someone, or something, else. Yet dreadful though all of this had been, nothing was as bad as the overwhelming sense of solitude. If it was true that a drowning man reviewed his whole life in the minute or so it took him to die, it was also the case that a man staring at the floor for six months revisited again and again and again every decision he had ever taken, every mistake he ever made, every girl he ever slept with. He was bound to his past like Prometheus to his rock, constantly reminded of his failings, waking each morning to be devoured alive.

Prominent among the spectral presences was the shade of his father, who moved through secret doors inside the chambers of his memory, turning up when he was least wanted, asking questions to which there were no answers. He had never understood the nature of their relationship. Perhaps they didn't have one. Perhaps they had just lived in the same house. He told himself that if his mother had survived, everything would have been different. She would have given him love and understanding. The farm would have known laughter as well as whiskey fumes. But that was just fantasy. After she died giving birth to him, the old man, like Miss Havesham in *Great Expectations*, became suspended in time. His long silences, interrupted only by prayer and periodic torrents of abuse, had persisted for more than twenty years.

Not that his own life since had lacked variety. There had even been moments of sublime black comedy. A week after his father died, as he lay face down in France, unable to attend the funeral, his fiancée, Siobhán, wrote to him from Dublin to tell him she was sorry, but she couldn't cope with his injuries and was breaking off their engagement. 'I know I must seem heartless,' she had written, 'and I want you to know how dreadful I feel about leaving you like this. I can only ask you to see the situation from my perspective.' He saw it well enough. Given everything else that had happened, the blatant egoism of her decision had made him laugh out loud – which hurt. The duty nurse, who had read him the letter in her heavily accented English, only half understanding it, thought he was out of his mind and summoned the doctor, who gave him a sedative.

The last he heard, Siobhán had married a hedge fund manager whose brother played cricket for Ireland. Cricket! Well, good luck to her. It had been a foolish relationship to begin with, which would never have lasted. She'd have divorced him inside of three years, pausing only to take him to the cleaners.

But time, as the cliché had it, was the great healer. Having never believed it, he now knew it was true. The scars on his back would always be there, but the ones inside his head had begun to close. He could feel life returning, like sap rising in a tree after a long winter. It had come back not only in the muscles of his back and the wasted sinews of his arms and legs, but in his altered view of the world and its possibilities. He had learned things about himself that he could never have known otherwise. He was less carefree since Iraq, less self-obsessed. He was more thoughtful, more discriminating. But the other side was always there, too. There were things he had learned that you weren't supposed to know until you were old. The fragility of human life and the despair that hid around every corner, waiting to declare itself, was something he could not dismiss. The only thing he could be sure of was that he was different now – new-forged – and he would have to be satisfied with that.

He felt a hand on his arm. A woman standing next to him in the gallery asked him in English if he was all right. Her voice seemed to come from somewhere else. It was then he realized that he had been gazing for a several minutes into the cold, sceptical eyes of Innocent X. He turned to the woman, who happened to be an American. 'Yes, I'm fine,' he said. 'I was just trying to work out what he was thinking.'

'I wouldn't know,' she said, moving away. 'I'm a Baptist.'

Smiling to himself, he backed out of His Holiness's presence and made his way down a long, brilliantly lit gallery until he was moved to halt in front of a double portrait of two lawyers by Raphael and *Salome with the Head of John the Baptist* by Titian. Both were extraordinary. The glistened as if they had only just been completed. But it was the Caravaggios he had come to see.

Earlier in the day, determined to show his uncle that he was not a complete prat when it came to art, he had taken the opportunity to view *Judith with the*

Head of Holofernes in the Palazzo Barberini, at the bottom of the Via Veneto. It was easily the most terrifying painting he had ever seen. According to his audio guide, Holofernes was an Assyrian general who had threatened the destruction of Israel. So no change there. Judith, a wealthy and beautiful Jewess, seduced him, then cut off his head as he slept. Must have been employed by Mossad, he reckoned. Holofernes had woken up just too late to avoid his fate. His killer, looking as if she found the task frankly distasteful but necessary, had slit his throat with his own sword, then just carried on sawing while a leather-faced crone stood ready to wrap up the head in a sheet. The victim's blood shot out thickly from his gaping neck, soaking his sheets and pillow, while his stifled scream echoed across the gallery.

Uncle Declan had warned him that Caravaggio was obsessed with capital punishment. At least a quarter of his paintings featured severed heads, some of them based on his own pain-racked features. Perhaps he had had a premonition. Following some dismal murder or other, he'd passed his last years as a fugitive. The story went that he'd been hunted down by unknown enemies who in the end had got their man.

But the two canvases Dempsey sought out in the Pamphilj could not have been more different. The first showed a penitent Mary Magdalene, the 'bad girl' of the New Testament, with her head bowed and arms loosely folded in her lap. The idea, evidently, was that she was repenting of her past and turning to Christ, but to Dempsey it was more like she ached for something that had been taken from her. There was certainly more to her melancholy than a renunciation of high living. But then he looked at the painting next to it, *Rest During the Flight into Egypt*. At first, he didn't think much of it. For a start, the Sinai looked less like a desert than a glimpse of the Garden of Eden, which made no sense. As Mary cradled the baby Jesus, Joseph, looking distinctly world-weary – as well he might, given the recent turn of events – held up a music score so that a half-naked angel violinist could play not a lullaby, as he first thought, but the Song of Songs.

But then he looked closer – and that's when it got interesting. It was the same girl in both paintings. Had to be: the same red hair and generous figure, head turned down, eyes closed. As Mary Magdalene, her arms were empty, clutching only empty space. But in the second work, she held her baby close to her heart – and it made all the difference in the world. Art, Dempsey was coming to realize, was not always about what it was about. Had the model, obviously well known to Caravaggio, maybe lost a baby? Was the artist giving us, in fact, a before and after portrait of loss? Whatever the truth, there were obviously two Caravaggios, one a consummate artist, a sensitive observer of the human psyche; the other haunted, fatalistic and disabled by self-loathing.

Just like that, Dempsey felt he had found a friend.

10*
4 October 1603

Jesus said: 'So secret is predestination, O brethren, that I say to you, truly, only to one man shall it be clearly known. He it is whom the nations look for, to whom the secrets of God are so clear that, when he comes into the world, blessed shall they be that shall listen to his words …' The disciples answered, 'O Master, who shall that man be of whom you speak, who shall come into the world?' Jesus answered joyous of heart: 'He is Muhammad, Messenger of God.'

—The gospel of Barnabas, Chapter 163

There were summonses in Rome that you could ignore and those you could not. Those from the office of the Camerlengo fell very definitely into the second category. A constable of the *sbirri* had pounded on Caravaggio's door. When the artist answered, wiping sleep from his eyes, he was told that he was to present himself that afternoon at the Palazzo Battista on the Via Monseratto.

'What for?'

'No prizes there, Merisi,' the constable said, with a sneer. 'To answer charges about your scurrilous personal behaviour. From what I hear, His Eminence wants to find out whether or not you're a heretic who should have his head cut off. So I wouldn't worry about it. Just routine.'

The constable, a thug Caravaggio had run across several times in the last year, sniggered before adding: 'I wouldn't advise you to keep His Eminence waiting. He can be very *persuasive* with people who get on the wrong side of him. Know what I mean?' Leaning forward, he wrinkled his nose, making snuffling noises like a bloodhound. 'And something else: I'd have a wash first. He's very particular about that.'

Caravaggio felt his blood run cold. 'I'll be there,' he said. 'No need to send for reinforcements. Now oblige me, Constable, and fuck off.'

It was just after three according to the clock in the Piazza Firenze when he reached the front door of Battista's residence. It was no more than a hundred paces from the Corte Savella prison, where Beatrice Cenci had been tortured before her execution, which did not seem a good omen. The last time he had felt this nervous, he realized, was October 1601, when he was arrested for brawling in Trastevere and carrying a sword without a permit. On that occasion, he had spent two terrifying nights in the cells of the Tor di Nona. The offence was his fifth of a serious nature since coming to live in Rome in 1592, and the head of the *sbirri*, enraged by the boldness and seeming impunity of the city's self-styled *bravi*, was determined to make an example. He had been thrown into the prison's deepest, dankest dungeon, known as the 'pit', where, as he lay in the darkness, all he could hear were the screams of the damned. Twenty-four hours later, he was brought out and shown the instruments of torture by a priest of the Holy Office, which had made him piss himself. If Cardinal Del Monte, prompted by the Colonna family, his father's employers, hadn't acted to free him, he had no doubt that he would have been hung up by his arms, with stone weights attached to his feet – an ordeal known as *strappado* – until he confessed to whatever crimes the *sbirri* needed to clear up and which they found it convenient to attribute to him. His next appointment, his last, would then have been with the headsman on the Ponte Sant'Angelo – a prospect that filled him with mortal dread.

It wasn't that long ago that he didn't worry about death – or at least knew how to laugh about it. Not any more. Now it was as if the darkness was pressing down on him, making his head hurt, transferring the grotesqueries of his dreams into his waking life. Others had noticed it. His temper these days erupted with alarming suddenness, clouding his judgment, causing him to inflate every slight, real or imagined, into a question of honour. Not long ago, he had thrown a plate of hot artichokes into the face of a waiter who couldn't say which were cooked with butter and which in oil. Not content with humiliating the fellow, he had then drawn his sword and threatened him, for no good reason. It was if a demon possessed him. The only thing that sustained him, and kept him from thoughts of suicide, was his unshakeable conviction that he was the greatest painter in Italy since Tintoretto, perhaps since Titian. This might have been hard for some of his rivals to accept, but it was true. Perhaps because they agreed with him, the others refused to leave him alone. Everything he did, every canvas, every drawing, was placed on the dissecting table of their vanity and minutely examined for flaws, mostly of a moral nature. Fellow painters praised him in public, but in private they spread poison about him and undercut his prices. The Church, meanwhile, suspected him of something close to heresy, as if his vision of Christ and the Apostles was motivated by something other than devotion. He couldn't understand it. More than that, he didn't understand himself.

He remembered how he had bounded into the home of Cherubini full of confidence and self-assertion. That wouldn't work with Battista, said to be cold and cerebral, but, above all, ruthless. No one had the ear of the Pope the way Battista did. Not even Pietro Aldobrandini, the cardinal-nephew, wielded as much raw power.

The bare bones of his story were well known. The son of a Sienese banker who made a fortune working for Venice during its long struggle with Genoa, Battista was rumoured to have paid 85,000 scudi into the papal exchequer in return for the post he now held. The previous record, according to Orsi, was 70,000 scudi. But it was worth it. With the revenues of the Holy See and the Papal States now bigger than ever, the Camerlengo's control of taxation, gifts and the issue of coins made him a pivotal figure in the economy of Europe far beyond the papal domains. Not even the Medici or the bankers of Switzerland dared defy him. Battista was the master of all he surveyed, and his surveys were no less than the audit of Christendom.

Yet closest of all to the heart of the Camerlengo was said to be his control of the finances that governed the war with the Ottomans. In recent years, while the Turks re-armed and prepared for a renewed offensive in the Mediterranean, money from Rome aimed at the maintenance of strong defences had steadily declined. Battista argued that no other course made sense. To wage war on a grand scale in perpetuity led only to bankruptcy. Let the Sublime Court spend its strength on a course that ultimately spelled ruin; Europe would not make the same mistake. As the power of Spain reduced and the cohesion of France continued to be challenged by religious division, some, like Longhi, thought it strange that Battista took so sanguine a view. But he was not alone. The Pope, with his background in ecclesiastical law, saw Protestantism and civil unrest, not Islam, as the greatest threat to the Church. The Ottomans, in his opinion, had had their wings clipped at Lepanto and could safely be left to the emperor and the Knights of Malta.

Caravaggio, waiting in the entrance hall of Battista's palazzo, prided himself in the sophistication of his political views. He mixed, after all, with princes and prelates, who frequently confided in him and even asked his opinions. But today he had to steer well clear of such matters. Instead, he rehearsed over and over in his mind what he would say if challenged to defend himself against the charge of heresy. The Camerlengo was supposed to be an ascetic, who preferred to say Mass in his own chapel, away from the crowds, and had even turned his back on wine. There certainly weren't many paintings in his hallway, and none of religious subjects, save for a large and distinctly second-rate Abraham and Isaac. In their place were elegant vases, woodcuts and a series of framed maps. The only sign of ego was a portrait of Battista himself, by Annibale Carracci, that occupied an alcove to the left of the main staircase. As rendered by Carracci, he looked strong-willed and calculating, with furrowed brow and fleshy lips: not a man to be crossed.

After a wait of some twenty minutes, a door to the right opened and a young priest emerged. He was of medium height, with no distinguishing features whatso-ever, dressed from head to foot in black. 'His Eminence will see you now,' he said in an unexpectedly high voice, 'and if you wish to survive the experience you will keep a civil tongue in your head.'

Caravaggio said nothing, merely nodded. The priest, who did not give his name, led the way into a broad *loggia* lit down one side by floor-to-ceiling windows through which a formal garden and fountains could be seen. Beyond, in the middle of a summer's afternoon, it was insufferably hot and humid; within the walls of the palace it was cool and inviting. Their footsteps echoed on the marble tiles. Suddenly, the priest halted and turned to his right towards a set of heavy oak doors on which he knocked firmly, yet politely.

A voice called out, '*Entrato!*'

'Your Eminence,' the priest said, pushing the doors open, 'the artist Merisi.'

'Ah yes. Come in, Merisi. Let me have a look at you.' In contrast with the high treble of the priest, Battista's voice was low and booming.

Caravaggio did as he was bid. The priest retreated, closing the double doors.

The cardinal was seated behind a large, ornate desk, an ironic smile fixed on his face. 'Father Acquaviva did not exaggerate,' he said after a lengthy pause. 'You look like one of the men I employ to catch rats in my basement.'

Not the best of starts. 'I'm sorry to offend you, Your Eminence. But I did in fact wash before I set out.'

'Really? And what about your clothes? When did they last see soap and water?'

'I'm afraid I tend to buy clothes and wear them until they are … well, as you see me now. Then I throw them away.'

'I see. Remarkable. Quite remarkable.' The Camerlengo, in his early sixties, sturdily built with broad shoulders, wore a scarlet cassock fashioned, Caravaggio thought, from pure silk, with a lace trim. His shoes were brilliant red, with silver buckles. It was impossible not to notice his dark, penetrating eyes. If the eyes were indeed the windows of the soul, Caravaggio told himself, then this man's soul was as black as anything in Dante's *Inferno*. The cardinal's pate was bald on top, with a fringe of dark hair that matched his black beard. His skull cap sat next to him on the desk. But what was most obvious about him was his malformed left arm, perhaps three inches shorter than it ought to be, ending in a hand the fingers of which were retracted, like a claw. Already, a portrait of the man was forming in the artist's head.

But then he realized that Battista was still speaking.

'Perhaps you should rethink your sartorial strategy. After all, you are not a swineherd. Your calling brings you into contact with nobles and princes of the Church. You should dress accordingly.'

'Yes, Eminence.'

'And if you sweat a lot, wash more frequently.'

'I shall endeavour to follow your advice.'

'That would be wise.' The cardinal looked cool and relaxed. He did not invite his guest to take a chair. 'Now tell me, why do you keep being arrested? What is wrong with you? You insist on fighting every week as if your life depended on it. Yet the offence given, or imagined, rarely justifies more than a rebuke. Are you incontinent, Merisi?'

'*What?*'

'Can you not hold yourself back? Must every slight be met with a rapier thrust?'

'These are not easy times,' came the mumbled reply.

'What was that? Speak up, man.'

'I said, we don't live in easy times, Eminence.'

'Is that so? Is it really? Then let me make things easier for you. I have spoken to Cardinal Del Monte and he agrees with me that this cannot go on. Should you come to the attention of the *sbirri* once more, to the extent that I have to be informed of your behaviour, you may expect to be arrested and detained. Should your offence be grave, you will meet with the full rigour of the law. There will be no further dawn amnesties. Do I make myself clear?'

'You do, Eminence. As a church bell.'

'I am glad to hear it. I should regret having to add your name to the list of those being investigated by the Holy Office, but I shall not shrink from it. Your constant street brawls, your whoring, your lack of respect for established traditions in art have become a source of public scandal. Your appearance, meanwhile, is an affront to decency. Why are you not married? What age are you?'

'Thirty-two, Eminence.'

'Are you a sodomite?'

'No, Eminence, I am not.'

'That's something, I suppose. You know that the penalty for sodomy is death! But let that go – for now. The thing is, you offend the dignity of the Church, Merisi. More particularly, you offend me – and I can assure you that that is not a good position to be in.' The cardinal squinted at his victim as if he couldn't quite make him out. 'Men have died for less. Women, too.'

Caravaggio could feel the veins in his neck begin to swell. Having to repress his natural instincts like this was almost more than he could endure. He wanted to punch the self-righteous prick in his smug, jowly face and tell him what he thought of him. But this time he knew better. 'No, Eminence,' he said, between clenched teeth. 'I can see that.'

'Good.' Battista picked up a letter from his desk. 'I have a note here from Master Laerzio Cherubini. You know him, I think: an esteemed legal adviser to the Holy See and a devout Catholic. He complains that your rendering of the death, or dormition, of the Virgin, commissioned for the church of Santa Maria della Scala, is an affront to the Council of Trent, verging on blasphemy. He adds that you were exceedingly rude to him in the presence of a bishop and implied that he frequented brothels.'

'Master Cherubini is a pompous buffoon, Eminence, and no expert on what is blasphemous and what is not. He is also a liar and owes me 230 scudi.'

Battista smiled thinly, reminding Caravaggio of the priest who had shown him the instruments of torture in the Tor di Nona. 'An interesting response. And what about Superior General Acquaviva, who has made a similar complaint about you in relation to a different painting, this time of *The Supper at Emmaus*?'

'The Father General and I must agree to disagree.'

'He says you are a heretic.'

'That is not a view shared by the Holy Father.'

Battista's stare turned to ice. 'So in both instances, the critics are wrong and you are right, is that it?'

Caravaggio felt his mouth go dry. 'We each have our point of view, Eminence.'

Before the cardinal could respond further, the young priest, obviously his private secretary, appeared unannounced through a different door and whispered something in his master's ear. Battista nodded. 'There is something I must attend to,' he said, 'but I have not finished with you. You will wait for me in the hallway. Oblige me by not murdering anyone in my absence.'

Caravaggio bowed and went out to resume his seat in the main reception area. After five fretful minutes, he could sit still no longer. Getting up from his chair, he examined Battista's portrait, recently completed, by the look of it. If anything, Carracci had been generous to his subject. He had captured the power, but not the cruelty of the man – except, perhaps, in the eyes. No doubt that was deliberate. To the right of the portrait was a table on which sat a series of carvings by Ottoman artists, which Battista must have brought back with him from his time in Constantinople. Wasn't that where he'd been? He wasn't sure. These led the way to the framed maps, showing each of Europe's great powers, from England in the west to Turkey in the east. Caravaggio followed the frames along an oak-panelled corridor until he reached the door of what was obviously, given the cross and coat of arms carved into the panelling, the cardinal's private chapel. After the briefest of debates with himself, he opened the door, expecting to find there the usual range of religious art. Instead, as his eyes adjusted to the gloom, he saw that there were no paintings whatsoever and that, for some reason, the cross on the altar had been laid flat.

That was when he heard the voices – which startled him, for the chapel had appeared to be empty. He listened, keeping perfectly still so as not to reveal his presence. They didn't sound like priests at a sung Mass. What he heard was much more soaring and rhythmic. He was intrigued. Edging forward, but still careful to remain hidden from view behind a pillar, he let his eyes search out the source of the incantation. What he saw made him draw breath. The Camerlengo and his secretary were on their knees, prostrating themselves on mats rolled out across the stone floor. It was they who were reciting the strange prayers. Caravaggio felt a chill came over him. What in God's name were they up to? They weren't even facing the altar, but were bent in the direction of the south-east. Both had their backs to him and gave no sign that they knew he was there. Only after several seconds did he realize, with a start, that the language they were using was Arabic.

He drew back, swallowing hard, feeling his stomach start to heave. As he did so, he caught sight of a third figure, standing at the rear of the chapel. A young priest, with dirty-fair hair. He didn't appear to have noticed Caravaggio. What clearly transfixed him was the bizarre sight of the Camerlengo of the Holy Roman Church apparently worshipping Allah. As Caravaggio watched, the man's mouth fell open and his eyes bulged. For several seconds, as his mind struggled to take in the scene being played out in front of him, he looked on in silence, as if hypnotized. Then, as the full significance hit him, he gasped. The sound was surprisingly loud and the heads of Battista and his secretary instantly came up from the floor and spun round towards the source of the interruption. For a brief moment, the two sides met each other's gaze, then Battista's voice roared out: 'Stop! Stand where you are!' For once, the prelate's command fell on deaf ears. The priest panicked. Turning quickly on his heels, he ran back the way he had come, the sound of his retreating footsteps echoing along the stone passage.

Battista and his secretary scrambled to their feet. The secretary reached beneath his cassock and produced a curved dagger. The Camerlengo, suffused with a cold fury, nodded. 'Quickly! He mustn't get away. If the Pope should hear of this, our plans will be in ruins. You must stop him. Go, Ciro! Hurry!' Both men surged towards the chapel's rear door.

Unseen, on the near side of the aisle, Caravaggio retreated, clicking the side door shut behind him and hastening back to the hallway. He was shaking uncontrollably. Only with a supreme effort of will did he restore some outward semblance of calm. This was something he should not have seen – should very definitely not have seen. It was dangerous; quite possibly fatal. As he ran back along the corridor, his mind tried to make sense of it – hoping to reveal some harmless explanation of the events in the chapel unconnected with heresy. But there was only one, inescapable conclusion. The Camerlengo was not the man he purported to be, but something else, something alien – a traitor to the Christian cause. There was a plan – no doubt a plot. This much Caravaggio knew. Yet he also knew, with total clarity, that if he were to say so, no one would believe him. Battista would have him arrested and tortured, then beheaded. The one available course, if he was to avoid his fate, was to say nothing and do nothing – not until he had had time to think. He stumbled on, regaining his chair in the *corridoio di ingresso* only just in time. Seconds later, looking red-faced and flustered, Battista burst through a set of double doors. Striding over to the window by the front door, minus his pectoral cross, he stared up and down the street outside.

Caravaggio's legs had turned to water. He coughed. Battista looked round.

'*You!*'

'Yes, Eminence. You asked me to wait.'

'So I did. Tell me, did a priest come through here a minute or so ago?'

'No, Eminence.'

'So you saw nothing?'

'No, Eminence.'

'Then get out!' came the reply, laced with vitriol. 'Get out now!' Caravaggio rose, bowed and leaned his head forward. Without thinking, the prelate extended his right hand to receive the *baciamano* – the kiss of fealty – except that, as he suddenly realized, his ring finger was bare. Embarrassed, he withdrew his hand beneath the sleeve of his scarlet cassock and turned away. Caravaggio, not daring to lift his gaze, was left to wonder if Battista had registered the sweat on his brow or the sound of his heart thumping in his chest.

That night, he got hopelessly drunk in the Turk's Head, ignoring the whores and the hustlers, reliving over and over again in his mind the terrifying scene he had witnessed. He had stumbled upon a terrible secret – one that he wanted to proclaim to the rooftops but dared not mention, not even to his closest friends, on pain of death. He felt cursed. It was inconceivable to him that the Camerlengo – the man charged by the Pope with funding the war against the Turks – could actually *be* a Muslim. But he couldn't deny the evidence of his eyes. His first impulse had been to run to the Apostolic Palace to warn the Pope that he had been betrayed. But that would only have played into Battista's hands. What proof did he have? None. Battista would counter that he had summoned the artist to warn him that if he didn't mend his ways, he could end up before the Inquisition. Who would the Pope believe, the prince or the pauper? It would be he, not Battista, would be put to the question. Perhaps if the priest, his co-witness, were to step forward, things would be different. He might then have the semblance of a chance. But the man had fled and must surely now be in hiding, in fear of his life. His next thought had been to confide in Del Monte. The cardinal was his friend and had been a member of the Sacred College for fifteen years. Everyone knew him as a man of probity and rectitude – though also a reckless homosexual! But what could even he do without evidence of the crime? Del Monte always thought the best of people and would probably conclude that his favourite painter had gone quite mad. In any case, the Pope owed a debt of loyalty to Battista. It was an open secret that it was because of funding from the Camerlengo that the Aldobrandini – unknowns from the poorer reaches of Florence – had grown so rich so quickly. It was Battista, acting for His Holiness, who had brokered a series of advantageous marriages for the family, with the Pamphilj and the Doria. He had also ensured that the cardinal-nephews were granted the most lucrative benefices in Rome.

No. It shamed him deeply to acknowledge it, but if he wished to live, silence was his only option.

It was a hot, sticky night, yet he was shivering. He hadn't eaten, he realized. All he had done was drink. Well, why not? At least wine helped dull the senses. He called for another jug of red. At the sound of his voice, a young whore he knew slightly tugged on his sleeve and asked him if he was looking for a good time. This was not what he needed to hear. Enraged beyond reason, he twisted round, wrenched her hand from his clothing and propelled her across the cobbles into a neighbouring table.

A young man with a wispy beard jumped up. There was wine spilled down his doublet. 'You're that fucking painter, aren't you?' he said. 'The one they call Caravaggio! Well, what the hell do you think you're playing at? If you know what's good for you, you'll apologize to me *and* the girl.'

Caravaggio snorted. He couldn't explain how, but his dagger had appeared in his hand and, jumping up, he now thrust the point of the blade against the young man's throat. 'Don't even think about it,' he whispered into his ear. 'My advice to you on an evening such as this, facing a man such as I, is to turn round, say nothing and fuck off.'

The youth drew back, his face white with fear. His right hand hovered nervously over the pommel of his sword. In a flash, Caravaggio reached out and cut clean through the belt that held the sword in its scabbard. The weapon clattered to the floor. 'Go home, boy,' he breathed, his face flushed with rage and shame. 'Go home and pray for Rome.'

Two of the youth's friends, seated at the same table, looked for a moment as if they might intervene. They were, after all, three to one. But a stern look from a couple of *bravi* seated opposite made them change their mind.

Caravaggio wiped his nose and face with the back of his hand and swayed off into the night, still talking to himself. It was as he made his way, tortuously, towards the Piazza Navona, his limbs suddenly drained of their strength, that he heard the sound of running feet. *Not that bloody boy!* he thought, turning round in the direction from which he had come. *Spare me that.* Before he could turn round, a stranger, his breath heavy and laboured, lurched into him from behind, practically knocking him off his feet, sending the knife flying. He struggled to regain his footing, cursing loudly. 'Who the fuck ..?' he began. But then he halted. There was a full moon overhead, and as the other man recovered his balance Caravaggio recognized, with a start, who it was. Mother of God! It was the priest from Battista's chapel – the one who could help him save the Catholic Church from treachery. He reached out unsteadily in an effort to restrain the fellow. This was the very person who could help him make sense of the afternoon's events. But his lunge was too slow and too awkward. The man, with wine on his breath, his eyes bright with fear, pulled away and staggered off into the darkness.

'Father! Wait! Hold on there! We need to talk!'

But he was too late.

As he stooped to recover his dagger, the drink he had taken finally caught up with him and he fell over. This was the moment when a second man appeared out of the shadows – tall and broad-shouldered, with a monk's tonsure, brandishing a heavy, two-edged sword. The newcomer glanced at Caravaggio, who stared back at him, almost as if he knew him, before moving off in pursuit of his quarry. Three minutes later, filled with a premonition of what he would find, Caravaggio came upon the the priest's body sprawled on the cobbles, arms outstretched. A step or so beyond the body lay the head. The eyes stared wildly, the mouth gaped, as if still calling out to God for mercy. For a moment, Caravaggio didn't know what to do or think. Then, instinctively, he pulled out the small sketch pad and chalk he always kept in one or other of his capacious pockets and began to draw the victim's face. The terror in the man's eyes would, like the frozen gaze of Beatrice Cenci, haunt him forever.

11*
Conclave minus 13

Franco Lucchese, from La Spezia, spent five years in Italy's *Reggimento d'Assalto Paracadutisti*, where he attained the rank of sergeant and was his unit's finest markman. Blonde-haired, just five feet, nine inches tall, he was built like a boxer, with the stamina and fighting skills to match. He had joined the army at the behest of his local Mafia *capo*, Renzo Giacconi, who wanted his *sgarriste*, or 'soldiers', to have the skills necessary to remain competitive in the post-9/11 world. But after serving six months in a military prison for breaking an officer's jaw, he was discharged and returned to general gangland duties. It was in 2009 that he was introduced by his boss to Cardinal Bosani, also from La Spezia – *Spèsa* in the local dialect – and finally discovered his true calling: assassination.

Lucchese was an intelligent man, entirely uninterested in ideas. This was his strength. He asked from life no more than a comfortable apartment, money in his pocket, women who understood his needs and someone to tell him where to go and whom to kill. He and his master were a perfect match. Bosani had a killer he could depend on. The fact that Franco believed he was doing God's work, however odd it sometimes seemed, only added to the satisfaction he derived from his work. As he told his confessor, Father Giacomo, who had ministered to the Mafia in Spèsa for more than thirty years, his role was to remove God's enemies and bring forward their appearance before the Seat of Judgment.

'And the Camerlengo has told you this?'

'Absolutely.'

'Very well. *Ego te absolvo.*'

Even so, when he was instructed by Bosani to 'silence' Cardinal Rüttgers, he had to admit it was unsettling. It was not right, surely, to murder a prince of the Church.

'Do not distress yourself, my son,' the Camerlengo had assured him. 'His Eminence is not an evil man. You will be sending him to God. But his politics, which are of the far left, mean, regrettably, that he has become a danger to the Church he serves. Next week, the cardinal electors must find a pope who can restore the purity of the Christian message in our divided continent. Rüttgers has said that he would work against this sacred mission and help install a pontiff who would offer hope to the Muslims. Is that what we want, Franco?'

'No, Eminence.'

'Very well. So take this and do what I ask of you.' He handed the Mafia soldier an envelope stuffed with euros and a tiny bottle, labelled as a throat spray. 'God will watch over you and guide your hand.'

'Thank you, Eminence. May I now have your blessing? And I should like it in the old form.'

'Of course, my son.' Bosani kissed the assassin on both cheeks, then raised his right hand in benediction. '*Misereatur tui omnipotens Deus, et dimissis peccatis tuis, perducat te ad vitam aeternam. In nomine Patris, et Filii, et Spiritus Sancti. Amen.* Almighty God have mercy on you and, having forgiven you your sins, bring you to life everlasting. In the name of the Father, the Son and the Holy Spirit. Amen.'

Next day, as darkness fell, Franco hid in the courtyard of the Collegio Teutonico di Santa Maria dell'Anima, known as the Anima, due south of the old Tor di Nona. The college and hospice, centred on Germany's national church, was founded in 1350 and contained the bones of the first German-born Pope, Adrian VI.

Wearing a clerical collar and soutane beneath his jacket, the Italian betrayed no sign of his true calling. Once he was sure that he was alone, he scaled the walls of the hospice and, using a floorplan given him by Father Visco, concealed himself on a ledge outside Rüttgers' bathroom. It was midsummer and the hinged window was open, so there was no need for him to break in. It was also big enough to allow him to gain entry without having to contort himself. His feet would land on a small matt placed next to the basin. All he had to do was oil the hinges, using a tiny can of 3-in-One, to ensure they didn't squeak. The bathtub, he noted with satisfaction, was located at the opposite end of the room, half concealed by an alcove that housed the toilet.

Rüttgers, he had been assured, liked to conclude each day with a bath, which he much preferred to the more usual shower. This evening, the cardinal was attending a function at the secretariat of the German Bishops Conference, on the Via della Conciliazione. He was expected home no later than eleven.

Franco sat down on the ledge outside the window and waited.

At nine minutes past eleven, he heard the bedroom door open. A minute after that, the cardinal – at least he assumed it was the cardinal – entered the bathroom, used the toilet and began to run the bath. Then he left again, – presumably to get undressed.

Franco listened. Another five minutes went by until Rüttgers re-entered the bathroom and, in gingerly fashion, lowered himself into the bath. The Italian said a quiet prayer and stood up. Pushing slightly at the window, he was able to look in and see the German prelate lying back, eyes closed, totally relaxed.

I hope you are in communion with God, Franco thought. *You will be meeting him soon.*

Checking that the 'throat spray' was in his pocket, the Mafia soldier removed his shoes, pushed open the window to its full extent and, one after the other, slid his legs over the sill. Seconds later, his feet touched down on the mat next to the basin. He had to move quickly now. If Rüttgers happened to turn round for any reason and call out, the result could be disastrous. He reached into his pocket and removed the spray. Reaching the bathtub in two measured strides, he reached down with his right forearm and caught his victim in a simple headlock.

The German's eyes opened wide in shock and his mouth gaped. It was the work of a moment for the killer to direct the fast-acting poison down his throat that he had been told would precisely mimic the symptoms of a stroke. Rüttgers shook violently for several seconds. His faced reddened, then, abruptly, he slid down into the water and expired without a word, his face etched with pain. Franco released him, blessed himself and made his way back to the window and onto the college roof. Ten minutes later, as dusk fell, he lowered himself back down into the college courtyard and made his way via a side gate into the Via della Pace.

Closing the gate behind him, he turned round and walked headlong into a young man making his way thoughtfully in the direction of the Vatican.

'*Mi scusi*,' said Franco, extending a steadying hand. 'I should watch where I'm going.'

'*Prego, Padre*,' said Liam Dempsey, on his way to see his uncle. 'Don't give it another thought. *Buona sera*.'

Franco smiled back warmly. '*Buona sera*, my son. And God bless you!'

It was all a question of organization. Seated in his private office in the Governorate, the Camerlengo ran his eyes once more down the list of names in front of him.

The *papabile* were the cardinals deemed most likely to form the short list from which the next Pope would be chosen. There was an African, an American from Philadelphia, a Philippino and three from Latin America – a Brazilian, a Peruvian and a Mexican. The rest, inevitably, were European, half of them Italian. These were the ones that interested Bosani.

The trick, once the conclave began, was to see to it that his own inner core of candidates, just three in number, were kept constantly in the forefront of voters' minds. This required that his associates – cardinals not themselves papabile but looking for preferment within the Curia – should know whom to nominate, whom to support and when to move on.

Bosani himself, acting alongside the former dean of the Sacred College, could not be seen to intervene directly on the day. Most of his work would be carried out in the run-up to the conclave. He had already 'interviewed' the three cardinals he judged most suitable and most likely to initiate conflict and was satisfied that all three would act under his direction. To this end, he had coached his various associates, including conservatives from Africa and the new Archbishop of Jakarta, about the signals he would give as voting got underway, involving mainly the way he raised his hand, or his eyebrow, or smiled or frowned. But it was mainly up to the Europeans, acting as a bloc, to ensure that the also-rans remained just that and that the radical challenge from Latin America was deflected. He had been preparing his people for months and was sure they would not let him down. An hour ago, Visco had informed him that the tally of cardinals on whose support he could count had risen to forty-seven. Just fourteen more names were required to ensure victory and he had no doubt that, one way or the other, these would be forthcoming.

The beauty of his case was that he was preaching overwhelmingly to the converted. European churchmen were deeply worried about the explosive growth of the Muslim population across the Continent. Every year that passed saw another rise in the percentage of Islamic voters. The number of mosques had increased by leaps and bounds, often at the expense of disused churches. At the same time, Muslims were more and more assertive, some even calling for the local imposition of sharia law and the establishment, in the fullness of time, of a continental caliphate. Priests felt themselves under pressure in the streets and exerted pressure in their turn on their bishops and archbishops to do something. Bosani was pressing at an open door.

He said a silent prayer, touching his fingertips to his forehead, mouth and heart. He had been a Muslim now for more than forty years, and until Rüttgers, no one had suspected him. It had been hard. Only a tiny handful within the faith knew of his true allegiance, which had meant long, lonely years without honours or recognition of his role. Only rarely had he been able to worship in a mosque.

Not once had he been able to declare his faith in the open; never had he been free to take a bride. But soon, *insh'Allah*, he would gain his reward: nothing less than the beginning of the end of the Christian heresy. Concealed in the top drawer of his desk, next to a copy of the Bible, was a leather-bound volume of the Holy Qu'ran. Bosani opened the drawer, drew the book to his lips and kissed it. As he did so, his eyes met those of his illustrious predecessor, Cardinal Orazio Battista, whose portrait, by the artist Guido Reni, rescued from the Vatican's secret archive, hung on the opposite wall. 'I will not fail you, old friend,' he whispered. 'Your death will be avenged long before I join you in Paradise.'

A complex of thoughts swirled around his skull. Not everything was in place. His final incentive to the cardinal-electors to elect a militant Pope had yet to be agreed. It was for this reason that he had met secretly in the central mosque with Yilmaz Hakura, of Hizb ut-Tahrir, the banned Islamic Freedom Party. Hakura was an experienced operator, previously identified with Al-Qaeda. Until now, the actions he had organized in Europe were small in scale, intended as much to alert Muslims to their strength as to frighten Christians. But that would soon change.

It was because of Rüttgers' mention of Hakura that Bosani had confirmed his instructions to Franco. The German was already a thorn in his side and an almost certain opponent in the conclave. But his suggestion, amounting almost to an accusation, that he, the Camerlengo, was in contact with a known terrorist was something that could not be tolerated. Too much was at stake. The era of transformation was at hand.

With Rüttgers out of the picture, a potent threat to his position would be removed and the electoral pieces could be left to tumble into place. He replaced the Qu'ran on the side table and picked up instead a well-thumbed copy of the Hadith. The Prophet – peace be upon him – could not have been more clear. The unbelievers in the new order would be given every opportunity to turn to the true faith. If Europe heeded Allah's message, they could choose to embrace Islam and enter eternity. Alternatively, they could pay the *jizya* tax and continue to worship in their own way. But should they refuse to accept the primacy of Islam, then they would pay with their lives and achieve only damnation. This was not his will, it was the will of God.

Bosani did not regard himself as an extremist. He believed himself to be a realist, assisting Europe to achieve its salvation. It was his most sincere wish that the unbelievers should repent their sins and commit themselves to Islam, in which case a way would be opened for them – for prayer and charity, *salat* and *zakat*, were among the Five Pillars. But as a realist, he knew that the revolution for which he had worked all his adult life would only be achieved by way of armed Jihad. Europeans prided themselves in their smug conviction that since the defeat of

Hitler and the rise of the EU, they had risen above mass conflict. They were wrong. All that was needed was the right cause, the right man and the right sequence of events. To this end, a militant pope was essential – one who, under the direction of his faithful secretary of state, backed by the Curia, would urge European governments and the general population to drive out Muslims, or confine them to ghettoes, like the Jews of old. Such a pope, believing Catholicism to be the manifest will of God, would quickly incur the righteous wrath of Islam. Muslims across the Continent would rise up, to be struck down by sectarian mobs, supported by the police and the armed forces of thirty nations. In response, liberals would demand the pope's abdication and a new policy of integration, thus playing into the hands of the extremists on both sides, neither of whom would embrace compromise. It would be at this point that Iran, Iraq and Saudi Arabia would declare themselves the protectors of Europe's Muslim people, withholding oil from the EU and pouring money and volunteers into the cause. Finally, it would be the Turks, 90 million strong and guardians for 1200 years of Isamic power, who would come to the aid of their brothers and sisters. In the fighting that followed, many thousands would die. The result, however, was assured – ordained by Allah and proclaimed by His Prophet. America might wish to intervene, but would be deterred by its own internal unrest and the real threat of a nuclear response. Truly, it would be the end of history. The last pope – the Antichrist – would die in despair in the Castel Sant'Angelo, watching as his empire crumbled into dust.

Bosani felt an almost erotic charge pass through his body – an intimation, surely, of the ecstasy to come. Truly he was blessed to be given a central role in these events. But his real reward awaited him in heaven. Once more, he picked up the Qu'ran and drew it to his lips. 'Allah be praised,' he whispered. Then he returned to his list of names.

The body of Cardinal Rüttgers was found next morning. An elderly nun became concerned when he failed to emerge from his bedroom for breakfast even though she had knocked twice. It was a young priest, Father Beckmann, who found him, his head almost entirely submerged in the bathwater, his face twisted in a manner that suggested the sudden onset of a stroke. The Vatican chief physician, called in by the Camerlengo, ruled that he had had suffered a massive, if unexpected, pulmonary embolism and drowned after losing consciousness.

His death sent sent shock waves through the Vatican. Rüttgers was one of the most popular men in the Church, who, in the event of a protracted stalemate in the forthcoming conclave might even, it was said, have been considered papabile. What could possibly have gone wrong? A healthy man, not yet fifty, he had rarely troubled his doctor. On the contrary, he regularly disappeared for days on end in the Black Forest and just two years previously had climbed the Matterhorn alone, without oxygen. Fatalists pointed out that God worked in mysterious ways; realists said that what mattered now, at a pivotal moment in the Church's history, was that he should be replaced as German primate as quickly as possible.

No post-mortem was conducted. After a hasty funeral Mass in the German Church, Rüttgers' corpse, in a sealed coffin, was interred in the historic Teutonic Cemetery, hidden from public view between St Peter's Basilica and the Pope Paul VI audience hall. Complaints from the cardinal's archdiocese, led by members of his family, that he should be buried in his own cathedral in Freiburg rather than locked away behind high walls in the Vatican were overridden. Instead, it was decided that his embalmed heart should, in due course, be sent back to Stuttgart in a glass box.

Superior General O'Malley was doubly disturbed by the news. He had known the German for many years. When they last spoke, just forty-eight hours previously, he appeared in rude good health and certain to add a liberal voice to the deliberations over a new pope. Amid a swelling chorus of anti-Muslim rhetoric, his was one of the few liberal voices left in Rome. Now there was talk that his successor as head of the German Church would be Cardinal Wolfgang Von Stiegel, a hardliner, with views on the future of Catholic-Muslim relations similar to those of Bosani. O'Malley was further concerned when he recalled what his friend had told him only two days before his death: that Bosani was a monster, who appeared to have no qualms about orchestrating a new crusade against Islam. The Irishman couldn't help wondering if Rüttgers' death might not have been accidental, but refused to allow himself to follow that line of thought lest it lead to an unacceptable conclusion. The last time there had been speculation about a possible murder in the Vatican, following the dreadful and unforeseen death of Pope John Paul I, the trauma had run long and deep, doing great damage to the Church's image in the world. Even so, speaking privately to his nephew Liam he revealed that recent events had an eerily familiar ring to them.

Pope Paul VI died on 6 August 1978. His fifteen-year reign had proved more eventful than the experts predicted. Not only had he overseen the deliberations of the Second Vatican Council – a latter-day Council of Trent, inaugurated by Pope John XXIII – but he had opened a dialogue between the Church and Islam and established the Secretariat for Non-Christian Religions. Among the cardinals attending the conclave called to elect his successor was Albino Luciani, the son of a socialist glassblower from Murano and his devotedly Catholic wife, Bartola, a scullery maid. Luciani grew up to be a priest, then a bishop, and by the time of his election, at the age of sixty-five, was the Cardinal Patriarch of Venice.

Years before, following the publication of a book by O'Malley on the Ottoman and Byzantine legal systems, Luciani, then in Venice, had written the author a letter in which he wondered whether secular law, without faith, could ever hope to hold society together. The Patriarch and the Jesuit later met at an exhibition in Venice celebrating a thousand years of contact between that city and Islam. The Italian remarked on the fact that the Ottomans of the Sublime Port and the Venetians, in their watery republic, had never, in five hundred years of conflict, relaxed their defences, yet always kept trade links open and maintained a sense of mutual respect. This, not confrontation and hatred, was surely the way forward, he said. In the days leading up to the papal conclave, Luciani and O'Malley – now vice-rector of the Irish College in Rome – met once more, this time after Mass in the Jesuit mother church, known as the Gesù. Luciani reflected ruefully, but with understanding, on the long decline of the Church in Asia Minor and expressed his personal regret that Pope Paul had chosen to abolish the patriarchate of Constantinople, with which his own seat in Venice was inextricably linked.

It was clear to the Irishman that Luciani had a sense of mission but considered himself in no way papabile. He had no idea that others saw special qualities in him and took a different view. Accordingly, he was deeply shocked when, on 26 August after one of the shortest conclaves in history, he was elected pope, taking the regnal name John Paul I.

Throughout Rome, and across the Catholic world, the rejoicing, and relief, was obvious. The cardinal electors – more than had attended any conclave in the Church's long history – had wanted someone of a pastoral disposition after the cold and cerebral pontificate of Paul VI. During a session in the Sistine Chapel made almost unbearable by the intense heat, the various hardliners quickly cancelled each other out until, finally, only Luciani was left. Two future popes, Karol Wojtyla of Kraków and Joseph Ratzinger of Munich, helped prepare him for his new role, which proved to be no easy task. 'May God forgive you for what you have done,' the Italian told them. But then the declaration was made by Cardinal Pericle Felici, the ranking cardinal deacon. '*Habemus Papam*,' he announced, almost in tears. 'We have a pope.' The bells of St Peter's rang out and, after the new pontiff had given the crowd his blessing, looking like a man in a daze, the applause was so great that he was forced to come out on to the balcony a second time.

Even the cynics were won round. This shy, modest intellectual would purge Rome of its wickedness and usher in a new age of openness.

12*
28 September 1978

Thirty-three days after becoming Pope, John Paul I was dead. He was found by an attending nun, propped up in bed, reading a book. The official explanation for his sudden demise was a myocardial infarction, a form of heart attack, which his physician in Venice dismissed as inconsistent with his known medical history. The issue could not be resolved because the body was embalmed within fourteen hours – a process that effectively obliterated the evidence. Rumours began to circulate almost at once that the Holy Father was murdered – possibly because he had resolved to deal with the mounting scandal of the P2 Masonic Lodge, a Mafia-led organization linked to the Vatican; possibly because he had proved less pliable to certain interests in the Curia than had been supposed.

Among those said by some to have been involved were two prominent archbishops, Cardinal John Cody of Chicago, under investigation for alleged financial impropriety, and Cardinal Jean-Marie Villot, from Lyon, the century's longest-serving Camerlengo, an authoritarian figure whose theological conservatism put him at odds with his new master. It was Villot, pre-empting all investigation, who called in the embalmers. They arrived on the scene within an hour of the Pope's death. Their first task, to be carried out before rigor mortis set in, was to restore a sense of serenity to His Holiness's features, distorted by the pain of his passing.

O'Malley didn't know what to think. All he knew for certain was that one week prior to Luciani's death he had been summoned to the private papal apartment where the new Pope told him in confidence of his fears about the true nature of Church government. He had learned that the P2 affair, with its links to the

Vatican's own bank, the Banco Ambrosiano, was much more than a local scandal, and had the potential to split the Church. If even half that he had heard were true, he confided, there were men in Rome, including senior figures in the hierarchy, who saw profit, power and control of the Italian state as more important than the law of God. But even that wasn't all. So-called liberation theology in Latin America turned out to be more about Marxism than mankind's relationship with God. 'These priests seek justice,' the Pope complained, 'but only justice here on Earth. There is little talk of salvation, none at all of life everlasting. Our Lord is being denied His divinity by His own priests. It is as if He were no more than a more sensitive, less aggressive incarnation of the late Che Guevara.'

But while these discoveries had unnerved the Italian, he had somehow found the time, and the strength, to focus as well on a quite separate emerging crisis, the growing unrest of Muslims around the world. It was in this context, against the backdrop of rising oil prices and the Islamic revolution in Iran, that he specially sought O'Malley's advice.

The Pope seemed to be reeling from a sequence of blows. The sheer extent of the challenges facing the Church had shocked him. But he was not unnerved. Instead, relying on prayer and a new team of hand-picked advisers, he seemed determined to tackle the issues as they arose and, if God so willed it, to bring each to a conclusion. The tragedy, as O'Malley saw it, was that he was not given the chance.

The Jesuit's unease refused to subside. On 5 October, the day after the papal funeral, O'Malley called Father John Magee, an Irish priest who served as His Holiness's private secretary, seeking some insight into what happened. But Magee, one of the first on the scene, failed to return his call and refused afterwards to discuss the matter. O'Malley then discovered that Lamberto Bosani, a newly appointed Monsignor and deputy head of the Secretariat for Non Christians, had had an audience with the Pope during the evening that preceded his death. He wrote to Bosani, like himself an authority on the Muslim world, but received an anodyne reply. He said he had visited the papal apartment only briefly to suggest possible dates for an important inter-faith conference, but left after five minutes when staff advised him the Holy Father was unwell and planned to have an early night.

The mysterious death of John Paul I was the longest-running news story of the year. Some reports said that he died in his bed while reading, or possibly writing; others that he was found on the floor of his private bathroom with vomit stains on his clothing. To O'Malley, it was inconceivable that anyone in the Pope's service could have poisoned him. These weren't the Dark Ages. Popes weren't monsters, with enemies at every turn. Yet *something* had happened. Was there a link to the P2 affair? Was Opus Dei involved in a clean-up operation? Did someone remove incriminating papers from His Holiness's bedside? Conspiracy theories abounded.

The official story was that, having prayed with his staff, Luciani retired to bed and died, quietly and serenely, consoled by St Thomas à Kempis' *The Imitation of Christ*. In that case, why the rictus of pain, which at least one of the embalmers reported?

O'Malley had no answers.

But the Vatican, like Nature, abhorred a vacuum. On 4 October, following a three-day lying in state and a funeral Mass conducted by Cardinal Carlo Confalonieri, dean of the Sacred College, Albino Luciani, the 'Smiling Pope', was entombed in the grotto of St Peter's Basilica and attention turned to his successor.

Twelve days later, at the conclusion of the year's second conclave, the Polish Cardinal Karol Wojtyla, Archbishop of Kraków, was elected Pope, the first non-Italian to sit on the Throne of Peter since the Dutchman Adriaan Boeymans, Adrian VI, in 1522. Once more the bells of St Peter's rang out joyously. '*Habemus Papam*,' the proto-deacon announced. 'We have a pope.'

But still O'Malley's sense of loss would not go away. He had expected much from the Venetian and mourned his passing as if he had lost one of his own family. The opening remarks of Cardinal Confalonieri's eulogy rang in his ears:

> We ask ourselves, why so quickly? The Apostle Paul tells us why in the well-known and beloved explanation: "How deep his wisdom and knowledge and how impossible to penetrate his motives or understand his methods! Who could ever know the mind of the Lord?"

13 *
1605

The death on 3 March of Clement VIII, after a pontificate lasting thirteen years, went unmourned by most of Rome. Thieves, beggars, whores and Jews had good reason to rejoice. But his passing could not have come at a worse moment for Cardinal Battista. When the news was brought to him, he was just about to board a ship from Civitavecchia for Malta, where he was due to conduct talks with Alof de Wignacourt, Grand Master of the Knights of St John. Instead, he returned at once to Rome to preside over the *sede vacante* and organize the conclave.

He would not have missed the conclave at any price. Even so, he was irritated at having to put off his trip to Valletta. De Wignacourt was a good soldier. More than that, he had a fine appreciation of naval tactics and had built up a Hospitaller's fleet that, in alliance with Venice, could well frustrate the Ottomans in their bid to recapture the eastern Mediterranean. Battista wished to find out for himself how strong a fleet it was and ways in which that strength might be reduced – possibly through the lease of ships to the papal navy that might then, mysteriously, be lost or kept far from any potential action.

But the Camerlengo had another purpose for visiting Malta. He planned afterwards to travel south to Tripoli, in Libya, for a secret meeting with his patron in the Sublime Port, Safiye Sultan, grandmother of Sultan Ahmed I. Brought to the royal court as a teenage concubine, Safiye was a native of Albania. Beautiful and strong-willed, of peasant stock, she had risen to be chief consort to Sultan Murad III, and, as *Valide Sultan*, or queen mother, exercised considerable power during his reign and that of her wayward son, Mehmed III. A notorious sybarite, like his father, Mehmed was best remembered in Istanbul for having had some fifty of his half-brothers and sisters strangled by deaf-mutes to ensure there could be no pretenders to his throne. No fool, he astutely left affairs of state to his mother, widely reckoned to be the cleverest politician in the empire. Upon Mehmed's untimely death, in December 1603, Safiye's direct authority came to an abrupt end, but as effective head of the Ottoman secret service she remained a formidable operator. Her principal objective was the recovery of Hungary for the Empire, parts of which, in spite of an unexpected victory by her son over an Austrian-led alliance in 1596, had since defected to the Hapsburgs, and the restoration of Turkish sea power. Battista, by far her most important spy, was the key to both enterprises. The brief she wished to give him was threefold: to prevent the formation of a new Holy League, the isolation of Venice from the papacy and a reduction in the strength of the Hospitallers' fleet.

With Battista obliged to remain in Rome, she spoke instead with Luis de Fonseca, from Toledo, one of the most senior Knights of Malta and the Camerlengo's closest confidant. Fonseca had been captured as a boy during the Ottoman conquest of Cyprus and converted secretly to Islam. The Spaniard listened carefully and agreed that as soon as a new pope was elected he would travel to Rome to pass on her orders to the Camerlengo.

'The West is growing in strength,' Safiye told him. 'If we do not strike soon and take Vienna, I fear we never shall. As for the Christian navies, we have done all that we can to match their technology, particularly their firepower, but they may simply be too many for us.'

Fonseca did his best to reassure her. 'Your Highness should not trouble herself,' he said. 'Battista will soon have the new pope in his pocket. He has already instructed the Spanish ambassador that Madrid's first priority should not be the Mediterranean – which he has told him can easily be left to Venice – but the war against the Dutch Protestants and their English allies. At the same time, His Eminence and I will see to it that, when the time comes, the Hospitallers' fleet is dispersed to the four winds.'

The Valide Sultan nodded. 'Let us hope that you are right,' she said. 'The empire that ceases to grow creates the circumstances of its decline. But the will of Allah cannot fail. I expect great things from you and the Camerlengo. A place of honour is being prepared for each of you in the Yeni Valide mosque being built even now in Istanbul. Your names shall live forever in the memories of the faithful. I urge you to be worthy of the honour.'

The Spaniard bowed. 'We shall not fail you,' he said.

Fonseca could not have known it, but five hundred miles to the North preparations for the papal conclave were not in fact going according to plan. Battista had lobbied hard and paid extensive bribes from the Vatican's own treasury to ensure the election of Camillo Borghese, the cardinal-Vicar of Rome, as successor to Pope Clement. But then the unexpected occured. Using a fortune of 300,000 écus provided by the king of France, Cardinal Pietro Aldobrandini, the former cardinal-nephew, had backed Borghese's rival, the strongly pro-French Cardinal Alessandro de' Medici, Archbishop of Florence. Battista was outbid and de Medici was duly crowned Pope Leo XI on Easter Sunday, 1605.

It was not, as things turned out, a catastophe for Battista. France and Spain were now at each other's throats and in no position to threaten Ottoman power. But then, even as the Camerlengo worked hard to consolidate a policy of divide and rule, de Medici died, aged seventy, having reigned for a mere twenty-seven days. Aldobrandini, still only thirty-four and too young to take the prize himself, was completely thrown by the unexpected turn of events. Lacking the funds necessary for a second round of bribery, he gave in with as much grace as he could muster. 'We live at God's pleasure,' he told Battista. 'We know neither the day nor the hour.'

Battista in reply offered the thinnest of smiles. 'Nor yet, Eminence, the state of our bank accounts when they are most needed.'

At the year's second conclave, the ill-preparedness of the French camp told quickly. Battista spared no effort and at the second time of asking secured the succession of Borghese. The new pontiff, taking the name Paul V, did not suffer fools gladly. He was also more mindful of his dignity than almost any other pope in the last hundred years. An ecclesiastical lawyer by training, for whom religion was a matter of observance rather than devotion, he quickly buried himself in Church business and privilege. His first concern was the promotion and elevation of his family. Once that was secured, he banished to their dioceses the hundreds of absentee cardinals and bishops who were the scandal of Rome, thus, at a stroke, preventing scores of his enemies from plotting together. Borghese, unlike his famous predecessors of the previous century, was inward-looking, preoccupied with his role as sovereign of the Holy See. To him, the Papal States were his garden and the Ottomans a remote and alien distraction. His one foreign adventure would centre on events much closer to home than the Sublime Port.

The Most Serene Republic of Venice was celebrated for its lagoon but extended west to Verona and south along the Dalmatian coast as far as Dubrovnik. The entire edifice was built on trade. While the Doge could call on an effective army and a large, efficient navy, these existed primarily to sustain the city and its hinterland as the richest entrepot in Europe, independent of the Papal States. Rome had long wished to bring Venice to heel and even to add it to its dominions. When the Doge and the ruling Council of Ten passed laws restricting the property rights of the clergy and required them to seek planning approval before building new churches, Pope Paul decided to act. Advised by Battista, he excommunicated the government and placed the whole of the Republic under an interdict, suspending public worship and denying the sacraments to its citizens. The Turks were delighted. Safiye Sultan was able to tell her grandson, Ahmed I – still just fifteen years old, but impatient to make his mark – that if he wished to expand the prestige of the empire, now was the time.

Less success accrued to Battista from his dealings with de Wignacourt. The wily Grand Master was not happy with the Camerlengo's proposal that half his fleet be based in the Balearics to protect Spain from the Barbary pirates. Nor did he see the necessity for more than a modest flotilla to be deployed in the Atlantic against the same Moroccan raiders. But he did agree to a secondment of ten ships, and Battista had to be happy with that.

The cardinal's one undoubted triumph was not of his own making, but an inspired response to events. Shah Abass I of Persia, whose empire had for many years been in conflict with the Ottomans, invited a delegation of Western diplomats to Isfahan and, to their great surprise, proposed an alliance with Europe against the might of Turkey. At first, the new Pope was keen to proceed. He could see value in dividing Islam against itself. But Battista would have none of it. 'Holy Father,' he argued, holding out his pectoral cross between the fingers of both hands, 'such an alliance would surely be contrary to the law of God. Can we permit our soldiers to fight alongside the Persians – whose heathen beliefs are, if anything, more anathema to us than those of the Ottomans? Would Our Lord wish us to make common cause with an oriental power that denies his very divinity?'

It worked. Abbas's overture was politely rebuffed and nothing was done. Pope Paul returned his gaze to the parish politics of Rome. In a letter to Safiye Sultan, sent via Fonseca, Battista boasted that by his action he had saved the empire, and the true faith, from possible destruction at the hands of its enemies.

Across the Tiber, Caravaggio had no triumphs to savour. Instead, as his money ran out, he spent more and more of his time reassessing his career. In some ways, he was his own worst enemy. He liked to shock. He liked to disturb. He saw no point in art that was merely devotional. Where his rivals drew from an established palette of ideas and images, he tried to engage his public in an argument. He was also an impresario, for whom art was, above all, theatre. Patrons knew this. That was why they came to him. They wanted it to be said of them that they were free and independent thinkers. The trouble was that in recent years the arguments he started often ended up as rows, with consequences. A new puritanism, not unlike that said to be stalking England, had entered Rome with Paul V. Orthodoxy, not exploration, was back in vogue. These days, a patron would as likely as not wait to see what the opinion-formers in the Curia had to say about a painting before adopting that opinion as their own. This was good, or at any rate profitable, if the response from the top was positive, but disastrous in the event of a thumbs down.

The way Caravaggio saw it, the consensus among the greybeards was that he was an unsettling, possibly heretical figure, whose influence, formerly given free rein, ought now to be curbed. His own view was that his critics were medicocre men, steeped in the banality of greed, who recognized his genius but would rather die than admit it. The result was that his situation was becoming desperate. His canvases hung in churches, in the halls of cardinals and princes, even in the Vatican itself. But as his enemies and rivals observed with relish, he no longer had the wherewithal to open a knocking shop in Ortaccio.

He thanked God for Orsi, his flagbearer and truest friend, who did what he could for him, settling his wine bill and securing him several private commissions. Longhi, too, mentioned his name all over town. After he was thrown out of his lodgings in the Vicolo Cecilia e Biagio for non-payment of rent, it was the poet who found him refuge near the Piazza Colonna with the lawyer Andrea Ruffietti.

His eviction was a humiliation. Even now, he trembled with rage at the memory of it. It was his own fault. He should have known better than to venture out, with drink taken, wearing a sword. He had been arrested for the same offence just weeks before and warned about his future behaviour. Then again, if bloody Lena Antognetti, that daft little strumpet, who everybody *knew* was his woman, hadn't got herself pregnant by that bastard lawyer Pasqualone, there wouldn't have been any need for a confrontation. What was he supposed to have done? Pasqualone was boasting that he'd won out in an affair of the heart against the great Caravaggio. People were sniggering. Even then, if the damned fool hadn't stepped out in front of him in the Piazza Navona, he might have got away with it. But there he was, plain as day, smelling of cologne, dressed like an undertaker. It was the work of an instant to smack him in the back of the head with the hilt of his sword. It wasn't a proper wound, it was a challenge Anyone else would have turned and faced him. But not Pasqualone. Instead, he screamed for the *sbirri*, who came running, almost out of nowhere. 'The painter Caravaggio' had tried to murder him, the little worm had told them. Well, that was it. He should have done for him there and then. But remembering the warning from Battista, he decided not to hang around. Instead, within a matter of hours, he was on the road to Genoa, where the Doria family had offered him work.

As it happened, the commission in Genoa, for an ambitious sequence of frescoes, didn't interest him – though it would have made him a rich man. He had never trusted himself at frescoes – all that wet plaster – and was concerned, in addition, that if he stayed out of Rome too long he would be forgotten. Instead, he took the advice of Doria's lawyer and apologized fulsomely to Pasqualone for his insolence. Groveling was not in his nature, and it rankled with him to beg the forgiveness of a man who had set out to cuckold him. But life away from Rome was, if anything, more unbearable. Two weeks later, after learning that his apology – posted by Pasqualone in the portico of Santa Maria Maggiore – had been accepted, he journeyed south once more to pick up his career.

His return proved as tempestuous as his leaving. His landlady, he discovered, had evicted him from his lodgings and disposed of his possessions as if he were an impecunious student. He had protested, of course. He even threw stones at her windows, causing the small crowd that gathered to erupt with laughter – though whether it was *with* him or *at* him, he wasn't sure. To add insult to his injury, an inventory of his worldly goods, seized in lieu of rent, was pinned by the official receiver to what had been his front door: a bed; several stools ('one broken'); a guitar; a violin without strings; two swords; a couple of daggers; two large, unfinished paintings; a mirror; three devices used for tightening canvases; a painting on wood; a wooden tripod … and an unopened letter. As a litany of his misfortune, it made dismal reading. No clothing was mentioned, which surprised some people, but not those who knew him. According to Orsi, Guido Reni, a second-rate painter but a first-class cardsharp, had remarked to anyone listening in the Turk's Head: 'Any clothes Michelangelo owns, he's wearing.'

The whole episode had soured him. How had it come to this, that he should end up a figure of fun to the populace? Most of the city's other artists weren't fit to tie his bootlaces. Only Annibale Carracci was worth a damn. But they knew how to work the system. That was why they were in favour and he was not.

Using the silk scarf around his neck to wipe the grime from a window of the tiny living room of his temporary lodgings – accommodation that he had moaned was better suited to a servant than a master – Caravaggio stared out at the street beyond. It was a late evening in May. The Piazza Navona was no more than fifty paces away and as the sun drifted beneath the horizon, the human comedy, as ever, played out before him. The fishmonger opposite, wiping his streaming nose with a corner of his apron, was disposing of his unsold stock, the pungent stench of which completely overpowered the scent of Alyssum flowers drifting down from an overhead balcony; an old man wearing patched-together rags, looking as if he had made the narrowest of escapes from an outbreak of the plague, sat on an upturned box plucking at a lute, while an equally diseased-looking monkey on his shoulder held out a miniature basket; a fat-bellied fire-eater, wearing an extravagant turban, exhaled a foot-long tongue of flame, then smiled hopefully at his audience through a mouthful of missing teeth.

Caravaggio turned away. He had had enough. Was that how people saw him – a tradesman or street entertainer, applauded one day, forgotten the next? There was no hiding the fact that his life had gone from bad to worse. Paintings for important patrons remained unfinished; the *sbirri* never let up on him, accusing him of brawling and affray, looking for the chance to lock him up and toast his feet over a brazier of burning coals. He was losing control. Not long before, he had returned home in the early hours wounded in the ear and throat, with blood streaming down his jerkin. He had no idea what happened and had taken to telling anyone who asked that he had fallen on his own sword while drunk, which could even have been true. Fate, though, took no account of the aggregation of circumstance. It was while he was recovering from his wounds, absorbed in self-pity, unable even to lift a brush, that he had been awarded one of the most important commissions of his career.

St Peter's Basilica, the largest church in Christendom, remained a work-in-progress. Thirteen popes so far had come and gone, and still the construction went on. To be displayed in St Peter's was the ultimate accolade for any artist and Caravaggio was determined to seize the opportunity. It was Cardinal Del Monte, his former patron, who had spoken for him – which was typical. Del Monte gave painters the latitude they needed. He knew better than anyone that the wind blowing through the Vatican had changed and was careful these days whom he promoted. But the opportunity was exceptional and only Caravaggio, he felt, could do it justice. The canons and cardinals in charge of the basilica had decided that a vacant altarpiece in the northwest corner should be assigned to the Confraternity of the Palafrenieri, or Papal Grooms – bankers, merchants and lawyers, mostly – who shamelessly used their connections to advance their careers. The Grooms' patron saint was St Anne, the mother of the Virgin Mary, widely venerated as a virtuous woman. It was well known that Caravaggio had been planning a St Anne canvas for at least the last two years, and it was this fact that Del Monte used as his trump card.

The question was, was the artist up to it?

'I can do this,' he told Orsi over a pitcher of wine in the Turk's Head. 'I know what you're thinking. You're thinking I'll miss the deadline or produce something they can't accept. But I won't. The Palafrenieri may be a bunch of bastards, but they'll still get my best work, Prosperini, depend on it.'

'I don't doubt it,' Orsi said. 'You've never produced anything second-rate in your life. But, for God's sake, try to remember who's paying you. This lot aren't only hypocritical and pompous, they're vindictive and they're greedy – and they have the ear of the Pope. Give them what they want, Michelangelo. Don't tempt fate.'

It took him three months. He worked on it every day and almost every night, sometimes until dawn. Finally, it was done and, with huge Vatican fanfare, the *Madonna dei Palafrenierni* was placed over the vacant altar. Three days later, at the height of one of the most vicious whispering campaigns in the city's artistic history, it was removed.

The whole of Rome, it seemed, had queued up to have a go at the man who for years was their favourite son. The Virgin's dress was disgracefully low-cut, an Austrian archbishop said. How had he put it? 'Her dumplings were boiling over.' Another prelate, clearly familiar with his model, complained that St Anne had been represented as a retired whore. But particular ire was reserved for the figure of the Christ child, who, with his Holy Mother was pictured stamping upon a serpent – evidently the Devil – while his infant penis jutted out towards the congregation.

Was that a provocation too far? Caravaggio asked himself. What was too far, anyway? And who got to draw the line? Whoever it was, he had crossed it. What incensed him was that, privately, the artistic community of Rome, led by Del Monte and Guistiniani, acknowledged that the composition was a masterpiece. They loved it. But the canons of San Pietro – as self-serving a group of hypocrites as any in Christendom – weren't having it. They were affronted, they said, and all they would pay him for his months of labour was seventy-five scudi. But that wasn't the end of it – as he never thought it would be. Like *Death of the Madonna*, the painting itself was quickly sold on – at a handsome profit. The next thing he knew, it was in the private collection of Scipione Borghese, the cardinal-nephew, along with five other of his works, including *David with the Head of Goliath* and a recently completed portrait of the Pope. Scipione's homosexuality was an open secret in Rome. His worldly ambition would have shamed Nero. Not only did he set the artistic standards of the age, he also worked with the Church to fix the prices. Everyone, it seemed, could make a profit out of Caravaggio except Caravaggio himself.

Later that night, having once again measured his considerable debts against his meagre resources, the artist climbed the narrow stairs to his studio. Using the candle that had guided his way, he lit five of the lanterns he employed for painting at night. Some of his detractors held it against him that the colours he used were too rich and overly accentuated. They accused him of cheap trickery and of using light like a stage prop. Caravaggio ignored their strictures, which he dismissed as jealousy. He had no doubt of his place in the pantheon, alongside da

Vinci, Michelangelo, Titian and Raphael. Nor did he doubt the fact that his rivals, including his friends, were, at best, second-rate.

But while none who knew him doubted the sincerity of his vision, especially his devotion to the art of *chiaroscuro*, of which he was the acknowledged master, Caravaggio had another, practical reason for eschewing the subtleties of daylight. His nightmares, always frequent, were now constant. The horrors of the Cenci executions had been joined by a recurring dream in which he himself was dragged from a prison cell – or else set upon in a church – and decapitated, either by sword or axe. The worst dreams were those in which he remained conscious after his head was struck from his shoulders, so that he gazed up at his executioner – often a thick-bearded Turk who grinned as he wiped the blade of his scimitar – unable to speak, or even to blink, waiting for the eternal darkness to enfold him. That was when he woke up screaming and clutching at his neck, mistaking the sweat that poured down his face for blood. So it was not merely that he was fascinated by the interplay between light and shade. He also wished desperately to remain awake.

As soon as he had he lit the fifth lantern, he moved to the window, looking across to the Piazza Navona, and closed the shutters. Then he began to sort through a series of canvases propped against the back wall, covered by several sheets of sacking. Selecting one – some six and a half feet wide by four and a half feet high – he dragged it out to the large easel he had set up in the centre of the floor. As soon as it was installed – no easy matter – he adjusted the lanterns so that they lit the entire surface equally. Then he stood back and stared.

He had worked on the painting for more than three years, ever since it was commissioned by Ciriaco Mattei in the late autumn of 1602. Large and luminous, more dramatic than anything he had accomplished since *Judith and Holofernes*, it featured the scene in the Garden of Gethsemane in which Jesus was identified by Judas and taken into custody by soldiers acting for the high priest. Mattei had agreed to pay 250 scudi for the finished work but had long since given up asking when, if ever, it would be ready.

As he gazed at the painting, to which he had given the name *The Betrayal of Christ*, a chill moved through his body and hairs on his arms stood up. How many times had he reworked the image of Judas? How often had he begun to obliterate the figure of the fleeing man, only to halt before he reached the face and hands? As for the witness on the right, holding a lantern, which he had added at the last at the expense of the Apostle John, what was he doing there and what was he trying to say?

The painting was a triumph. He knew that. But it could also be his death warrant. The question was, could Mattei be trusted to keep it from public view? He swallowed hard, rubbing his fingers down the thin stubble of his beard, remembering as if it were yesterday the portentous scene he had witnessed in Battista's chapel. The audacity of the composition struck him anew, as it did every time he looked at it. Judas' left arm, with which he clutched his Saviour, was several inches too short, with a claw-like hand. Caught in the very moment of betrayal, the fallen Apostle was burly and bearded. The pink-skinned crown of his head was bare, giving it the appearance of a cardinal's zuchetto. But it was the figure on the far left, ostensibly a fleeing disciple, whom those who knew the truth would have found the most disturbing. For it was unmistakably the murdered priest from Trastevere, his expression taken directly from the chalk sketch Caravaggio made minutes after he was killed. To the right of the canvas, meanwhile, shedding light on the ghastly scene, stood the unmistakable figure of the artist himself – perplexed and afraid, unable to intervene.

For twelve months now he had wrestled with the demons the canvas evoked in him. He had thought many times of burning it. Once, he had even drawn a knife to it, as if it were his enemy, only to stay his hand at the crucial moment and collapse into tears. He could no more destroy it than he could accuse Battista of betraying his sacred trust. He had tried to rework the central figures, turning them into the conventional tableau of Christ and his disciples. But that had proved impossible as well. It was as if the Lord himself was directing him to leave it as it was.

Disconsolately, he sat down on a small, three-legged stool and once more considered his options. His debts were mounting. He hardly dared show his face in the Campo Marzio. He had even been forced to release Bartolomeo from the terms of his apprenticeship, meaning that there was no one to mix his paints or fill in backgrounds, or make his supper. Just yesterday, his benefactor Ruffietto had informed him that the house in which he had rooms was up for sale and he must be out by Christmas. What was he to do? Where was he to go? The seventy-five scudi he had been paid by the canons would do little more than settle his bar bills and buy new paint and brushes. The simple fact was that he desperately needed the cash Mattei would provide once he handed over *The Betrayal*. But that wasn't all. The problem went deeper. As much as he needed the money, he also needed to be rid of the painting, which he had begun to think of as having a life of its own. He couldn't destroy it. He knew that now. It was as if it no longer belonged to him, but rather to history. But nor could he live with it.

He mopped his forehead with an oily rag and with a supreme effort of will came to a decision. Tomorrow he would visit the banker and offer him the painting. But there would be one important stipulation: it could not be shown in public, not even to friends, so long as the Camerlengo was alive. If Mattei would agree to that – and there was no guarantee that he would – he would accept just half the agreed fee – 125 scudi. If not, then, God help him, he would have to burn it.

The candle in one of the lanterns guttered out and he could hear a mouse scuffling beneath the floorboards. Standing up, he blew out all but one of the remaining candles, using the one still lit to guide him next door to his bedroom. There, he lay down, fully clothed. A shaft of moonlight cutting across from an unshuttered window silvered the right side of his face leaving the other side in darkness. He could hear an owl hooting. Then sleep came like a falling axe.

14*
Conclave minus 12

Rome in the middle of the papal campaign was buzzing with gossip. Superior General O'Malley, dressed in chinos, sandals and short-sleeved shirt, had taken time off to be with his nephew in the Scholars Lounge, an Irish bar behind the Gesù, where those who knew him left him alone and others just thought him a passing tourist. As additional insurance – for he knew that if Father Giovanni could get to him, he would – he had switched off his mobile and shoved it deep in a pocket of his trousers.

It was another hot, still day. The air conditioning in the bar was set to low in conformity with the latest energy-saving measures imposed by the EU, and the two men selected a table away from the windows. Dempsey fetched a couple of pints of Guinness from the bar and brought them across.

'Cheers!' he said, pulling his chair back with the toe of his shoe.

'*Sláinte!*'

He sat down. They raised their glasses and each took a sip. Both then wiped their upper lips with the backs of their hand.

'So how are you today?' O'Malley asked. 'How's your back?'

Dempsey hesitated. 'I'm okay,' he said, turning his glass slowly on the table in front of him. 'The physiotherapy seems to have worked. With any luck, I'll be back to normal by Christmas.'

O'Malley nodded. 'I'm glad to hear it. You've had a rough time of it right enough. Now tell me about Maya Studer. How's that going?'

'Slowly. She's very much her own woman – not the sort to be rushed. But maybe you'll get a chance to meet her … lunch or dinner, something like that.'

'I'd be delighted.'

'It's not as if she can meet dad.'

'No.'

O'Malley took a sip from his Guinness, staring at his nephew over the top of the glass. 'Your father didn't hate you, you know,' he said. 'You mustn't think that. He simply couldn't understand what happened.'

'Right. It's a funny thing, though. Here you are, the head of the Jesuits, and yet you don't seem to mind that I don't go to Mass any more.'

'I wouldn't say that.'

'No, but you don't take it personally. Dad lost himself in religion after my mother died. That and the drink. When I told him I didn't really take the church stuff that seriously and was leaving Galway to join the army, he took it as a personal rejection of him – which it never was. Not really. He thought I was doing it just to get back at him for something – maybe for the beatings, or the times I'd come down in the night and find him slumped on the sofa with an empty whiskey bottle beside him and a burnt-out fag in his fingers.'

O'Malley remembered the last time he'd spoken to his brother-in-law. He'd been drinking, as usual. He'd wanted to know if God would reunite him with Kitty after he died. O'Malley hadn't known what to tell him.

'He didn't have it easy either. Your mother was his world. When he lost her, he didn't know where to turn, except to the drink – and the Lord. Not an unusual combination in my experience – though if it's one or the other it's generally religion that misses out. There's many a priest in much the same boat.'

'I think he blamed me for her death,' Liam said.

O'Malley looked away. 'What makes you say that?'

'Well, she died in childbirth. If it hadn't been for me ...'

The priest reached for his glass. 'Don't be talking that way. How could it possibly have been your fault. You were hardly born.'

'Original sin?'

'Liam, please. You don't know what you're talking about.'

'I only know what I saw in his eyes.'

There was a pause while both men both finished their pints.

'My shout,' said O'Malley.

When the priest got back to the table, he found his nephew staring out the window. Three North African men were walking past, talking animatedly to each other. Behind them trouped their wives, dressed in hijabs, holding on to at least half a dozen young children. But Liam was looking right past them, like they weren't there. He placed the glasses of stout on the table. 'What's bothering you, Liam? Is it what I said? If so, I'm sorry.'

'I just wish I'd called him, or he'd called me. It shouldn't have ended like that.'

'Your father was a proud man. I think maybe you take after him. You both had a lot to put up with. Too much, if the truth be known. The difference is, there were no therapists in his day, no counsellors. And no anti-depressants. He was on his own.'

'What do you mean, "if truth be known"?'

'Nothing,' O'Malley said hastily, remembering his promise. 'Just a figure of speech.'

The result was a piercing look, which made the priest feel distinctly uncomfortable. 'Yeah, well here's to him!' Dempsey said at last, raising his glass.

'I'll drink to that.'

They smiled ruefully at each other over the tops of their glasses. 'So what else is happening?' O'Malley asked, anxious to break the mood. 'Do you think the Catholic Church is finished or are we in with a chance?'

'You're asking *me*?'

'Why not?'

'Aren't you the Black Pope?'

'Only when it suits me.'

'Okay. So what do you reckon about this stuff about St Malachy? You must have seen it. It's in all the papers. The internet's full of it.'

The Jesuit sighed. The prophecies of St Malachy, a twelfth-century archbishop of Armagh, had come to light in 1590 after allegedly being lost for five hundred years. Detailed, yet obscure, the prophecies purported to list every pope up to and including the next one, who would not only be the last, but quite possibly the Antichrist, whose arrival would herald an era of unparalleled tribulation for the world.

As a Jesuit and an Irishman, O'Malley found the myth of Malachy doubly irksome. 'You're surely not taken in by that old malarky,' he said. 'Come on. Just because we're Irish doesn't mean we have to take pride in a lie.'

'I didn't say I believed it, I said everyone's talking about it.'

'Including you, apparently. It's ridiculous, Liam. For a start, the "prophecies", supposedly handed personally to Pope Innocent II in 1139, were almost certainly a late-sixteenth century forgery. They were intended to secure the election of Cardinal Gorolamo Simoncelli as the successor to Urban VII. That's all.'

'You're kidding.'

O'Malley took another swallow of Guinness. 'Actually, I'm not. Simoncelli was from Orvieto. The Latin name for his hometown is *Urbs Vetus*, which means "Old City". According to Malachy, the next pope would be *ex antiquitate urbis* – from the old city. Claude-François Ménestrier, a Jesuit, showed later it was a fix – and, face it, who am I to contradict a man with SJ after his name?'

'You seem to know a lot about it,' said Dempsey. 'For a man that doesn't believe it, I mean.'

O'Malley shrugged. 'I did a paper on it in my fourth year at Maynooth. The thing is, it keeps on coming up. Now, with the last name on the list pending, it's becoming an obsession. Do you remember *The Da Vinci Code*?'

'Vaguely.'

'Sold by the truckload, in a hundred languages. Complete tosh, of course. It claimed Jesus got married and raised a family. The Holy Grail was in there, too. But the thing is, millions believed it. I tell you, it was the Devil's own job to persuade most of them it was only a story. Amazing what some people will swallow.'

Dempsey grinned. 'So did it work?'

'Did what work?'

'The *Urbs Vetus* business.'

'Oh, that. No. Niccoló Sfondrati got the job, took the name Gregory XIV. Much good it did him – he was dead inside of ten months.'

'A stressful job. So what did the Prophecy crowd say when Sfondrati ended up as Pope?'

'They pointed out that he was from Milan, which is one of the oldest cities in Italy, and that his father and grandfather had both been senators, which comes from the Latin, *senex*, for –

'– old man.'

'Exactly.'

'Inventive.'

'I'd prefer to say, desperate.'

'You're not a subscriber, then?'

'I believe in God, not word games.'

'And God doesn't play Scrabble. Is that it?'

'Nor dice. Einstein was right about that. I'd say Patience was his game.'

Dempsey shifted in his chair. The scars down his back were burning, which they did when he sat still for any length of time. 'I'm sure you're right,' he said. 'But that doesn't mean people aren't anxious.'

'People are always anxious.'

'True. But this time they're worried that the next pope will be Petrus Romanus – the Antichrist – and that after he's done with us it's Judgment Day and the End of the World.'

'That's what they said the last time. According to Malachy, Benedict XVI was the last pope but one … except that he wasn't.'

Dempsey looked gleeful. 'Ah, but that's where the fun starts. Someone on the internet claims to have spoken to a leading cardinal who was present at the last conclave, and according to him the result was a fix, contrary to the wishes of a majority of the cardinal electors. If that's true, then the man they buried last week wasn't Pope at all, but an imposter – an antipope.'

'Bollocks.'

'Is it? I've seen the record. Did you know that in the two thousand years or so of Church history, there have been no fewer than forty antipopes?'

'Nearly all of them in the wake of the Great Schism and the move to Avignon. There hasn't been an antipope for more than five hundred years.'

'So you say. Not everybody out there agrees with you.'

O'Malley threw up a despairing hand. 'Please,' he said. 'Can we just drop this? Right now I have more urgent matters to contend with.'

'Such as what?'

'Such as the future of the Catholic Church and the prevention of war between Europe and the Muslim world.'

'Is that all?'

'I'm serious, Liam. You probably know that with the death of the Pope all Curial posts were placed in abeyance. That means, for example, that Cardinal Bosani is no longer Secretary of State. But Bosani is also Camerlengo, or High Chamberlain, of the Church, a post he acquired last year on the death of the previous incumbent.'

'Go on.'

'Centuries ago, the Camerlengo was the second-most powerful man in Rome, in charge of taxes and estates and all kinds of appointments, civil and religious.'

Dempsey nodded. 'But then along came the *Risorgimento*. The Papal States were incorporated into a unified Italy and the popes retreated into the Vatican.'

'Exactly. But it wasn't just the popes who lost out; their henchmen suffered too. The Apostolic Camera, controlling the finances of a country bigger than Portugal, with a standing army of nearly 15,000 men, was overnight robbed of all purpose. From being both finance and defence minister of a major European state, the Camerlengo became overnight like a figure out of comic opera.'

'Except that you're not laughing.'

'No. One crucial responsibility remained. The Camerlengo acts in place of the Pope during the *interregnum*. Not only that, he organizes and presides over the conclave that elects his successor. What if I were to tell you that, with this power at his elbow, Cardinal Bosani wishes to secure the election of a pope who will adopt an aggressive stand against Muslim expansion in Europe?'

'I'd say he'd have the support of 90 per cent of Catholics across the Continent.'

O'Malley leaned in closed to the table. 'But what if it meant driving out immigrants and establishing a fortress mentality of a type we haven't seen since the Turks stood at the gates of Vienna in 1683?'

'That would be something else.'

'Never doubt it. So don't talk to me about St Malachy and his loony prophecies – not that he wrote them anyway. I'm more worried that Bosani will get his man – whoever that may be – onto Peter's throne and launch us all into a real-life clash of civilizations.'

'The Fifth Crusade? Oh, come on. Now who's being fanciful?'

'It's not an exaggeration, Liam. It could happen.'

'But the Curia wouldn't let it … would they?'

'It would depend how it was sold to them. Look around you. The Muslim population of Europe has grown out of all proportion in the last thirty years. Marseille is virtually an Arab town. There are more observant Muslims in the UK than there are Catholics. Here in Rome, where the biggest mosque in Europe is less than two kilometres from St Peter's Square, it's possible sometimes to imagine yourself in an Arab souk.'

Dempsey offered a wry smile. It was true. The world capital of the Catholic faith was now 10 per cent Muslim, with no sign of any slowdown. In some districts of the city there was a mosque on almost every corner.

O'Malley continued. 'Muslims these days are confident of their strength. They're done with life in the shadows. Spit on them and they'll spit back. Desecrate their cemeteries and they'll take to the streets. They've reached the point where they want major concessions to their culture and way of life, and equality of esteem for their places of worship. You might think this a simple matter of natural justice – and you'd be right. I support them in this without any reservation. Yet Christians – those of us that are left, that is – can't help asking, where's the *quid pro quo*? In most of the Muslim world, Christianity is either banned or heavily restricted. Missionaries are outlawed. If they're caught preaching the Gospel, they risk deportation, flogging or a prison sentence. In some places, converts are condemned as traitors to the true faith and stoned to death.'

He looked around him as if to ensure there was no one listening. 'But that's not the half of it. Here, among indigenous Europeans, fear, resentment and animosity are widespread. People are starting to feel like strangers in their own countries. Nobody's happy. Look at Turkey. The Turks have been denied what they see as their rightful place in the European Union. They feel insulted – and who can blame them? They think, well, if secularism isn't going to give us a future in Europe, maybe it's time to give Islam a chance. So the women have taken to the veil again and the legal system installed by Atatürk is on its last legs. But it doesn't end there. Hizb ut-Tahrir, with its calls for a restoration of the caliphate, is operating openly in Istanbul, as it is across much of Europe. It's almost as if the Hadith are coming true and there's going to be a second Muslim conquest of Constantinople.'

Dempsey looked blank. 'What are the Hadith?' he asked.

'The sayings, or wisdom, of Muhammad, as taken down by his followers. There's a school of thought, based on the Hadith, which claims that Istanbul – which was run by a secular administration for almost a century – is about to witness a full-blown Islamic revival and that this will be followed by a period of rapid religious expansion climaxing in the conquest of Rome.'

'Jesus Christ!'

'Exactly. Jesus – Isa to Muslims – is supposed to return to Earth a year or two after the fall of Rome to battle the *Dajjal*, or Antichrist, who will have laid the world to waste. Eesa wins the victory and in the final judgment curses the followers of the *Dajjal*. After that comes the End of the World.'

Dempsey looked hard at his uncle. 'And how exactly does that differ from what Malachy says? In the important particulars, I mean.'

'It doesn't.'

'So what do you make of it?'

'I wish I knew. The only thing I know for sure is that we live in dangerous times. I've never been more despondent. All that's needed to set off the ticking bomb is a pope who thinks that the best way to shape the future is by returning to the values and attitudes of the twelfth century.'

Dempsey threw back his shoulders to ease the pain in his back. He didn't like to be reminded of ticking bombs. 'I hear you, Uncle. But it'll never come to that. Canute had more chance holding back the waves than a modern pope has of stemming the tide of history. The cardinals must know this. Most of them aren't European anyway. They're from all over the show. What they're looking for is a man who can rebuild the universal Church, or at any rate thinks it's a good idea. They'd have to be off their heads to believe that restoring the Holy Roman Empire is an idea whose time has come.'

A wry smile from O'Malley greeted this last remark. 'Neither holy, nor Roman, nor an empire, I wish I had your faith,' he said.

'And I wish I had yours, Uncle. History's a big beast. We think we can harness it and take it in the direction we choose. But every now and again it breaks loose and smashes anyone and anything that gets in its way. So even if I'm wrong and you're right and we're all off to hell in a handcart, what the hell can we do to stop it?'

O'Malley clasped his hands in front of him and leaned forward in his chair. 'That's what I want to talk to you about,' he said.

Dempsey groaned.

15 *
26 May 1606

It was after nine in the evening and the sun had gone down to the west of the Villa Mattei, the weekend retreat of Ciriaco Mattei in the exclusive Monte Celli district. Set among trees next to the church of Santa Maria in Dominica, the handsome four-storey residence looked north to the ruins of the Temple of Claudius and east to the Archway of Dolabella, built in AD 10 for the consuls Caius Junius Silanus and Cornelius Dolabella.

As candles were lit, Mattei sat at the head of his table in the central salon, next to his principle guest, Cardinal Orazio Battista. The banker was in an expansive mood. He had just concluded a deal with the Medici in Florence providing for the opening of a jointly run outlet in Bruges. In addition, his mistress, who had recently returned to her hometown of Lucca to visit her sick father, was on her way back to Rome and would join him in his bed the following night.

So, as far as Mattei was concerned, all was well with the world. The death of his revered brother, Cardinal Girolamo Mattei, two years previously had been a bitter blow both personally and to his standing with the Curia. But he had shown the Holy Father – all three Holy Fathers, in fact – that he remained an extremely useful conduit for funds and financial information and had quickly regained the confidence and affections of the Apostolic Palace.

The Camerlengo, seated to his right, was not one of his favourite prelates. He'd heard too much about him to trust him, let alone like him. But as the most intimate confidante of the new Pope, Paul V, and with the treasury and military power of the Papal States at his disposal, Battista would always be a welcome guest at his home.

A brace of chandeliers, festooned with candles, had just been hoisted to the ceiling above the dining table, revealing, in a pleasing light, two paintings by the artist Caravaggio. One was *The Supper at Emmaus*, so severely adjudged by Father General Acquaviva; the other was a rendition of the young John the Baptist, showing him naked in the presence of a spectacularly long-horned ram.

Mattei very much admired the *Emmaus*, beardless Christ or no, but he positively loved his John the Baptist. Seeing the Camerlengo's eyes strain in the direction of the two canvases, he could not help asking his opinion.

'I must tell you, Eminence, I consider these two to be works of the first rank – equal to anything by Titian or Raphael. May I hope that you concur?'

'That depends. Who's the artist?'

'Michelangelo Merisi – called Caravaggio. I believe you and he have met.'

Battista frowned, causing his brow to furrow thickly like a new-ploughed field. 'Indeed we have, Don Ciriaco. An ill-tempered scoundrel. It would not surprise me to learn that he was also a blasphemer. But tell me, that one there, the one of the boy, what in heaven's name is going on?'

'Why, it's a portrait of John the Baptist as a youth. Your Eminence will no doubt recall that he ran naked in the desert, living off locusts and honey.'

'You don't need to lecture me on the scriptures. I am well aware of the Baptist's early life.'

'Then you will appreciate that he spent much of his time, before he encountered Jesus, in the company of his flock.'

Battista threw a chicken bone into the pot in front of him and scowled. 'The man Merisi is a drunk and and a whoremonger, and quite possibly a sodomite. It's a mystery to me why you and others of your rank continue to have dealings with him.'

'Ah, but he paints like an angel,' Mattei replied.

Battista was unmoved. 'I need hardly remind you, Signor Mattei, that Lucifer was once an angel.'

'Indeed. But I would venture to suggest that Caravaggio, though no paragon of the virtues, has not yet fallen so far from grace.'

' "Not yet" is the operative phrase,' Battista replied.

'A harsh judgment, Camerlengo, if I may say so. I have spoken with him many times, and it has always seemed to me that, though deeply troubled, he remains a true believer in Our Lord. You would agree with me, I am sure, that such is not always the case, even here in Rome.'

At this, Mattei's nephew, Cosimo, a young lawer recently returned from his studies in Perugia, piped up: 'But Uncle, why don't you just show His Eminence the painting you keep upstairs – *The Betrayal of Christ*. That's as inspired as any religious work I have ever seen, either here or in Florence.'

Battista's ears pricked up. 'What's that? To which painting does the boy refer? I know of no such work.'

Mattei smiled to cover his embarrassment. 'I assure you, Eminence, it is a slight affair – a painting of no importance.'

'Not so, Uncle,' said Cosimo. 'It's truly marvellous. I should say it's the pride of your collection. It just astonishes me that you don't show it off. Even I wouldn't have seen it if I hadn't visited you one afternoon in your bedroom when you were ill with gout.'

Mattei shot his nephew a look like death, but it was too late.

'Take me to it,' Battista said. 'I should like to see this so-called masterpiece.'

'But Your Eminence, it's upstairs, away from the light. Really, you shouldn't trouble yourself. Allow me to fill your … oh, but I see you've hardly touched your wine.'

'Upstairs, you say. Then let us proceed. I am not yet so old that I cannot negotiate a set of stairs.' The cardinal beckoned to a servant with his stubby left arm. 'Bring lanterns and candles. Hurry! At once!'

Mattei realized that further prevarication would only make matters worse. He and Battista, preceded by servants bearing lanterns, followed by the general retinue of dinner guests, proceeded up the ornate main staircase of the villa to the host's sumptuous bedchamber, with its unrivalled views across the Eternal City. 'It's over there!' Mattei said, casually, as soon as there was sufficient light to pierce the gloom. Every eye followed the direction of his gaze. The wall opposite his elaborate four-poster bed was dominated, even overwhelmed by *The Betrayal of Christ*.

The yellow light from the servants' lanterns flickered across the canvas. Notoriously short-sighted, Battista squinted and pursed his lips. Then he strode closer to the painting, mounted in a golden frame. Several seconds went by. As the burly figure of Judas moved into focus, his left arm several inches too short, his bald spot mimicking a cardinal's zuchetto, Battista's jaw dropped in shock.

'So … what do you think, Your Eminence?' Mattei asked. 'An interesting use of colour …'

'I am sorry to say that your nephew has got it completely wrong,' the cardinal replied, managing with an extraordinary effort of will to curb his indignation. 'Our Lord looks as if he has just been caught cheating at cards. And take note of the wretch with the lantern, looking as if he's led the way. If I'm not mistaken, it's the creator of this abomination, shamelessly associating himself with the betrayal in the garden.'

Mattei looked as if he was about to say something, but in the end merely nodded his head.

'Your Eminence is, of course, an expert.'

As most of those gathered around the painting looked from the figure of Judas to that of the cardinal, the gaze of one man – an elderly Jesuit – remained fixed on the figure of the fleeing man. Eventually, he remarked in a loud voice, only slightly slurred from drink, that this fellow definitely reminded him of someone, if only he could put a name to the face. 'It will come to me,' he added. 'It's on the tip of my tongue.'

While the old man struggled with the remains of his memory, Battista pulled his cape around him with a flourish, covering his left arm. It was late, he informed Mattei. He had to go. It was a signal for the other guests to depart as well, for no one wished it to be said of them that they stayed behind to gossip about the former chief prosecutor of the Inquisition, a man whose temper was as short as his reach was long.

Minutes afterwards, as he was about to step into his carriage, his departing guest informed Mattei that he wished to purchase *The Betrayal of Christ* in order to destroy it and safeguard future generations from contemplation of its blasphemy. 'How much will you take for it?' he demanded.

The banker considered the potential profit involved in such a transaction and was tempted. But in the end he could not bear the thought of Caravaggio's masterpiece being burned, as if it were a heretic. 'It is not for sale, Camerlengo,' he said at last, his voice almost cracking with the strain.

'Don't be absurd. Every man has his price, and you are a banker. One hundred scudi.'

'I am sorry, Eminence, but it was a particular favourite of my late brother the cardinal. I couldn't possibly ...'

'Two hundred.'

'I have to decline.'

'Five hundred.'

Mattei was sweating now. 'Your offer is most ... most generous. But, Eminence, I beg of you, you ask the impossible. I would beg you instead to accept my personal assurance that this canvas will be kept hidden from public view.'

'I have your word on that?'

'You do. So long as I am alive, the painting shall remain hidden.'

Battista almost spat out his reply. 'Be in no doubt, Mattei, that I shall hold you to your promise. And may God help you if you fail.'

16*
Conclave minus 11

The Vatican Secret Archive, set up by Pope Paul V in 1610, was not, in fact, secret at all. Legitimate scholars and interested journalists had for many years been able to access its material simply by filling in a form, presenting suitable ID and turning up at the stated time.

The problem, as Dempsey had been warned by his uncle, was that you had to know where to look. For the archive was also a labyrinth.

At first, his task looked simple enough. He wanted to know how far back Cardinal Bosani's interest in Islam went and at what point he had become so stridently anti-Muslim. The young receptionist at the Salla degli Stampati – a Sicilian, he thought, with thick glasses and prominent teeth – was impressed by the Irishman's letter of introduction, signed by the Superior General of the Society of Jesus. But, then, having studied Dempsey's written request, he shook his head.

'*Mi dispiace*. I am sorry, *Signor*. But the information you seek is embargoed for the next fifty years at least.'

'Really? And why would that be?'

The receptionist looked at him as if he were a child. 'His Eminence is the most senior member of the Curia – a former Secretary of State as well as Camerlengo. No files relating to his life and career will be available for inspection until a minimum of twenty-five years after his death.'

Dempsey had no time for the Church's self-importance. 'But I am merely seeking the sort of information that would be available in the public domain.'

'Then that is where you should look for it.'

'Right.' The Irishman thought quickly. 'Listen,' he said, 'the Father General, my uncle, is preparing a sermon, to be delivered in the Gesù. His congregation will include many cardinals of the Sacred College, among them, I feel sure, the next Vicar of Christ. His sermon will discuss the current state of relations between the Catholic Church and Islam. The Camerlengo, as you will know, has been deeply involved in this process for many years. There must be speeches, press releases, a record of which countries he visited and who he met. That is all I'm looking for. I'm not suggesting that His Eminence murdered anyone or conspired to start a crusade.'

The receptionist smiled. 'No, of course not. I understand. You say the Father General has requested this information?'

'That is correct.'

'Very well. Wait here. I will see what I can do.'

As soon as he was alone, having checked that the second receptionist on duty was busy with someone else, Dempsey sat down at the now vacant computer, which was logged on to the archive's state-of-the-art Vatican intranet. Moving his fingers as quickly as he could, he cross-checked the name 'Bosani' against the words 'Islam', 'Muslim', 'Ottoman' and 'Qu'ran'. What came up was both routine and entirely unexpected. Buried among the hundreds of references to speeches, meetings and appointments, was a reference, highlighted in red, noting a connection with a Cardinal Orazio Battista, Camerlengo during the time of Popes Clement VIII and Paul V. According to the computer record, Bosani had called up everything he could find about Battista within weeks of his arrival in Rome in 1977. The details, which must originally have been inscribed in card files, had obviously been transferred to the computer archive some years before. Battista, it transpired, had been a leading prosecutor in the trials in 1599 of the astronomer Giordano Bruno and of the Cenci family – both of which had ended in the defendants' torture and execution. Both cases, he noted, were cross-referenced as 'controversies'. Bosani had evidently held on to the original files and the corresponding microfilm for several years, returning them, according to an asterisked footnote, only after the personal intervention of the Cardinal Prefect.

It was crazy stuff. How a Church so rooted in violence and deceit could pretend to itself that it was the faithful expression of God's will was a mystery to Dempsey – but not one he had any desire to solve.

One file still said to be missing, declared 'lost', was listed as 'Most confidential … For the eyes of His Holiness only'. No details were given, only that it related to an investigation carried out by the Inquisition on the Pope's personal order. All that remained of the file was its classification tag and the brief two-line description of the content. For a reason not given, the entry was cross-referenced to a painting by Caravaggio, *The Betrayal of Christ*, apparently lost for some two hundred years. Bloody odd, he thought. What could be the possible connection between Caravaggio and a suspect cardinal? And why might Bosani have held on to the file?

Maybe there would be some mileage in this stuff after all.

He heard footsteps. Fortunately, the archive had a marble floor. Hastily returning the computer to its home page, he stood up and moved to the other side of the desk. The young receptionist walked towards him, beaming.

'I have found what you wanted,' he told him. 'All public knowledge ... nothing about murder or crusades.'

He laughed, and Dempsey joined in.

'If you could just fill in this form, I'll give you a reader's pass and a number. Then you should make your way to the Old Study Room on the *piano nobile* and take a seat at desk number seven. The papers you asked for will be brought to you there.'

'Thank you ever so much,' Dempsey said. 'You really are most kind.'

'*Prego*. It is nothing, Signor. May God reward your efforts and those of your uncle, the Father General.'

Five minutes later, Dempsey was at his assigned desk, idly switching his table lamp on and off, when another member of the library staff, a women this time, in her forties, coughed politely and smiled down at him.

'You are number seven?' she asked.

'I am,' he replied, feeling slightly Kafkaesque.

'The papers you requested, Signor. When you have finished, please take them to the desk over there and sign out.'

'I shall do that. *Grazie*.'

'*Prego*.'

The pile of papers the woman had delivered were bunched together in a manila file and looked about as interesting as a company report. The bulk of it, as he expected, was made up of newspaper and magazine clippings, many from *Time* magazine – which seemed to take an inordinate interest in the affairs of the Holy See – and, of course, *L'Osservatore Romano*. There were also copies of speeches and news releases from the grandly named Pontifical Council for Social Communications – the Vatican press office. In addition, there were several reports in Arabic, with translations into Italian, emanating, so far as he could tell, from the governors of the central mosque in Rome, plus one, dated November 1989, from the official Egyptian newspaper, *Al-Ahram*.

He took out a notebook and pencil and began to write. Bosani's involvement with the Secretariat for Non-Christians, set up by Pope Paul VI, began, he discovered, within two years of his ordination. He had taken Islam as part of his degree in Bologna in the 1960s and spoke Arabic fluently. As a young priest, he travelled widely in the Muslim world, visiting Saudi Arabia twice, in 1970 and 1977, at a time when even getting an entry visa couldn't have been easy. But then, judging by his trajectory, he was never destined to be an ordinary priest. After three years as a curate, in La Spezia, he spent two years at Cairo's Al-Azhar University, the oldest and most famous institute of theology and law in the Muslim world, founded in 988, where he took classes in the Qu'ran and Islamic law. Unless you knew a religion from the inside, he told a conference in Vienna years later, you could never hope to understand its appeal or assess its claims.

Over the years, obviously an administrator rather than a pastor, he had risen quickly to become head of the semi-autonomous Pontifical Commission for Religious Relations with Muslims. According to a published memo from the office of Rome's mayor, it was Bosani who had most influenced Pope Paul VI to approve the construction of the city's central mosque, the largest in Europe, paid for by the king of Saudi Arabia. A letter from the governors of the mosque, sent out as a press release, confirmed this and thanked the Monsignor (as he was then) for his 'invaluable support'.

Years later, following the death of John Paul I, Bosani had continued on a positive note, persuading the new pontiff, John Paul II, of the importance of improved relations with the Muslim world. An article in *The Boston Globe* reported that it was due to Bosani's efforts that the Pole, a deeply conservative Catholic, whose countrymen had spent centuries defending Christendom against the Ottomans, ended up visiting the Great Mosque in Damascus – the first-ever head of the Church to enter a Muslim place of worship. The Pope had also, the *Globe* reminded its readers, kissed the Qu'ran publicly on at least two occasions, confirming it as a work of Holy Scripture, and spoken many times of Muslims as his 'dear brothers and sisters'. In recognition of his contribution to religious understanding, Bosani was consecrated a bishop in 1983 and then, at the Consistory of 26 November 1994, a cardinal deacon, later elevated to the status of cardinal priest. Bosani recalled with evident pride, in a speech to seminarians in his native La Spezia, that, after his death, His Holiness was eulogized as a 'hero' of Islam. 'Worshippers in mosques across the Arab world remembered him in their prayers. In Egypt, three days of mourning were declared. The Arab League and the governments of Jordan and Lebanon even lowered flags to half-mast and hurried to send representatives to the funeral.'

All of this, characterized by an almost evangelical tolerance, appeared strangely at odds with the Camerlengo's new-found reputation as fanatically anti-Muslim. What had brought about his dramatic, 180-degree change of direction? Dempsey read on. While retaining his interest in Islamic affairs, Bosani had moved into the heart of Vatican bureaucracy in the mid-1990s, rising to be sub-dean of the College of Cardinals, then, after the death of Benedict XVI, Secretary of State and Camerlengo. There was nothing in his speeches or public writings that provided a clue to the shift in his attitude; nor, so far as he could tell, did it immediately follow the terrorist attacks by al-Qaeda against the United States on 11 September 2001. The first indicator of his aggression did not in fact emerge until the arrival of Pope Benedict four years later. The German pontiff's disastrous speech, delivered in Regensburg in 2006, in which he appeared to condemn the 'evil and inhumanity' of the Prophet and his intent 'to spread by the sword the faith he preached', was the first public sign of the new hard line. Under intense international pressure to recant, the Pope had moved quickly to clarify his position and reassure Muslims, but the damage was done.

Dempsey looked at his watch: a quarter past twelve. Time to go. He needed to talk to his uncle – and Maya. Packing up the documents and placing them back in their folder, he returned them as instructed and signed out. On his way out of the building, via the Porta di Santa Anna, he stopped at the Salla degli Stampati and thanked the young Sicilian who had gone out of his way to assist him.

'*Prego*,' came the reply. 'It is my job to help, and I am always, of course, at the disposition of the Father General.'

They shook hands. As Dempsey disappeared out of the main door, the receptionist took out his mobile phone from his trouser pocket and tapped in a number.

He waited. On the second ring, a voice answered. '*Pronto!* Vatican Security Office. Who do you wish to speak with?'

17*
28 May 1606

The heat in Rome was building but had not yet reached the intensity of high summer. Caravaggio and his friend Onorio Longhi were on their way to play racquetball at a court just off the Via della Scrofa, not far from the painter's old lodgings by the Palazzo Firenze. They were among Rome's best-known *racchetti*, difficult to beat on their home court. But as they approached the playing area, where they faced a challenge from the artists Guido Reini and Orazio Gentileschi, it wasn't so much the game that occupied their thoughts, but their chances of coming out of it alive.

A bitter feud had existed between Caravaggio and Longhi on the one hand and the powerful Tomassino clan on the other for at least a year. The exact origins of the dispute were forgotten, though obviously rooted in gambling, women and drink. But in recent weeks the enmity had swollen to dangerous proportions, threatening to turn the quarrel into a vendetta. Following a dispute over the favours of Fillide Melandroni, Caravaggio – who had recovered something of his former verve following the discreet sale to Mattei of *The Betrayal of Christ* – found himself goaded on an almost daily basis by Ranuccio, the youngest of the three brothers, whose family controlled everything that went on in the Campo Marzio. Longhi had been attacked in the street only a week earlier, receiving a slight rapier wound to his shoulder. Caravaggio's continued occupation of the apartment owned by the lawyer Ruffietto didn't help. He should have been out by Christmas, except that the sale of the building had fallen through. The artist's continued presence in the area was viewed by the Tomassoni as a deliberate provocation. It was an open secret that any further 'insults' would end in bloodshed. That was why Longhi had asked Petronia Toppa, a veteran army officer from Bologna, to join them as back-up. Toppa was a burly fellow who liked nothing more than a good scrap – whether with swords or fists, it made no difference to him. He also owed Longhi fifty scudi, which helped. As the three men turned off the main street in the direction of the *teatro rachette*, a small crowd began to gather, keen to see what would happen next. A quartet of *sbirri* held back, knowing both sides to be well connected, biding their time.

What Caravaggio didn't know was that Ranuccio had particular reason that day to vent his spleen. Twenty-four hours earlier, he had been approached by a represent-ative of Cardinal Battista – a tall, hooded monk – who had given him one hundred scudi and the Camerlengo's personal assurance that he would not be prosecuted were he to kill the artist Michelangelo Merisi.

'His Eminence understands that Merisi has wronged you on many occasions in the past. He wishes you to know that his sympathies are with you entirely in your detestation of a man who is both a braggart and a heretic. Merisi is a man who must swiftly be brought to justice, and the Tomassoni, with their proud record in arms in service of the Church, are viewed as righteous in this matter. Absolution is assured.'

The emissary handed over the cash.

Rannuccio nodded. He required no further urging. He knew what he had to do. Placing the money in a strongbox, he alerted his brothers and fetched his rapier.

It was Toppa, following behind, who called out a warning. Caravaggio, his hand firmly on the hilt of his sword, spun round in time to see Ranuccio moving towards him, blade drawn, his brother Giovan Francesco and two cousins one pace to the rear. Straightaway, in a loud, theatrical voice, Ranuccio accused Caravaggio of carrying on an affair with the 'little whore' Melandroni, who, he observed, with a flourish of his rapier, was riddled with the pox.

Caravaggio took stock of the scene. He felt oddly calm. Ranuccio was a braggart, but no slouch with the sword. There was a definite glint in his eye, as if he meant business. Immediately behind him stood his older brother, Giovan Francesco, and a pace or two further back, two of their cousins, both aged around thirty, well known as 'enforcers'. It was an ambush, no doubt about that. The ques-tion was, how far did they wish to press it?

Ranuccio meanwhile had halted, standing with his legs apart, drawing a semi-circle in the dirt in front of him with the point of his sword. 'You are in Campo Marzio,' he boomed. 'That is Tomassoni territory, as understood by the Senate and People of Rome. And you, Merisi, are not welcome here. I advise you, as the coward you are, to leave at once or face the consequences.'

Following this, there could be only one outcome. Caravaggio sighed, looking to left and right to locate his seconds. Both nodded to him. He drew his sword and tested the point against his thumb, Then, in an equally oratorical voice, he answered Ranuccio, reminding him that he owed him twenty scudi from the previous year and that he would do better to pay his debts than slander a good woman.

The small crowd drew its breath.

There was no further preamble. With an oath, Ranuccio launched himself at his enemy. Caravaggio stood his ground, shifting his weight from one foot to the other, trying to anticipate the angle of the attack. His opponent's opening lunge was hasty and amateurish, probably because of the rage he felt, and the price he paid was a swipe across his back that slit open his doublet, though without injuring the flesh beneath.

'Olé!' Caravaggio called out. The crowd laughed.

It would be the only flash of humour that day. Now the contest grew serious. Neither man was a mere *bravazzo* – a swashbuckler or 'cutter'. Both were skilled with the rapier and neither was in a mood to grant quarter. In the subsequent exchange, it was Ranuccio who fared the better, opening a nick in his opponent's throat and driving him steadily backwards. But then Caravaggio feinted to one side, catching Tomassino in the hamstring of his right leg with the point of his blade as, for the second time, he continued past at full stretch. Enraged, and ignoring the flow of blood that immediately stained his tights below the knee, the Roman halted, reversed direction and renewed his attack. Caravaggio parried, giving ground but confident that he had gained the upper hand.

The fight soon settled into a pattern, with each side advancing, retreating and riposting as if directed by a choreographer. Both were breathing heavily. It was becoming clear, though, that the injured Ranuccio was out of ideas. Caught unawares by a sudden change in the line of attack, he stumbled, missed his footing on a cobblestone, and fell heavily. Caravaggio's nostrils flared as he looked down at his stricken opponent. Every fibre of his being called out to him to finish it. He wanted nothing more than to end the existence of a man whose slanders had made his life a misery. Instead, he stayed his hand. This was not out of generosity, but so that no one, most obviously the *sbirri*, could accuse him of reckless murder. His intention was to attack with renewed ferocity the moment Ranuccio regained his feet, ignoring any plea for mercy. This would add to the kudos that came his way.

It was a decision he would regret for the rest of his life, for all at once, from a prone position, his enraged and humiliated opponent lashed out and stabbed him in the foot. Caravaggio winced. The pain was excruciating. Teeth bared, he uttered a throaty growl and, without further conscious thought, thrust downwards, driving his blade straight into his opponent's stomach. A gasp rose up from the onlookers, who then fell silent, for they knew at once that the wound was mortal. Ranuccio swayed back onto the cobbles holding both hands to his stomach so that the blood spilled out between his fingers. The light in his eyes began to dim. But though he almost fainted with the effort, he still spat his venom at Caravaggio, taunting him that soon he would join him in hell.

'The Camerlengo has put a price on your head, Merisi. If you are not … cut down like a dog in the street, you will die on the scaffold. Even now, an axe is being ground for you. There can be … no escape.'

Caravaggio's eyes narrowed. 'What are you saying? Did Battista pay you? Did he tell you why he wants me dead?'

Ranuccio tried to speak, but couldn't. Instead, he started coughing blood. Caravaggio didn't know whether to try to revive him or to throttle him. Before he could make up his mind, he felt a searing pain in his head. Ranuccio's brother, Giovan Francesco, had attacked him without warning from behind, seeking instant revenge for the loss of Ranuccio. A cut three inches long opened up behind his right ear. As he fell, helpless, to the ground, it was the action of the redoubtable Toppa that saved his life. As Longhi hauled Caravaggio to his feet and pressed a handkerchief against his skull to staunch the flow of blood, the former army captain took on all three surviving Tomassoni, only giving up when his sword arm ceased to respond and he could no longer hold his weapon.

It was at that point that the *sbirri* intervened and arrested him.

Ranuccio died thirty minutes later, having being given absolution by his parish priest from the nearby church of San Lorenzo in Lucina. As Caravaggio, bleeding and barely conscious, was taken for emergency treatment to the shop of the barber Lucca, Longhi fled the city. Witnesses, paid in advance by the Tomassoni, testified to the papal police that Caravaggio had initiated the duel. Several pointed out that as Ranuccio lay prone, the artist had driven his sword into his body with the obious intent of killing him. Within hours, an official investigation was launched. Battista protested to the Pope that Caravaggio had finally shown his true colours. He was joined in his denunciation by the Farnese family, in whose service the Tomassoni had fought against the Huguenots in France. The artist, a suspected heretic, they said, was notorious for his brawling. Now he had murdered the scion of a valiant family and for that crime alone must pay with his life.

No one listened to those who said it was the Tomassoni who were to blame for what happened. A young *bravo* who volunteered that Ranuccio had brought his death upon himself by violating the gentleman's code of honour was told to get about his business. A plea for mercy by Del Monte fizzled out when Battista drew His Eminence aside to point out to him that his frolics with boys could very easily be brought into the public domain, 'with the most unfortunate consequences'. Everything then happened in a rush. By order of the Apostolic Palace, a hue and cry was ordered. Caravaggio was to be hunted down and brought to immediate account.

Before the *sbirri* could make the arrest, however, fate intervened. Alerted by Costanza Colonna, the Marchesa di Caravaggio, Prince Marzio Colonna offered the artist sanctuary on his estate in the Alban Hills.

The Merisi had been in the service of the Colonna for more than half a century. Marchesa Costanza in particular, on a visit to the family seat at the base of the Quirinal Hill, was convinced that the son of her longtime *uomo di fiducia* was a genius in the service of God and his protection a sacred trust. He was spirited away under the very noses of the *sbirri*, hidden beneath a pile of offal in the back of a butcher's cart. Ranuccio had not exaggerated. Caravaggio's failure to answer a papal summons had automatically rendered him a fugitive and a *banda capitale* was now in force – a death warrant that anyone could act on with guaranteed immunity from prosecution.

In the midst of what became a citywide manhunt, no one noticed the unexpected death, apparently from food poisoning, of the elderly Jesuit who recognized the fleeing man in *The Betrayal of Christ*. The late Father Alfonso di Conza was a modest man, who taught Latin and Greek to seminarians and was known for the gentleness of his sermons in churches around Rome. It was after twelve o'clock Mass on the Monday following his dinner at the Villa Mattei that he returned to the Jesuit residence on the Via Marco for lunch. The cook told him she had something special for him today left by an anonymous well-wisher – a delicious lamb stew, with tomatoes and basil, which he ate hungrily. One hour later, he complained of stomach pains. By mid-afternoon, his sickness had turned to diarrhoea, then to dysentery. By midnight, he was dead. Father General Acquaviva awarded his old colleague a Requiem Mass, but attributed his death to overwork and bad meat. No one asked, but if they had inquired they would have learned only that Di Conza was buried in the Catacombs, with none but his sister and a small group of parishioners in attendance.

As news reached the Curia of Caravaggio's flight from the city, Cardinal Battista discussed developments with his fellow Muslim, Fra'Luis de Fonseca, now a chevalier of the Knights of Malta, who for the second time that year was visiting Rome from Valletta. The Knight was puzzled that Caravaggio had managed to get away. Battista scowled. 'We picked the wrong people,' he said, referring to Ranuccio and his brothers.

'So it would seem. When choosing an assassin, Your Eminence, it is generally wise to exclude those who are reckless or who have an interest in the result.'

This cold analysis did nothing to improve the cardinal's temper. 'Let us hope you do not repeat the error, my friend. For I am informed that the fellow has long held ambitions to join your order and become a Knight. He believes apparently that membership will instil discipline into his life and give some structure to his faith.'

'If you are right,' Fonseca replied, 'then his life is forfeit, for he will find me ready and waiting.'

Battista nodded, then glanced towards the window. 'The sun is about to set,' he said, 'We should pray.'

18*
Conclave minus 10

The Swiss Guard sentry, in his dark blue uniform and beret, offered Maya a crisp salute and a shy smile as she approached the Cancello di Sant'Anna, the main commercial gateway into the Vatican. It was coming up to six o'clock in the evening and a steady stream of cars was crawling towards the exit. The gate itself, overlooked by stone eagles dating from the pontificate of Pius XI, was heavily shielded and reinforced, and though it might not have been evident to visitors, the sentries on duty were heavily armed. To Maya's left as she crossed the invisible line that separated Rome from the sovereign territory of the Holy See stood the guards' barracks. Her parents' apartment was on the second floor. But she didn't go left. Instead, she turned immediately right, off the narrow pavement into the church of Sant'Anna, to which Caravaggio's *Madonna dei Palafrenierni* was taken after its removal from St Peter's, before it was bought by the Pope's nephew, Cardinal Borghere. She liked to sit in the church for a few minutes each day, and on this day in particular she needed time to think.

The previous night, after an afternoon spent walking from the Piazza Navona, by way of the Caravaggios in the French Church and drinks in some bar she had never heard of called the Scholars' Lounge, she had gone back with Dempsey to his apartment, where they had made love for two solid hours before falling asleep, exhausted, in each other's arms. It was the first time they had had sex together, which still surprised her. But where in the past the pleasure had been mainly physical, mixed, if she was honest, with the thrill of conquest, this time there had been an intensity that she had never previously experienced. It had made her cry.

Maybe this was how you discovered love: not in an accumulated awareness of shared likes and dislikes, or the realization that you appreciated the other person's sense of humour – which was how the women's magazines liked to present it – but rather, as in the great nineteenth-century novels, like a burst of lightning or a sudden epiphany, in which your life and awareness of everything was heightened and transformed. When she woke up, hours later, she was surprised at first to find a man's arm resting on the small of her back, just above the crease of her buttocks. Then it all flooded back. Dempsey was still asleep but Maya's mouth was dry as a bone. She was desperate for a glass of water, followed by a coffee. She also wanted him to wake up so that she could tell him what she was feeling. It was like in that old movie, *When Harry Met Sally*: when you realized you wanted to spend the rest of your life with somebody, you wanted the rest of your life to start as soon as possible. But she knew it wouldn't be easy. Drawing back the sheets, she saw for the first time in the light of day how terrible his scars were. He had told her on their second date about what happened to him in Iraq and she was fully prepared to be shocked. Yet the truth was that in candlelight, after two bottles of wine, several pints of Guinness and any number of grappas, she had hardly noticed. If anything, the ridges on his back had only added to the excitement.

But now, looking down, she was able to appreciate how close he had come to losing his life and now painful, and lonely, it must have been for him in that isolation ward in Marseille. As carefully and gently as she could, so as not to waken him, she replaced the sheet over his damaged flesh and went to prepare some breakfast.

She was not a good Catholic. Her tastes at school and university had run much more to boys, loud music and basement bars than priests and Mass. But today, sitting on her pew in the church, lit by the lanterns above set into the eight-sided dome, she found herself offering a small prayer.

Sant'Anna was more than a tourist attraction. It was the parish church of the Vatican. And when a loudspeaker informed those present that the next Mass, due to start in three minutes, would be conducted in French, Maya rose to go. Back outside in the street, a bespectacled Guard – from the village of Küssnacht, she seemed to recall – halted the stream of traffic heading towards the gate so that she could cross over to the barracks. Over his right shoulder rose the tower of Nicholas V, and then the massive bulk of the Apostolic Palace itself.

'*Guete Obe*, Christian,' she said, greeting him in Schweizerdeutsch, the almost impenetrable dialect of German spoken in the north and centre of Switzerland.

'*Guete Obe, Fräulein*,' he replied, blushing. He was, she realized, no more than twenty-one.

Maya had fallen in love with the barracks almost the moment she first set foot inside. The earliest portion of the building dated from 1492, when the Pope was Alexander VI, the notorious Rodrigo Borgia. But most construction had taken place during the reign of Julius II, the Warrior Pope, under whom the Guard became a permanent feature of Vatican life. Behind the front office, somewhat incongruously, was the dry-cleaner's, specializing in the maintenance of the Guards' elaborate costumes. Beyond that again was the refectory, its walls decorated with frescoes glorying mighty deeds with sword and halberd. The Armory was another favourite. This was where the steel helmets, two-handled swords and halberds carried in pontifical processions were stored, along with the Corps' colours and drums. Upstairs were the dormitories, and beyond these again the officers' quarters, including the spacious apartment of the Commandant and his family.

The sergeant at the desk was from Unterwalden, one of the original cantons of the Swiss Confederation. 'Guete Obe, Fräulein Studer,' he said.

'Good evening, Sergeant Weibel. Is my father home?'

'I believe so. I saw the colonel head upstairs twenty minutes ago.'

'In uniform or out?'

The question elicited a rare smile. 'He was wearing a suit, Fräulein. I think he had just come back from a meeting at the Governorate.'

'A busy week ahead. Lots to prepare for.'

'Most definitely. But the election of a new pope is always a time for celebration, is it not?'

'A chance to polish up your breastplates.'

'Ja, ja. Of course. But also our 226s.'

The Swiss-made P226 Elite semi-automatic handgun, with its beavertail grip and short reset trigger, had become the standard issue of the Swiss Guard, which these days also trained with assault rifles and Heckler & Koch machine pistols. 'Yes,' said Maya. 'But let's hope the conclave doesn't end in a shoot-out.'

The sergeant, a two-time pistol-shooting champion in the Swiss army, shrugged. 'You know our motto, Fräulein: *Acriter et Fideliter* – Honour and Fidelity. These days, we must be prepared for anything.'

Upstairs in the apartment, as Frau Studer prepared supper, the colonel was reading his paper while keeping half an eye on the evening news in German. Maya went into the kitchen to say hello to her mother, then returned to the living room, where, for the third time that week, she turned down the air conditioning before taking a seat on the sofa next to her father.

'You must have got home very late last night,' he said disapprovingly. 'I didn't hear you come in.'

'Actually, I stayed at a friend's house.'

'Have I met her?'

'Him, father. He's a "him".'

'Aah!'

Studer sighed. He knew better than to seek to impose his religious views on his daughter. At least, he reasoned, her overnight stays were few and far between, which was as much as any father could hope for these days.

Berlin, according to ZDF, had elected a new mayor, and for the first time his deputy would be of Turkish origin. She nodded in approval. That was progress, and long overdue. In Strasbourg, the European Parliament was acting to reduce national vetos in respect of the EU budget. Did that mean more democracy, or less? She wasn't sure. The president of the United States, on a visit to Beijing, had confirmed that China would take the lead in the development of the next generation of short-haul jets by the jointly owned Boeing Corporation. In another development, an historic church in Würzburg had been deconsecrated and would shortly re-open as a mosque .

The world had changed so profoundly in the years since she was a child that the Europe and the Switzerland in which her parents grew up seemed almost as remote to Maya as the Austro-Hungarian Empire. Today's Europe was thoroughly cosmopolitan and multi-cultural, governed increasingly from Brussels by the democratic equivalent of diktat. Switzerland continued to be an anomaly, on the margins of the EU. But with close to 40 per cent of its population now of Middle Eastern, African or East European descent, it could no longer claim to be the land of William Tell. Two of her father's Halberdiers were ethnic Africans; five members of the national parliament were Muslim, and another a Hindu. As the old ways faded, it was to be expected that there would be a reaction by traditionalists to changes that seemed to cut across the very definition of Swiss-ness. Older people – but some younger people, too – were concerned especially about the huge increase in the country's Muslim population, which had led not only to the widespread wearing of the hijab and a surge in Muslim-only schools, but also to demands for Muslim cantons, with sharia law.

Behind the high walls of the Holy See, none of this was visible. As commandant of the Swiss Guard, the colonel, like all of his predecessors, dating back to 1506, was considered a member of the 'pontifical family', holding the rank of a Chamberlain of His Holiness. Yet the Guardia Svizzera Pontifica was much more than a papal adornment. With his one hundred officers and men – the *Hundertschweizer* – Studer was responsible not only for ceremonial duties but for every aspect of papal security, which, ever since the attempted assassination by a deranged Turk of Pope John Paul II, included intelligence, crowd control and electronic surveillance.

These days, the Guards only wore their breastplates and steel helmets on solemn occasions. Their red, blue and yellow 'gala' uniforms, designed not by Michelangelo, but by a gifted commandant in 1914, were still very much in evidence, and remained a firm favourite with tourists. But in the twenty-first century, proficiency with small arms, keen eyesight and the ability to spot a potential threat, whether an individual or among a multitude, were what marked out the finest recruits.

Not that the Guards either looked or acted like a SWAT team. Life in the centuries-old barracks had a strict but seductive rhythm, not unlike that of a monastery. The Guardsmen, who normally served two to three years, were not only professional soldiers, but also practising Catholics, who viewed their calling as a great honour. Maya's father regarded his own role as a rare privilege rather than a distinction. It was not that he lacked an ego or sense of self-esteem. It was more that as an army officer, then a director of the family bank, he had commanded respect for thirty years. This time round, virtue was its own reward.

As they watched the news, an item came on about the return of the heart of the late Cardinal Rüttgers to his cathedral in Freiburg. The cardinal's sister was distraught. Her brother, she told an earnest young interviewer, had been in perfect health when he left for Rome. She couldn't understand what happened to him. How could it be God's will that a man of just fifty-one, newly elected to lead Germany's Catholics, should have died so suddenly? And why, she wanted to know, had the Church prevented the return of his body to his family and homeland? She had written to Cardinal Bosani, the Camerlengo, to request his body for burial next to his parents. But Bosani said no, he must be interred in Rome. No explanation was given. There hadn't even been a post-mortem. All they had been sent was her brother's heart, filled with formaldehyde, 'like a pickled peach'.

At the mention of Bosani's name, Colonel Studer looked up from his well-thumbed copy of the *Neue Züricher Zeitung*. Maya noticed him twitching.

'What's the matter, father?' she asked.

'Nothing,' he said. 'It is nothing.'

'You don't like Bosani, do you?'

He placed the newspaper next to him on the sofa, keeping half an eye on the television screen. 'It's got nothing to do with liking. He's a hard man, but we live in hard times. I just wish that poor woman had been able to take her brother's body back with her to Germany.'

'I'd have thought she'd be proud of the send-off they gave him. Wasn't there a funeral Mass in the Vatican? Didn't Bosani himself preside?'

The colonel, relaxed for the evening in an open-necked shirt and chinos, curled his lip. 'Oh there was a Mass all right, but the Camerlengo seemed merely to be going through the motions. He has a lot on his mind at the moment, of course. The conclave is just around the corner. But I still thought it could have been better done.'

'Did you know Rüttgers?'

Her father made a face. 'I wouldn't say I knew him. But we'd run into one another every now and then. The first time, about three months ago, I noticed him talking to one of my guardsmen, which strictly speaking is not permitted when they're on duty. But the young man seemed so uplifted by the conversation that I couldn't bring myself to reproach him. Instead, I spoke with the cardinal himself, who told me he had been pleased by my appointment and asked after my family, you included.'

This surprised Maya. 'He knew about me?'

'And your brother. He grew up just over the frontier from us in Schaffhausen, near Singen. He even had a Swiss cousin, from Steckborn, married to a watch-maker. He told me he used to attend Mass at the Münster at least once a month when he was a teenager.'

'So he would have passed our house on the way to the church.'

'That's what he told me.'

'Interesting. How did he seem the last time you met him?'

'That would have been shortly before he died. He was on his way into the Camerlengo's office. Evidently, the two of them had a difference of opinion. He looked really downcast, as if something terrible had happened. I asked him if he was all right. Maybe he wasn't feeling well, I thought. But he said he felt fine – never fitter. It was just that he wasn't looking forward to the process of electing a new pope. "But Your Eminence," I said, "it is surely a great honour to be able to choose Christ's Vicar on Earth." He looked at me, with a look that I won't forget. He looked sad, but pained as well. "My dear Colonel," he said, "you have no idea how desperate things have become. The Church these days is hardly even Christian anymore. It's as if it has been infiltrated by outsiders pursuing their own agendas." '

'Did you ask him what he meant by this?' Maya asked, astonished by Rüttgers' candour.

'No,' the colonel replied. 'It wasn't my business to ask. After all, no one was suggesting a crime had been committed. I just wished him well and told him I would pray for him. He blessed me and went on his way. Three days later he was dead.'

'But that's extraordinary. I've never heard of such a thing.'

'I agree. And when I heard a couple of days ago that he had been buried in a sealed casket in the Teutonic Cemetery, without any proper ceremony, I thought, well, that's it – they've washed their hands of him.'

Maya was silent for a moment. On the television screen, the pictures were now showing a huge demonstration in Tehran demanding the destruction of the state of Israel and recognition of Islamic sovereignty across the region. Relations between Muslims and the West seemed to be deteriorating with each passing day.

She turned back to her father. 'Do you think Bosani was sorry when Rüttgers died?'

'Sorry? I really can't say. Priests deal with issues of life and death on a daily basis. To them dying is just a means of exchange. To ask Bosani if he mourned the death of a fellow cardinal would be like asking a banker if he thought a rise in interest rates meant the end of capitalism. What I do know is that he kept us well away from the body and then raced through the funeral process. I have no doubt that he felt Christian charity at the loss of a brother-in-Christ, but when I watched him as they carried the body out of St Peter's Basilica towards its final resting place, I can't pretend that he looked anything other than relieved.'

19*
Conclave minus 9

The south clock of St Peter's had just begun striking twelve as Dempsey bounded up the steps of the Jesuit headquarters on the Borgo Santo Spirito. He had intended to report to his uncle the previous night on what he'd found in the Secret Archive. Instead, he'd met up with Maya and they had spent the entire evening together, ending up in bed at his flat. It had been a tremendous emotional as well as physical outpouring and the result was that today he felt like a new man. By comparison, he decided, sorting out the apostolic succession would be no trouble at all. It was just a matter of who made the first move.

The receptionist, seated in his cubby hole on the left of the small entrance hall, looked up from his sports paper, recognized the Father General's nephew and buzzed him straight through. Ignoring the lift, Dempsey took the stairs two at a time to the fourth floor and made his way, echoingly, down the marble corridor to the door marked *Superiore Generale*. His uncle had been at work since eight o'clock, putting the final touches to a Jesuit initiative intended to counter the spread of evangelical Protestantism in Brazil. He had hoped he could postpone this until after the conclave, which took obvious precedence. But a conference was due to take place in Rome in one week's time. All the arrangements had been made. Air tickets were booked and hotel rooms reserved – and given that, by pure coincidence, the conference coincided with the most exciting few days in the Catholic world, the emergence of a new pope, no one was willing even to consider an alternative date. So he had just buckled down and got on with it. No sooner had he finished drafting his introductory speech than the new Provincial from Belgium was waiting, ready to fill his head with woe over the impending breakup of his country into separate Flemish and Walloon nations. Would this mean a division of the existing province into two distinct jurisdictions, he wanted to know. Given that he was from Brussels and had a foot in both camps, which job would fall to him? O'Malley made clucking noises and promised to get back to him as soon as possible. He remembered his own time at the University of Louvain – or Leuven as the locals called it – which he had very much enjoyed. It depressed him to think that two Catholic peoples, living in the fulcrum of the new Europe, could no longer stand the sight of each other. Finally, when he got the chance, he had run through the list of invitations to the traditional High Mass in the Gesù that would precede the conclave – striking out a couple of names he thought unsuitable or irrelevant and replacing them with names of his own. Father Giovanni, badly in need of a haircut, was hunched over his computer in the outer office, answering emails and fielding calls from around the world on his video screen. Dempsey's arrival, unannounced, did nothing to improve his humour and the young Irishman had almost to force his way past his desk, piled up with papers, in order to get to his uncle.

'Liam, there you are! Come in, come in,' O'Malley said. Then he saw the harassed features of his secretary, standing in the doorway, running his hands distractedly through his hair. 'It's all right, Giovanni. This will only take ten minutes; then, I promise you, you will have my undivided attention.'

'A busy day, Uncle Declan?'

'Don't get me started. Take a seat. I hope your trip to the Secret Archive wasn't a waste of time?'

'Far from it. You letter of introduction did the trick. I was made to feel like a cardinal-nephew. I saw lots of old press reports, a mountain of speeches and news releases, even a couple of letters in Arabic from the central mosque. But the real paydirt only appeared when I got a couple of minutes of my own on the library computer.'

'I thought they were restricted.'

'Well, he'd gone off to arrange for a load of papers to be brought to me and his screen was just sitting there. I didn't see the harm.'

'Don't say any more. Probably better that I don't know. Anyway … what did you find out?'

Dempsey ran down Bosani's history and demonstrated how his reputation for tolerance towards Islam, established over several decades, had taken a U-turn during the time of Benedict XVI.

O'Malley listened closely to his nephew's analysis. Dempsey stressed that the transformation in Bosani's position did not coincide with the terrorist attacks on America and the emergence of al-Qaeda. Rather, it had only happened with the arrival of a new pope. He wondered if it might not have been Benedict who influenced Bosani rather than the other way round. But O'Malley had met the German pontiff after his controversial 2006 speech and was struck by the depth of his penitence. 'The Holy Father,' he said, 'was concerned that Muslims around the world were turning to violence in pursuit of their ambitions, but he never intended to suggest that this was the will of God or of Mohammad.'

'Then why did he quote the emperor, who made exactly that claim?'

'Palaiologos? That's what I'd like to know. It was an error of judgment – but who was responsible? Who put the idea in his head?'

Dempsey thought for a moment. 'Is there no chance you could raise the issue with Bosani himself? You're one of the most senior priests in the Catholic Church. How could he say no to you?'

'I'm not sure what good it would do,' O'Malley said. 'In his present frame of mind, he might own up. Who knows? It's possible. Or he could lie … yes, even princes of the Church can lie. Either way, we would be no further forward, except that now he would know we were on to him.'

'And play his cards more carefully?'

'That's what I'd do.'

'You're a cunning man, Uncle.'

'I'm the head of the Jesuits. We're trained to be cunning. It's in the blood.'

'And what's in Bosani's blood?'

'That's what we're here to find out.'

Dempsey reached into his inside pocket and took out the notebook into which he had copied the material on the library stubs linking Bosani to Battista, the one-time head of the Inquisition. He turned to the relevant page and handed it across, with its reference to a mysterious file intended for the Pope's eyes only. His gratification came when his uncle whistled through his teeth as he took in the significance of what he'd read.

'Odd, don't you think?' Dempsey said. 'Battista was obviously a nasty piece of work, who'd burn you soon as look at you.'

His uncle took up the train of thought. 'Ashes to ashes, dust to dust. And for some reason he was under investigation on the orders of Paul V. Why would that be? I wonder.'

'No idea. It doesn't say. And, of coure, the file itself is missing.'

'I see. And the last man to look at it was ..?'

'Who else? His Eminence Lamberto Bosani, 23 January 1977.'

'Fascinating.'

'And that's not all.'

'Go on.'

'There's some sort of a connection – I don't know what – between Battista and a lost painting by Caravaggio, *The Betrayal of Christ*.'

A shock of recognition crossed O'Malley's face. '*The Betrayal of Christ*? Are you sure?'

'That's what it said. Sometimes known as *The Taking of Christ*, painted sometime in the early 1600s.'

'I know it.'

'You *know* it? But it's been lost for centuries. That's what it said in the file.'

A look of amused disdain crept over his uncles' features. 'It may have been "lost" when that note was written,' he said, 'but in the 1980s it hung over the sofa in the parlour in Dublin where I read my *Irish Times* each morning.'

'What? You mean the Jesusit house in Leeson Street? You're having me on.'

'No, it's true. It was "discovered" in 1990. The Residence hadn't been done up for something like thirty years. It smelled like a mixture of your grandmother's front room and the snug of Dohenny & Nesbitt's. Anyway, we took the art down and got the decorators in. The rector, Noel Barber – do you remember him? I think I took you along on a visit once – suggested we ask the National Gallery to do an evaluation. "Why not? You never know," he said. The upshot was that a couple of days later, this chap Benedetti – one of those little round Italian fellas you'd think was weaned on spaghetti – turns up, looking bored, like he'd been asked to run a village stall version of the Antiques Road show.

'He wanders round, turning up his nose at the dross he's looking at. Not that I blamed him. But then he sees this big painting propped up against the wall in the library, where we took it for storage. He got down on his hunkers and stared at it. The look that came over his face was priceless. It was like all his Christmases had come together. To cut a long story short – and take it from me, it was a long story – it turns out to be the missing Caravaggio, *The Betrayal of Christ*. Apparently it had hung in the Mattei family's palazzo in Monte Celio for a hundred years or more, hardly ever seen. The Mattei were big-time nobility – they produced more cardinals than you could shake a stick at. But after Napoleon's invasion of Italy, they fell on hard times and the Caravaggio was one of a job lot sold off to a passing Scotsman called Nisbet, who kept it for years on his estate in East Lothian. The image I have is of it hanging next to a stag's head in the library, half hidden by an aspidistra. Anyhow, another century goes by until an Irishman, Captain Percival Lea-Wilson – a Protestant, needless to say – buys it at auction. It was listed as by the Dutch artist Gerard Honthorst, who lived in Rome at the time of Caravaggio and painted in a similar style. This was around the time of the Easter Rising and the War of Independence, and in the way of these things Lea-Wilson, who worked for the British and wasn't what you'd call an ardent Republican, gets himself shot. In 1920, I think it was. It was his widow, a pediatrician, who very generously donated the picture to us. Turns out she'd been comforted in her distress by a Jesuit priest and felt grateful to us.'

'Amazing. So is that where it is now – back in Leeson Street?'

O'Malley raised a pitying eyebrow. 'The Jesuits may be crazy,' he said, 'but we're not mad. No. After authentication, the painting was given to the National Gallery on permanent loan. It's the star turn of the collection, and if you had anything else in your head except girls and guns, you'd know that.'

'It must be worth a fortune.'

'A hundred million euro, that's what they tell me.'

Dempsey whistled. 'Jesus Christ!'

'Exactly,' said his uncle, 'and we weren't going to betray him a second time by selling him off to the highest bidder.'

'But what's the connection with Battista? I don't know the painting. To be honest, Caravaggio's no more than a name to me, like Goethe or Nietzsche. I'm guessing, though, that the scene in the Garden of Gethsemane must have been painted a hundred times by a hundred different artists. So what's special about this one, and what's the link between two cardinals separated by more than four hundred years?'

'As to the first,' said O'Malley, 'the painting is astonishing. The first time I saw it after it was restored, it took my breath away. But as to your second question, I've no idea. That's what we're going to find out.'

After Dempsey left, O'Malley picked up the phone and asked to be put through to the provost of the German College, Monsignor Josef Steinbrück. It had suddenly occurred to him that Rüttgers might have confided any fears he had about Bosani to his fellow countryman, with whom he had been staying in Rome.

Steinbrück came on the line almost at once.

'Father General,' he began, in his heavily accented Italian. 'It's been a long time. What can I do for you?'

O'Malley got straight to the point. 'It's about Cardinal Rüttgers.'

'What about him?'

Did the German sound defensive? O'Malley wasn't sure.

'It's just that I was wondering if he left, you know, any kind of testament.'

'Testament? What are you talking about?'

Now he really *did* sound defensive.

'Well, the thing is, I knew him pretty well. We'd corresponded for years. And in his last week or so of life, he seemed terribly unsettled. He seemed to believe that the Church was going through some awful crisis.'

Steinbrück snorted. 'And when exactly was that not the case, Father General? I am sixty-four and I must say I have never known a time of ease or tranquillity.'

'Quite so,' said O'Malley, who sensed he was getting nowhere. 'But he didn't saying anything to you, did he?'

'Nothing out of the ordinary. It is well known that he and the Camerlengo disagreed over the best approach to the Islamic question, but other than that he seemed fine. His death was, of course, a terrible tragedy, but one that comes to us all.'

'Indeed. Just one other thing. I recall that His Eminence kept a journal. He began it during his years in Brazil. He showed it to me once. It was most insightful. You didn't find his diary, I suppose … in his bedroom or in his suitcase?'

The provost didn't hesitate. 'A journal? No, no. Absolutely not. There was nothing like that.'

'You are certain?'

'Totally. And it was I who sealed his room pending the arrival of the Camerlengo. I would have seen it straight away. But now, Father General, with all due respect, I have to speak now with three of my seminarians whose ordinations are almost upon us.'

'Of course, of course. I'm sorry to have troubled you. Once again, my condolences on your loss. The cardinal was a fine man and an outstanding Christian.'

'There is no doubt of that. And his replacement as head of the German Church, Cardinal Von Stiegler, will be no less of a leader.' The provost cleared his throat. 'We should meet for lunch, Father General, maybe after the new pope is installed. Until then, goodbye and *Auf Wiederhörn*.'

'*Auf Wiederhörn*,' echoed O'Malley, replacing the phone on its cradle. His conversation with Steinbrück had proved extremely interesting. So Bosani had been one of the first on the scene and immediately took charge of the clean-up operation. What was that about? He flicked through the old-fashioned Roladex on his desk, squinting at the numbers that came up until he found the one he wanted.

This time, the voice that answered was warm and welcoming. Father Hermann Scholz S. had been a senior tutor at the Anima for ten years or more. He and O'Malley had previously served together in Chicago and, of course, as a Jesuit, the German was bound by his oath of obedience.

After a brief exchange of pleasantries, conducted in English, O'Malley asked Scholz if he had heard anything about a journal belonging to Cardinal Rüttgers.

'Oh yes,' came the immediate response. 'In fact, as His Eminence's confessor and intimate secretary in Rome, I can tell you that he kept it up to date until the very day of his death.'

O'Malley tried to keep the excitement out of his voice. 'I don't suppose you happen to know anything about the last few entries.'

'You're not suggesting I would read a private diary?'

O'Malley sighed. 'Don't play the innocent with me, Hermann. I know you too well. Did you read the final entries?'

The German paused. 'I did,' he said at last.

'And ..?'

'And they were much as you would expect. It's common knowledge that he and the Camerlengo fell out rather spectacularly a few weeks back.'

'So, what did he say? What did he write?'

'Well, that was the funny thing. His final entry didn't touch on polemics or theology – unless you count an odd reference to Bosani's eyes.'

'His eyes?'

'Yes. Rüttgers had planned to deliver a speech in the university – it would have been this week, I believe – in which he urged increased dialogue between the Catholic and Islamic faiths, but demand also a much greater tolerance of Christianity in Muslim lands. When he told Bosani this, the Camerlengo turned away, he said, but not before Rüttgers saw a hostile look in his eyes that seemed to betray a contrary view.'

'Strange.'

'Most definitely.'

'What did you make of it?'

'It's hard to say. It could simply be that he had allowed his own antipathy to the Camerlengo get the better of him. I mean, how could any Christian leader not want greater freedom for the Church in places like Saudi Arabia, Pakistan or Iraq?'

'Quite. What else? What else did he say?'

The German thought for a moment. 'He noted that he had asked His Eminence if it was true that he had met recently in Rome with someone called Yilmaz Hak-something-or-other. Does that mean anything to you?'

'Yilmaz Hakura. He's a leader of Hizb ut-Tahrir.'

'The Islamist party?'

'Exactly.'

'But they're banned, aren't they?'

'That doesn't mean they don't exist.'

'You must forgive my naïveté. I don't get out much. Well, the Camerlengo evidently said that there had been no such meeting – which hardly rates as a surprise. Rüttgers wrote afterwards that he was sure of his facts. And then he added something really strange. I remember it exactly. "Betrayal starts and ends with the self. Judas was acting out his destiny. The question is, who – or what – controls Bosani?"'

'Extraordinary. And how do you interpret that?'

'I have no idea. I only know that it chills the blood.'

'As if he sensed that there was something very wrong at the heart of the Church, but couldn't quite identify it.'

'As you say, Father General. Have you noticed that the greatest mysteries in life seem to attach to saints and sinners? Perhaps good and evil share something of the same nature.' He sighed, as if disturbed by the implication of what he had said. 'One last thing, and make of this what you will, but the late cardinal also mentioned a painting he'd seen that belonged to the Camerlengo. It wasn't hung in the public rooms in which he receives visitors, but in his private drawing room in the Governorate.'

O'Malley was intrigued. 'Painting? Which painting?'

'A portrait, signed by Annibale Carracci, of one of Bosani's predecessors as Camerlengo, dating from the early years of the seventeenth century. Carracci is a much underrated master, if you ask me – though not, of course, of the same rank as Caravaggio.'

O'Malley drummed his fingers impatiently. 'And the subject of this painting?'

'Ah, now that was inscribed on a small brass plaque fixed to the base of the frame. Someone by the name of Orazio Battista.'

'Battista?'

'*Ja, ja*. According to Rüttgers, Battista was once very powerful, but came to a sticky end. I looked him up in the Catholic Encyclopedia. There was no mention of him, which seemed strange. Even odder is the fact that the Carracci picture – which would be worth an absolute fortune … a drawing by him sold recently in Christie's for, I think, a quarter of a millions euro – isn't even listed in the inventory of the Vatican Museum. And when I consulted an official catalogue of Carracci's known body of work, there was no mention of it.'

O'Malley had forgotten that Scholtz was an art buff. 'I'd like to take a look at the diary for myself. Could you arrange to have it biked over?'

'I would, gladly, Father General,' Scholz said. 'Unfortunately, an official from the Vatican security service took it away for safekeeping the day before yesterday. He said it contained confidential references pertaining to the upcoming conclave and that it had to be kept out of the public domain.'

'Really? What did Rüttgers' family have to say about that?'

'They were told it was a Church matter, nothing to do with them.'

'I see.' O'Malley sucked his teeth. 'Just one more thing, Hermann. Without betraying the confidence of the Confessional, can you tell me what mood Cardinal Rüttgers was in the day he died?'

The Jesuit thought for a moment. 'I'd say he was a very unhappy man. Deeply depressed. Maybe whatever it was that caused his stroke affected his judgment. I cannot say.'

'Did he appear in any way physically unwell?'

'Physically? No, not at all. In fine fettle, I'd say. He made me feel old.'

'Okay, Hermann, I'm grateful to you. And I'd appreciate it if you kept our little conversation to yourself.'

'Of course, Father General.'

'I'm serious. Not a word.'

'You can rely on me. Is there anything else I can do ... ?'

'If there is, I'll let you know.'

O'Malley rang off. He walked over to the window of his office and stared up the street towards St Peter's. *Judas was acting out his destiny.* What in God's name had Rüttgers meant by that? It was the second time the fallen Apostle had cropped up in this affair. Was it a sign? If so, where was it pointing? *The question is, who – or what – controls Bosani?* This was both cryptic and infuriating. Even those who detested the Camerlengo and believed him to be a malign influence in the Church didn't question his bona fides. It was maddening. And now were now two paintings, both of the mysterious Cardinal Battista, the second of them, without any known provenance, in the private collection of the Camerlengo. What was the possible link between the two men and what did it mean for the future of the Church? As he gazed at the famous dome of the basilica, a thin crescent moon rose above Fontana's cross and lantern. For some reason, the sight of this filled him with unease.

20 *
July 1606

Six weeks had passed since Caravaggio became a fugitive from justice, and the artist was living in the magnificent household of Don Marzio Colonna in the hills south of Rome. The sword wounds inflicted by Ranuccio's brother, Giovan Francesco, had left him with a deep scar across his right temple, mostly hidden by his hair, but the wound to his throat had healed almost completely. Given that he had lost a lot of blood, he had made an impressive recovery.

The news from Rome, however, was not good. Longhi was in hiding in Milan. A warrant had been issued for his arrest as an accessory to murder. Toppa, the soldier, gravely wounded in a fight not of his making, had lost the use of his sword arm and been left to fend for himself, so was in no mood to speak up for Caravaggio. At the same time, Giovan Francesco, who had initially fled Rome, fearing arrest, had successfully petitioned the Pope for a judicial pardon. The magistrate appointed to the case evidently took into account Tomassoni's long service to the Holy See and accepted his claim that Caravaggio attacked Ranuccio and murdered him in cold blood as he lay on the ground.

A Monsignor in the papal household, who owed his elevation to the Colonna, confirmed to Prince Marzio that Caravaggio had been made the scapegoat for the entire sorry business. The Pope was appalled by what had happened, the Monsignor said. He thought he had come to know the painter during the sessions in which he had sat for his portrait nine months previously. But apparently he had been fooled. The Camerlengo, Cardinal Battista, had condemned Caravaggio not only as a murderer, but as a dangerous heretic, who fled the scene of his crime.

Once it was clear that the accused had no intention of returning to Rome, it was on Battista's orders that a *banda capitale* was issued.

Without the protecting hand of the Colonna, Caravaggio would never have survived, and he was grateful. His father, Fermo, had worked all his life for the Sforza branch of the clan, rising to be chamberlain in Milan, with a household and servants of his own. He became a trusted adviser and confidant – an *uomo di fiducia* – whose death deprived the family of valuable counsel. Partly out of feudal loyalty, but also because they recognized the genius of Fermo's boy, the Colonna, with vast estates throughout Italy, would always watch over him.

In an effort to repay his host for his kindness, but also because he could not stop himself, Caravaggio produced a series of canvases in Zagarolo that he then offered to Prince Marzio. Among these were a second *Supper at Emmaus*, much more solemn than the first, reflecting St Luke's description of the risen Jesus, now bearded, being invited by Cleophas and his unnamed companion to break bread with them: 'Abide with us, said the disciples, for it is towards evening and the day is far spent.' The prince accepted the gift, but then, unknown to the artist, arranged to have it sold in Rome and the proceeds held in trust. The second painting, which he kept, was a *Magdalene in Ecstasy*, no longer penitent but resigned to her fate, gazing into the darkness, her neck exposed, as if calling on the world to do its worst.

One evening, after waking yet again from the recurring nightmare of the Cenci, Caravaggio couldn't get back to sleep. He went downstairs to a back porch of the Palazzo, where he found Don Francesco, the prince's eldest son, seated on his own at a table, drinking wine and watching the fireflies.

Francesco was several years younger than Caravaggio and of a scholarly disposition. It had been assumed he would go into the Church, where he would unquestionably have secured a red hat. But it turned out that he planned to get married and have children and, after serving three years as a soldier, he had returned to Zaragolo to manage the estate.

'What is it this time?' Francesco asked, slapping at a mosquito on his forearm. The artist was standing before him looking like Prince Hamlet in the play of the same name by the English playwright, Shakespeare. 'Your life these days seems to be nothing but a sequence of nightmares and dark awakenings. Have you lost the will to be happy, Michelangelo?'

'You don't have a *banda capitale* hanging over your head,' Caravaggio replied gruffly.

Francesco nodded and poured him a glass of wine from the jug on the table. 'Come now,' he said. 'You are safe here. The *sbirri* do not dare to enter the territory of the Colonna.'

'No. But I can't stay here forever. I'm a city person. The countryside drives me mad. All that sky overhead!'

This made Colonna smile. It was said that Caravaggio almost never included the sky – or even daylight – in his paintings. 'Have you thought of returning to Milan?' he asked. 'The Pope's writ doesn't run there and you are held in high regard by my aunt, the Marchesa Costanza.'

The painter appeared to consider this option. He wore a loose-fitting night-shirt, much cleaner and fresher than anything he had been used to in Rome. The female servant assigned to look after him had appealed to her master about the state of his clothes and the result had been a complete new wardrobe. 'Milan's worse,' he said at last, as if delivering a definitive judgment from which only a fool would dissent. 'Big and empty. Have you ever sat through a Milanese winter?'

'Well, what about Naples? We could set you up there readily enough.'

The artist drained his glass in a single swallow. 'That's a thought.'

Italy's largest and most populous city was a a place entirely unto itself, far outside the Pope's domains. The Colonna, who owned several estates in the region, were close allies of the Spanish viceroy, who ruled on behalf of King Felipe III.

Francesco poured a second glass of wine for his guest and another for himself. 'But face it, Michelangelo, geography alone won't solve your problems. You are pursued as much by demons inside of you as by the *sbirri* or Cardinal Battista. You need to find peace, and I'm not convinced that simply opening a new studio in Naples, or anywhere else, will give you what you want.'

Caravaggio's eyes narrowed. This assessment of his state of mind had obviously hit home. There was a long silence before he spoke again. 'What would you say,' he asked at last, 'if I told you that I planned to become a Knight Hospitaller?'

The young Colonna made a face. 'I'd say that, regrettably, you have ideas above your station.'

'What! Just because I'm not a noble? I'm as good as you, Francesco, and better than Giovan fucking Francesco, who's been pardoned by the Pope, even though he tried to kill me, just because he fought in France alongside the Farnese.'

Francesco reached out a reassuring hand. 'Calm down, my friend. No one is seeking to belittle you. All I am saying is that the Knights of Malta are drawn from the nobility of Europe. You know this as well as I do. Their bloodlines are examined as if they were stallions.'

'And what good will that do them when the Ottomans return with a hundred thousand men and lay siege to them in Valletta?'

A derisive laugh greeted this remark. 'Then,' said Colonna, 'Malta will be ankle-deep in the bluest blood in Christendom.'

The two men drank the wine in their glasses and wiped their mouths with the backs of their hands. Francesco reached for a fresh jar and removed the muslin top.

'But seriously,' Caravaggio said, slapping a mosquito that had begun to feed on his arm, noting with interest how the blood stained his fingers. 'Do you really think I could move to Naples? And if I did, could you make inquiries for me with the Knights? A letter from your family would carry great weight with the Grand Master.'

'I will see what we can do. Now drink up before we're eaten alive.'

Two minutes later, his head spinning, Caravaggio leaned conspiratorially across the table. 'Do you want to know a secret, Francesco – a secret that I have never told anyone?'

By now, both men were slightly drunk.

'Go on,' Francesco said.

Speaking hesitantly, with great deliberation, looking around him every few seconds as if a spy might be hidden among the olive trees, Caravaggio proceeded to relate the story of how he had discovered the Camerlengo in his private chapel worshipping Allah. He described the murder the same night of the only other witness – 'a priest of God!' – and how his painting, *The Betrayal of Christ*, intended as testimony to posterity of what he had seen, had been viewed by Battista just days before the events in the Campo Marzio. He concluded his confession by recalling Ranuccio Tomassoni's last words to him, taunting him with the fact that the Camerlengo had paid to have him killed.

As he finished his story, he gripped his friend's wrist and Colonna could see the fear in his eyes. 'There will be other assassins, Francesco. Battista will not give up. He won't stop until my head is loosed from my body.' As if anticipating his fate, he ran a finger down his neck and slumped back in his chair. Francesco said nothing, not knowing how to respond.

It was Caravaggio who broke the silence. 'You are to tell no one about this, Francesco – not even your father. It would put all your lives in danger. Promise me.'

'You have my word. But depend on it, my friend, if anything should happen to you and I find out it was the work of the Camerlengo, I will see to it that you are avenged.'

Caravaggio put a hand to Francesco's shoulder and muttered something about him being a good man. Then he slumped across the table and fell asleep, snoring.

21*
Conclave minus 8

The civil administration building of the Holy See, known as the Governorate, was like no other government offices on earth. A handsome, rather elegant structure, it looked from the outside more like a luxury Riviera hotel from the 1920s than the home of a leading multinational executive – an impression compounded by its ornate formal gardens, acres of surrounding parkland and immaculately tended paths.

The building appeared serene on the surface. Inside, it was an ants' nest. In the week leading up to the papal conclave, its corridors pulsed with gossip as the workforce, both lay and religious, traded opinions on the identity of the next pope. Those who knew the Vatican as an absolute monarchy, in which power devolved from the top, would have noted the lack of an authoritative voice. But the fisherman's ring was broken. While officials continued to deal with routine problems and queries from around the world, at the higher-function level there was only silence. The Secretary of State, the cardinal prefect of the Congregation for the Doctrine of the Faith; the heads of the dicasteries and the pontifical councils: none remained in place. All those who wished to continue in their previous roles, and those who hoped to replace them, had to await the emergence of a new head of state to learn their fate.

All save one. No such uncertainty attended the ambitions of the Camerlengo, whose power, uniquely, reached its peak during the *sede vacante*. Sat at the ornate desk of his spacious corner office, Cardinal Bosani took a moment to reflect on the luxury of his position.

As Secretary of State, his principle base had been the Apostolic Palace. But he preferred it here, removed from the basilica and the Sistine Chapel, with its view, however distant, of the central mosque. It had always amused him that the very word *governoratoro* derived from the Arabic word *muhafazah*, meaning administrative unit. The Ottomans employed a similar term, as did the Nazis. Even amid the presumed purity of its position as the font of supreme power in the universal Church, the Vatican was historically compromised.

Rome in summer was unbearably hot and humid. Today, though, a light breeze blew across the city and there was a freshness in the air that brought welcome relief to the city's three million inhabitants. Bosani rose from his leather-covered chair and moved across the parquet floor of his office to the windows that looked over the sumptuous lawns as far as the west end of St Peter's Basilica. A few weeks ago, a Monsignor from Spain had asked him, only half joking, when he thought they would be adding minarets to Michelangelo's masterpiece. That had made him laugh. 'Don't worry,' he had replied, 'I think we have ten years at least.'

Looking north, he could just make out a group of cardinals moving in stately fashion along the Via del Governatorato in the direction either of the Sistine Chapel or, more likely, one of the half-dozen or so top-class restaurants that lay just outside the Vatican walls. Squinting a little, he thought he recognized the distinctive loping walk of Cardinal Georges Delacroix, Archbishop of Reims, accompanied no doubt by his diminutive friend, Cardinal Alfonso Salgado from Valencia. The two men, ironically, were liberals when it came to the issue of Islam – so much so that ten years ago he would have courted them in the cause of religious tolerance.

Not any more. Bosani allowed himself the ghost of a smile, bearing the points of his teeth. Bigots were what was needed today. Under the revised rules of the papal conclave, as promulgated by John Paul II, a protracted stalemate during the election of a pope could now be broken by a simple majority vote. If all went well – if all, in other words, went extremely badly for the establishment of consensus among the cardinal electors – he would need just sixty-one votes to secure the emergence of a pope who would strike fear into the hearts of Muslims. At the last count, he already had fifty votes in his pocket, with several cardinals 'undecided'. Tomorrow, following his planned lunch at Checchino, in Monte Testaccio – exclusive, yet discreet – he expected the number of undecided to fall by two. Delacroix and Salgado were liberals mainly because they feared what would happen to them and the Church if a pro-Christian, anti-Muslim policy were to be proclaimed from the Throne of Peter. But they were also ambitious. Both wished to be relieved of episcopal responsibility in the midst of such turbulent times; both had hinted strongly that they would welcome positions in the Curia. Bosani would accommodate them. Or perhaps he would not. It would depend. Either way, they would have served their purpose.

As he took in the sweep of the pontifical gardens, his eyes fixed for several seconds on the seclusion of the Teutonic Cemetery to his right, containing the remains of the late Cardinal Rüttgers. The German's probing inquiries had posed an unexpected threat at a critical time. It wasn't simply that he was intelligent and doctrinally adept; he also possessed a disquieting intuition. But he had been dealt with and, insh'Allah, all was well.

Bosani steeled himself mentally for the hurdles that still lay ahead. He prayed to God to help him and give him strength, remembering how the Prophet had patiently built up his forces before his triumphant return to Mecca.

It was as he raised his hands in prayer that he heard the footsteps behind him of the ever-faithful Visco.

'I'm sorry to interrupt you, Eminence. I just wanted you to know that I have booked your usual table for tomorrow at Checchino. I have informed Cardinals Delacroix and Salgado and they will both be there.'

Bosani turned round, beaming. 'Excellent,' he said. 'Anything else?'

'There is another letter from the sister of Rüttgers.'

The Camerlengo frowned. 'Draft a reply for me to sign. But make sure that I don't have to hear from her again.'

'Not a problem.' A short pause followed. 'There is just one more thing. I hesitate to mention it.'

'Go on.'

'It's just that a young historian has been engaging in some troubling research in the Secret Archive.'

Visco now had Bosani's full attention. 'What sort of research?' he demanded.

'He has been consulting details of your career, including your student days and your work to establish the central mosque. More to the point, he has discovered a connection between you and your illustrious precedessor, Cardinal Battista.'

'How is that possible?'

The priest looked embarrassed. 'When our people destroyed the files about the unfortunate business with Battista, they did not, it appears, wipe every trace. They were operating at a time when the computerisation of the records was far from complete and it appears that the classification stubs, indicating the fact that Your Eminence was the last one to examine the now missing file, were transferred as jpegs of the originals.'

'And what was on these ... jpegs?'

'A brief description of the subject nature of the files, nothing more. They referred to an "investigation" ordered by Pope Paul V ...'

'But no mention of the nature of the investigation?'

'None – save that His Eminence was the subject.' Visco paused and looked down at his feet. 'There was also a cross-reference to *The Betrayal of Christ*.'

Bosani shot Visco an angry look. 'This "historian" … what is his name?'

'Dempsey … Liam Dempsey – from Ireland.' He handed over a high-resolution picture of the Irishman taken by the security cameras in the Archive as he sat at the receptionist's computer screen.

Bosani stared at the picture. 'Who is he? What's he doing in Rome?'

'That is what is interesting, Eminence.'

'Explain.'

'His uncle is Declan O'Malley, Superior General of the Jesuits. He provided the letter of introduction to the Library.'

'O'Malley!' Visco could see that his boss had begun to twist the episcopal ring on the fourth finger of his right hand between his left thumb and index finger – a sure sign that his temper was building. 'And you tell me the nephew of Declan O'Malley has established a link between me and Battista? And that he has been putting together an account of my movements and interests over the last twenty years?'

'I'm afraid so.'

Bosani exhaled heavily. 'That is unacceptable, Cesare. Unacceptable! And how exactly do the Jesuits fit into this?'

'I'm working on that. I have asked Father Haddad …'

'– The American?'

'Actually he is Lebanese. But he has American citizenship.'

'Yes, yes. But how can he assist us?'

'He is our ears and eyes in the Society of Jesus.'

Bosani looked doubtful. 'Is he any use? He must be eighty if he is a day. Anyway, I thought he had a drink problem.'

Visco ran his hand down his chin. 'He has got over that, insh'Allah, and he has known the Father General for many years.'

'Very well. But see to it that we find out everything we need to know. I have never trusted O'Malley. He cares nothing for the Church, only for his faith. Such men are dangerous.'

'The matter has been dealt with, Eminence. There is no need for concern.'

Bosani frowned. 'But the facts he has already – what about those?'

'I assure you, everything is in hand. The Archive has been told what to do and what to say. If you want my opinion, Eminence, I sincerely doubt that after today Mr O'Malley will have the stomach to bother us again. It is much more likely that he will be on the first plane home to Dublin. In the meantime, to answer your question directly, it would appear that the apartment he is staying in here in Rome is about to be … burgled.'

'Franco?'

'Naturally.'

'That is something. But we cannot afford to relax our vigilance. Time is precious and too much is at stake. Tell my friend from Spésa that for the next few days he is to keep a close eye on that young man. If he steps out of line even once, I am to be informed.'

'Of course.'

'And when Haddad has spoken with the uncle, tell him to report directly to me.'

'Yes, Eminence.'

The cardinal picked up his pen and signed a couple of letters, both to leading cardinals newly arrived in Rome from the United States. 'Have these delivered at once,' he said. 'Time is running out. There is serious business to be done in the next week and we can't afford distractions – particularly if they involve the Jesuits. I shall rely on you to take all necessary steps. Do you understand me?'

Visco met his master's gaze. 'Perfectly,' he said.

'Very well, then. Let us get on.'

The prefect of the Secret Archive, Monsignor Domenico Asproni, was a small man and he stood on the balls of his feet as he faced up to the much taller figure of Dempsey. 'Here is the problem,' he said. 'When our archivist, alerted by Security, sought to retrieve papers yesterday relating to Cardinal Orazio Battista – documents which you had precisely identified through the improper use of our internal computer network – what did he find? He found that they were gone. Papers that had been securely filed for more than four hundred years were now missing.'

Dempsey had been summoned to the prefect's office an hour before. He had assumed he would receive a formal reprimand for his flouting of the rules the previous day. But he had not expected to face a criminal charge. He threw up his hands – a gesture that he had learned conveyed indignation to Italians much better than words. 'So what are you saying? That I'm a thief? Is that it?'

'The papers have vanished, Signor Dempsey. The file is empty. All that remains is a classification stub and a brief indication of the subject matter.'

'Nothing to do with me. I only came across his name by accident. Who was Battista, anyway? And why is he suddenly so important?'

'I think you are in a better position to provide that information than I. My question to you is much more simple and direct. Where are the documents? What have you done with them?'

Dempsey bunched his fists and tried to remain calm. This was a put-up job. It had to be. 'What have *I* done with them? According to the computer record – which was all I got to see – the file on Battista had been missing for nearly forty years. The last person to see it was Cardinal Bosani, in January 1977.'

The prefect shook his head. 'I have checked. What the computer says is that the file was identified by you yesterday morning and has since disappeared.'

'That's ridiculous.'

'Is it, Signor Dempsey? Is it, really? I will grant you that this was an audacious theft. I cannot begin to imagine how it was achieved. But that is a matter for the police to resolve. We have no wish, as you can imagine, to bring embarrassment to the Father General of the Company of Jesus, who, as your uncle, provided you with a letter of introduction. I had hoped that you would appear before me this morning suitably contrite, bringing with you the missing file. Regrettably, you have not chosen that option. In the circumstances, my advice to you is to get yourself a good lawyer. The unauthorized removal of historical documents from the Apostolic Library, one of the world's greatest repositories of knowledge, is a serious business – very serious indeed. You have left me with no alternative than to report this crime, and you as the sole suspect, to the Vatican Security Service. You may expect its officers, assisted by the detective branch of the Carabinieri, to call you in for questioning.'

Dempsey swallowed hard but stood his ground. 'In that case, Monsignor, since you have obviously concluded that I am a thief and a liar, I shall await your pleasure. You already know where I live.' He turned to go.

'Just one more thing. Do you have your identity card?'

'That's no business of yours, if I may say so.'

The Monsignor pressed a button on his desk. Seconds later, the door to his office opened and two burly security men entered.

'I would remind you, Signor Dempsey, that I represent the government of a sovereign state and have full jurisdiction in this matter.'

Dempsey hadn't thought of that. Passports were no longer necessary for EU citizens travelling within the Union. The latest generation of machine-readable ID cards provided a complete record of the holder's police or criminal record, if any, plus credit rating, service and medical record and educational and employment history. Without it, life could be extremely difficult.

Asproni folded his arms. 'I am waiting,' he said.

Dempsey sighed. He took out his wallet, removed the card and handed it across. 'I'll expect that to be returned to me in the morning,' he said.

'That will be for the police to decide, not me. *Arrivederci*, Signor Dempsey.'

'*Ciao.*'

Minutes afterwards, as he walked out the main door of the library, Maya returned his phonecall. He told her what had happened. She couldn't understand it. This wasn't the sort of thing that happened to people she knew.

'What's going on?' she asked him. 'What did you do to provoke them?'

'Nothing,' Dempsey said, a tone of indignation creeping into his voice. 'I was just doing my uncle a favour. Now I've been framed.'

'That's ridiculous.'

'I wish it were. But look, is there any chance you could meet me later on at my apartment?'

'I suppose so. Someone needs to talk some sense into you. For what it's worth, though, there's something very strange about Bosani's behaviour.'

'What do you mean?'

Dempsey listened as Maya gave him an account of what her father had told her about the Camerlengo and Cardinal Rüttgers. 'It was as if he didn't care about Rüttgers or what happened to him,' she concluded. 'And when the poor man's sister asked for his body to be sent home to Germany, Bosani refused point-blank. Instead, he had him entombed behind the walls of the Teutonic Cemetery. My father was shocked. He told me he had never witnessed such a lack of Christian charity in a man of God.'

'I think we need to talk to my uncle,' Demspey said.

At that moment, however, Superior General O'Malley was busy pursuing his own inquiries. Briefcase in hand, he had walked the five hundred metres or so from the Borgo Santo Spirito to the Governorate, where he announced to the front desk his intention to visit the Office for Civil Records.

The young man on duty was suitably respectful. 'Of course, Father General. If you could wait one minute, I'll arrange for someone to meet you as soon as you exit the lift.'

'No need,' the Irishman replied genially. 'It's a routine matter and I require no special assistance.'

'Very well, Father General. You know the way?'

O'Malley had already ascertained that Bosani's office was on the fourth *piano*. 'Of course. *E grazie.*'

'*Prego.*'

He felt vaguely guilty about the lie he had told. But God, he was sure, would forgive him. Taking the lift to the fourth floor, he checked again that he had remembered to bring a corkscrew with him. It was always the details that let him down. A pretty young nun looked embarrassed as he nervously fingered the end of the opener. He smiled at her reassuringly. When the lift stopped and the doors opened, he looked up and down the long corridor, not sure in which direction to proceed. It was a passing Monsignor, a portly man in his late forties, who assisted him.

'Father General, you look lost,' he said, speaking English with an American accent.

'I suppose I am, really,' O'Malley replied. 'I'm looking for the office of the Camerlengo.'

'I see. Unfortunately, His Eminence is extremely busy at the moment. Do you have an appointment?'

'Of course!'

That was his second lie.

'In that case, simply turn right and walk to the far end of the corridor. The Camerlengo's office is in the corner. You can't miss it.'

'Thank you.'

'No problem.'

Thirty seconds later, O'Malley halted at a door on which were inscribed the words *Camerlengo de la Santa Iglesia Romana*. Prior to Bosani, the Camerlengo had not kept an office in the Governorate, which was the seat of purely civil administration. But the current occupant of the post, who until the death of the Pope had also been Secretary of State, had announced that he wished to separate his two roles and had immediately commandeered a suite of rooms for his personal use.

O'Malley didn't knock. He just walked straight in. An earnest-looking young priest looked up from his desk in surprise. Opposite him, dressed in a black coarse-weave habit, sat a tall friar, built like a rugby forward, the dark fringe of his tonsure marking him out as a Benedictine.

'*Permesso*,' O'Malley said, smiling briefly at the monk, who scowled in reply. 'I'm here to see His Eminence.'

'I'm sorry, Father General, but that is impossible …'

'He will see me, I think.'

'Yes, but …'

'If you could just bring us a couple of glasses, Father …'

'Visco. I am His Eminence's Intimate Secretary.'

'Of course. Two glasses then, Father Visco. And thank you.'

Bosani's private office was straight ahead and, again, O'Malley didn't hesitate. It was only as he entered the inner office that he noticed that there was no one behind the desk.

Bugger! It hadn't occurred to him that Bosani might simply not be there.

But then he heard a familiar baritone voice. 'Cesare, is that you?' The voice emanated from behind yet another door, this time to his left. O'Malley charged in yet again and two seconds later found himself staring down at the figure of the Camerlengo seated bareheaded in an old-fashioned leather armchair. He was reading a copy of *Cumhuriyet*, the Istanbul newspaper, which he immediately threw down, looking slightly alarmed.

'Father General!'

'Camerlengo!'

'What are you doing here?'

'God's work, I hope.'

By now, Bosani had grabbed his skullcap from a small table next to his armchair and was labouring to his feet. Jamming the cap on his head, he glared at O'Malley. 'But I am …'

'– Reading the newspaper. Yes, I can see that. Only, the thing is, I need to talk to you, Your Eminence. I have things on my mind.'

'What things?'

'And to make it easier, I've brought you something.' He snapped open his briefcase. 'It's a bottle of Cinque Terre, from the estate north of La Spezia on which, I believe, your father worked for some years. It's a wine you must have grown up with, but not so common these days.' He paused, showing Bosani the label. 'I hope you don't mind, but I asked your secretary, Father Visco, to fetch a couple of glasses.'

At this point, Visco put his head around the door.

'Speak of the devil,' O'Malley said.

'The Father General asked me to bring some glasses.'

Bosani shot his assistant a fierce look. 'Just put them down,' he said, 'then leave us.'

Visco slunk out.

As O'Malley fumbled in his cassock for the corkscrew, Bosani decided it was time to take command of the situation.

'Father General,' he began, 'I appreciate your kindness, but I really am exceptionally busy just now …'

The Jesuit, dressed from head to foot in black, waved away the Camerlengo's protest and drew out the cork with a discernible pop. He sniffed the bottle. 'An excellent bouquet,' he said, 'with a faint tang of the sea. But then, I don't need to tell you that.'

He poured two glasses and handed one to Bosani.

'Good God!' the cardinal said, holding the wine as if it were a poisoned chalice. 'It's not even lunchtime.'

'But very nearly,' said O'Malley, smiling genially, 'and it is an exceptionally hot day.'

Bosani drew back, exposing the points of his teeth. 'The quality of the day has nothing to do with it,' he began. 'I must ask you to desist in this matter. I am shortly to host a lunch in the Apostolic Palace for the cardinal electors of Latin America. After that, I shall be engaged in discussions with the former dean of the College of Cardinals. I'm afraid the future leadership of the Church must take precedence over a bottle of wine – even if it is Cinque Terre.'

O'Malley's eyes narrowed. There was no doubt about it: Bosani was a very odd fish indeed. It was rare for any Catholic prelate to refuse a glass of wine. For an Italian to say no – especially one who had grown up in the trade – was almost unheard of. It was almost as if ...

'Very well,' he said, abruptly. 'Then let me state my business directly. As you know, when I became a member of the Company of Jesus, I took an oath of loyalty and obedience to the Pope and his successors – an oath that I take extremely seriously. It is for that reason that I need to know from you that a certain rumour is not true.'

'You speak in riddles. What rumour?'

'The rumour that you, Your Eminence, are doing everything in your power to secure the election of a violently anti-Muslim pope – one who would more closely resemble the Antichrist than the Servant of the Servants of God.'

Bosani's face had by now turned purple. 'How dare you? This is intolerable. Who have you been talking to?'

'Is it true, then?'

'I don't know what you're talking about.'

'Don't you?'

Bosani's eyebrows met in the middle as he struggled to contain his anger and indignation. 'No,' he said, 'I do not, and I must tell you that I very much resent your insinuation.'

It was then that O'Malley noted that the Camerlengo was not wearing his pectoral cross. Nor was there any other crucifix or holy object in the room. He examined the features of the elderly Prelate, trying to divine his true nature. It was impossible to tell. Confronting Bosani, he felt like a prosecuting counsel. 'There is something I must know, Eminence ... something that has been bothering me. When the late Pope Benedict delivered his address in Regensberg, you were his closest advisor on the politics of the Muslim world. Had you opposed the substance of his talk, you would have had the opportunity to make your feelings clear.'

'What is your point, Father General?'

'My point is, Eminence, did you concur with the Holy Father's presumed attack on Islam? Were you, in fact, as some have suggested, the inspiration behind his words?'

'You are talking about events in the past …'

'… which have relevance to the Church's future.'

Bosani bristled. He had reached the limits of his patience. 'I don't have time for this,' he barked. 'And I will not be questioned in such a manner.'

'Then answer me just this: what is the virtue that you, as convenor and co-chairman of the upcoming conclave, most earnestly wish should characterize our next Holy Father? Because, you see, I have been invited to write an article about the election for a newspaper in America.'

It was his third lie. Next he would hear a cock crow.

'The proceedings of the conclave are confidential,' Bosani spluttered. 'You know that very well.'

'Only when in session, Your Eminence, or, thereafter, in relation to the votes cast for each candidate. What I am seeking is an indication from you, as Camerlengo of the Holy Roman Church, of the qualities considered essential at this particular moment in our history. You are, after all, at the centre of events and uniquely qualified to pronounce on the question. Specifically, what possible benefit could accrue to the Church from a potentially violent confrontation with Islam? There are those, I know, who pray for conflict, believing that a new crusade is the only way to take Christianity back to its roots. But we live in a new world. The United States, for the moment, has withdrawn hurt from the global stage. The vacuum it has left is being filled by aggressively Muslim states, such as Iraq, Saudi Arabia, Iran and Pakistan. What if the war did not go in our favour? What if Europe, in its arrogance, found itself under a concerted assault from the Muslim world?'

For several seconds, the two men stared at each other. Rüttgers' fatal words, written less than an hour before his death, raced through O'Malley's head: *Betrayal starts and ends with the self. Judas was acting out his destiny. The question is, who – or what – controls Bosani?*

It was a revelation. But a revelation of what?

It was the Camerlengo who spoke next. 'You may be assured, Father General, that, so far as I am concerned, the chief characteristic required of the next Pope is that he be a staunch defender of the Church and its heritage. Beyond that, I can only pray for God's guidance. Now, if you don't mind … '

He indicated the door.

'Of course. Would you like me to leave the wine with you? I'll pop the cork back in and you can keep it in the fridge.'

'Just leave. In the name of God, go!'

O'Malley nodded, noticing as he did so a space in the wall opposite the cardinal's armchair that had obviously been occupied until recently by a large painting – presumably the portrait of Battista by Annibale Carracci. He could tell this not only because of the two metal hooks that still protruded from the wall but because a rectangle of paint, previously obscured, registered a deeper tone of Apostolic white. For a moment, he thought of asking Bosani what had prompted him to remove the canvas, but then changed his mind. Better, he decided, not to give too much away too soon.

'I wish you God's peace, Eminence,' he said. 'I shall pray that you and your colleagues elect a worthy – and suitable – successor to the Throne of Peter.'

'A sentiment that I might equally wish upon the Company of Jesus.'

O'Malley smiled in appreciation of the *bon mot* and withdrew, closing the door behind him. As he did so, Father Visco moved at speed in the opposite direction.

22*
September 1606–July 1607

The 'voices' had started in the last few days of July. Caravaggio remembered the first time he heard them. He was looking down from the loggia next to his room, where he had set up his easel. Prince Marzio's estate manager was talking to the head vintner, a man called Mario, who was worried that a series of afternoon rain showers, combined with an unusually hot sun, would scorch the grapes and reduce the harvest. Caravaggio took little interest in such matters. He only cared about wine when it appeared in his glass. It was as he turned back to his canvas, a study of Francesco Colonna, that Ranuccio Tomassoni first spoke to him.

'*Why do you bother, Merisi? Don't you know how it will end?*'

'Who's that? Who's there?'

Francesco Colonna looked up from the chair on which he was seated. 'Who are you talking to, Michelangelo?'

The painter started. He swallowed hard and looked about him. 'Nothing, Francesco. It was nothing. I thought I heard your father's estate manager call up to me.'

'Maybe he wanted your advice on the balance of light and shade in the vineyard.'

'Yes. Very likely.'

Afterwards, as he took a walk through the estate, keeping close to the house in case someone on the road should recognize him, he heard Ranuccio a second time, except that on this occasion he was joined by Cardinal Battista and the executioner who had taken the head of Beatrice Cenci.

'*We are coming for you, Merisi.*'

'*Kill him now,*' Battista ordered. '*Bring me his head.*'

The executioner didn't speak, but Caravaggio had felt his breath on his face. That was when he had started to run.

Now they spoke to him almost every day. At night, when the headsman struck his axe against Beatrice's neck, Battista and Ranuccio were seated next to him looking up at the scaffold.

Ranuccio, with the blood still pouring from a wound in his stomach, grinned at him. '*You'll be next, Merisi. We're coming for you. It won't be long now.*'

Battista pressed his fingers to his lips. '*Allahu Akbar!*' he said.

Worried about the well-being of their guest, Prince Marzio Colonna and his son took time to discuss what should be done.

'He needs to see a doctor,' Francesco said. 'Perhaps also a priest ... a confessor. He is deeply troubled and I fear for his sanity.'

'That's all very well,' his father replied. 'But I don't want anyone else knowing he's here. It's been hard enough to keep the servants from gossiping. Word has reached the village of the murder of young Ranuccio, killed by an artist. We have to face facts, my son. The Camerlengo is determined to arrest Michelangelo, and if he should end up in front of the Holy Office I wouldn't give five scudi for his chances.'

A look of resignation crossed Francesco's face. 'Will the Pope not pardon him? He must know the death was the result of a duel freely entered into by both sides.'

Prince Marzio shook his head. 'The Holy Father feels he was let down. Last year, you will remember, Michelangelo painted his portrait. The result pleased him greatly. During the sittings, the Pope accorded our friend the rare privilege of discussing with him issues affecting both the Church and Rome.' He paused. 'I am told that one of the issues raised was the possibility of his becoming a Knight of Malta.'

'Really?'

'It seems Michelangelo felt that taking his vows as a Knight would allow him to redeem himself from a life ill-spent.'

'And how did the Pope respond?'

'He said he would consider it. That is why he feels so betrayed.' The prince grimaced as a thought occurred to him. 'But even if His Holiness could be persuaded to show mercy, Battista will not hear of it. He is as cold as ice on the subject. His view is that a capital crime must meet with a capital response.'

Francesco put his hands behind his head and blew out his cheeks in frustration. 'So what can we do?'

'Truly, I think Naples is the only answer. Apart from anything else, if one of Battista's spies should ever find that we are hiding him here, it is we who will be in trouble.'

'Father, no! Battista would not risk confrontation with the Colonna.'

'Not on his own, I'll grant you. But with the added authority of the Pope and the excuse of a *banda capitale*, who can tell? Remember what happened to the Cenci. That was less than seven years ago.'

It was then, in spite of his promise, that Franceso Colonna told his father of his late-night conversation with the artist and of the bizarre allegiance of Cardinal Battista to the faith of Mohammad. He did so partly to demonstrate the injustice of the charge laid against their guest, but also to underline the urgency of their situation.

As he listened, the prince felt a chill run down his spine. The idea that one of the highest-ranking members of the Sacred College could be an enemy of the Church was alarming, but not entirely without precedent. During the crusades, there had been instances of monks and clergy deserting Christ and adopting the Muslim faith. He remembered his own father telling him about a leading Benedictine, Fra'Marino, a confidant of Pope Sixtus V, who had abandoned the Church in the 1580s and fled to Constantinople. The story went that he had come across a copy of the long-lost Gospel of Barnabas hidden in the papal library. While translating it into Italian, he had reputedly become convinced of its claim that Jesus was not the Son of God, but a prophet, who would be followed by another, a divine messenger, bearing revelations that would transform the world. Such a view was deeply heretical, undermining the entire basis of the Christian faith. But if Battista believed it and was working for the Ottomans, it could change everything, not just for Caravaggio but for Italy and the Catholic Church. He turned back to his son.

'This is dangerous talk,' he said. 'Even the conversation you and I are having could result, if it were made known to Battista, in both of us being brought before the Inquisition.'

'Not if we acted first. Every accusation must be heard by a tribunal. Is that not how it works? The Camerlengo would be hoist by his own petard.'

Prince Marzio made the sign of the cross. 'Is this what you want, Francesco? To take on the second-most powerful man in Rome in a life or death struggle? Think what might happen if the case went against us.'

'I understand, Father. But what if Michelangelo is right? We have a duty not only to him, but to the Church.'

For several seconds neither man spoke. It was the prince who broke the silence. 'I don't know what to believe,' he said, his voice dropping to a whisper. 'All I know for sure is that the Camerlengo is an extremely powerful and vengeful man. But you are right. As Colonna, we have obligations that are greater than our personal

well-being. What is it the French say? *Noblesse oblige*. So I will make inquiries …
discreet inquiries. My connections inside the Curia and the Apostolic Palace have,
after all, been established over many years, and I am owed some favours.'

Francesco placed a hand on his father's arm. 'Thank you, father. I am sure you
have made the right decision.'

Prince Marzio had turned pale. He seemed to have aged five years in as many
minutes. 'Let us hope so, Francesco. As for our friend, it is too dangerous for him
to remain in Zagarolo. He must leave us – and the sooner the better.'

Three days later, mounted on a three-year-old gelding, accompanied by two
servants on packhorses, Caravaggio set off by an inland route for Naples, 150 miles
to the south. In addition to the servants, he was provided by the prince with a letter
of introduction to his cousin, supplies for the journey and a sum of two hundred
scudi – the price obtained from a Florentine banker for the *Supper at Emmaus*.

Francesco Colonna didn't tell Caravaggio straight away about the extent of his
father's knowledge of the business with Battista. It was only as he was on the point
of leaving that he drew him to one side and confessed the truth.

'I realize,' he said, 'that you swore me to secrecy. But my father is involved in
this, as are all my family, and I felt it would have been a disservice to him to keep
him ignorant of the truth.'

Caravaggio felt a brief spasm of indignation, but then immediately relented.
'So what did he say?' he wanted to know.

'He said he would make the most discreet of inquiries and, in the event of
discovering any evidence to support your claim, bring it to the attention of His
Holiness.'

'But does he believe me?'

'He does not believe that you are a liar, if that is what you think. But he finds
the accusation so bizarre, so outlandish, that he cannot properly take it in.'

'I don't blame him. But I saw him with my own eyes, Francesco. Otherwise I
would never have believed it myself. If anyone had told me that the Camerlengo
was a secret Muslim, I would have said they were mad, or lying, or both.'

Colonna shrugged. 'What is important now is that you take care and always
watch your back. And if I should learn anything, I will be in touch. I can do no
more than that.'

'Of course not. And once again, thank you – and please thank your father
also. I shall be forever in your debt.'

At that, the two men shook hands and embraced. They never saw each other
again.

The first day of the journey south passed uneventfully. By choosing the upland route, through Campania, travellers avoided the intense heat of the coastal plain. But the narrow, twisting track, overhung by trees, was hazardous. On the second day, a little south of Ferentino, two brigands, dressed in rags, appeared out of nowhere and barred their path. One of them pointed a matchlock at Caravaggio, calling on him to unsling his saddlebags and throw them onto the ground. The artist, feinting fear, began to fiddle with the buckle, but then, as the fellow relaxed his guard, kicked at the extended gun barrel, sending it tilting into the air, at which point the servant behind with the pistol discharged his weapon. The would-be thief crumpled in a heap, whimpering and clutching his leg. The second man backed off into the undergrowth.

Three days later, after spending one night at an inn in Frosinoni and another at the famous monastery of Monte Cassino, Caravaggio arrived at last in Naples.

The moment he entered the city, his mood lifted. The sights and sounds exhilarated him. Even the smells of horse dung, chamber pots and rotten vegetables cheered him. Naples, with its 200,000 inhabitants, was the great survivor of Italian urban living. Laid out along roads first built by the Greeks centuries before Christ, it teemed with life. On the high ground were the grand palazzi of the Spanish governing class and the native nobility, said to be the tallest residential buildings in Europe. Great churches and public buildings occupied the many piazzi, with their fountains and statues. Market stalls lined the streets. There were taverns and brothels on every corner – the latter not constrained by papal decrees. Above the busy skyline, the city's cathedral, on the Via Dumo, rose more than 150 feet into the air, while beneath the streets water flowed in aqueducts built for the Emperor Caesar Augustus.

Caravaggio had been warned to take extra care in Naples. The mob was a constant presence – as were gibbets, from which dangled the fly-blown, bloated corpses of thieves and murderers. From time to time, as they progressed, ignoring beggars, cat-calls and the imprecations of whores, he and his little party were obliged to move to one side as groups of Spanish soldiers appeared, armed with arquebuses and pikes, led by officers who shouted out orders in heavily accented Italian to clear a path.

The painter breathed it all in. Then, having given a professional guide ten baiocchi, he and the two servants began to thread their way, tortuously, to the ornate Via Toledo, where the immense Palazzo Colonna, home of Prince Luigi Carafa Colonna, was to be found. Having reached the gate, surmounted by the arms of Italy's most illustrious family, he announced his presence to the guards, who admitted him and his servants to the front courtyard. After a short delay, a liveried flunky emerged. The scent of jasmine and bougainvillea filled the air.

Cool water from fountains, in the forms of gods and nymphs, played into ponds teeming with goldfish. Parakeets and toucans from South America, housed in a wrought-iron cage, screeched their protest at the new arrivals.

Caravaggio dismounted from his horse and looked about him with satisfaction. 'Take me to your master,' he said, brandishing his letter of introduction. 'I have come from the home in Zagarolo of Prince Marzio Colonna, who requests of his cousin, Prince Luigi, that I be given food and lodgings and all due consideration.'

The servant took the letter without a word and disappeared back into the house. Minutes later, an elegantly dressed gentleman in his fifties emerged blinking into the sunlight. He was tall, with a greying beard and moustache, and dressed in the Spanish style.

'So you are Michelangelo Merisi,' he said, looking as if he were much amused by the prospect. It was Prince Luigi himself. 'I bid you welcome to my house, where you may be assured of the protection of the Colonna. Come in and make yourself at home. I have heard so much about you.'

The artist bowed and indicated his companions. 'These two fellows have accompanied me all the way from Zagarolo. I should count it a distinct favour if they could remain overnight before returning to the home of your cousin, Prince Marzio.'

'Of course.' Prince Luigi nodded to his major domo, who nodded in turn to a footman. The two servants, caked with dust and utterly exhausted, turned to their beasts and began to unload their cargo. Before disappearing into the palazzo with his host, Caravaggio gave each of the men ten scudi and thanked them for their trouble. They looked, he thought, suitably grateful. Minutes later, he had forgotten them.

Naples was everything he had hoped for – and more. For the next two years, idolized by the mob, courted by the rich and powerful, Caravaggio rose to fresh heights of creativity. Neapolitan nobles, leading prelates of the Church and the Spanish governing class vied with one another to offer him commissions. The fact that he was an indicted murderer and a fugitive from papal justice only added to his allure. People everywhere wanted to meet him and experience the frisson of his notoriety.

But the uplift that came from the restoration of his freedom and the satisfaction of living in Europe's biggest city soon palled. Though his career flourished, Caravaggio was plagued by the persistent belief that he was a sinner destined for hell. He wished desperately for absolution. More than that, he longed to forgive himself. His shifting dispositions became a talking point among Neapolitans of all classes. No one who knew him could be sure from one minute to the next what mood he would be in or how long it would last. He could be laughing and joking in the tavern, with his hand running up the thigh of a young whore, then, abruptly, fly into a rage or be consumed by self-pity. Friends learned to be circumspect. It was one thing to be a bosom companion of 'the greatest painter in Italy', it was another to be the object of his scorn.

Governing his mood were his 'voices', which still spoke to him, though he tried earnestly to block them out. So long as he was working, he held on to his sanity. But he couldn't paint twenty-four hours a day. The consequences of his continuing, uresolved dialogue became a matter of public scandal. Mindless of his personal safety, he got into a wearisome series of fights in taverns and whore-houses. He also drank too much, hoping to dull the pain that drove him on.

Prince Luigi despaired of his guest. But then, one evening, he looked in to his studio and watched for an hour as the artist laboured over a vast *Flagellation of Christ*. After that, he would not hear a word of criticism.

All the while, Caravaggio knew that Battista would not rest. The Camerlengo, he was convinced, would hunt him down. At some point, when he least expected it, an assassin would come up behind him and drive a blade between his shoulders. Perhaps, like the priest, he would leave his head grinning in the gutter. But it wasn't only apprehension that moved him. Grief-stricken over his misspent life, he was consumed increasingly with a need to atone and do some service for Christianity. The fact that he had fled Rome after the business with Tomassoni preyed on his mind. He should have stood his ground, he told himself. He should have denied the charges against him and taken his chances in the papal court. Here in Naples, surrounded by luxury, able to indulge his talent to an extent previously impossible, he was sickened by himself. Worst of all was his knowledge that the future of Christian Europe could be altered by Battista and that he had done nothing to prevent it. An honest Muslim was one thing. Everyone had heard the stories about the nobility and tolerance of Salahadin. In Spain, it was said, the Moors had allowed Christians and Jews to follow their religions unmolested. But a traitor, who concealed his intentions, was something very different. An insidious man like Battista was a blot on the affairs of men. Caravaggio knew that he couldn't hide for ever. He had to rescue his good name with the one person whose opinion he truly valued: himself. Yet the question was, what could he hope to achieve? He had left it too late. No one would believe him if he made an accusation without evidence. They would say that he was slandering the reputation of an honoured prince of the Church simply to save his neck and win favour with the Pope. Not only that. To press a charge at all, he would have to return to Rome, which meant that first he must receive a guarantee of safe conduct. But how would he achieve that with a *banda capitale* hanging over his head?

One possibility remained. He had still not given up the idea of becoming a novitiate of the Knights of St John, in Malta – a proposal he had once discussed with the Holy Father. But how could he hope to achieve such an ambition? In Prince Luigi's private chapel, he prayed for guidance.

Two weeks later, in the middle of the afternoon, his prayers were answered. His studio, on the second floor, had windows on two sides, one overlooking the street, the other the main courtyard. Alerted by a combination of horses' hooves, carriage wheels and men shouting, Caravaggio looked out of his courtyard window just in time to see the gates swing open to admit, first, four armed horseguards, in uniform, then a carriage bearing on its side the arms of the Marchesa di Caravaggio.

Overjoyed, he threw down his brushes, telling his models to take the rest of the day off, and ran down the stairs two at a time. Prince Luigi was already there to welcome his aunt, the unquestioned matriarch of the Colonna, daughter of the great Admiral Marcantonio Doria, the victor of Lepanto.

'Luigi,' she said, as a footman rushed to place a stool beneath the door of the carriage. 'Let me take your arm, for I am no longer as young as I used to be.'

'You are forever young in our hearts,' said Don Luigi with a flourish. 'But I had no idea you were coming and have not prepared.'

'I came as quick as a letter ever would. And I have no doubt, nephew, that your generous household will prove more than adequate to my needs.'

Don Luigi bowed. As he did so, the Marchesa could see, standing behind him, shifting impatiently from foot to foot, the artist Caravaggio. Striding towards him, she held out her hand, which he kissed with as much gallantry as he could muster.

'My lady,' he began. 'I had thought never to see you again.'

'You should not underestimate me, Michelangelo, nor my family. Word came to me from my cousin Don Marzio that you were in trouble and I have hastened to be by your side.'

'I do not deserve the honour, but I am deeply grateful.'

The Marchesa nodded before turning approvingly to her nephew. 'And you, Luigi. I know that you have already played your part. That is as I would expect. But now, it is much too hot to be standing outside. In this heat it is little wonder that your famous birds are not singing. Let us go inside, where I hope I may have a drink of clean water followed by a glass or two of the estate's most excellent wine. After that, it is my intention to retire until it is time for supper. It has been a long journey from Rome.'

'Of course, aunt,' said Don Luigi, smiling. He turned to lead the way inside. At the same time, his major domo clapped his hands and a variety of servants came running.

Moments later, the prince turned to Caravaggio. 'This must be your lucky day, Michelangelo,' he said. 'If my aunt has decided to take you into her embrace, who would dare stand against her?'

Later, over dinner, the Marchesa revealed the cause of her visit. 'I have with me a letter signed by the Pope in which His Holiness grants Michelangelo the promise of his pardon.' She paused. The prince and Caravaggio waited respectfully. 'But,' she went on, 'there are two conditions. The first is that you, Michelangelo, should repent fully of your sins and over the next year perform work in the service of the Church. The second is that you should present yourself in person to obtain the Pope's absolution. I shall place in my nephew's safekeeping the laisser-passer provided by the Vatican, in the name of Cardinal Gonzaga. In the meantime, you must give yourself to God.'

Caravaggio could hardly believe what he was hearing. It was the second chance he had prayed for so earnestly ever since arriving in Naples.

'But what work should I do, my lady? I have fallen so far from grace.'

The Marchesa sipped from her glass of wine, then dabbed at the corners of her mouth with her napkin. 'I remember the day you were born – just three days after Lepanto. It was the feast day of Saint Michael the Archangel and it was I who suggested to your father that you be given the name Michelangelo.'

Caravaggio knew the story but listened as if hearing it for the first time. 'Your contribution to my life, my very survival, is something for which I shall always be grateful,' he said.

Still elegant on the brink of old age, the Marchesa looked at him and smiled. 'Do you believe in fate?' she asked him.

'I believe that each of us has a role to play, given us by God.'

'And what is yours, Michelangelo?'

'That is a question I ask myself every day.'

'Then let me provide the answer. You were born to paint. You were born to make the world see with new eyes. You were born for greatness. I knew it the first time I saw you. On the day your mother went into labour, as I walked down the steps of the palazzo, a rainbow appeared in the sky, and as I watched it came down just in front of the house in which you had been born only hours before. It was a sign. It was as if Christ himself had anointed you.'

'I don't understand.'

She stretched a hand to his face and stroked his cheek. 'When the rest of us are long forgotten, you, Michelangelo Merisi da Caravaggio, will be remembered. Your art and your struggle will live for all time.'

'That is flattering, my lady. But look at me. I am a fugitive, on the run from justice. Anyone who chooses may kill me. Every day I must look round me for the assassin who may be out there. When I go for supplies, or to the tavern, or to ...'

'... or to the brothel?'

Caravaggio looked down, unable to meet her eyes. 'As you say, my lady.'

'Then listen to me. In life, there are many who never know persecution. They come to no one's attention. They are not even important enough to have enemies. Others are hounded by the fates. You are one such man, Michelangelo. My son Fabrizio is another. Both of you have a destiny to fulfil, and those of us who are less troubled have a duty to see to it that you are not robbed of your achievement.' She found herself examining his hair, his beard and his clothes and concluding that time spent in her nephew's household had done much to civilize him. Eventually, she said: 'I am told that you have expressed a desire to join the Order of St John, in Malta.'

'That is correct, my lady ... if they will have me.'

'Oh, they will have you, Michelangelo. I have already taken soundings and am informed that the Grand Master would be more than happy to benefit from your genius. In return, he will consider you as a Knight – or at least as a novitiate. But only if you show a willingness to live a pure life and place your art at the order's service.'

'I should be honoured.'

'Then it is decided. I am sure my nephew will add his voice to mine in this matter.'

Prince Luigi nodded. 'Of course, aunt – and I shall also be pleased to write to the Grand Master, pleading your case.'

The Marchesa murmured her approval and patted her nephew's hand. Then she turned back to the artist, whose eyes, she noticed, were more deeply sunk in his head than she remembered when he was a young man setting off to conquer Rome.

'Join the Knights, Michelangelo. Learn discipline and attain peace. But most of all, paint! Will you promise me that?'

'I will, my lady.'

'Very well. Now go. I have business to discuss with my nephew. We will meet again in the days ahead. In particular, I wish to see what paintings you have made in the last year. But be assured, arrangements will be made.'

A month later, word was brought to Caravaggio that he should present himself the next morning, 21 July, with such goods and chattels as he intended to bring with him, to the quayside in Naples. There, he was told, he would be met by the general of the galleys of the Knights Hospitaller, who would convey him to Valletta for an audience with the Grand Master himself, Alof de Wignacourt.

It was everything he had dared to hope and Caravaggio wasted no time. Having packed up his few possessions, and leaving behind him a magnificent portrait of his host, he made his farewells to Prince Luigi and set off for the port.

The Marchesa accompanied him to wish him God speed and *bon voyage*. But she had another reason for venturing into the stink of the harbour. She wished to speak with her errant, yet illustrious son. For there on the quayside, waiting to greet them, was a man almost as infamous as Caravaggio: Fabrizio Sforza Colonna.

23*
Conclave minus 7

O'Malley's encounter with Cardinal Bosani had convinced him that the Camerlengo was a dangerous adversary pursuing an obscure and intensely personal agenda. He was alarmed and deeply uneasy, but none the wiser. What possible reason could the highest-ranking cardinal in the Church have for meeting in secret with Yilmaz Hakura, a known terrorist? It made no sense. Hakura, by all accounts, wasn't a man to be reasoned with. He wasn't like Martin McGuinness, the one-time IRA commander, who had famously done a deal with his lifelong enemy the Reverend Ian Paisley to bring peace to Northern Ireland. Hakura didn't understand compromise; he believed in suicide bombers, assassination and Jihad.

A thought, unbidden, had taken root in the Irishman's mind. It was dark and disturbing, like a storm still far off that you knew was coming. He tried to summon the thought to the forefront of his brain, but couldn't get hold of it. It kept sliding away. He was reminded of the summer when he was ten years old and used to spend hours every day at an amusement arcade in the Galway resort of Salthill. Inside a glass box, next to a booth housing a mechanical gypsy fortune-teller, was a heap of toys, one of which, a plastic GI Joe, he really wanted. To win it, he had to manipulate a small, chromium-plated crane, lowering its grab into position, then hoisting the prize towards the delivery point. Again and again, over six weeks, he had failed. The prongs of the grab always sprang open at the last moment. But in the end, on the last day of the summer, he had done it, slowly lifting the elusive toy soldier, then inching it towards the slot. It had been one of the highlights of his childhood – a triumph that had lived with him over the decades since.

He concentrated. Again and again he tried to recover the thought that was eluding him. Over and over again, he almost got hold of it, only to see it slip back into the darkness of his unconscious.

He shook his head and screwed up his eyes. Maybe Rüttgers had got it wrong about Bosani and Hakura. Maybe it just a simple case of mistaken identity. The trouble with detective work, O'Malley decided, was that it threw up as many questions as answers. He needed to know more and there was only one way to find out.

Descending during his lunch break into the cavernous archive of the Curia Generalizia, he called up the Society's files for the reigns of Popes Clement VIII and Paul V, who, between them, save for the 26-day reign of Leo XI, reigned from 1592 to 1621. To his astonishment, there was hardly anything about Cardinal Orazio Battista. A former prosecutor with the Inquisition, he was awarded his red hat in an addendum to the first and only list of cardinals created by Pope Innocent IX at the Consistory of 18 December 1591. The Pope himself died shortly after and Battista, according to the Jesuit record, remained in Rome until sometime in 1610 or 1611, when he apparently died of the plague. O'Malley next consulted the official archive of the Catholic Hierarchy and was surprised to discover that, apart from the date of his creation as a cardinal priest and the date of his death, there was nothing in the record to mark his passing. Whereas the Jesuit account placed Battista as Camerlengo for eleven years, from 1599 to 1610, the official account, updated annually, granted the title to Cardinal Pietro Aldobrandini, the cardinal-nephew of Clement VIII, who, as it happened, was a well-known patron of Caravaggio.

Why the discrepancy? Digging deeper, O'Malley pulled up the Society's official calendars for 1599 and 1610. These were dusty volumes, bound in leather, in which the events of each day were recorded in Latin, by means of a quill pen dipped in a mixture of soot, wine and walnut oil, held together with gum. It was pretty dismal stuff, he had to admit: a list of Masses held and who the celebrants were, plus comings and goings ... the Father General to Brindisi; a visit by the French Provincial General; the admission of novices; a new coadjutor agreed; three deaths. But there were other references, too, in faded red ink, recording events in the Church outside the Society, including the creation of seven cardinals on 31 March 1599 and the death, on 13 December of that year, of the Camerlengo, Cardinal Enrico Caetani. A week later, on 20 December, the same hand noted the appointment as Caetani's successor of ... His Eminence Orazio Cardinal Battista.

There was no mention of Aldobrandini. And yet, if memory served, the cardinal-nephew had been the most important figure in the Curia of his time. Elsewhere, in the official record of the Sacred College, against the name of Aldobrandini, was the information that he had been Secretary of State – a new post in those days – who had also served as Camerlengo from 1599 until his death, on

10 February 1621. The cardinal's funeral oration, O'Malley couldn't help observing, was delivered by Father Angelo Galluccio, SJ.

It was bloody odd. Turning back to the Jesuit archive, he eventually found an entry for Gallucio, who turned out to have been a papal lawyer, consecrated a priest in 1597, attached to the office of the Secretary of State from 1614 until his death in 1635. Several of his papers were available in a grey box last opened, O'Malley imagined, at the time of Galileo. He unfastened the small metal clip and slowly drew back the lid, sneezing as he did so. The interior of the waxed box was surprisingly dry. The papers themselves, four in all, were yellow with age, but still decipherable. One was an account of a trip to Venice during the interdict imposed on the city by Paul V. Another addressed a jurisdictional dispute between the Archbishop of Paris and a leading Benedictine abbot. The third looked to be even drier than the paper on which it was written: an account of the processes used to distribute the income from the Lateran cathedral during the pontificate of Gregory XV. But it was the last, the oration given by Gallucio at the Requiem Mass for the soul of Cardinal Aldobrandini on 10 February 1621 in the Basilica of Santa Maria sopra Minerva, that caused O'Malley to utter an impatient grunt.

His practised eyes skipped down the florid encomium. Aldobrandi, unsurprisingly, turned out to have been a paragon among men, raised to the cardinalate by his uncle, who early on recognized his nephew's sterling virtues and Christian calling. Yes, yes, but where were the references to the offices he held?

Ah! At last. There it was. Archbishop of Ravenna, Abbot commendatario of Rosazzo, prefect of the Office of the Apostolic Signature, governor of Ferrara, cardinal nipote, or cardinal-nephew, and head of the diplomatic service – the man who in 1598 had triumphantly negotiated the incorporation of the Duchy of Ferrara into the Papal States.

Nothing about being Camerlengo of the Holy Roman Church from 1599 to 1621. It could be that he had subsumed the office into that of Secretary of State, rather as Bosani had done. But in the 1600s, the office of Camerlengo was the most powerful job around. Gallucio, an obvious bureaucrat and yes-man, would never have left it out.

No. It was now clear to O'Malley that someone else – most obviously Battista – had been Camerlengo for at least part of the time generally ascribed to Aldobrandini. At some point he had obviously been airbrushed out of history. But why? Who would have benefited? And what possible connection could there be to Bosani?

He was not done yet. Turning finally to the personal papers of Father Claudio Acquaviva, Superior General of the Society from 1581 to 1615, O'Malley discovered a letter received from a Father Alfonso di Conza, SJ, dated May 28, 1606.

He adjusted the ancient Anglepoise lamp fixed to the study table at which he was seated and peered at the text, realizing with a tremor of excitement that it had probably not been read by anyone other than its intended recipient. It was written in the formal Italian of the period, but the author's meaning was clear.

Father General,

I write to inform you that I was present two nights ago at a dinner given by the banker Ciriaco Mattei, brother of His Late Eminence Cardinal Mattei. In the midst of the discussions that attended the meal put before us, Don Mattei was prevailed upon by the Camerlengo, Cardinal Battista, to permit him to inspect a canvas Mattei kept in his bedchamber, painted some time before by the artist Michelangelo Merisi, known from the place of his birth as Caravaggio.

It would be safe to say that the work did not please the Camerlengo, who at once pronounced it second-rate and an abomination. Notwithstanding this negative apprehension of Master Caravaggio's depiction of the betrayal in the Garden of Our Lord Jesus, the cardinal afterwards declared his intention to buy the work and was clearly vexed when Don Mattei declined to sell. In my hearing, the Camerlengo then warned Don Mattei to keep the canvas out of public sight, which he agreed to do.

I mention the above because, Father General, I have to report that the figure of Judas in the painting was uncommonly like the Camerlengo himself, right down to His Eminence's foreshortened left arm. More troubling still, on the left of the arrangement was to be seen the figure of a fleeing man, his mouth open, his eyes terrified. I knew at once that I had met this man, knew him even, but it was only later, in my sleep, that his identity revealed itself to me.

The man, Father General, was our servant of God, Fr Marcel d'Amboise, from St Brieuc, in Brittany, a scholar who chose to perform his pastoral duties among the poor of Trastevere but was called on from time to time to translate documents for the Curia from Armenian and Turkish, both of which languages he spoke fluently. I must now tell you that Fr d'Amboise was murdered on the night of October 4, 1603. He was pursued through the streets and alleyways of his parish and his head savagely struck from his shoulders by an unknown assailant. No motive has yet been ascertained for the crime, nor did the sbirri appear anxious to make inquiries.

I cannot make sense of these facts, but present them to you fearing that harm was done to Fr d'Amboise lest he reveal some knowledge concerning Cardinal Battista of which he perhaps had possession.

I ask God to offer repose to his soul and, if He so wills it, to deliver the truth of his death that justice might be done.

Requesting, Father General, that you should remember me in your prayers, I remain,

Your servant and brother in Jesus,
Alfonso di Conza

O'Malley was overwhelmed by his discovery. In the days when he used to read his *Irish Times* in the parlour of the Jesuit House in Dublin, the depiction of the fleeing man in Caravaggio's then unrevealed masterpiece was all but obscured by centuries of tobacco smoke and grime. But once restored by Benedetti, the painting – now hanging in a place of honour in the National Gallery - had been as remarkable to him for its harrowing portrayal of the figure running terrified from Gethsemene as it was for its rendition of Judas' betrayal. Now he knew the reason why.

There was still one missing piece in the story. He turned to the card index and looked up the entry for Di Conza. This referred him to the calendar for the year 1606, in which was another entry in red ink: Father Alfonso di Conza, born Siena 25 March 1544; died 30 May 1606 – apparently from food poisoning. That was all. He had been a member of the order for forty-one years, since 11 August 1565, but, like Father d'Amboise, he had survived his curious encounter with Cardinal Battista by less than forty-eight hours. It was incredible: two murders of two priests, each of whom had fallen foul of Battista, and no one seemed to think it strange.

As he absorbed the significance of this latest information, his mobile phone began to vibrate in his pocket. It was Father Giovanni, reminding him that he had an urgent appointment with an insurance broker – something about health care costs for the staff of Boston College.

'Yes, yes, Giovanni, don't worry, I'm on my way. Just give me five minutes.'

'Your taxi's waiting.'

'Very well, then … *two* minutes.'

He glanced back at the files. Acquaviva was in the view of many the most dynamic leader the Jesuits ever had. He'd brought in thousands of recruits and expanded the order across Europe and South America. He was also remembered for his part in the long-running dispute with the Dominicans over grace and free will, which became so bitter at one point that there were even fist fights and the Pope had to order both sides to desist. But no doubt Acquaviva had meetings as well. According to the accounts for 1606, he had been summoned to Venice on urgent business on the morning of 30 May and probably wouldn't have read Di Conza's letter until weeks, even months, later, by which time the poor man was long dead. Acquaviva could well have reasoned that there was nothing to be done.

Caravaggio to him would have been a lost cause – possibly an artist whom he viewed with suspicion. Or perhaps he was overwhelmed with business and simply chose not to take a view. Then, as now, Vatican bureaucracy had a lot to answer for.

24*
Conclave minus 6

Dempsey knew exactly what he was going to do when he got home after his confrontation with the head of the Secret Archive. He was going to have a glass of wine, watch the news, take a bath and wait for Maya to turn up. Beyond that, he hadn't a clue. All he knew for certain was that he'd had enough of putting his own security on the line. His apartment, on the shabby but fashionable Via della Penitenza, at the bottom end of the Janiculum Hill, was one that in his past life he would never have been able to afford. But the renewed surge in land prices in Ireland, especially near Galway, the fastest-growing city in the nation, had changed everything. It was an irony. His father had worked long, unsocial hours all his life and rarely managed a night out, never mind a shot at getting married again. Yet if he had only sold the farm during the first land-boom that came in with the new century – the one that had ended in the crash of 2008 – he'd have been a millionaire twice over.

He hadn't mentioned to Maya that he had money. For a start, she was from a Swiss banking family, which meant that her standards of what constituted wealth probably weren't the same as his. In all likelihood, she'd just think he was comfortably off. But there was also the fact that he didn't want to seem part of a world he despised, where money was what people valued about you and studying for a PhD in history was viewed as the equivalent of trying to improve your golf handicap.

Not that his doctorate was exactly at the forefront of his thinking right now. Walking down the Lungotevere Gianicolense, with its view across the river to the heart of the old city, he was wondering how he had allowed himself to be drawn into a dispute within the higher reaches of a Church that he no longer even believed in. What difference would it make if Bosani got his way and a new pope was elected who took a hard line against Islam? Europeans – indigenous Europeans, that is – were already up in arms about the huge growth in the Muslim population. There were articles in the papers every other day. Afternoon television, in the interludes between gameshows and soap operas, regularly featured debates involving academics, clerics, civil rights activists and Muslim spokesmen in which the explosive growth of Islam was the central theme. The rights of immigrants to live in their own enclaves governed by sharia law, or to convert churches to mosques, or to organize street protests against Israel and in favour of the Palestinians, were set against the demands of native Italians to be masters in their own country. There was no doubt that if the Pope raised his voice in support of a Christian Europe, it would make headlines. But would it really bring society closer to Armageddon that it already was? Dempsey didn't think so. A thousand years ago, popes could launch crusades; five hundred years after that they were able to broker the Holy League. But today, well into the second decade of the twenty-first century, the vicars of Christ were powerless. They didn't even enjoy the spurious glamour of being prisoners anymore, as they had been in the years after the *Risorgimento*. They were neither threatening nor tragic. If anything, they were a photo opportunity.

It was intriguing, yet deeply frustrating. Cardinals in Rome still thought of themselves as players on the world stage. That had to be force of habit. But it was the influence these same prelates had closer to home that was of deeper concern to him. The prefect of the Secret Archive obviously meant business, and now that the police had been called in, anything could happen. The last thing he wanted was to end up in court. On the other hand, Uncle Declan was depending on him and he couldn't let him down. Who else was there to help? Not Father bloody Giovanni, that was for sure. So it came down, like some sort of third-rate Shakespearean play, to a matter of family honour: the Omali versus the Bosani. If he owed it to no one else, he owed it to his father to stick by the Father General. Besides, it wasn't as if the Church was going to put him on the rack. They weren't going to *murder* him. A fine and a rap on the knuckles was all they had left in their armoury. So his best plan was to organize himself and work out his next move. He'd talk to Maya about it. She'd help put him straight.

He had just passed the Carabinieri barracks in the old Palazzo Salviati, halfway to the Ponte Mazzini, when he became aware of shouting in the distance and heard the characteristic wail of Italian police sirens. Behind him, a column of police vans was powering out of the heavy stone gateway of the Salviati courtyard and wheeling right onto the embankment. They passed him, one after the other, in a blur of flashing lights. What the hell! He increased his pace, curious to know what was happening. Two minutes later, as the crowd noise ahead of him continued to swell, he found his path blocked by a police cordon. The vans that had passed him were discharging groups of riot police, wearing steel helmets and body armour and carrying shields, now making their way in formation through the barrier. Immediately behind the cordon, local residents had gathered, with that lynch-mob look about them that made Dempsey wonder at first if maybe the police had just arrested a child murderer. But it wasn't that. Instead, a little way ahead, outside Rome's main prison, the Carcere di Regina Coeli, built on the site of a seventeenth-century monastery, a demonstration of some sort was underway. He drew closer. Several thousand protestors, flying the distinctive black and white flags of the banned Islamist party, Hizb ut-Tahrir, were chanting and waving their fists. Some threw rocks at the the police, which bounced off their plastic shields. But when the crowd parted to allow a young man in a checkered mask to run forward and hurl a petrol bomb, the response was instantaneous. As a helicopter clattered overhead, the riot squad began drumming their batons against their shields and moved forward in a broad phalanx.

'What is it? What's going on?' Dempsey asked an elderly Roman wearing a beret and smoking an evil-smelling Sicilian cigarette.

'They arrested a load of Arabs,' he replied, coughing and spitting the result onto the pavement. 'It's the gang that killed that poor gardener at the Lateran cathedral.' He coughed again. '*Bastardi!*'

By now, as the police line continued to advance, the demonstrators were pelting them with anything they could find. The real threat, however, came from a group, chanting Allahu Akbar – God is great! They carried baseball bats and moved in a tight military formation. Aware of the danger, a senior officer directed a detachment of his men to move right and force a path through the protestors. As they did so, a hail of petrol bombs came down, one of which struck a police car, enveloping it in flames.

Things were getting serious. Dempsey was reminded of riots in Kirkuk involving rival mobs of Sunnis and Kurds. A crowd-control officer ordered the Italian crowd to move back. But it was obvious that some of the locals, women as well as men, wanted to pitch in on the side of the police.

One young woman in a short skirt and tight-fitting T-shirt was particularly vehement. 'They come over here because their own fucking countries are shit. Then they tell us they don't want our culture, they want theirs and they throw bombs into our churches. Now they're attacking the police.'

'*Esattamente!*' said a man in his thirties, wearing a dark suit and sunglasses. 'Fuck them!' A roar of approval greeted his expletive, which he had delivered in English. Emboldened, the man turned to taunt the demonstrators. 'Send them back where they fucking came from,' he shouted, brandishing an extended forefinger. 'We don't want them here – *facce di merda!*'

At this, all the Italians raised their fists and surged forward.

Dempsey could tell that the situation was about to get out of hand. He backed away, saying nothing, and turned right, down the side of the jail along the Via delle Mantellate, where women prisoners were housed. As the first CS gas grenades exploded behind him, he made his way to the Via San Francesco di Sales, with its turnoff into the Via della Penitenza.

Relieved to have escaped the mayhem, he headed for a large, three-storey villa with a red roof. His two-bedroom apartment occupied the basement, the entrance to which was at the bottom of a steep set of steps. He squinted into the mail box by the front door of the main household – nothing, as usual – and descended the steps. Then he reached into his trouser pocket for his house keys. That was when he realized that the door was open, or at least ajar. Instantly, he was on his guard. There could only be one explanation. This was Rome after all. *Fucking hell!* he thought. *I've been burgled.*

He went inside, moving with caution in case the intruder was still inside. But whoever had been there was gone. Now he checked his possessions. It was as he feared. His laptop computer, his digital camera and €500 he'd left in the drawer by his bed were missing. So were all the notes he had taken in the Secret Archive. Whoever the burglar was, he was a professional. There were papers strewn around and every drawer in the apartment was open. But nothing was broken or vandalized, and he was sure there would be no fingerprints. The intruder had simply forced the locks on his front door, then conducted a systematic search until he found what he was looking for. The money would have been a bonus, nothing more.

He felt a complete fool. He hadn't bothered to activate the alarm when he went out that morning. His view was that any half-decent burglar would have known how to deal with it, disabling the siren after its first piercing shrieks, to the general satisfaction of the neighbourhood. Even so, it might have been some sort of deterrent.

He reached into his jacket pocket for his mobile, discovering as he did so that he had missed a call fifteen minutes earlier, probably because of the noise of the street demonstration. He rang his voicemail. It was a detective from the Rome City Police, called Drago. He and a colleague from the criminal investigation department of the Vatican gendermerie wanted to interview him at police headquarters at nine o'clock next morning in connection with a suspected theft from the Vatican library. He was advised not to be late.

He sat down on the edge of the bed. Jesus Christ! That's all I need. Then he called Maya to give her the latest bad news.

'Do you still want to stay with me tonight?' he asked her after he had finished.

'I think someone should,' she said.

25*
July 1607: Malta

Fabrizio Sforza Colonna, the son of Costanza, Marchesa di Caravaggio, was the sort of man around whom legends grow. Descended from three of the most illustrious families in Italy, the Colonna, the Sforzi and the Doria, who combined in the 1570s to lead Catholic Europe in its defence against the Turks, he was both the brightest star of his generation and the errant son. Five years before, in 1602, he had been charged with a crime so grievous that it had never been uttered in public. Speculation had since rehearsed every possible malefaction, from the murder of a priest, to the rape of a nobleman's twelve-year-old daughter, to incestuous relations with his mother. Yet so powerful was his family name and so glittering his own accomplishments as a young army officer that the Pope could not bring himself to put him to death. Instead, he was sent as a prisoner to Malta where he was placed in the charge of the Grand Master of the Knights of St John, Alof de Wignacourt.

A year later, after he had been released from jail and accepted as a novitiate, word came from Rome that, with the coronation of Paul V, Fabrizio once more enjoyed papal favour. He was appointed Joint Prior of Venice with his uncle, Cardinal Ascanio Colonna, and made an officer in the Hospitaller fleet. By the time he was instructed to pick up Caravaggio from Naples and bring him to Valletta, he had been promoted to the post of general of the galleys and was in the middle of a rebuilding programme aimed at repelling any assault by the resurgent Ottoman navy.

Two years younger than Caravaggio, with blonde hair and a flamboyant moustache, Fabrizio was to the depressed and despondent artist the very embodiment of hope. It didn't matter that he was tired and rootless, hunted like an animal and uncertain of the nature of his own soul. Like Fabrizio, if he simply submitted himself to God and the Hospitallers, he could start afresh and remake himself in the image of a Christian Knight.

'My mother is full of your praises,' Fabrizio told the artist as he directed the loading of cargo onto the galleass *San Giovanni*.

'The Marchesa is most kind. I am indebted to your entire family.'

Fabrizio placed a comradely arm on Caravaggio's shoulders. 'She believes in you, Michelangelo. We all do.'

'She also believes in you, Fabrizio. She says you have a destiny.'

'Then let us hope neither of us disappoints her.'

With only a light wind blowing, the voyage from Naples to Valletta on the new galleass took two days. Fabrizio had been promised a consignment of Turkish slaves to work the oars, but it turned out only twenty or so were available, and not all of these were strong, so he took the opportunity to test the new sails.

It was as they passed through the Straits of Messina, heading south, that Fabrizio caught his famous guest observing the performance of his second-in-command.

'You're wondering where you've seen him before – am I right?'

'He does seem somehow familiar.'

'Let me introduce you.' He called the young man over. He could not have been more than twenty, slim and well-constructed, but with a haunted look in his eyes.

'Michelangelo Merisi,' said Fabrizio, indicating Caravaggio. 'A fugitive from papal justice, under sentence of death for a murder he did not commit.' Then he turned to his ship's mate. 'Bernardo Cenci – the only surviving member of his family, bound as a galley slave for life by Pope Clement VIII.'

Caravaggio gasped. 'I was there! 11 September 1599. I saw your family die. I saw you faint and watched as you were carried off into servitude. I still have nightmares about it.'

'As do I, Master Merisi,' Cenci said. 'But I have heard the story of your own misfortune from General Colonna and wish you to know that I am at your service.'

'I am deeply grateful, but I do not deserve the honour.'

'They say that you spoke to my sister as she was about to mount the scaffold.'

'Yes. She asked me if I intended to draw her.'

'And did you?'

'I began to … but then I was sick.'

'I pray for her every day. As well as for my mother and my brother.'

'They will be rewarded in heaven.'

Cenci stared out in the direction of Reggio Calabria. 'Perhaps,' he said. 'But I must go now. I have have work to do.'

The *San Giovanni* berthed just before midday on 13 July. Caravaggio looked up at the mighty Castel Sant'Angelo, which jutted into the Mediterranean like the prow of a gigantic ship. Stone steps ran up from the Grand Harbour to the shops and houses clustered around the market place. On the wharf, groups of weather-beaten fishermen mended their nets. A couple of prostitutes sidled up to the water's edge looking for business, but seeing Fabrizio on board with two armed constables moved them along.

As the artist and the admiral mounted the steps, above their heads the sound of a church choir drifted into the midsummer air from the nearby Cathedral of St John.

'A new Knight is being initiated today,' Fabrizio said. 'Just think, Michelangelo, in another year that will be you. Then all your troubles will be over. The Pope will pardon you and you'll return to Rome in triumph.'

'I'll believe it when I see it,' was Caravaggio's response.

Grand Master Alof de Wignacourt had rushed through the initiation of his latest Knight, a young Portuguese nobleman, so as not to be late for the arrival in his court of the most famous artist in Italy. The Frenchman, at the age of sixty-five, remained an impressive figure, strong enough to practice with a heavy mace and crush a walnut in his mailed fist. Broad-shouldered, with a deep chest and the legs of a prize fighter, he could still fit into the armour made for him ten years before and was vain enough to be bothered by a wart on the right side of his nose.

There were not many left who had fought during the great siege of Malta in 1565, when the Knights had held off an entire host of Ottomans for four months, with the loss of one-third of their number. De Wignacourt, from Picardy, was not one of the few. He had arrived in Malta the following year, brimful of the virtues of chivalry, and, having earned his spurs at Lepanto, spent years as captain of Valletta, then head of the order in France, before being installed as Grand Master in 1601. Most recently, he had been appointed a prince of the Holy Roman Empire, according him the right to be addressed as His Serene Highness. It was a style, or 'dignity' that he did not require of his brothers but that was expected of ambassadors, fellow monarchs and, most obviously, representatives of the Sublime Porte.

As a Frenchman, well acquainted with life in Paris as well as Rome, de Wignacourt was constantly looking for ways to add lustre to his remote island realm. The construction of St John's Cathedral, as sovereign church of the order, was now all but complete. The Oratory, in effect the Knight's Hall, was another matter. Still unfinished, its greatest lack, in the opinion of the Grand Master, was a painting commensurate with its status as home to the most illustrious order of chivalry. Caravaggio would fill that void with distinction, and he, Alof de

Wignacourt, would take the role of Pope Julius II, the patron and protector of Michaelangelo. It was a pity, of course, that the painter was a murderer on the run from papal justice. But then, had not the same been true of Fabrizio Colonna? And look at him now: general of the galleys, preparing a fleet of the latest class of vessels to take on the Turks and repeat the glory of Lepanto. Perhaps, de Wignacourt said to himself, one of Caravaggio's most magnificent works would yet be a representation of the destruction of the Ottoman fleet in which, beneath their banners and among the swirling smoke of battle, he and Fabrizio stood proud on the fo'c'sle of the *San Giovanni*.

He had been debating with himself over whether or not to descend from his palace to the harbour to welcome his guest in person. But then he thought, no, his elevated status required that the artist should come to him. Accordingly, he now stood next to the fireplace in his audience chamber, striking a pose – a pose he had to hold for some time as Fabrizio and Caravaggio drank a glass of wine at a nearby tavern.

But at length, his sergeant-at-arms approached and announced the arrival of 'the artist Caravaggio'. De Wignacourt at once assumed his commander-in-chief look, which he liked to think combined far-sightedness and vision with a close attention to detail.

'Master Caravaggio!' he began. His voice was deep and resonant, for which he had always been grateful. 'Please step forward. I bid you welcome to the headquarters of the Order of St John of Jersualem.'

Caravaggio bowed. 'Thank you, Grand Master. I am honoured.'

'And you, General Colonna: welcome home. How is our new flagship?'

'A miracle of engineering, Grand Master. The best I have ever seen. Once the others in her class are delivered, we shall be more than ready to take the fight to the enemy.'

'I'm glad to hear it. And what of you, Master Caravaggio? What do you bring to our island fortress – apart from a rather interesting aroma?'

'I bring my craft as a painter. Further, I offer myself in your service as a novice.'

'As to that, I can as yet promise you nothing. There are, as you will be aware … complications. Yet I have some hopes of your preferment. In the meantime, we have a cell prepared for you and a studio with good light overlooking the harbour and cathedral. And the strand on the far side of the point offers most excellent sea bathing. If there is anything you need, you have only to ask.'

'I am most grateful.'

'Have you given any thought as to what your first subject might be?'

Caravaggio rubbed his nose with the back of his hand and looked thoughtful. 'Naturally, I shall offer a work relating to the life and death of St John the Baptist, the order's patron saint. But I was wondering, Grand Master, if you might accord me the singular honour of allowing me to paint your portrait, dressed as if for battle. I see there is a vacant space above the fireplace where you now stand. I would humbly suggest to you that such a space could best be occupied by a painting of one of the most illustrious Grand Masters the order has ever had.'

De Wignacourt, who had already decided that he should be painted in full armour, no matter how uncomfortable the experience, shut his eyes and plucked at his beard, as if pondering the option. 'It had not occurred to me,' he said, 'that you might be interested in painting me, a humble custodian in God's service. But by all means, if you think it would redound to the credit of the order …'

Caravaggio bowed again, this time more extravagantly than before. As he came up, his eye caught Fabrizio's gaze. They understood each other perfectly.

26*
Conclave minus 5

The sprawling, grey brick headquarters of Rome's state police, known as the Questura, occupied most of one side of the Via St Vitali, off the Via Nazionale in downtown Rome. Patrol cars and scooters filled the street outside. A couple of uniformed officers stood lazily on guard at the main entrance.

At exactly nine o'clock, Dempsey made his way up the steps into a large marble reception area, where he explained to an overweight young woman behind a thick glass partition that he had come to see Detective Sergeant Drago. The woman, who was in the middle of eating a sandwich, asked for his name, then picked up the phone and punched in Drago's number.

After a brief conversation, she pointed vaguely in the direction of the rear wall. 'Wait over there. Sergeant Drago will be with you presently.'

'*Grazie.*'

'*Prego.*'

Two North Africans in handcuffs stood in the corner, watched over by a bored-looking officer with a handlebar moustache. One of the two had a cut lip, the other nursed a black eye. A gypsy, probably Romanian, with several teeth missing, stood next to them.

After a couple of minutes, a stocky, dishevelled man in his forties, with greasy hair and his shirt hanging out at the back, walked in and looked straight at Dempsey.

'Are you Dempsey?' he asked in Italian.

Dempsey nodded.

'The name's Drago,' he said. 'Follow me.'

They turned right out of the reception area into a broad corridor. A flight of stairs led up to another, narrower passage that extended at least a hundred metres in both directions. 'This way,' said Drago.

The detective's office was near one end. It had a grey door. Inside was a single desk, with a computer terminal. Staring out the window overlooking the street was a smartly dressed, somewhat younger man, with dirty fair hair. 'This is Agent Scajola of the Vatican Security Service,' said Drago. He pointed at a hard chair in front of his desk. 'Take a seat.'

Scajola still hadn't turned round. He did so now, revealing a pinched face with fleshy lips. 'So you are Dempsey,' he said, in English.

'Keep it in Italian,' said Drago. He looked at the Irishman with faint contempt. 'You do speak Italian, I suppose.'

'*Naturalmente. Quando a Roma ...*'

The two Italians exchanged glances, as if to say, we've got a smartarse here.

Drago sniffed loudly. 'Agent Scajola has been talking to the Vatican's chief librarian, who tells him you stole valuable documents from the Secret Archive dating back nearly four hundred years. Is that true?'

'It's true that the librarian says so.'

Drago looked away for a moment, then spun round. 'Don't try to be clever with me,' he snarled. 'Just answer the question. Did you steal the missing papers?'

Dempsey strained to keep his temper. 'No,' he said. 'I did not steal the missing papers.'

'Then where are they?' Scajola wanted to know.

'As I told Monsignor Asproni, they were listed as missing as long ago as 1977.'

'That's not what the records say.'

'Then the records have been tampered with.'

Scajola looked down at his shoes. 'What were you looking for in the first place? Why did you go to the museum?'

'I'm a historian. My uncle, the Superior General of the Jesuits, plans to deliver a sermon in the Gesù and wished to know more about the life and career of Cardinal Bosani.'

'And why should he do that?'

'Because he and the Camerlengo have a philosophical disagreement about the future direction of the Church in respect of its attitude towards Islam.'

'And you thought it might help things along if you "borrowed" confidential material that properly belongs to His Holiness the Pope?'

Drago snorted. 'He means you took it.'

'I've already told you. I took nothing.'

Scajola said: 'But you did "steal" three minutes on the library's computer, contrary to the stated regulations, which were explained to you in advance.'

'Yes, I admit that. It seemed harmless enough at the time, but I agree now that it was wrong.'

'So you don't deny it.'

'I've already said so.'

'You admit to abusing the confidential records of a sovereign state.'

'To accessing them – yes.'

'Once a thief, always a thief.'

'Once a thug, always a thug.'

Drago drew back his hand and slapped him in the face – hard. Demspey rubbed his cheek, which stang. 'I wouldn't do that again, if I were you, Sergeant,' he said calmly. 'Unless you want to spend the night in the local hospital.'

The Italian's face twisted into a scowl. For a moment it looked as if he was about to launch himself at Demspey. But Scajola put out a restraining arm.

'I will put a proposition to you, Signor Dempsey. According to the information I have seen, the disputed material was in the file of the library until you removed it. So why don't you do us all a favour and give it back? That way, things will go easier for you. You could say that you were a scholar who in your enthusiasm got carried away and did something you now very much regret.'

'But that's not what happened,' Dempsey said. 'I didn't steal anything. Matter of fact, I'm the one who's been burgled. My apartment was broken into yesterday and my computer, my camera and my private papers were stolen, as well as €500.'

The Vatican man examined his fingernails. 'Very convenient, wouldn't you say? You would have us believe that, contrary to the evidence, it is you, in fact, who are the victim here. Next you will be claiming police harassment.'

Dempsey's expression in response to this cynical interpretation of events registered, he hoped, a precise mixture of irony and contempt. 'My uncle – ' he began.

'Ah yes, your uncle. Let me tell you something, Signor Dempsey. It is only out of respect for your uncle, the Father General, that you are not being handed over to my colleague here to cool your heels in a Roman cell.'

'In which event,' said Drago, 'we'd soon see who ended up needing medical attention.'

'I was going to say,' said Dempsey, ignoring Drago, 'that my uncle will gladly confirm the nature of the request he made to me. Of course, should you decide to detain me, then he will have no option but to explain what has happened to the media.'

Scajola considered the implications of Dempsey's threat and appeared to rethink his strategy. 'This matter remains under investigation by both the Vatican and the Polizia di Stata. In the meantime, you will sign this form guaranteeing that you will stay out of the precincts of the Vatican and do nothing to discredit the administration or governance of the Holy See.' He extracted a form from the inside pocket of his jacket. 'There is about to be a papal election. This is a crucial moment in the history of the Church ...'

'Exactly. And that's why – '

'– And that is why,' the officer resumed, 'you will keep your nose out of our affairs. Should you ignore this warning, you will be arrested at once and charged with the theft of historical documents from the library of the Holy See. Pending trial, you will be held in a remand prison ...'

Drago offered Dempsey a crooked smile. '... where I could always ask my colleagues to offer you their most personal service.'

Dempsey sighed. 'I don't doubt that their hospitality would be second to none. My only wish, as you can imagine, is that some day I may be in a position to return the favour.'

Twenty minutes later, having consulted with Drago and the vice-prefect of the Secret Archive, Scajola reported back to the Camerlengo.

'Do not trouble yourself, Eminence. The matter has been taken care of. If this Dempsey steps out of line again, he will answer to me directly.'

'I am glad to hear it,' says Bosani. 'The Irish, as you know, tend to be a little direct in their methods and are also subject to fantasy.'

'Should he interfere in any way with your plans, Camerlengo, he will find that our reality is worse than his nightmares.'

Bosani sighed with pleasure. Sometimes, he realized, there was a ruthlessness about Catholicism that Islam lacked.

27*
1608: Malta

In the months that followed his arrival in Valletta, Caravaggio worked almost ceaselessly at his art. His full-length portrait of the Grand Master showed its subject 'standing and armed', holding his staff of office, his plumed helmet borne beguilingly by a page. The armour he wore – reputed to be the mostly costly in Christendom – was not his own, but that of his famous predecessor, Jean de la Valette, commander of the Hospitallers during the Great Siege. The symbolism was clear: the life and death struggle with Islam was far from over and de Wignacourt was determined on victory for the Holy League. The fact that la Valette's armour was slightly too small may, according to Fabrizzio Colonna, have accounted for the subject's slightly other-wordly gaze into history. But however constrained he may have felt at the time, the Frenchman was delighted with the result and immediately commissioned a second portrait in which he posed, seated this time, out of armour but wearing his Knight's habit.

During the early sittings, Caravaggio, who had begun to recover something of his old confidence, said little about his ambition to join the order. Instead, he provided de Wignacourt with lively accounts of the princely class in Rome and Naples, in whose affairs the gossip-starved nobleman had an almost insatiable interest. Only gradually, as the two men became familiar with each other and relaxed, did the talk turn to the artist's longer-term plans.

The Grand Master was convinced that attracting Caravaggio to his isolated court was quite the cleverest thing he had ever done and was wary of doing anything that might rob him of his prize. At least, he told himself, he had succeeded in his first objective, the progressive removal of layers of grime from the fellow's body and his adoption of a novice's habit, changed every three days. Now the brothers could at least bear to be in the same room with him. But there was still, alas, the niggling matter of the murder in Rome. Overturning a *banda capitale*, proclaimed by His Holiness, was no easy matter. As he watched the artist accord him immortality in a world in which death came often as a thief in the night, the Frenchman decided to get straight to the point

'What do you propose I do about the murder of Tomassoni? You killed him in a duel then fled the city to avoid arrest, leading, *in absentia*, to a death sentence that to date has not been revoked. I wish very much to assist you in your quest, but I can hardly pretend these facts don't exist.'

'I understand your position,' Caravaggio replied, wishing that he could confide in his patron the truth about the Camerlengo's treason. 'But it was Tomassoni who attacked me. If I hadn't defended myself, he'd have murdered me. And I should point out that the *banda capitale*, though issued in the Pope's name, was in fact signed by Cardinal Battista, who has made no secret of his dislike of me personally – and of my art.'

'Battista, indeed.' De Wignacourt was intrigued. 'I have only met His Eminence once, and that was before he became Camerlengo. But Luis de Fonseca, my *Cavaliere di Giustizia*, has often commended him to me as a most stalwart defender of the Church and a sworn enemy of the Turks.'

Caravaggio appeared to consider this. It really was hard for him not to blurt out the truth and to hell with the consequences. He drew a deep breath. 'Yet I have heard it said that the Camerlengo regards the Muslim threat as ended and is no supporter of the Hospitallers.'

'It's true,' de Wignacourt agreed, 'that His Eminence tried recently to divide our fleet – a ploy that I neither understood nor condoned. Yet this very week, upon his return from Isfahan, Brother Fonseca praised him to me for having persuaded the Pope not to form an alliance with the Persians – an arrangement that, according to Fonseca, would have been tantamount to a pact with the Devil.'

Caravaggio bristled. Twenty-four hours earlier, at their first meeting, Fonseca had deliberately snubbed him in the Knights' Hall, remarking to two of his confrères, both Germans, on the remarkable sight of 'a servant in gentleman's attire'. All three had sniggered and Caravaggio had felt his hand go to his sword, only to realize that it wasn't there. Swords and other weapons were worn in Malta only by members of the order and the local *sbirri*. So, biting his tongue, he had simply smiled and moved on.

But the issue of an alliance with the Persians was one on which he saw no reason to hold back. 'You are a man of action, Grand Master, and I a poor painter.

But it seems to me that the Persians and the Holy League, led by the Knights of Malta, could, together, have dealt the Ottomans a blow from which they might never have recovered. As for the Persians, is it not true that they have always looked east, to India and Mesopotamia? Seen from Isfahan, the Christian states must appear distant and alien. Why would the Shah, with the eastern world at his mercy, turn instead on Europe?'

De Wignacourt smiled benevolently. 'Ah, Master Caravaggio. But you know so little of empire or of the Muslim mind. Empires must always continue to grow. The moment they stand still, they are in trouble. For followers of Islam, the ultimate goal is the conquest of Europe and the establishment of a caliphate in which we poor Christians would be reduced to the status of slaves. They may never achieve their objective, but they must always believe it possible.'

'Is not the same true of us?' Caravaggio asked. 'You, sir, are a soldier of Christ. To you, the retaking of the Holy Land must be an equivalent goal.'

'– And I must always believe it possible. Yet I do not propose to waste my ships and the armies of Europe in a vain attempt to recapture Jerusalem. That would bring ruin to us all and, even if achieved, might last no longer than a single generation.'

'So deadlock is both our tactic and our strategy?'

The Grand Master threw back his head and laughed. 'Precisely. You have understood. Who knows, Master Caravaggio? You may make a Knight after all.'

The next day de Wignacourt instructed his ambassadors to Rome and the Holy See to sound out opinion in the relevant quarters about entering Caravaggio as a novice. Precedent showed that it had once been possible to create Knights without the proof of nobility in all four lines now considered de rigeur and, more to the point, exclusive of any reference to alleged criminality. The Grand Master now wished it known that he would consider it a singular favour were he to be allowed to make an appointment just once under the old rules.

The request did not fall on deaf ears. There were many in the Vatican and among the ruling class in Rome ready to welcome the Prodigal's return. Prelates hoping to adorn their churches with the splendour of great art were joined by rich merchants and princes who yearned to have their images recorded for posterity by a painter equal to the task. Unfortunately for all their hopes, the decision was left to the Camerlengo, who scrawled '*No! Refuitato*' – rejected – on the letter of supplication, adding that it was the Grand Master's Christian duty either to carry out the sentence imposed by the *banda capitale* or else to send the malefactor back to Rome in chains. Battista had, as it happened, learned only latterly of the artist's arrival in Malta. It was Fonseca, newly returned from Isfahan, who brought the news. Now, having disposed of what was in effect a request for a papal pardon, the cardinal sent word to Fonseca reminding him of his undertaking to remove once and for all the greatest single threat to their mission.

In the meantime, de Wignacourt had decided on a more direct approach. There would be no intermediaries this time. Instead, in a personal petition couched in the dignity of a prince of the Holy Roman Empire, he asked the Pope to allow the award of a Knight's habit to a repentant sinner, whom he did not name, who had committed unintentional homicide in a 'brawl'.

To the surprise of some, the pontiff on this occasion chose to listen not to his chamberlain – whose presumption of power had begun to get under his skin – but to Cardinal Del Monte, Caravaggio's first and most loyal benefactor, and Borghese, the cardinal-nephew, who owned a number of the artist's works and hoped to acquire more. The argument in favour of allowing the Grand Master's request was telling. First, at a time of increased danger from the Turks, it would add to the personal loyalty owed by the Hospitallers to the Throne of Peter. Second, it would permit the return to Rome of the one painter whom even Julius II would have regarded as the equal of Leonardo and Michelangelo. A letter of 'exceptional permission' was despatched to Valletta within days. Enclosed, under the papal seal, was a second letter, from the cardinal-nephew, addressed to the painter, urging him to complete his novitiate as quickly as possible, and afterwards to make his way to the Villa Borghese, where lucrative commissions and a 'secure' life awaited him.

Battista fumed, but in the end decided that it didn't matter. Caravaggio was a thorn in his flesh, but he would be dead long before he could return to Rome. Besides, there was one other loose end he still had to tie up, requiring an early visit to the Alban Hills. Soon, insh'Allah, he would be able to report to the Safiye Sultan that the last remaining threat to their joint enterprise had been removed.

14 July 1608 was the day chosen by de Wignacourt for Caravaggio's admission to the order. It was one year and a day since the artist's arrival in Valletta – an interval deemed just long enough for him to have completed his novitiate. Not everyone was happy about the honour accorded the son of a mere retainer. Many of the Knights, believing themselves part of an élite anointed by God, were affronted, thinking him to be no more than an *arriviste*, lacking both military training and breeding. Out of deference to this opinion, the ceremony of induction, held in the Oratory of the Cathedral of St John, was short and to the point. Fabrizio Colonna, to no one's surprise, was the artist's principle sponsor. What was wholly

unexpected was the identity of Colonna's seconder: Luis de Fonseca, Cavaliere of the Knights of Giustizia and one of the most aloof figures in the order. Some saw Fonseca's decision as a sign of the deep bond between him and de Wignacourt; others, more cynical, wondered if the Spaniard was not simply reinforcing the authority of a position to which he ultimately aspired. Either way, the effect was the same. The oath was administered by the chaplain general, allowing the Grand Master to welcome his protégé on behalf of the 'entire community', which could now, he said, 'glory in this adopted disciple and citizen'.

Admitted as a Knight of Obedience, a sub-division of the Knights of Giustizia, Caravaggio swore to lead a life of Christian perfection. He dedicated himself to the Virgin and to St John the Baptist, kissed the white linen cross embroidered on his habit and, having undertaken to lead a life marked by poverty, chastity and obedience, swore an oath of lifelong allegiance to de Wignacourt and his successors.

Then, following High Mass, he got back to work.

Before he could leave Malta and return to Rome, he had several important commissions to finish, the most important being an alterpiece, *The Beheading of Saint John the Baptist*, for the same oratory in which he had been invested. This was to be a massive work, some seventeen feet by twelve, and the artist, out of gratitude to de Wignacourt, spared no effort to ensure that it was one of the pinnacles of his career. He had painted the Baptist many times and would return to the subject, in more macabre fashion, before he died. But on this occasion, in honour of the Knights, he determined on a canvas about which there could be no argument and no controversy.

Previous depictions of St John's last moments, by artists from every corner of the Christian world, had focused either on the moment when the victim waited for the headsman's sword to fall, or else on the presentation of his head to the dancer Salomé, at whose request the execution was carried out. Caravaggio took a different course. He would show St John helpless on the stone flags of the prison yard, his throat cut, his blood draining almost onto the frame of the painting. The executioner, concerned only to get the job done, reaches behind him for a second blade in preparation for the act of decapitation. As prisoners look on in horror and Salomé holds out her salver, the Messiah's cousin surrenders to his destiny.

The completed canvas, recognized by all who saw it as a wonder of the age, was due to be installed in the Oratory in late August, just in time for the subject's feast day. Caravaggio felt satisfied. He was more at peace now than he had been for several years. It was as if he had been redeemed and cleansed of his sins. But the nightmares didn't stop and, still, gnawing at him, was the sensation of Death at his heels. To distract himself, he took to slipping out at night to visit taverns, even brothels – acts that he did not associate with sin. But try as he might, he could not rid himself of the conviction that Fate was stalking him, merely awaiting the opportunity to strike.

Sometimes, when he spent too much time in his own company, his voices told him what to do. It was they who told him to sign his newly acclaimed masterpiece in the Martyr's blood, using the same paint that rendered the rich, red flow from St John's gaping neck. He had never previously signed any of his paintings. He had never felt the need. It was in token of the pride he felt in his new status that he now styled himself F. (for Fra) Michelangelo. It would be as Brother Michelangelo, a servant and soldier of God, that he would return to Rome and expose to the Holy Father the treason of Cardinal Battista.

It was Fabrizio Colonna who brought Caravaggio the news. Prince Marzio Colonna had died suddenly in his palace in Zagarolo. He had been in good health in the weeks prior to his death and there was no explanation to offer.

Fabrizio took out an envelope, sealed with wax bearing the arms of the Colonna. 'My cousin Francesco sent you this letter,' he told the artist. 'He said it could be conveyed by no one but me and that it was intended for you alone.'

Caravaggio offered his condolences, which were deeply felt, then took the letter and immediately retired to his cell to read it. It was dated 30 July.

My dear Michelangelo,

I have entrusted this letter to my cousin Fabrizio, who undertook to deliver it to you personally. If anyone else, for any reason, has handed it to you, you should at once be on your guard.

Three days ago, my father, Don Marzio, died unexpectedly. He had been in excellent health, though in low spirits on account of the information of which he had been in possession since your time at Zagarolo. You will recall that he undertook to conduct discreet inquiries regarding the matter raised. He had thought the persons to whom he turned in Rome would be receptive to the information he imparted. Regrettably, it is now clear that in at least one instance, his trust was misplaced. Three days before his death, my father was a guest at the Palazzo of Cardinal Pamphilj, the Vicar General. There were several Cardinals and other Prelates present, including the Camerlengo, who paid particular attention to my father and sat next to him at dinner.

That night, my father, having retired to his own residence in the city, was taken violently ill. Two days later, he was dead. Doctors – in whom I place no great reliance – spoke of an 'infection'. Others, they said, had recently exhibited the same symptoms and also succumbed – though I know of none.

You will understand, my dear friend, the thoughts that currently occupy my mind. Not only do I grieve sorely for my late father, but I am bound to wonder as to the true cause of his affliction.

I advised you once to take great care, and I repeat that warning now. Should you ever make it back to Rome, or to Zagarolo, the hospitality of the Colonna will once more be available to you. In the meantime, I commend you to God's protection.

You must trust also to Fabrizio.

Your friend,
Francesco

The letter threw Caravaggio into a deep and abiding depression. Don Marzio was a good man and a loyal friend and it pained him greatly that he should have been responsible, however unintentionally, for his death. He would write to Franceso at once and express his most deeply felt condolences. But there were also clear implication for his own safety. He planned to leave Valletta within the month, following the feast day of St John. He had produced five paintings, intended as gifts for St Peter's and the papal apartments, and drafted an application to the Pope seeking formal pardon for the death of Ranuccio, while at the same time pledging himself, as a Knight of Malta, to the Christian cause. Now he felt sure that Battista would be waiting for him, ready to strike his head from his shoulders. Beyond that, he was convinced that, upon his death, the Camerlengo would feel emboldened to strike at the Holy Father himself.

Over the next weeks, Caravaggio spent long hours in the taverns by the Grand Harbour, where his argumentative nature, brawls and other noisy encounters did not go unnoticed. De Wignacourt was aware of what was happening but put it down to a surfeit of grief for his great patron, Don Marzio.

Luis de Fonseca had not, meanwhile, forgotten his undertaking to Battista that Caravaggio would not leave Malta alive. On a hot evening, towards the end of August, knowing the artist to be drunk, he deliberately barged into him on the steps leading down from the Knights' refectory. Complaining in an outraged voice that Caravaggio had almost knocked him him over, he demanded an immediate apology. Caravaggio refused, insisting that it was Fonseca who had knocked into him. The lofty Hospitaller, known for his piety and nobility, then accused the newcomer of behaviour unbecoming a Knight. He accused him of public drunkenness and required him, in the hearing of several fellow Hospitallers, to deny that he was on his way into the town to pick up a whore. At this, provoked beyond reason,

Caravaggio began to draw his sword and lunged forward. Fonseca, an experienced combatant, easily sidestepped the approach and called on his colleagues, as witnesses, to arrest his assailant.

At a preliminary hearing next morning, Fonseca recounted how Caravaggio, drunk, deliberately lurched into him on the step, then, when challenged about the affront, as well as his flagrantly immoral behaviour, tried to run him through with his sword. Witnesses, all associates of the lofty Cavaliere di Giustizia, were happy to confirm the substance of the accusation. Mortified, de Wignacourt was left with no option but to place his newest recruit under arrest pending a court martial.

There were several cells in the fortress of Sant'Angelo that would hold a brother securely without undue humiliation. Fonseca, newly returned as an ambassador of both the Grand Master and the Pope, insisted that the accused be thrown into the deepest dungeon, a pitch-black, underground hell-hole, known as the *guva*, accessible only from above. With the *banda capitale* already in effect, the Spaniard was confident of a swift conviction followed by the condemned man's execution. But he would take no chances. Should it begin to look as if Caravaggio might win his freedom, his secondary plan was to poison the painter in his cell and attribute the death either to suicide or God's will.

On the third night of his incarceration, plagued by bad dreams and shivering with cold, Caravaggio was visited by his accuser, who descended into the pit by rope, carrying a blazing torch to light his passage. The Knight drew his sword, which he thrust against the throat of the weakened painter, calling on him in a loud voice to confess his crimes. 'If you admit to your error and deceit,' he said, 'a simple beheading awaits you. If not, you will be stretched on the rack and your tongue cut out before you are hanged, drawn and quartered. The choice is yours.'

Caravaggio, his eyes half blinded by the flames of the torch, summoned up just enough strength to spit into the Knight's face. At this, Fonseca flicked the point of his blade so that it nicked the prisoner's neck. 'The scent of blood always attracts the rats, Merisi,' he hissed. *Sotto voce*, he added: 'In the name of Allah the beneficent and Mohammad His Prophet – peace be upon Him – I wish you eternal peace.'

Hearing these words spoken, Caravaggio recoiled in panic. No! It couldn't be true. Fonseca as well! Now truly he was doomed. Falling back onto the cold stone of his cell, he put his hands up to his face and felt the warm tears stream through his fingers.

Another week went by, during which Caravaggio remained in the *guva*. A tribunal was meanwhile announced, to open in three days' time, during which the accused would be permitted to enter a plea of guilt or innocence. By now, Fabrizio Colonna was convinced that his friend's case was hopeless. Many of the

Knights, the Germans especially, were intensely jealous of their new comrade-in-arms, believing him to have secured membership of the order without the proper pedigree or proof of valour. They pointed to the fact that he drank too much and spent time in the company of whores.

'Unlike you, you mean?' Fabrizio had said to one of these, a bone-headed brute from Swabia. 'You are obsessed with your lineage – as if the fact that your antecedents in all four lines never had to soil their hands with honest work absolved you from every obligation of truth and charity. But be sure, my friend, when the war comes, you shall stand with me in the front line. We shall see then how deep lies your nobility.'

The next thing that happened was that Battista, alerted by Fonseca, sent word to de Wignacourt upholding the *banda capitale* in relation to the murder in Rome. Fabrizio, in response, wrote to Mario, younger brother of the late Ranuccio Tomassoni, begging him to tell the truth of what had happened in the Campo Marzio. The letter was put on a felucca bound for Rome the following day. Mario, said Fabrizio, was a man of honour. He would surely testify that Ranuccio had engaged freely in a duel, possibly over the honour of the girl he hoped to marry.

De Wignacourt, unsure how to proceed, consented to this, so that the case brought by Fonseca was placed in abeyance. Caravaggio, however, was to remain in his cell, where he could reflect on his behaviour.

Before taking action on his own account, Fabrizio made one final appeal to Fonseca.

'You know this man,' he said. 'You know that the balance of his mind is disturbed. But he is a genius, who has brought glory to our order and will continue to do so if given the chance. I beg you, do not condemn him to a felon's grave on a mere point of Knightly etiquette.'

Fonseca sneered. 'Well, Colonna,' he said, 'I cannot deny that you know wherof you speak. You yourself stand before me as a murderer. Now you beg leniency for another of your kind.'

'So you will not withdraw your charges?'

'I will see him hanged first.'

As he replied, Fabrizio gazed deep into the eyes of the Knight of Justice. 'And having done so, sir,' he said, 'you will answer to me.'

Shortly after his encounter with Fonseca, Fabrizio visited his friend, bringing food and clean water, and told him to be ready to escape the following night. 'Listen for me,' he said. 'I will tap three times on the metal cover of your cell. As soon as you hear my signal, you must summon up all your strength and be ready to leave.'

Twenty-four hours later, having sent drugged wine to the one overnight guard, so that he dozed at his post, Colonna, accompanied by Bernardo Cenci, banged three times on the metal cover of the guva with the hilt of his sword. The noise below was unmistakable. Then he drew the cover aside and lowered a rope down into the dungeon. The artist was weak from the meagre prison diet and shivering with cold. Yet somehow, with Colonna and Cenci hauling at the rope and Caravaggio hanging on for dear life, the ascent was made. Next, having replaced the cover, Colonna lowered his friend from a window down the sheer walls of the fortress towards the rocks and sea at its base. Here, a small boat lay waiting, which picked up the fugitive and conveyed him to Colonna's galley, tied up in the Grand Harbour.

The next morning at dawn, before Caravaggio was even missed, Colonna set sail for Sicily. The voyage was properly scheduled and aroused no suspicion. Six hours later, in the middle of the afternoon, they arrived off Syracuse. Fabrizio had undertaken to have his personal possessions, including three paintings, conveyed from the port to the house of his friend, the artist Mario Minniti. He would also, he said, send word of what had happened to his mother, the Marchesa, and his uncle Luigi, in Naples. In the meantime, he urged the two-time fugitive to remain hidden in Syracuse and under no circumstances to draw attention to himself. Newly fed and clothed, armed with a sword and pistol and provided with ready cash, he was disembarked into the same small boat in which he had escaped to the Grand Harbour. The oars were taken by Bernardo Cenci, to whom the artist made a solemn vow that he would do all in his power upon his return to Rome to re-establish the good name of his family. Cenci shrugged. It was clear that he did not believe in miracles. As he pushed off towards the shore, the galley continued into the harbour to pick up wine and Turkish slaves intended for the Grand Master's service.

In Valletta, the escape caused uproar. No one could explain it. Though Fonseca suspected Fabrizio's hand in the affair, he could prove nothing and was reluctant to make a second charge of Knightly dishonour, especially against a scion of the most powerful family in Italy. The escape was seen at once as an affront to the dignity of the order, which had given sanctuary to the artist and even invested him as a Knight, trusting in his reformed nature. De Wignacourt, humiliated beyond measure, felt he had no choice but to convene a tribunal of inquiry, which promptly came up with nothing. No one knew how the escape was achieved. There was no evidence of struggle and the drugged guard, a trusted man, had awakened at least an hour before the alarm was raised unaware that anything untoward had occurred.

The Grand Master next convened a meeting of the General Council of the Order at which it was agreed unanimously that Caravaggio should be deprived of his Knighthood and habit and declared an outlaw. Fonseca, as head of the Knights of Giustizia, to which Caravaggio, as a Knight of Obedience, was tied, requested permission to hunt him down. Permission was granted. According to the Council's ruling, the artist was 'expelled and thrust forth like a rotten and fetid limb from our Order and Community'.

28*
Conclave minus 4

It was after seven in the evening when Maya's father, Colonel Studer, arrived home from a joint meeting with the Vatican secret service and the Gendarmeria Vaticana, the papal police. He was in a stinking mood.

Maya looked up from her laptop on which she was reading a blog from Stuttgart about the death of Cardinal Rüttgers.

Studer got straight to the point. 'That young man of yours – the Irishman. What does he think he's up to? The Vatican security service and the Rome police suspect him of stealing historical documents from the papal archives. He has been barred from the library and warned that he is under formal investigation. In the end, I had no alternative but to reveal that my daughter and he are having … an *affair*. Can you imagine how I felt? They didn't know where to look. I was hopelessly compromised – I who have taken an oath to safeguard the Holy Father's personal security. What must they have thought? I cannot believe that you have allowed this to happen. But this cannot go on. Listen to me, Maya, I don't want you to see him anymore. Do you hear me? Not while you live under my roof.'

Maya was used to her father's occasional impersonations of a nineteenth-century martinet, which she never took entirely seriously. She drew a deep breath and started to explain what really happened.

Her father – a fair man, but a natural conservative, used to siding with the secular authority – brushed his daughter's version of events to one side. 'That's not what the security service says. And why would they lie?'

'They are not lying. But they're wrong. I don't know what's happening. But

Cardinal Bosani is not what he seems. It wouldn't be the first time in the history of the Church. Four hundred years ago, there was another Camerlengo, also not what he seems, who was secretly investigated by the Pope. Back in the late seventies, when he first came to Rome, Bosani removed the files relating to this man. These are the same files that the security people and the Rome police now say were stolen by Liam.'

'But that makes no sense, Maya. What are you saying? That Bosani is … what? Working to destroy the Church? That is the logic of what you are saying. Are you out of your mind? Do you want me to have to resign over this? Think of the disgrace. The first ever colonel of the Swiss Guard to have to surrender his post! It is unthinkable.'

Studer stormed off into his study and Maya was left wondering what on earth she could do to repair the damage. An enemy of the Church? That thought had never occurred to her. But she dismissed it almost as quickly as had her father, and for the same reason. It was preposterous. The truth was almost certainly a lot more prosaic. Bosani was just a misguided hardliner, no different from so many others she had met down the years. After several minutes, she called Dempsey on her mobile. He answered on the third ring.

'I need you to listen to me,' she began. 'I've just been talking to my father, who spent much of the afternoon with the Pope's security people discussing you. He was utterly humiliated. I feel so guilty. I've placed him in an impossible position. He's convinced we've got it all wrong. He says Bosani is exactly what he seems and everything else is a product of our imaginations.'

Dempsey interrupted her. 'I'm sorry about your father,' he began. 'I truly am. I had no intention of ever involving him in this mess. It just happened. But there are bigger issues at stake here. What if we're not wrong? What if we're right and there really is a conspiracy to undermine the Church?'

This was not what Maya wanted to hear and her voice when she replied was laced with scorn. 'A *conspiracy*? Is that the next thing? For God's sake, Liam, listen to yourself. Who are these conspirators? What do they want? Why have they decided to blame everything on you? It makes no sense.'

At the other end of the phone, Dempsey felt himself grow tense. 'I wish I could tell you, Maya. I wish I knew. My uncle doesn't know what to think. He's like your father. His every instinct is to support the Church and protect its doctrines. But what if there's a Church within a Church? What if there's something going on that has nothing to do with the last two thousand years of Christian history?'

The thought of this made Maya's head spin. 'I'm sorry, Liam, but this has to stop. My father is right and it's not fair that he should bear the burden of our arrogance. Good sense and reason seem to have gone out the window. Paranoia has taken over.'

Dempsey wasn't going to let her get away with that. 'Is it paranoid to think that Rüttgers was murdered? He was a strong, healthy man. He was determined to prevent Bosani from getting his way at the conclave. Or what about me? Was I paranoid to imagine that I had been framed by the Vatican and accused of stealing documents that had in fact been seized by Bosani in the 1970s?'

'I don't know, Liam. I don't have answers to your questions.' Maya could feel a headache coming on. 'But it's obvious that we're being drawn into an area in which we are powerless. If we carry on like this, we are the ones that will be hurt. My father, too. Is that what you want?'

Dempsey gave up. He didn't know what to think. 'Maybe you're right,' he said, lamely. 'I'll call you tomorrow.'

'Don't bother,' she said.

On the opposite side of St Peter's Square to the Swiss army barracks, O'Malley was calling in some favours. It would have been easy for him to go the Vatican library and use his privileged access to make inquiries about Bosani and his sinister predecessor, Battista. But he didn't want to arouse suspicion or provoke a response. Instead, after a lengthy meeting with the provincial general for Poland, and just as Studer set out for his appointment with the Vatican security service, he called an old friend in the Rome police whose experience of the Vatican went back three decades.

Ispettore Superiore Raffaele Aprea was the sort of man O'Malley found it easy to get along with. He was a lapsed Catholic, wary of the Vatican's special pleading down the years, but he was also a realist, who knew better than to offend the Curia. They had met fifteen years before when O'Malley was vice-rector of the Irish College. The Irishman had helped him with an investigation into the murder of a paedophile priest, and since his return to Rome as head of the Jesuits they had dined together on the first Tuesday of each month.

At O'Malley's request, they met for lunch in their usual restaurant off the Via Cavour, next to the basilica of Santa Maria Maggiore. As soon as they had ordered, Aprea, a large, shambling figure, whose burly physique concealed a mind sharp as a switchblade, invited O'Malley to unburden himself. 'I'll consider your penance afterwards,' he said. When the priest was done, the chief inspector sat back in his chair, hands clasped on his stomach. To begin with, he said, he wasn't impressed by Dempsey's *modus operandi*. 'What did he think he was doing? Did he think the Vatican wouldn't mind that he was using their computer like that and prying into business that doesn't concern him?'

O'Malley poured the wine, an expensive Barolo they would each regret ordering as soon as the bill came. 'I'm not defending my nephew's way of doing things, Rafi. He's young and impulsive. But he's no thief.'

Aprea chewed very deliberately on a morsel of osso buco, then put down his fork. 'And you honestly think he's on to something?'

'Yes, I do. Quite what that something is remains to be seen. But I can't believe the Vatican would be leaning on him like this if they didn't have something to hide.'

'In my experience, the Vatican leans on anyone and everyone they don't like. They way they see it, it's like a scattergun. If you spread enough shot around, you're bound to hit something.'

The Irishman pulled at his dog collar, which he still found constricting even after forty-five years. 'Tell me honestly, Rafi, do you think there are real criminals inside the walls of the Holy See? I mean the sort of people who would stop at nothing.'

'You tell me, Declan. You're the Black Pope.'

'Don't give me that. Because I have to tell you, it worries me that there may be individuals working right in the bowels of the system – priests, bishops, even cardinals – who consider that a crime committed in God's name is no crime at all.'

'Well, of course,' the policeman replied, 'it all depends on what is a crime and what is not. The Vatican is a sovereign state, after all. What's a crime in the Via Cavour may not rate the same definition in the Via del Governatorato. And even if it is a crime, it's no sin – not if you've got your confessor on hand or you believe you have a special line through to God.'

'Do you have anything in particular in mind?'

'You know as well as I do that the death of John Paul I was no accident.'

'I know no such thing.'

The two men looked at each other, each sipping at their wine. Rüttgers' final, mysterious diary entry had been looping through his head for the last few days: *The question is, who – or what – controls Bosani?* O'Malley pressed his fingertips to his forehead, as if trying to deter a migraine. 'Even if I agreed with you,' he said, 'is there any way to prove it?'

Aprea shook his head. 'After all these years? No chance. Even if they'd let us in to open an investigation – which they wouldn't – we'd run straight up against a brick wall. Most of those who knew the answer are dead. The rest are keeping quiet.'

'*Omerta?*'

'You said it, not me.'

'But what if there's something going on now; something that we could prevent? What if there's a conspiracy to elect a pope who would provoke war with the Muslim world?'

As he spoke, O'Malley could see his friend draw back in disbelief. Perhaps he hadn't explained himself properly. 'Look,' he said, 'I know what I'm saying must sound like the ravings of an old fool, but I'm really worried.'

Aprea leaned back in. 'Maybe the problem is that you are too close and cannot see the wood for the trees. The way I see it, a pope who stands up for the Catholic Church against Islam may be ill-advised. He may even be crazy. But unless there's something you're not telling me, there's nothing criminal about it.'

This detached appraisal evoked a sigh from O'Malley. 'You're right,' he said. 'But there is a background to this. I suppose I'd better tell you everything.'

'That would be useful.'

Only when O'Malley had finished his explanation did he notice that, between them, he and Aprea had finished off the Barolo.

The chief inspector ran his stubby fingers through his thinning hair. 'I think we should order two grappas.' He signalled to the waiter.

'So, can you help?' O'Malley asked once the waiter had brought the drinks.

'I can try. But I'll tell you this much now. This can't be true, Declan – it just can't be. One cardinal murdering another; the Secret Archive framing the nephew of the Father General of the Jesuits; the Camerlengo consorting with a known Islamist extremist; the whole Church being dragged into supporting a lunatic as pope. If that's the way things really are, the whole world's in trouble and we've got – what? – less than a week to stop it.'

'Three days, to be accurate,' O'Malley said.

While they waited for their desserts, Aprea used his secure mobile to ask a colleague in the anti-terrorist police, DIGOS, if there had been any reports recently of Yilmaz Hakura or of Hizb ut-Tahrir operating in Rome. The man called back three minutes later. An undercover officer working in a housing project in the north of the city claimed to have seen him outside a hardline mosque about a month earlier, talking to some of the usual suspects. But he had vanished before backup arrived and the only evidence was a fuzzy photograph taken by the undercover officer using the camera on his mobile phone. Image enhancement suggested that the man might well have been Hakura – which would fit in with the prison protest and the bombing of the Lateran cathedral. But no further sightings had been made and the trail was now cold.

Next, Aprea called an expert from the Polizia Postale division of the Questura, responsible for computer crime. The officer was to join him in an hour's time at the office of the prefect of the Secret Archive, Monsignor Asproni. Aprea telephoned Asproni himself and told him that he and a colleague would be along shortly to continue the investigation of the missing papers case. At 3.35 precisely, the specialist, complete with bag of tricks, sat down at the Monsignor's desk and logged on. Aprea observed him closely, acutely aware of his own technical limitations. After a couple of minutes, the specialist emitted a satisfied grunt. The 'file missing' signal attached to the Battista papers had been overlaid on top of a previous indicator, since deleted. Using software developed by Britain's MI5, he was able to recall the original message, thus confirming Dempsey's claim that the Battista file had gone missing years before. Aprea said nothing to the prefect, but later, in Asproni's office, asked him who in the library had the authority and access to amend computer entries, especially when a file went missing or had maybe been stolen.

The Monsignor took off his glasses and rubbed his eyes.

'There could be five or six such people,' he said, 'plus myself and the vice-prefect. But that's only the start. Before any substantive change can be made to the record, it is necessary first to inform me or my deputy. And any kind of investigation that's carried out would, needless to say, have to have my personal sanction.'

Pressed to do so, the prefect then drew up a list of the names of those with authority to make online changes.

'Could a switch be made without your knowledge?' Aprea asked.

'Of course,' the priest replied. 'But that would be quite irregular and most unethical.'

'*Assolutamente*,' Aprea said. He thanked Asproni for being so helpful and told him they'd be in touch.

Outside, he asked the specialist, 'What do you think?'

'I think anything's possible. It's a clever enough system, but the ones in charge aren't necessarily the ones who know how it works.'

'So you think we can rule out the Monsignor and his number two.'

'I'd say so. But who knows? Maybe they've been to night classes.'

'And Dempsey?'

'He's in the clear – at least so far as the charge of theft is concerned. Those papers went missing back in the 1970s, before he was even born. Unless he's invented a time machine, the most they can get him for is unauthorized use of a computer.'

Aprea thanked his colleague and took out his mobile to give O'Malley the news.

At the same moment, at a terminal on the library's reception desk, a message flashed up. The Battista file had been tampered with again. The security guard on duty picked up the telephone.

That evening, as he left his office to head home to his nearby apartment, O'Malley was surprised to find his nephew sitting on the Curia's front steps.

'Liam! What are you doing here? I was about to call you.'

'I had a row with Maya.'

'Aaah! What about?'

'A bit awkward, actually. Her father was called to a meeting with the Vatican security service today. They told him about their inquiries and he had to admit to them that the person they are currently investigating in connection with the alleged theft of historical documents from the Secret Archive – i.e. me – is currently conducting a relationship with his daughter.'

'Well, I can see how that wouldn't look good.'

'No. And it didn't look any better when they told him I was embroiled in some sort of smear campaign against Bosani.'

'Oh, dear Lord. The poor man. I must call him.'

'I wouldn't, if I were you. The long and the short of it is that Maya thinks I'm mad, or paranoid, or maybe both, and she doesn't want to hear any more about anti-Islamic conspiracies. Matter of fact, she doesn't want to hear anything more from me, full stop.'

'She'll get over it.'

'You're speaking from experience, are you?'

'That's not fair, Liam.'

'No, I suppose not. I just wish I hadn't let you talk me into this in the first place.'

'I had no idea it would come to this.'

Dempsey stood up. 'Yeah … well, it's serious now. Where are you headed?'

'Back to my apartment. I've got a lot to think about – more after what you've just told me.'

'I'll walk with you.'

'Fair enough.' They turned right, down the hill past the Santo Spirito hospital, towards the Jesuit Residence, named for Sant Pietro Canisio. 'As it happens,' O'Malley said, 'I've got some good news for you.'

'Oh yes?'

'Yes. A friend of mine, a top detective with the Rome police, has looked into your case. He got a computer expert who was able to confirm your claim that the missing papers had in fact disappeared back in the 1970s – before you were born. So you're off the hook.'

At this, Dempsey brightened considerably. 'Do the Vatican crowd know about this?'

'They will,' his uncle said. 'My friend says he'll make the call himself.'

'So I'd have a clean slate?'

'Clean as a whistle.'

'That's something, I suppose. So what else is new? Anything more on Bosani?'

'Do you really want to know?'

'Tell me. Otherwise I'll just spend all my time thinking about Maya and how stupid I've been.'

'Well, if you're sure.' O'Malley related the story of Rüttgers' diary and how the provost of the German College had denied its very existence. The journal, he said, was now in the hands of the Camerlengo.

'Interesting. So what you're saying is that Rüttgers didn't just disagree with Bosani, he doubted the basis of his faith?'

'That's what he wrote.'

'So who's this fellow Hakura?'

'A bad lot. One of the most dangerous Islamists around. They say he learned his trade in Baghdad and wants to introduce suicide bombings to Europe.'

'Jesus!'

'Exactly.'

'And Rüttgers believed Hukura met Bosani?'

'You can see why I'm worried.'

'But why would he do that?'

'I've no idea.'

'It'd be like Churchill inviting Stalin to celebrate the setting up of NATO. This gets curiouser and curiouser. Anything else?'

O'Malley told him about the portrait of Cardinal Battista in Bosani's private office.

'If you ask me,' said Dempsey, 'Battista's the key to all this. According to Caravaggio, it was Battista who betrayed Christ, and now we have Bosani keeping a portrait of the same fellow in a place of honour in his private apartment – a portrait that ought to be worth millions but doesn't officially exist.'

'Yes,' said O'Malley. 'The problem is, we don't know what the link between them is. If we work that one out, we'll have a window into what it is that Bosani's planning.'

'A tough one.'

'Very. So what do you say? Are you game? It's entirely up to you. I wouldn't dream of pressuring you.'

Dempsey laughed at that one. He was in two minds. On the one hand, with an intensity that he could feel in the pit of his stomach, he realized that he didn't want to lose Maya, a girl unlike any other he had ever known. She had made her opinion on the Bosani business admirably clear. On the other, how could he abandon his uncle and walk away from a possible rendezvous with history? He thought hard, then came to a decision. 'I'll help you,' he said. 'But on one condition.'

'Name it.'

'I'd like you to call Maya for me and explain what's happened. Maybe if she hears it from you, she'll simmer down.'

'I'd be glad to. The three of us could meet up, maybe have dinner. Like you say, the whole business might not seem so crazy coming from the Black Pope. I'd make it clear to her that the Rome police are now convinced of your innocence and that, in any case, we wouldn't expect her to do anything to compromise her father.'

'Would that work?'

'In my experience,' O'Malley said, smiling.

'In that case,' said Dempsey, 'I'm in.'

O'Malley did not even try to conceal the relief he felt. With Liam at his side and Aprea sleuthing in the background, maybe they were in with a chance. But the Vatican was a labyrinth, in which it was easy to lose sight of reality. Or maybe it was more like one of those Russian dolls, in which different personalities and identities were constantly revealed and you never knew what was true and what was lies. Intrigue, not faith, was the fuel that propelled the governance of the Church, and those who stood against it weren't assured of their survival.

It was something O'Malley had known for a long time. Ever since 1978: the Year of the Three Popes.

29 *
25 September 1978

John Paul I had been on the Throne of St Peter's for thirty-one days. Declan O'Malley, SJ, was in his third year as vice-rector of the Irish College in Rome. During their previous meeting, the two men had discussed a fresh approach to the relationship beween Islam and the Catholic Church. But then events beyond the new Pope's control had moved to centre stage.

The phone rang a few minutes after eight in the evening, just as O'Malley was sitting down to dinner in the college's small refectory on the Via dei Santi Quattro. All calls after six o'clock were switched through to the office of the rector, Monsignor Eamonn Marron, as well as to the old bakelite instrument that stood on the sideboard in the priests' dining room. After a moment, Marron, a White Father, came back and tapped O'Malley on the arm. 'It's for you,' he said. 'The Pope.'

O'Malley spluttered into the glass of wine he had just raised to his lips. 'You're having me on,' he said.

'I'm not,' said Marron, smiling. 'It really is the Holy Father, and if I were you I wouldn't keep him waiting.'

The Jesuit jumped up, knocking over his chair, and ran to the phone. 'Holy Father,' he began, speaking Italian, 'what an unexpected honour.'

'I hope I'm not disturbing you,' came the voice, sonorous and musical, down the line from the apartment high over St Peter's Square.

'Good God, no, not at all. But whatever can I do for you? You have only to ask.'

'I would like you to come over to my private lodging. Can you do that?'

'Of course, Holy Father, of course. Do you mean now?'

'If that would be convenient.'

'I'm on my way.'

O'Malley was in such a rush that he didn't replace the receiver properly and it was left to the rector, standing behind him, to tell His Holiness that his intended visitor had already quit the room. 'Most kind of you, Monsignor,' the Pope said. 'Father O'Malley is, I think, a man of action. Is that the phrase? I shall await his arrival. In the meantime, please pass on my blessings to all your staff and residents and know that I intend, God willing, to visit the college as soon as it can be arranged. Goodnight, my son.'

The rector muttered his thanks, bade the Pope goodnight and put down the phone. Then he walked back to the dining table in a daze.

Luckily for O'Malley, there was a cab rank just around the corner from the college and the Irishman was quickly on his way across the city. Ten minutes later, as the taxi, an elderly Mercedes, swept along the Via Conciliazione, Mussolini's homage to civic and religious virtue connecting Rome directly to the Vatican, he couldn't imagine what it was that the Pope wished to talk to him about. They had corresponded once, years before, about the peculiar relationship between the Ottomans and the Venetian Republic. But that couldn't be it. And on the single occasion on which they had actually met, in the Gesù, six weeks ago, it had mainly been the oppressive summer weather they had discussed, as well, he remembered, as a few words about the increased violence in Northern Ireland. But remarks he had made about the situation in Iran had struck O'Malley at the time as particularly far-sighted. The then patriarch remarked that the Muslim revival, based on oil, plus the expected coming to power of Ayatollah Khomeini in Tehran would spell deep trouble for the West. The resulting revival of Shia Islam would have long-term consequences, he said. Since then, the Lebanese civil war had broken out, resulting in the shelling of Christian communities by the Syrians, the invasion of the south of the country by Israel and, in the end, the expulsion of the PLO. O'Malley had been particularly concerned by the kidnapping and murder that year of two Irish peacekeepers by the South Lebanon militia, officered by Christians but increasingly Shiite in composition. The Arab oil producers were meanwhile consolidating their use of the oil weapon against the West, demanding a new attitude from America and Europe in their dealings with Islam. At the same time, demonstrations by pro-Khomeini zealots in Tehran were growing daily more intense and the feeling was that the Shah would not survive the year. Luciani was deeply concerned by the deepening sense of crisis in the world. But with the upcoming conclave dominating everybody's thoughts, including his, there had been no time for more than a cursory discussion of the events and where they were leading.

O'Malley wondered if the new Pope wanted to revisit these themes. If so, his own prospects could be much altered in the days ahead.

They were almost there. 'Drop me here,' he said to the cab driver as they approached the entrance to St Peter's Square. 'I think I can manage the rest on my own.'

He got out, remembering to include a small tip along with the fare, and walked through the gateway. At the far side, he looked again in admiration and astonishment at the vast piazza, with St Peter's Basilica straight ahead, its dome oddly receding the closer you got to it, and the Apostolic Palace to the right. Picking up his pace, he approached Bernini's Colonnade and eventually halted at an enormous bronze door.

All of a sudden he realized that he didn't have a written invitation, or indeed any proof of who he was. He had never owned a car, so he didn't even have a driving licence. The two guards in their flamboyant blue and orange costumes closed their halberds against him.

'I'm here to see the Pope,' he began, somewhat unconvincingly.

At this, an older man stepped forward, dressed in a smart suit, with a small papal badge pinned to his right lapel. 'Father O'Malley, is it?' O'Malley nodded. 'I'm Colonel Von Altishofen, commandant of the Guard. Please step this way; the Holy Father is expecting you.'

Two minutes later, after walking through several marbled halls and ascending a set of winding stairs, they arrived at a broad corridor with a tiled floor. The colonel led the way, then halted in front of a simple door. The two guardsmen on duty moved smartly to one side and the commandant pushed down on the handle.

The papal reception room was certainly comfortable, and definitely spacious, with some fine furniture and a collection of religious paintings that were obviously of the first rank, including, he thought, one by Raphael. But this, evidently, was not where he would meet the Pope. Instead, the colonel knocked twice on a second door before ushering him into a much smaller room containing two sofas, a couple of armchairs, an inlaid armoire, a coffee table and various lamps, as well as a surprisingly large television set. On one of the sofas, nearest the window, sat the Supreme Pontiff of the Holy Apostolic and Universal Church. He looked small and frail, dressed in his white silk robes, but offered a friendly smile to his visitor.

'Father Declan O'Malley,' said the colonel stiffly.

'Thank you, Colonel. Most kind of you. That will be all.'

And then they were alone.

It was immediately clear to O'Malley that his host was under considerable strain. His skin was almost deathly pale and his eyes looked exhausted, as if he had been reading constantly and had no time for sleep. Three key issues dominated his thinking. First, the shadowy P2 Masonic Lodge, linking certain highly placed figures in the Hierarchy, even the Curia, to the Mafia and international banking, had to be confronted without delay. Second, the spread of so-called Liberation Theology in Latin America was threatening papal authority. 'This unholy mix of Marxism and Christian thinking cannot be tolerated,' Luciani told O'Malley. 'And it is your own order, the Jesuits, who must find the way forward.' But it was in connection with the third question – what the Pope judged to be an impending conflict between the Church and Islam – that he had invited the Irishman to join him.

Seated on an armchair opposite the pontiff, O'Malley was taken aback by the extreme candour of Luciani's words, evidencing, he feared, a startling naivety. Surely, he told himself, the Holy Father must know that he couldn't take on all the problems of the Catholic Church in a single campaign, however well-intentioned. That wasn't how it worked. It was, rather, a matter of give and take, of reciprocity and compromise.

But it was not for him, even as a not-so-humble priest, to contradict the wishes of Christ's Vicar on Earth. 'I am at your disposition, Your Holiness,' he said simply. 'How can I help?'

The Pope, seeming to appreciate a sympathetic voice, told his guest that he still remembered the monograph O'Malley had written about the historical relationship between the Ottoman Empire and the Republic of Venice, which he said spoke rationally and compassionately about the problems faced by both sides.

'I made inquiries and was told that you spent several years in Constantinople – I'm sorry, I mean of course, Istanbul – and were considered an authority on Muslim society.'

'That,' said O'Malley, 'was before I was exiled to Milwaukee.'

The Pope nodded. 'Ah yes. A retreat house, I believe. How was that?'

'Actually, I enjoyed it very much.'

'I'm glad to hear it. Those of us who spend so much of our lives in the great metropolises dealing with institutional matters can learn much from pastoral work.'

O'Malley offered a half-smile. 'But not, alas, the imperatives of inter-faith dialogue. The truth of the matter, Holiness, is that I'm out of touch these days. I try to keep abreast, naturally. I read what I can. But I'm afraid my global contribution has been, well … limited.'

'I understand,' the Pope said, blinking hard as he spoke. 'What is important is that you know the history of Islam. You've studied what really happened, not simply imbibed the myths. That is rare. And you have an Islamic sensibility, I think, that guards against prejudice.'

O'Malley did not demur from this analysis. He was not without ego. He was also intrigued. 'In what way may I be of assistance?' he asked again.

The Pope clasped his hands in front of him. As he spoke, the vast bulk of St Peter's Basilica, built over the tomb of the Apostle, loomed to his right through the open drawing-room window. 'In the past,' he began, 'Islam always advanced in parallel with an empire. There were the Turks, of course – your friends, the Ottomans. But also, before them, the Seljuks, the Umayyads, the Abbasids and, in Persia, the Safavids. Things are different today. Conventional conquest is no longer realistically possible, so the caliphate, desired by many, must be established by other means.' He turned his head sharply, so that he now faced O'Malley directly. 'How do you assess the situation in Iran?'

'I think the Shah is finished. And when the ayatollahs take over, anything is possible. I would expect an Islamic republic to be established, with strict application of sharia law. The next few years should prove critical.'

'Exactly,' the Pope said. 'And when this happens, the tumult will quickly spread and Europe will once again find itself a battleground. I have no wish to be alarmist. Muslims worship the same God as we do and have the same rights and freedoms. But I am concerned that if we do not open our minds, and our hearts, soon, it may be too late to prevent the situation from getting out of hand.'

O'Malley was fascinated by what he was hearing. It was said by some that the Holy Father's problem was that he was provincial and out of touch. Apparently this criticism was well wide of the mark.

The Pope twisted the fisherman's ring on the fourth finger of his right hand, as if it did not quite fit. 'Have you visited the site of Rome's new mosque?' he asked.

'Yes, Holiness. Indeed I have, and I believe it will be the most beautiful, as well as the largest, in Europe.'

The pontiff's eyes narrowed behind the thick lenses of his glasses. 'But why so large? Do you know that it can be seen from the terrace of the Castel Sant'Angelo? I looked for myself. It seems that they wish to challenge us. Is it possible that the next great global conflict, after the Millennium, will not be between belief and unbelief, as has been the case in the present century, but rather between what remains of Christian certainty and a resurgent, possibly militant Islam?'

'I do not just think it possible,' O'Malley replied. 'I consider it almost inescapable. That is why it is so important that we here in Europe, especially, perhaps, here in the Holy See, demonstrate our repect for the faith of Mohammad. We should make it clear that while we cleave as ever to our belief in the Lord Jesus and His Holy Mother, we nevertheless acknowledge that we are all children of the one God, equally deserving of His mercy.'

The Pope's face lit up at this, making him look particularly vulnerable. 'That is it exactly,' he said, clapping his hands together. There was a pause. 'But there must be a *quid pro quo* from the Muslim world. Do you recall that at our last meeting, in the Gesù, I mentioned my regret that the patriarchate of Constantinople had been abolished?'

'I remember it well.'

'I intend to restore it.'

'But that's wonderful.'

'I'm glad you approve. But whereas in the past, certainly since 1453, it was a vestigial archdiocese, almost an honorific, my proposal is that it should become a true bridge between East and West, between the Church and Islam. Of course, an archbishop – or in this case a patriarch – must have a flock. He must have churches. It has always seemed to me a tragedy that the parishes of Asia Minor, so closely identified with Paul and Barnabas, have for the last five hundred years been allowed to wither on the vine. I wish to promote some recovery in their position.'

'That may not be easy, Holiness.'

'No, but the Turks wish some day to join the European Community. This could be one means of smoothing their path.'

'Even so ...'

'Even so, there are two sides to a street. There are things we can offer Islam and things they can offer to us. We need to learn to do more than co-exist. We need to recognize our common heritage.'

'You should have been a politician, Holiness.'

The Pope looked away. 'But I am, Father General – as are you.' Again, he twisted at his ring. 'You know, by the way, that I wanted to be a Jesuit when I was young?'

O'Malley was genuinely surprised. 'No, I hadn't heard that.'

'It was in 1933. I was at the seminary in Belluno. My bishop, Monsignor Giosuè Cattarossi, who had confirmed me fourteen years before and knew me well, didn't think I was suitable material.'

'He must have had a premonition that your life would take a different course.'

'No doubt. Now tell me, when does the next issue of *La Civiltà Cattolica* come out?'

The reference was to the Jesuits' principle newspaper, edited each week in Rome. 'Next Thursday, I believe,' O'Malley replied.

'Would there be time, do you think, to include an article by me on this subject?'

'On the Patriarchate? Of course, Holiness. I have no influence myself. The Society has always considered the paper a prerogative of the Italian membership. But I cannot imagine that they ...'

'Excellent. Very good. Perhaps you could ask the editor to contact me.'

'Of course.'

It seemed a natural end to the conversation and, after a short pause, O'Malley rose to leave. As he did so, the Pope spoke again, appearing, the Irishman thought, a little hesitant.

'One more thing, before you go. Have you met Bishop Bosani?'

'From the Secretariat for Non-Christians? No, Holiness, I have not yet had the pleasure.'

'Ha! Yes. "Pleasure" is one way of putting it. He is very ... energetic. Full of ideas. Not, though, the easiest man to get along with. He does not approve, I think, of restoring the Patriarchate. I get the feeling that he is pursuing his own agenda, which he prefers not to confide to me. So be it. What matters is that I am looking for a personal adviser on relations with the Muslim world – a cross between a representative and a confidant. And I should like to know, Father O'Malley, if would you be prepared to accept the role? The choice is between you and Bosani, who, it must be said, has his advocates within the Curia. He knows how the system works and which levers can be pulled with what results. But I have to say, at this stage, I favour you.'

O'Malley drew back, genuinely moved. 'You do me great honour, Your Holiness, but I ... I beg you to reconsider ...'

This show of reluctance made the Pope giggle. It was a musical, almost child-like sound. 'No, no, my son. Diffidence did not work for me and it will not work for you either. Put simply, it would be a great weight off my mind if you were to stand next to me on what I am sure will become one of the great issues in the years ahead. You would have to be promoted, of course. A Monsignor at the very least.'

'How is that possible? I am a Jesuit ...'

'... And thus bound by your oath of allegiance to me.'

To this there was no answer. The new Pope may have been straight as a die, but he was also slippery as an eel. As a courtesy, he told O'Malley, he would raise the issue of his appointment as a senior adviser with the cardinal secretary for Non-Christians. 'I wish to restore the Patriarchate of Constantinople as quickly as possible. And I intend it to be residential, with proper diocesan authority. A true bridge into the Islamic world – just as the new mosque here in Rome connects Muslims to the Vatican. To achieve this, we have to deal with Turkish and Muslim sensitivities, and I believe that you are the perfect man for the job. Get back to me as quickly as you can. Do I make myself clear?'

O'Malley nodded. He said he would speak with the editor of *La Civiltà Cattolica*, as well as to the head of the Irish College and the Superior General of the Jesuits, and report back in person at the end of the week.

Three days later, it made no difference. The Pope was dead.

30*
Conclave minus 3

Father Visco was disturbed when he read the report from Monsignor Asproni, prefect of the Secret Archive, indicating a wider police inquiry into the missing papers than he had expected – or wanted. He was puzzled. Scajola and Drago, young and devout, from good Catholic families, were personally selected for their loyalty to the Camerlengo, as well as their discretion. He telephoned both men on their personal mobiles to find out what was going on and was assured that neither raised the issue of the theft with anyone else.

'If I were you,' Scajola said, 'I would find out who Dempsey has been talking to – or maybe his uncle.'

'Agreed. But I need you to discover what information concerning this matter has reached your superiors. Drago should do the same.'

'Understood.'

Minutes afterwards, Visco knocked on the door of Bosani's office and walked in, taking with him his internal Vatican post, a small pot of espresso and a Meissen cup and saucer – all on a silver tray.

'I hope I am not interrupting, Eminence,' he said.

The Camerlengo looked up. 'Cesare! Not at all. Come in, come in. How are you? I must say, I feel confident today. Things are moving in our direction.' He paused, eyeing the priest up and down. 'But I know you and I recognize that hangdog expression. I hope you are not the bearer of bad tidings.'

'Not at all, Eminence,' the secretary replied briskly. There was no point in spoiling the cardinal's mood. 'Everything is in hand.'

The older man looked doubtful. 'So what do you have for me – apart from that coffee, I mean?'

'Oh … yes. My apologies.' He stepped forward and placed the tray on the cardinal's desk.

Bosani poured a half-cup of espresso and raised it to his lips, breathing in the rich aroma. 'Do you know, Cesare, one day – probably long after we are gone – Italians will corner the market in coffee throughout the caliphate.'

'It would make up for the decline in the wine market, I suppose.'

'Indeed. Pope Clement VIII had the right idea. Did you know that he came under pressure to ban it as the "bitter invention of Satan" simply because of its popularity among Muslims? His Holiness – the man, we must not forget, who promoted my illustrious predecessor, Battista – was not to be cheated. Coffee was so good, he ruled, that he would cheat the Devil by baptizing it.'

'I was unaware of that.'

'That doesn't surprise me, Cesare. For you are all business. That is your strength. So what do you have for me today? Have we heard from Delacroix and Salgado?'

'Their letters are at the top of your pile. They were hand-delivered five minutes ago.'

'Excellent. So there's nothing further to report?'

'Nothing that should concern you.'

'I'm glad to hear it. But remember, if that young man Dempsey continues to give us trouble, you should not hesitate to call on Franco.'

'I'm hoping it won't come to that.'

'So are we all. The Prophet – peace be upon Him – offered mercy to all, far and near, friend and enemy. But he also knew when to strike in defence of the faith. You understand me?'

'Perfectly.'

'That is good. Now leave me to read the letters from Their Eminences.'

As soon as his secretary left, clicking the door behind him, Bosani picked up a monogrammed paper knife from the paraphenalia arranged in front of him and slit open the letters from the French and Spanish cardinals. There were times, he had to confess, when he almost didn't want the Church to fall. His life here in Rome was almost … perfect. But God's will be done. He prised out the first letter – on scented paper, he noted – and began to read.

He had not been wrong about the two prelates. Though mindful of the strength of the Muslim lobby in their countries, they could see the benefits accruing from a policy that pitted the Catholic Church against the increasing arrogance of Islam. More to the point, perhaps, they were glad to note that, in the event of the arrival on the Throne of Peter of Bosani's candidate, places would be found for them in the uppermost reaches of the Curia. All priests divided into those who could devote themselves to pastoral care and those who were, in essence, managers. In Bosani's long experience, managers were increasingly in the majority. It was hard to care deeply, day after day, about a flock most of whom no longer even believed in the Christian story. Secularism now had such a grip across Europe that priests, instead of being central to their communities, were isolated and often lonely. The French and Spanish cardinals may have risen to the top of their national hierarchies, but they, too, had to face up to the reality of their irrelevance in the twenty-first century.

It would be different when the caliphate was restored. There would be respect for religion, which would once again be at the heart of society.

Bosani's one regret – though he did not expect it to to affect him personally – was the lack in Islam of a recognized priesthood, with an upwardly mobile power. To that extent, he had to admit, he was a Vatican man through and through. But then again, who knew how things would evolve in the future. Perhaps when the Vatican, twenty years from now, became the centre of European Islam and St Peter's was transformed into the new Hagia Sophia, the values of sound management and good organization would enter into the soul of Islam.

In the meantime, Delacroix and Salgado were content. He smiled and once more congratulated himself on his ability to see right into the hearts of his colleagues. Ten minutes later, he pressed the large button on his telephone console. Visco shimmered in like a ghost. This time he carried with him a small basin of hot water. A simple white towel hung from his left arm.

'Good news,' the Camerlengo announced. 'Our friends Delacroix and Salgado are safely on board. They will vote for our man and, as the primates of France and Spain, will surely bring most, if not all, of their fellow countrymen with them.'

'Allah be praised!'

'Precisely.' Bosani held his hands out in front of him, like a surgeon about to scrub up. Visco placed the basin of water on the desk and waited with the towel while the cardinal washed his face and hands. Next, he removed his shoes and socks and washed his feet. As soon as he was done, the prince of the Church rose from his chair. Visco, himself barefoot, had already fetched the prayer mats and rolled them out on the floor, facing Mecca.

'Is the door locked?'

'Of course.'

'Then let us remember our God and seek His guidance.'

It was the middle of the afternoon when Visco heard back from Sergeant Drago. In order to further his inquiries, he had, he said, managed to place a 'bug' in Dempsey's telephone at the apartment on the Via della Penitenza.

'Doesn't he used a mobile?'

'Local calls are free. It makes sense when he's at home.'

'And ..?'

'And he left a message this afternoon on the voicemail of a young woman.'

'Which young woman?'

'Well, Father, that's the strangest part. We traced the number and it turned out she was Maya Studer, the daughter of Colonel Otto Studer, commandant of the Swiss Guard.'

'*Merda!*'

'What was that, Father?'

'Nothing. You are sure of this?'

'Quite certain.'

'And what was the message?'

'It was to tell her to join him and his uncle – the Father General – tonight at the Caffè Giolitti.'

'The Giolitti? What time?'

'Eight o'clock.'

'Was that all?'

'I'm afraid so. Like you say, Father, most people these days use their mobiles. And listening in to those is … what is it the Americans say? … above my pay grade.'

'Very well. But keep me informed.'

'Of course, Father.'

Visco briefly debated with himself whether or not to tell Bosani about this latest melancholy discovery. He would have to, he decided. It was unavoidable. But not yet. Not until he had something to report. Instead, he called Franco on the cheap, pre-paid mobile he used for the purpose – a different one each time.

The assassin took the call in his exclusive downtown gym, where he had been working out for most of the afternoon. Later, after he had showered and changed, he planned to head out to a club in Trastevere where two of his younger associates and a group of well-brought-up young girls – one of them was the daughter of a cabinet minister – would be waiting.

'*Pronto!*'

'His Eminence begs a favour.'

'I am at your service.'

'The usual terms.'

'Of course.'

Visco then told him about Dempsey and O'Malley and the danger they posed to the election of a new anti-Islamic, pro-Italian Pope.

'We not not require you at this stage to deal finally with Dempsey. But there is no doubt that he is a thorn in our flesh. I need to know what he knows and what insights he may have into the nature of our campaign.'

Franco thought about this. 'What if I find that they have discovered your plans and intend to frustrate them? Time, after all, is pressing.'

'In that event, we leave the final decision to you. But in respect of Dempsey only. Do not approach O'Malley.'

'Understood.'

'You will be remembered in our prayers, my son.'

'And in my bank account.'

'As you say.'

'Then please tell His Eminence that I am on the case.'

'And may God go with you.'

A storm – rare this early in the season – was breaking over Rome. Dempsey had set out on foot to meet Maya and his uncle, expecting another balmy summer's evening, and was wearing only light cotton trousers, open-toed sandals and a t-shirt. But dark clouds were already racing in from the northwest as he closed his apartment door, and by the time he reached the Ponte Mazzini the first drum-rolls of thunder had begun to reverberate across the roofs and towers, followed by prolonged and heavy rain. *Like bloody Ireland*, he thought, as he hurried along, keeping to the inside edges of the pavements, dodging in and out of colonnades.

He didn't notice that he was being followed, at a discreet distance, by a stocky, thickset man dressed in a light-blue suit that, though crumpled and marked by sweat, looked as if it had cost its owner a small fortune. Franco Luchesse had been as good as his word. He had arrived at Dempsey's apartment less than a minute before the Irishman set out for wherever he was going. The ex-Special Forces sergeant hadn't been sure how things would proceed. If the Irishman had been home, he would have buzzed through on the entry phone, then, once the door was opened, shouldered his way in and 'persuaded' him to tell him everything that he knew – a sequence of events that could only have one outcome: the subject's death. He would have enjoyed that. Alternatively, had the apartment been empty, he would have made himself a sandwich, maybe had a glass of wine, and waited. As it was, Dempsey had come bounding up the steps just as he was checking to see there was nobody about. This had left him with no other option than to follow him – something he had become surprisingly good at over the years.

Dempsey was now scurrying along the Via del Pellegrino, still dodging the rain. O'Malley hadn't let him down. He had called Maya and explained to her that his nephew had been cleared by the police of the theft of Vatican documents. Afterwards, with her permission, he had spoken to her father and assured him that neither he nor Liam were engaged in activities in any way contrary to the interest of the College of Cardinals, still less the Catholic Church. Studer had rather grumpily accepted what he was told. He was, after all, a good Catholic and O'Malley was, after all, the Superior General of the Jesuits. As a result, Liam and Maya had been reconciled, which pleased everybody, except, possibly, Studer. A gathering at the Giolitti, originally intended to affect this reconciliation, was thus redefined. Now it would be a council of war.

By the time Dempsey reached the Pantheon, there was hardly anyone in the square. Everybody had crowded inside the cafés and bars, avoiding the unexpected downpour that danced off the cobbles and poured in sheets off the awnings. Running his fingers through his hair and brushing off his neck and shoulders, he walked on up the narrow Via Maddalena and turned right into the Via degli Uffici del Vicaro. The Giolitti, a favourite meeting place for Romans for more than a hundred years, was just a few metres along on the right-hand side.

He went in, past the ice-cream counter and turned left into the main *salone*, hung with crystal chandeliers.

'Over here, Liam!'

He looked down the rows of tables. Uncle Declan had secured one of the favoured window seats out by the far wall, overlooking the street. Perhaps they had recognized him as the 'Black Pope'. Being a Jesuit, even in these hard, secular times, was no disadvantage in Rome. Maya was seated next to him. She looked stunning.

He made his way through the throng of customers, dodging the waiters in their white jackets. 'What sort of weather do you call this?' he asked of no one in particular.

'A good night for the ducks,' his uncle said. 'Sit down. We saved you a seat.'

Maya stood up and kissed him lightly on both cheeks – a habit that still entranced him. She was dressed in a short denim skirt and a white, patterned t-shirt with the legend 'Spend an Eternity in Rome' emblazoned in English across her chest.

'You've already met my uncle, then,' he said, stating the obvious.

'Yes,' she said, grinning. 'I looked around and I saw this distinguished man dressed from head to foot in black, and I just took a chance.'

'Maya's been telling me all about you,' his uncle said.

'Oh yes.'

At this point, a young waiter approached, and Dempsey ordered a glass of Frascati.

'Just bring the bottle,' his uncle countered.

None of them noticed a stocky, hard-faced man with blonde hair who'd come in out of the rain a couple of minutes after Liam and occupied a nearby table, ordering a double espresso while seemingly engrossed in his copy of *L'Osservatore Romano*.

'I'm serious,' O'Malley said. 'Maya's been filling me in on her father's view of things. Did you know he's wary of you? A good judge of character obviously, the colonel.'

'Yes,' said Dempsey. 'I am aware of his opinion.'

Maya broke in. 'But if we can persuade him … that is to say, if I can persuade him that there's something not right here, something that might actually be working against the interests of the Church …'

'Then he might join us.' Dempsey finished the sentence for her.

'That would certainly be a bonus,' O'Malley said. 'But we must be careful. In the end, your father must reach his own conclusions.'

Dempsey pulled at the wet front of his t-shirt, which was clinging uncomfortably to his chest. 'I don't know if either of you has noticed, but I'm soaked.'

'You'll be fine,' said Maya, patting his knee.

'Water off a duck's back,' O'Malley said.

The waiter arrived with the Frascati. He filled Dempsey's glass and set down a small plate of olives in the centre of the table.

As he reached for an olive, Dempsey felt a twitch of pain run down his spine. His back had been aching for the last hour. Sudden changes in the weather often affected him like this. Scar tissue had a life of its own. Right now he didn't need to be in a chair, he needed to be in a heated pool doing forty lengths.

He looked up and realized that both of them were staring at him.

'Are you all right?' Maya asked, suddenly concerned.

'It's his back,' O'Malley said. 'The bomb …'

'Yes, I know,' she replied. 'He got me to massage it in bed this morning.'

At this, Superior General O'Malley looked shocked, and his nephew blushed to his roots. Coughing into his hand and giving Maya a look that said, 'Never, ever say anything about sex in front of my uncle,' Dempsey huddled forward in his chair. The heads of the other two drew in to meet him. 'Never mind me,' Dempsey said, 'Let's talk about how we're going to expose Bosani and get the conclave back onto a level playing field.'

The other two nodded and Dempsey continued. 'It seems to me that the first thing we need to establish is the hardest to prove. Is the Camerlengo of the Holy

Roman Church – the man charged with organizing the free and fair election of Christ's Vicar on Earth – bent on forcing a confrontation between Europe and the Islamic world?'

It was a stark analysis of their dilemma and for several seconds there was total silence.

But O'Malley wasn't finished yet. 'What – not to put too fine a point on it – if Bosani wishes to foment a new crusade? He wouldn't be the first to call for Holy War. There are extremists on both sides who see armed conflict as a means of redeeming a world steeped in sin. Crusaders and jihadis in the end are cut from the same cloth. All the pieces are in place. The Muslim world is seething. America and Israel are nuclear states. But so these days are Iran and Pakistan. Hammas and Hezbollah are growing in strength. The Taliban control Afghanistan. In Egypt, the Muslim Brotherhood is at the heart of government. Its astrologers are scouring the heavens for the proper alignment of the stars. In Europe the influence of groups such as Hizb ut-Tahrir is increasing almost by the day.

'The only loyalty of these groups is to the Ummah – the sovereign nation of Islam. Communities of Muslims, from England to Austria, including Italy, are turning away from the pretence of a European identity and looking for support to their fellow believers across the world.

'At the same time, half of the earth's remaining oil and much of its wealth is tied up in the Arabian Gulf, the spiritual home of al-Qaeda, where the governing elites have never been weaker. Seen from the ramparts of the Castel Sant'Angelo, to which the minarets of Rome's central mosque offer a daily reproach, it might well be argued that if we don't take Islam on today, we will have lost our last and greatest chance of victory.'

Less than a metre away, Franco had heard enough. He folded his copy of *L'Osservatore Romano* and placed a ten-euro note under his saucer. Then he stood up and moved away in the direction of the front door leading into the square.

Back in the bar, Maya voiced a thought that had been nagging at her all day.

'You will probably think I'm insane for saying this,' she began, 'but is it possible that we're looking at this the wrong way round?'

'What do you mean?' O'Malley asked.

She hesitated. 'What if Bosani isn't actually a Christian? He certainly doesn't act like one. What if he is something else?

This produced a rare guffaw from O'Malley. 'Now that really is crazy,' he said. 'The idea that one of the highest-ranking cardinals in the Catholic Church might actually be working against the faith is … well, it's just beyond belief. It's fantastic.'

But Maya stuck to her guns. 'It was something my father said that started me thinking. He'd gone to Rüttgers' funeral and was shocked when Bosani raced through the service like he was chairing a business meeting. There was no empathy, he said. He simply went through the motions. Papa was reminded of how angry and despondent Rüttgers was after the meeting with Bosani the previous week. He told him then that there were some in the Vatican who were hardly even Christian any more. It was as if it was being run by terrorists pursuing their own agenda.'

'Did he really?' O'Malley's face, previously animated, now wore an expression of profound sadness that Maya found deeply affecting. 'What a terrible comment on our stewardship.'

'But that wasn't all. Later, when he told me I was to have nothing more to do with Liam, he said something that stopped me in my tracks. He said that the logic of what we were saying about Bosani was that he was not Catholic at all, but something else.'

'Wow!' said Liam.

O'Malley's face turned pale as the implications of Maya's words struck home. 'Holy Mother of God!' he said. *The question is, who – or what – controls Bosani?* Rüttgers had known it, too. He just couldn't prove it – and for his insight he had paid with his life. Feverishly, the Jesuit replayed in his head all that he had learned of Bosani in the last few days. Starting with the absence of crosses in his chambers, all the evidence pointed in one direction. What was it Conan Doyle wrote? 'When you have eliminated the impossible, whatever remains, however improbable, must be the truth.' He turned back to the young couple who were staring anxiously at him. 'Your father was right,' he said. 'I've been blind. How could I have missed it? The lust for conflict; the obsession with Battista; the renunciation of alcohol; the meeting with Hakura … and all of that following on from his years in Egypt.' He threw up his hands. 'God forgive him!' he began. 'I don't want to believe it. I hardly dare to believe it. And yet nothing else makes sense. Cardinal Bosani, the cardinal in charge of the conclave to elect the next pope … is a *Muslim!*'

For several seconds, no one spoke. Then Dempsey whistled through his teeth. 'Jesus Christ, Uncle Declan! That has to be the weirdest thing I have ever heard. But I tell you this: it would make sense of what happened to Rüttgers. As Camerlengo, Bosani is in a perfect position to drive the Church towards its own destruction. Either there'd be the war of civilizations that you just described, which Islam seems to believe it can win, or else the papacy would end up so discredited that it would lose all authority and just vanish from history.'

'It would make Bosani the greatest spy of the last hundred years,' Maya said, with a hint of admiration in her voice. 'Think of it … he'd have to have been in place for years – for *decades* – advising popes and formulating Church policy. It's incredible. How could no one have noticed?'

It was Dempsey who jumped in with the answer. 'Because no one in the Church could ever conceive of such a thing. It would have been literally unimaginable.'

'So all this time, as he rose through the hierarchy, he would have been hiding in plain sight.'

'Exactly.'

O'Malley closed his eyes and slowly shook his head. He looked like a man who'd just been told he had a terminal illness. The realization that Bosani had duped the Church and betrayed Christ, while acting as a spy for God knows who – or what! – was almost unbearable to him.

Maya, by contrast, was energized by her insight. 'If we're right,' she said, 'if Bosani really is a Muslim, and he thinks we're on to him, he's going to be on his guard. And we don't have time to set elaborate traps. But he won't be acting on his own. This is a conspiracy and conspiracies need conspirators. So we've got to find another way in – something, or somone, he can't deny. But who do we go for? Who else is there?'

O'Malley looked up. 'There's his secretary, Visco, for a start. He sticks to him like glue.'

'Okay. So what if we could prove that Visco is a Muslim?'

'We've only got two days,' Dempsey reminded them.

'Prayer would be the obvious way in,' O'Malley replied, talking as if in a dream. 'It's a daily ritual, like a combination of the Mass, the creed and the rosary.'

'What happens exactly?'

'Well … the muezzin starts it off, live or recorded. He calls out "*Allahu Akbar*" – God is great – which he repeats four times. Then he sets out the fundamental articles of faith: that there is no God but Allah and Muhammad is His Prophet; that the faithful must pray and that they should show mercy; and then once again that God is great.'

'Sounds simple enough.'

'Not as simple as you'd think. Worshippers need to have purified themselves first by removing their shoes and washing their hands, face and feet. They start with the *Rak'ah* – that is, they bow. Next, they raise their hands to their ears, then fold their hands across their breasts, right over left, and bow. This is known as the *Qiyam*. The *Ruku*, which follows, requires them to bow down, hands on their knees, and then to stand again. The best-known part of the ritual – the one you tend to see in photographs – is the *Sajdah*, in which, as the Imam calls out that God is Great, There is no God but Allah and May Allah be Glorified, all of those taking part prostrate themselves completely, twice. Finally, as the worshippers straighten up, the blessing echoes round the mosque: "*As-salaamu allayakum*" – Peace be Unto You and the Mercy of Allah.'

'It sounds exhausting,' Maya said. 'Like a full-time job.'

'In some respects, it is. But no one is required to do anything they can't manage. It's like the Haj in that sense. All Muslims are enjoined to visit Mecca at least once, but only if they are able. The point about Islam – the part that's most often missed – is that it's about mercy and doing your best. God doesn't expect the sick and the dying, or the hopelessly indigent, to somehow crawl to Mecca. With prayers too, known as the Salaah, account is taken of circumstances and abilities.'

Dempsey seized on this. 'That would have to apply to Visco, wouldn't it? I mean, there's not likely to be a muezzin in the heart of the Vatican.'

'Not so far as I know.'

'So it would have to be a minimalist version of prayers.'

'I should imagine so. But if he's fit and true to his faith, he must still do his best to pray five times a day, every day.'

Maya thought about this. 'I doubt Visco lives in the Vatican. That's only for the Monsignors and above. He probably rents an apartment nearby. If we could find out where he lives, maybe we could break in and ...'

'Dear God!' said O'Malley. 'I don't believe I'm hearing this.' He turned to Dempsey. 'Are you not in enough trouble already?'

'Double or quits,' Dempsey said. 'There's a lot at stake.'

'We wouldn't have to take anything,' Maya added, reassuringly. 'Just have a look round, maybe plant an electronic bug in his briefcase. Then if he and Bosani engage in prayers – behind closed doors, no doubt – we'll hear them.'

'Then what?' asked Dempsey

O'Malley tugged at his dog collar. 'We'd hold a news conference and expose his conspiracy to the world. No matter what, there wouldn't be a hope in hell his man would get elected.'

Dempsey's right eyebrow rose quizzically. 'Who is his man, anyway?'

'I've no idea,' O'Malley admitted.

'You must have a list of possibles.'

'I'm working on it. There's any number of hardliners in the College of Cardinals. But this is all very new and there's no time to pin anyone down. Besides, from what you say, we don't know whether Bosani is pushing for the election of an anti-Muslim bigot or a genuine Islamist. My betting would be on the former.'

Maya said, 'It's unbelievable that we should have come to this. I can't imagine what my father will say.'

The Jesuit nodded. 'I'm having trouble myself. I hardly know how to respond. But, as I keep reminding myself, time is short and we have to explore every possibility. I'll carry on with the Battista link. You two think about Visco. Just be careful, that's all. And if you get yourself arrested, don't expect me to bail you out.'

'Fair enough,' said Dempsey, raising his glass. 'In the meantime, I give you a toast. To the next pope!'

O'Malley tugged furiously at the lobe of his left ear. 'Let's just hope he's a Catholic.'

The conversation, which O'Malley had begun to fear was taking on the characteristics of a conspiracy, continued for another twenty minutes or so until Maya looked at her watch and announced that she had to go.

'I promised my mother I'd be home for dinner,' she said. 'It'll be the last time we sit down together as a family until after the conclave.'

'Fair enough,' said O'Malley. 'And, anyway, I have to be going, myself. The superior of the order from Brussels is in town . He wants to know who'll be in charge if Belgium splits up into Flanders and Wallonia. Would you credit it?'

The rain had stopped but the streets of Rome were glistening. Dempsey suggested that Maya share a cab with his uncle while he made his own way home on foot. 'I'm already wet through,' he said. 'I'll jump in the bath when I get home – maybe put something in the water to ease my back.'

'But tomorrow we follow Father Visco, right?' said Maya.

'Right,' said Dempsey.

O'Malley looked pained and anxious. 'You know my views on this,' he said. 'Visco may well be a throwback to Catholic medievalism. But he's not a Muslim. And once we've established that, we'll have very little time to go after the real culprit in all this: Bosani. In the meantime, both of you, be careful. Promise me that. I don't want any more trouble with the Roman authorities.'

'You have my word on it,' Dempsey said.

They reached a taxi rank and a cab drew up beside them. Dempsey opened the rear door and O'Malley stood back to let Maya get in first. Half-smiling, he said: 'God knows what my enemies will say if it's reported that I've been seen in the back of a cab with a beautiful young woman.'

Maya blushed. Dempsey kissed her on the cheek then turned and embraced his uncle.

'Seriously, Liam,' O'Malley said. 'Watch your step. And look after Maya. A girl in a million, I'd say.'

'I'll do my best,' Dempsey replied.

As soon as the taxi pulled away, the young Irishman looked around to get his bearings. He didn't notice the sturdy figure of Franco moving out of a shop front opposite and keeping pace with him as he made his way from the Piazza della Rotunda towards the Via di Torre Argentina and the Ponte Mazzini. Rome felt fresh after the rain and he found himself wandering off his intended route until he realized after a while that he was lost. Attempting to get his bearings south of the Corso Vittorio Emanuele, he looked out for a street name and discovered that he was on the Via di Monserrato heading northwest towards the Vatican. A faded plaque mounted on a wall caused him to pause. Beatrice Cenci, it said, was taken from incarceration in a jail on this site to her execution on 11 September 1599 – 'an exemplary victim of unfair justice'. Who was Beatrice Cenci? he wondered. The name seemed vaguely familiar. Had Shelley written a poem about her? Or was that Byron? He couldn't remember and walked on, thinking instead about Maya.

A little way behind, keeping to the shadows, Franco had taken a rare executive decision. It was obvious that O'Malley had worked out the Camerlengo's plan to install a pope who would stand up for Italy and the Catholic Church against the Muslim invaders. It was also clear to him that the younger man, Dempsey, was O'Malley's 'muscle', ready to carry out his uncle's schemes. Father Visco had said that he should used his judgment, and in Franco's view no good could come from allowing the Irishman to continue with his inquiries. He knew too much already and was on track to find out much more. Moreover, his death would serve a double purpose. Not only would it end, once and for all, his intrusion into affairs that did not concern him, but, with time running out before the start of the papal conclave, it would be useful to have the older O'Malley preoccupied with family tragedy, unable to play any further part in the proceedings. As for the Studer girl, Visco hadn't said anything about her, so he would leave her alone – for now.

Dempsey had halted again, this time at the Spanish National Church on the Monserrato, before turning left into the narrow Via della Barchetta, one of those alleys that looked impoverished but where the houses, if they ever came onto the market, changed hands for millions of euro. Past an intersection with the Via Giulia, the Irishman paused for several seconds at a small water fountain, taking several sips from the flowing tap. Franco kept out of sight behind a van. The alleyway was dank with rain. Pools of brackish water gathered among the cobbles. The wing of a dead pigeon lay next to a discarded cigarette. On the right was a high wall with a metal rail on top. To the left was a row of small, flat-fronted houses, then yet another church. What was this one called? The Chiesa di Sant'Eligio degli Orefici. There was a tourist plaque on the wall, in Italian and English, which Dempsey stopped to read. The church, he discovered, had been planned, but not finished, by Raphael, back in 15-something-or-other. That was interesting. He tried the door, but, as usual after office hours, it was locked. What happened to a soul in need when the priest went home? He had no idea. But he could guess at the reason for shutting up shop. Burglars were now almost as ubiquitous in Rome as muggers. No one was safe. He turned away. Ahead of him, beyond a row of parked cars, was a grey wall, with steps leading to the Tiber. That was more like it. As he looked briefly to his left, down a blind alley, he realized that he was standing on a thick metal grating, bearing the initials SPQR. He found it amazing that after 2500 years, city property was still described as belonging to the Senate and People of Rome. It was somehow reassuring.

That was the moment when Franco launched his attack.

At the final second, Dempsey, his ears refined by months of listening out for the slightest suspicious sound in Iraq, heard the faint click of a knife blade snapping into place. He wheeled round. The advancing assassin's switchblade missed his neck by inches. Dempsey, now fully alert, came back fast. He directed a short punch into the Italian's throat, causing him to jerk back, but without losing hold of the blade, which he quickly swung back, cutting his adversary's left arm below the shoulder. Dempsey ducked down, wincing with pain. Then he sprang back up and directed his fist straight into Franco's groin. The Italian groaned and doubled over. As Dempsey muscled forward, he swayed to one side and drew a breath. He had to finish his man quickly. The city police frequently patrolled these deserted alleyways, a favourite haunt of muggers. Passing the switchblade from hand to hand, he dared Dempsey to make a move, but the Irishman's left arm was bleeding and his focus was purely on survival. Franco feinted to the left, then moved in for the kill. Dempsey responded with a high kick that caught the other man in his knife hand and sent the weapon flying. Franco grunted and kept on coming, taking advantage of the fact that Dempsey was now fractionally off balance, Punching him hard on the side of the face, he followed up with a left to the stomach. But Dempsey, though almost retching with pain, was still not ready to give in and jabbed the Italian between his mouth and nose, causing blood to gush from both nostrils. Following up with a head butt, learned in his schoolyard in Galway, he sent Franco spinning. Then, with the wound to his arm draining him of blood and energy, he turned and ran. Within seconds, he was up the embankment steps and gone. Franco rose quickly to his feet, gathered up his switchblade and drew a handkerchief from his pocket, which he used to staunch the flow of blood from his broken nose. Visco, he reckoned, would not be pleased by his performance this evening. Best, he thought, not even to mention it to Bosani. As for the Irishman, he had his measure now. Next time he would do the job right.

The Ponte Mazzini, which would lead Dempsey across the Tiber to his apartment, was less than a hundred metres away. But the Irishman was dizzy and weak. His head was spinning. He sat down on the kerb of the embankment, noticing as if for the first time that his left arm was streaming with blood. He needed to get to a hospital, he decided. But how? Which direction? He didn't know. He was confused. Standing up with difficulty, he felt in his pocket for a handkerchief to halt the bleeding. But he didn't have one. Who did these days? Instead, he clasped his right hand over the wound beneath his shoulder and wandered into the middle of the Lungotevere dei Tebaldi. An angry chorus of car horns greeted his arrival. Someone shouted at him from the pavement. He looked up and saw in the distance the illuminated statue of Garibaldi rearing above the botanical gardens on the opposite side of the river. That was when he lost consciousness.

31*
1609: Sicily

The arrival of Caravaggio in Syracuse remained a secret for less than forty-eight hours. Mario Minniti was a native Sicilian who took great pride in the culture and way of life of his home island. But he was also a natural metropolitan – a reveller, an inveterate gossip and a committed drinker. Like Caravaggio, he had been forced to flee Rome after a brawl, and like his friend he missed the hurly-burly of big-city life. When the opportunity arose to welcome as his house guest the man who was not only Italy's most celebrated artist – the one who had taught him mastery of light and shade – but also his one-time companion in debauchery, Minniti seized it with both hands. He organized a reception at his home to take place on the Friday night. Invitations were extended to fellow artists, the local nobility and representatives of the Spanish governor, all of whom flocked to attend.

Caravaggio himself remained in low spirits. He could barely remember what it was like to be carefree or happy. The days when he had played cards with Longhi and Orso and spent hours at a time with whores in Ortaccio seemed not so much episodes from his past as events in another life. Though relieved to have escaped the dungeon of Sant'Angelo, he felt he was sleepwalking towards his death. He dreaded God's judgment, which he felt sure would reject his penitence. He was also fearful that on Earth he might never get to confront Battista and reveal the truth of his apostasy. Most of all, he was afraid of the axe above his head that he knew was poised to fall, sending his lifeless and sightless head tumbling into oblivion.

A party was the last thing he needed, he told Minniti, an attitude that the Sicilian put down down to mere fatigue.

'Syracuse is not Rome, Michelangelo. You don't have to tell me that. But it is a town that knows how to have a good time. Believe me, by tomorrow, as you prise yourself away from at least two of the most alluring courtesans in Sicily and count up the commissions that have come your way from Church and state, you'll feel a different man. You'll be ready to work again and to put the terrible business of the last few years behind you.'

'But the Knights will pursue me.'

'Let them. I'll see to it that when you go for a drink or spend time in a brothel, or even step outside to take a piss, no man shall lay a hand on you. If these lofty Maltese sons of bitches think they can outflank Sicilians in their own backyard, they're welcome to try. But I promise you, they'll return to Valletta with their throats slit.'

Even Caravaggio had to smile at this.

In the event, the party was a great success. There had been no such star attraction in Syracuse since the time of Frederick II, the *Stupor Mundi*, or Wonder of the World, who, as Holy Roman Emperor, had denounced both Christ and Muhammad as 'deceivers of mankind'. Everyone, from the viceroy down to the humblest parish priest, seemed truly delighted that so great an artist should have ended up among them, and the result was that Caravaggio decided, yet again, to put his past behind him and rededicate himself to both pleasure and art.

Two weeks later, with Minniti, he embarked on a grand tour of Sicily, travelling north to Catania and Messina, then west, across the north coast, to the island's capital, Palermo. Everywhere they stopped, crowds gathered. Caravaggio took to making sketches of local worthies and handing them to their subjects free of charge. He also visited churches and palazzi, looking at paintings and frescoes, marvelling at the vitality and mongrel quality of Sicilian art. By the time he returned to Syracuse, he had more commissions than he could easily realize, including a sequence of alterpieces, *The Burial of Saint Lucy*, *The Raising of Lazarus* and the *Adoration of the Shepherds*, that he would dash off but would immediately be hailed as masterpieces.

Yet as his mood lifted, aided by drunken nights in Syracuse with Minniti and his many artist friends, events in the real world were closing in. In mid-July, some eleven months after his arrival in Sicily, word came from the harbour that three Knights of Malta, led by Fonseca, had arrived from Valletta asking for the whereabouts of the artist known as Caravaggio. The three were sent at once to Catania, where they were told their quarry was resident at an inn just off the main square. In the meantime, the painter was put on his guard and surrounded wherever he went by armed men in the service of a local smuggler. When Fonseca and his associates returned from Catania, they were met by an angry mob, carrying swords, daggers and any other sharp implements they could lay their hands on, and obliged to set sail at once. Townspeople jeered as they raised the sail on their felucca. From the cliffs above the harbour, several men and boys pelted the retreating craft with stones.

Minniti could not hide his satisfaction at the turn of events. 'Do you not see, Michelangelo, how much these people love you? You've found a home here. You mustn't even think of leaving.'

But Caravaggio, though deeply grateful, knew that his luck would not hold. Fonseca now knew where he was hiding. Battista would no doubt be informed. It could only be a matter of time before the Spanish governor received letters from the Holy See and the Grand Master requiring either his arrest or the carrying out of the sentence implicit in the *banda capitale*.

'There are things I cannot tell you, Mario – things that would be dangerous for you to know. You should be aware only that these men, and others like them, will pursue me to the ends of the earth. For your sake, and the sake of your family and friends, I've got to leave Sicily and return to Rome. Only if I am granted an audience with the Pope is there any hope for me.'

Minniti was saddened by his friend's determination, but could tell that he was impelled by more than mere fear for his survival.

'Then God go with you, Michelangelo,' he told him. 'We shall pray for you.'

Two days later, one year to the day after his arrival, Caravaggio made his goodbyes and descended once more to the harbour, where he boarded a ship for Naples. The following day, another ship left Syracuse bound for the same destination. Among the passengers was a short, burly fellow, an expert with both garotte and dagger. He was not a popular man, but there were few, even in Sicily, who dared risk their lives by confronting him. In the stranger's village of Canicattini Bagni, concealed beneath the floorboards of his cottage, was a strongbox containing one hundred scudi. According to Luis de Fonseca, the Cavaliere de Giustizia who had given him the money, another hundred would follow once his assigned task was carried out. The Sicilian, who was not a good sailor, went below almost at once. As the felucca pulled away from the harbour, he sat down by a porthole and took out a pitcher of red wine, some cheese and a half-loaf of bread. When he had eaten, he curled up and fell asleep.

32*
Conclave minus 2: morning

When Dempsey woke up, he saw a face gazing down at him. A woman's face. But he didn't recognize her. He screwed up his eyes and brought her into focus.

'Where am I?' he said.

'*Sono spiacente. Non capisco*,' she said.

'What?'

She looked at him inquiringly. Then he remembered he was in Rome and repeated the question in Italian.

'You are in the Ospedale di San Spirito,' she told him, relieved that he wasn't going to be a problem patient.

Ah! She was a nurse. That explained the white hat she was wearing.

'A police car nearly ran you down in the middle of the Lungotevere dei Tebaldi. You lost a lot of blood, but we have treated you and you should make a full recovery. You are a lucky man.'

Lucky? Dempsey offered her a lopsided grin. He had been accused of theft by the Vatican and threatened by the police. His home had been burgled. Now he had been stabbed by a mystery assassin. If this was luck, give him war every time. But she was right. The knife wound, she explained, had missed vital veins and arteries, so that an emergency transfusion, twenty-eight stitches and a course of antibiotics were all that was needed to promote recovery. But as a precaution he was being kept in overnight.

'Thank you,' he whispered. His eyes were heavy. It was difficult to stay awake.

'Sleep now,' she said. She was smiling.

Later, still aching but alert, he gave an account of what happened to a uniformed officer from the city police. A little after that, he was visited by a scruffily dressed detective from the office of his uncle's friend Ispettore Superiore Aprea, who told him that it was agreed now that he had real enemies, who obviously wanted him dead. In between, he spoke on the phone with O'Malley and explained what had happened.

The priest was shocked. He had called Demspey's apartment earlier that morning and then tried him on his mobile. But the home phone just rang and rang and the mobile was switched off. 'I feel terrible,' he said, 'exposing you to all this danger. What must you think of me?'

Dempsey drew a deep breath. 'Don't worry about it, Uncle Declan. You weren't to know. And I'm going to be fine.'

'Thank God for that. But have you talked to Maya? She'll be worried sick.'

'Maybe you could call her for me?' He gave him the number.

'I'll do that. You can expect the pair of us within the hour.'

They turned up forty minutes later. Maya was distraught and struggled to maintain her composure. He should drop the whole wretched business, she told him, and concentrate on getting well. O'Malley agreed. It was up to the police now. Aprea had opened an urgent investigation into the assault, with its background of burglary and the loss of historical documents from the Secret Archive. Dempsey's detailed description of his assailant would be put through the computer database, and a search was under way for any witnesses who might have seen a man acting suspiciously in the run-up to the attack. The problem was that the would-be killer was almost certainly a professional and would most likely not turn up on the files.

Later that day, after he and Maya had delivered Dempsey by taxi to his apartment – newly fitted with state-of-the-art locks and a sophisticated alarm system – O'Malley continued with his inquiries. The argument that Cardinal Battista was a secret Muslim in the time of Caravaggio was persuasive. Was it possible, he asked himself, that such a figure could exist in the modern age? Maya's argument, however paranoid it appeared, was at least consistent with the facts. O'Malley himself had watched Bosani recoil from a glass of wine like a vampire from a crucifix. He had also noted the sudden removal of a valuable portrait of Battista from the Camerlengo's inner sanctum. Finally, there was the fact that both Cardinal Rüttgers and Liam had witnessed Bosani in conversation with a known Islamist – a man wanted by the police of at least three Western countries.

But was it enough? Who would believe him? Bosani was one of the most powerful voices in the Church. Not only that, millions of ordinary Italians and other Europeans would prefer to believe that he was one of them – a Christian patriot.

While pondering his dilemma, O'Malley was interrupted by a knock on the door. It was Father Amin Haddad, an elderly Jesuit of Maronite extraction, who wanted to talk to him about the state of the Church, which he said was troubling him. O'Malley was at once on his guard. Haddad had always had a kindly aspect to him, but, as the poet MacNeice once observed of 'ordinary' people, there was a vagrant in his eyes. The Lebanese had lived the first twenty-five years of his life in Sidon and Muslims were among his oldest friends. He bade the old man take a seat, not wishing to give offence – or perhaps warn Bosani that he was on to him. Haddad mumbled his gratitude. He was concerned, he said, drawing his beard together beneath his chin, that in the present climate of global paranoia a new breed of Catholic was emerging that hated Islam and was determined to stoke up ancient fears. He had even heard, he confided, that members of the Curia could be involved – though with what end in mind he had no idea. O'Malley listened with the best patience he could muster. He, too, feared for the future, he said. For Europe was gripped by fear. All they could do was pray and hope that the spirit of God would descend on the conclave. Haddad looked vaguely annoyed and muttered something about the 'harsh rhetoric' of the Camerlengo, but O'Malley refused to be drawn in. 'We should remember His Eminence in our prayers,' was all he said. As soon as the priest had gone, O'Malley fell to wondering. Why should Haddad, with whom he had not spoken in months, suddenly turn up in his office like that? It didn't make sense. When faith and politics were mixed, there was no such thing as coincidence. Returning his thoughts to Battista, whom he felt instinctively held the key to the mystery, he used the internet to download a high-quality reproduction of *The Betrayal of Christ* and concentrated on the figure of the fleeing man. Dark thoughts began coursing through his head. He needed help and decided to call his old friend, Cardinal Henry McCarthy, one of those who had attended Bosani's recent gathering in Rome.

When the phone rang in his study in Dublin, the Archbishop was watching hurling on RTÉ television. 'Could you call back in half an hour?' he said plaintively. 'It's a close game – just a couple of points in it.'

'Sorry to spoil your evening, Your Eminence,' said O'Malley, 'but this is important.'

'More important than St Pat's making it through to the second round?'

'I'm afraid so.'

'Jesus Christ! Okay.' Using his remote, he muted the commentary from County Westmeath. 'What is it? Could it not wait until I arrive tomorrow night for the conclave?"

'I'm afraid not. It's about Cardinal Bosani.'

'The Camerlengo? What about him?'

'Do you trust him?'

'Do I trust him?'

'Yes.'

'Trust in what way?'

'Is he mad or what?'

'Mad? What are you driving at, Declan?'

Dear Lord, O'Malley thought. *If I don't cut to the chase, it could go on like this all night.* 'What I'm driving at, Your Eminence ...'

'And cut that "Your Eminence" crap, unless I get to call you "Father General". I mean, how long have I known you?'

'Right. Henry it is. Anyway, Henry, what I need to know is this: is the Camerlengo of the Holy Roman Church trying to provoke a war between Christian Europe and the Muslim world? Yes or no?'

There was a lengthy pause at the other end. O'Malley waited. At length, the familiar voice, with its flat midlands accent, came back on the line. 'He might be, Declan, he might be. I really don't know.'

'What's your instinct?'

'Well, if I were a betting man – which I am – I'd say that he wants a pope who isn't afraid to stand up for what he believes in, even if it means a confronta-tion with Turkey, Egypt, the Saudis, Iran, Pakistan, Afghanistan – just about any Muslim country you can name – to say nothing of the thirty million or so Muslims of the European Union.'

'But that's insane.'

'That's what I thought. But then I listened to him and I came to the conclusion that it might be no bad thing for the Vatican to start asserting itself again. Christ! These days the Church is looked on as if it were the spiritual arm of the United Nations instead of a living faith and the basis of Western civilisation for the last two thousand years.'

O'Malley refused to get drawn into this particular argument, which had a tendency to go round and round until it disappeared up its own fundamentals. 'But what if the result of a new strong man in Rome was an upsurge in terrorism across Europe? What if it led to armed confrontation with the entire Middle East, backed by the Islamic bomb?'

'Well,' said the cardinal, 'obviously that wouldn't be the ideal outcome.'

'But you think there's a middle course?'

'Yes, I do, as a matter of fact. Listen, old friend, I don't want to see people lose their lives. I don't want to see decent Muslim families in Dublin, or anywhere else, being turfed out of their homes or beaten up or intimidated. They've made their lives in the West and they've the same rights as the rest of us, and anybody who thinks differently will have me to answer to. But I'd be lying to you if I said I didn't want some formal recognition from Muslims that Europe, and the Western world in general, is governed by a Christian ethic. All these immigrants – they say they came for a better life: a job, a decent education for their children, money in their pocket. But then it turns that's only a part of it. Before you know it, they're demanding Muslim enclaves, Muslim schools, Muslim marriage customs, even their own legal system, with stoning for adulterous wives and flogging for those that get up to mischief behind the bicycle sheds.'

O'Malley thought about this. He could think of more than a few priests who had 'got up to mischief' with children, then escaped all punishment. But that was another question. 'It wasn't so long ago,' he said, 'that such customs and outlook were the official policy of the Catholic Church.'

'Ah, but we've come a long way since then. Sure look at the changes on contraception and gay rights. We'll have a married clergy before we're done, you watch. But the point is, that's for us to decide. It's not for newcomers of a different faith and outlook to come over here and impose their values on us. If they want to live under sharia law – if that's what's important to them – why didn't they just stay at home in the first place, where it's already enshrined in statute? What they're truly after, it seems to me, is revenge for the crusades and five hundred years of failure.'

'I can't talk about this now, Henry,' said O'Malley. 'But tell me this. The other day, when you were at that meeting with the other senior cardinals – the European ones, that is – did you notice any enmity between Bosani and Rüttgers?'

McCarthy snorted. 'Lord, yes. The two of them were at it hammer and tongs. Rüttgers – may he rest in peace – was all for integration and moderation and extending the hand of friendship. It could all be worked out, he said. No need for violence. But Bosani wasn't having any of it. I always thought he was the sort of fella would keep a pearl-handled Derringer up his sleeve. If a gun had sprung into his hand and he'd shot Rüttgers through the heart, it would have seemed entirely in character. Instead, he put him down in that particularly imperious way they teach you in Rome, as if the Curia had an exemption, signed by Jesus himself, from any of the usual requirements of Christian charity. He reminded me of those priests in Joyce preaching forgiveness while reaching for the switch behind their backs. Anyway, a couple of days later, after poor old Rüttgers drowned in his bath, you'd have thought from what Bosani said it was God's punishment on the man for his error.'

Just listening to McCarthy made O'Malley realize what it was he missed about Ireland. But he wasn't done yet. 'One more thing,' he said. 'How close would you say Cardinal Bosani is to understanding the Muslim world view? How steeped is he in Islamic thinking?'

'Jesus, Mary and Joseph! What are you implying?'

'I'm just asking.'

'Asking for trouble, more like. Okay, make of this what you will – and you're a Jesuit, so for you it's a full time job – but just between us, since you raise the question, I'd say Bosani would almost be happier as a Muslim. He'd be at home within its dense regulatory framework, preaching the kind of certainties that the Church seems to have lost hold of it in recent years. I don't need to tell you that he's not one to turn the other cheek. If he met Our Lord, I'm pretty sure he'd wanted Him to rethink the notion that the meek shall inherit the Earth. He'd put you in mind of those intellectuals who love the ritual and language of the Church and would be all for the Latin Mass and the pope with his triple tiara, but can't bring themselves to go to church of a Sunday because, when you come down to it, it's all piss and wind.'

O'Malley hesitated before he spoke again. 'And how would you react if that turned out to be an accurate description of Bosani?' he said at last.

'What? You mean if the man charged with organizing the election of the next Pope turned out not to be a true Catholic?'

'Exactly. Or believed in something else. Islam, for example.'

McCarthy gasped in astonishment. 'Sure if that was true, we'd all be fucked.'

'Thank you, Your Eminence. Concisely put, as always. Now bear with me. You will be familiar with Caravaggio's masterpiece, *The Betrayal of Christ*.'

'The one in the National Gallery that was lost for centuries? Of course. It's magnificent. But what about it?'

'Would you be surprised to learn that the figure of Judas laying hold of Our Lord as he hands him over to the Romans was in fact a representation of the then Camerlengo, Cardinal Orazio Battista?"

'Is that a fact?'

'It is. Though I only just discovered as much during a recent trawl through the Secret Archive. And would it further surprise you to learn that the fleeing man on the left of the picture – widely assumed to be St John the Evangelist – was in reality a depiction of a priest who was murdered within hours of discovering Battista offering prayers to Allah?'

O'Malley paused to let the significance of what he was saying sink in. In Dublin, Cardinal McCarthy pressed the off switch on his TV remote. 'Go on,' he said, his voice barely audible.

'What the Camerlengo failed to realize,' O'Malley continued, 'was that the priest, a Father d'Amboise, was not the only witness to his heresy. Caravaggio was also present, but hidden from view. Later on, when Battista discovered that the artist not only knew his secret but had fingered him as an enemy of the faith, he took steps to suppress the painting, which afterwards disappeared from history.'

There was another pause, broken by McCarthy. 'Why are you telling me this, Declan? What are you trying to say?'

'I'm not sure yet,' O'Malley replied, still struggling to come to terms with the logic of his own argument. 'But here's what our American friends would call "the clincher". The late Cardinal Rüttgers, the circumstances of whose death continue to disturb me, visited the private quarters of the Camerlengo shortly before he died. On the wall, in a place of honour, he noticed a portrait of Battista by Annibale Carracci, a contemporary of Caravaggio's. In 1611, by instruction of the Pope, this portrait – which in the current market could fetch millions – was consigned to the newly created Secret Archive and remained there, in obscurity, for the next four hundred years. The Holy Father wanted it out of his sight. Bosani wanted it next to him and we are entitled to ask why.'

Down the line from Dublin there came a sharp inhalation of breath.

O'Malley continued. 'I appreciate how bizarre this must seem, and I don't pretend that all the evidence is in. But events are moving very fast indeed. If I'm right in my suspicions, the implications for the Church could be profound. We could be on the brink of a turning point in history. Could I therefore ask you to exercise extreme care when you attend the conclave? Take extra care. Listen intently to whatever Bosani has to say. Watch his every move. Don't let him ride roughshod over the conclave.'

'Wait! Hang on there!" McCarthy's voice was rising to a crescendo. Are you telling me that the Camerlengo is planning some sort of Islamic *coup*?'

'I wish I knew,' O'Malley said. 'But if he is, you need to have your wits about you. The future of the Church itself could depend on it.'

'No pressure, then.'

'I'm sorry, Henry. I wish I …' O'Malley's voice trailed off.

McCarthy closed his eyes and uttered a silent prayer. Then he spoke, very slowly and very deliberately. 'We are all sinners. We are all flawed. But ever since I took my vows as a priest I have always done what I think is right for the Church. And may I be struck down and damned to hell if I ever follow a different course. I find what you have just told me to be literally incredible. If you were any other man, I would recommend that you visit both your confessor and a psychiatrist. But I have known you for forty years and I have never once doubted either your intellectual acuity or the strength of your faith. You may take it from me, Declan, that if it should become clear to me in the days ahead that Lamberto Bosani plans to turn St Peter's Basilica into a mosque, he'd better be ready for a scrap.'

O'Malley made the sign of the cross. 'I'm glad to hear it. I will pray for you.'

'And I for you, Declan. God bless.'

While O'Malley and McCarthy were on the phone, Franco, wearing glasses, his black hair cut back almost to the roots, visited Father Visco to report on the events of the previous evening. He was embarrassed and apologized for not taking care of Dempsey. 'You never told me he was an ex-soldier,' he said.

'I didn't know. I thought he was a historian.'

'These things are important, Father. You've got to do your research.'

'So what happens now?' Visco was nervous. He hated it when things went wrong. Franco was normally so dependable. 'Scajola telephoned a short while ago to tell me the Rome police have issued a wanted notice for a man answering to your description.'

The assassin scowled. 'In that case, what happens is that I disappear for a while. They'll be looking for me and it won't do anybody any good, not least the Camerlengo, if they establish a link between me and you.'

'Exactly. You should leave Rome immediately – this morning. Go to Genoa, or La Spezia. Anywhere. If we need you, we'll call you.'

Franco shrugged. He didn't like to leave a job unfinished, but he was glad he didn't have to face Cardinal Bosani to account in person for his failure.

The Camerlengo was calculating his next move. Though irritated that Dempsey was still alive, he reckoned the Irishman would be out of the picture for several days at least – which was all the time he needed to secure victory for his plan. Later, if necessary, he would have Franco attend to him. What mattered was that all the necessary pieces were now in place. Ten key cardinals had already undertaken to support his candidate; a dozen more were on the brink of declaring. Where they went, others would follow. What none of them knew, and could never know, was that, under the direction of Yilmaz Hakura, an unprecedented Muslim 'outrage', directed at Catholicism's heart, would take place on the opening day of the conclave. A suicide bomber, recruited from Islam's growing army of European converts, would blow himself up in St Peter's Square, thus, in accordance with Islamist teaching, guaranteeing himself a place in paradise. The slaughter, and the insult, would be like nothing that had gone before. Not only governments but the Christian peoples of Europe would demand that action be taken against the Islamists responsible, hiding in Iran, Iraq, Saudi Arabia or Lebanon. Their demand would be impossible to resist. After that, Bosani told himself, nothing would prevent the emergence of a new age of chaos in Europe.

33*
1610: Naples

Neither the Prophet, nor those who believe shall ask forgiveness for the idol worshippers, even if they were their nearest of kin, once they realise that they are destined for Hell.

—The Holy Qu'ran, 9:113

Caravaggio's return to Naples began better than he could ever have imagined. Fabrizio Colonna's mother, the Marchesa, received him with open arms and immediately invited him to stay at her palazzo in Chiaia, constructed against the Spanish viceregal walls, with spectacular sea views. Soon, all the nobility of southern Italy appeared to call. Commissions poured in. Scipione Borghese, the latest cardinal-nephew, was only the first of a long line of wealthy and influential men queuing up to buy paintings from the most celebrated, and now most notorious, painter in Italy.

But though he worked diligently and, many said, with divine inspiration, the canvases he produced demonstrated that he remained in the grip of a terrible obsession. *Salome With the Head of John the Baptist* was sent to Alof de Wignacourt in Valletta with a plea for the Grand Master's understanding. The work was accepted, but no response made. A bleak, despairing *Crucifixion of St Andrew*, commissioned by the Spanish viceroy, was interpreted by those who knew him as a plea for release from the prison of the world. Even more terrifying, his *Martyrdom of Saint Ursula* painted to order for Prince Marcantonio Doria of Genoa, showed the saint on the point of death, with the artist behind her, looking on. Caravaggio's shadowy self-portrait was the one thing about the canvas that was not original – for it was lifted straight from his previous masterpiece, done for Ciriaco Mattei, *The Betrayal of Christ*. He was reminding himself that he had seen too much already and had reached breaking point.

By now, his voices were becoming dominant. He was more and more convinced that he had a mission – to expose Battista and prepare the way for a Christian defence against the coming Ottoman onslaught. But he also believed that he was fated to die before he could achieve his purpose.

On the evening of 24 October, he woke from a sleep feeling more refreshed than he had done in months. He had just completed a canvas, and to clear his head and relax his tired frame he walked into Naples, to the Osteria del Cerriglio – a tavern as famous for its music and the beauty of its courtesans as it was for the richness of its food and drink. The time was approaching midnight. Caravaggio had just come down from one of the upstairs rooms, still holding the hand of the seventeen-year-old prostitute with whom he had spent the previous two hours, when the Sicilian sent by Fonseca, who for weeks had patiently bided his time, suddenly barred his path.

'Watch where you're going,' the assassin said, already reaching for the dagger in his belt. 'Don't you know when to make way for your betters?'

'If you are my better,' the artist replied, 'then I must be a very low fellow entirely, for you strike me as an ignorant oaf.'

At that, the Sicilian drew his blade and drove it straight at Caravaggio's heart. Taken by surprise, the painter sprang sharply to his right, but missed his footing and stumbled forward instead. The knife blade now swung upwards and opened a terrible wound from his chin all the way up the left side of his face, almost severing his ear.

The girl screamed. At once, three guards employed by the innkeeper bounded up the stairs. Seeing the Sicilian about to deliver what would have been a fatal blow, they grabbed him from behind and wrestled him down the stairs.

'This fellow tried to kill the artist Caravaggio,' one of the three called out.

'Find out who paid him, then slit his throat,' the innkeeper replied. He had been paid by the Colonna to keep an eye out for trouble and would do whatever he had to to justify their faith in his establishment.

The Sicilian, who was strong as an ox, broke free at this point and made for the door, easily knocking out of the way two men who tried to stop him. It was the innkeeper himself, another brute of a man, who brought him down from behind, using a heavy cudgel that split his skull, killing him instantly.

Surgeons called in by the Marchesa Costanza saved Caravaggio's life. But they could do nothing about the disfigurement. He was left with an ugly scar running up the entire left-hand side of his face, and the top half of his left ear was missing.

Throughout the long winter that followed, he slowly recovered his strength. But by now he was so paranoid that he slept with his hand on his dagger and woke up, screaming, at the slightest noise.

He spoke to Costanza and told her he was more determined than ever to return to Rome.

'There is nothing for me here, Marchesa. Only the running sore of fame and the prospect of death. I have business with the Holy Father. Only he can give me peace.'

Costanza tried to dissuade him, but failed. Instead, she wrote letters to the Pope and Cardinal Scipione, pleading his case and begging for a revocation of the *banda capitale*. Caravaggio meanwhile painted *David with the Head of Goliath*, with himself as the model for the giant, and sent it to Scipione in sign of atonement. It would prove to be his final work. The cardinal-nephew, almost out of gratitude, but also from self-interest, agreed upon seeing it to add his powerful voice to the chorus demanding a papal pardon.

Finally, in July 1610, word arrived from Cardinal Ferdinando Gonzaga, son of the Duke of Mantua and effective head of the Curia, that the sentence imposed three years before had at last been rescinded, conditional only on the accused's presenting himself in person in Rome. Retrieving from Prince Marzio the *laissez-passer* obtained for him by the Marchesa, Caravaggio at once booked passage for Rome.

A felucca was leaving for Rome, Livorno and Genoa three days later. The vessel, loaded with goods, including five recently completed canvases by Caravaggio, sailed north for two days, hugging the coast, until it put in at Palo, a tiny port near Civitavécchia, west of Rome. As he waited for his goods to be unloaded, Caravaggio set off to find a means of onward transport. That was when the tightly coiled mainspring of his life finally gave way. Reports of his disfigurement were widespread throughout Italy and he was instantly recognized. Within an hour, he was arrested by the commandant of the local papal guard, who, not knowing that the *banda capitale* was annulled, sent word to the Vatican that the infamous fugitive, Merisi, had been captured.

Next day, having spent the night in the cells, the artist argued his case before a local magistrate, brandishing his *laissez-passer*, signed by Cardinal Gonzaga, and insisting that he was on his way to meet the Pope. At noon, after paying a large bribe, they let him go. But by then, the felucca, with all his remaining wordly goods still on board, had embarked for Porto Ercole, fifty miles to the north. Desperate to retrieve the paintings, which were now his only currency, the painter set off in pursuit, telling the commandant that he would wait for Cardinal Gonzaga's men in the church in Porto Ercole. He was exhausted and all but broken in spirit. Anything that remained of his former confidence and swagger was gone.

Two days later, having wandered in high heat through a malarial swamp, he reached his destination, a spit of land under Spanish rule. He was burning with fever and badly dehydrated.

The end was close. But he would not give up. Not yet. Though terrified, he was determined to live long enough to impart his secret and expose Battista's treachery. Barely able to stand, his head concealed by a floppy hat, he staggered into Porto Ercole by way of the beach. Minutes later, he reached the harbour, arriving just in time to see the sails of the felucca billowing in the distance as the craft continued on its way to Livorno. It was a defining moment. But he was not surprised. If anything, he had expected it. Slumping down on to the edge of the harbour wall, he threw up his arms in surrender to God's will. Then he started to laugh, causing two fishermen mending their nets nearby to glance at each other, fearing that he must be a madman, or else diseased.

Overhead, the midsummer sun continued to beat down. He could feel his senses reeling and his mind begin to wander. Once more the voices came. *Give up, Michelangelo. Give up*. There is nothing you can do. Concentrating hard, telling himself that soon the worst would be over, he stood up and made his way slowly uphill, behind the waterfront taverns and fishmongers' shops, until he came upon the church of Saint'Erasmus. Inside, grateful for the cool provided by the thick stone walls, he prayed before a statue of the martyred saint before collapsing in a coughing fit onto the flagstones.

It was the parish priest who found him. Not recognizing him, for he was lying face down, he feared to touch him in case he was a plague victim and rushed off instead to raise the alarm. He barely made it to the church door. Three horsemen, a Monsignor in his distinctive red-trimmed cassock, and two brothers from the Order of Saint John the Beheaded, had just ridden up and now stared down at him from their mounts.

'I beg you,' the priest called out. 'Don't go into the church. For there is a stranger inside and I fear he may have the plague. I am on my way to fetch help in having him removed.'

The prelate, a powerfully built man in his forties, looked down scornfully. 'Do not trouble yourself, Father. Continue on your way, but do nothing and say nothing about the stranger. Do you understand me?'

The priest saw the papal arms, the crossed keys and the triple tiara on the sleeves of the Monsignor's cassock and mumbled his assurance.

'Very good. We have heard about this man and are come to take him with us to Rome. I suggest you pray for his immortal soul – and your own.'

The three riders dismounted. The smaller of the two monks took the reins of the horses and remained on the path outside the church door. His companions looked around them before disappearing inside. Caravaggio was lying, semi-conscious, his left hand reaching out to the statue of St Erasmus.

While the Monsignor looked on, the second monk, tall and broad-shouldered, reached into a bag slung over his shoulder and drew out a cloth and a canteen of water. He lifted the artist's head and leaned it into the crook of his arm before pouring cold water over his face and wiping it with the cloth.

Caravaggio began to come round. 'Drink,' said the monk. 'We are here to help you.'

'Yes, Michelangelo,' the Monsignor said, speaking softly, careful not to avert his eyes from the horrific scars marring the painter's once handsome features. 'My name is Monsignor Marinello and the man holding you is Brother Domenico. We have been sent by Cardinal Gonzaga, on the orders of His Holiness, to bring you home.'

At first, Caravaggio could only hear the words. The face looking down at him was a blur. But after several seconds, as the water from the monk's canteen trickled down his throat, the image of the priest's face began to move into focus.

'Is it true?' he asked, his voice hoarse and trembling. 'Are you really sent by the Pope?'

'Yes,' said Marinello, smiling. 'We have brought your letter of safe conduct. As soon as you are well, we shall travel together to Rome, where the Holy Father has pardoned you for your past indiscretions, committed without malice, for which you have already suffered enough.'

'I should like to confess, Monsignor.'

'Of course,' said Marinello. 'In a little while, as soon as you are better.'

'No,' Caravaggio insisted, looking suddenly angry. 'I wish it now!'

'Very well,' Marinello said. 'But you must conserve your strength.'

Caravaggio drew a deep breath and gripped hold of the priest's arm. 'Bless me, Father, for I have sinned.'

'How long has it been since your last confession?'

'Three months, perhaps longer.'

'Tell me of your sins.'

Caravaggio began to talk. The sins poured from his lips: lust, fornication, drunkenness, pride.

Marinello listened. There was no mention of the murder in Rome or the illegal flight from custody in Valletta. He must, he concluded, have confessed to these already – probably in Naples. So this latest list had to relate only to recent months. He and the monk exchanged glances.

When Caravaggio was done, Marinello made the sign of the cross and spoke the words of absolution. 'I absolve you from your sins in the name of the Father, and of the Son, and of the Holy Ghost. Amen.'

'And what is my penance, Father?'

'We shall come to that presently,' said Marinello, 'for yours has been no ordinary life and your sins are not such that a recital of the rosary will suffice. But you must accept that your reception into heaven and the company of saints depends very much on how honest you are with me about your claims in repect of Cardinal Battista.'

Caravaggio nodded and the monk raised him into a sitting position.

'First,' said Marinello, 'I have been charged by His Holiness to ask you some questions.'

'I am ready,' said Caravaggio.

'Is it true that you witnessed Cardinal Battista engaged in an act of Muslim worship?'

'Yes, Monsignor.'

'Tell me about it.'

Caravaggio did so, recalling for Marinello how he had seen the Camerlengo and his secretary prostrate themselves on the floor of Battista's private chapel, with the cross laid flat on the altar as they prayed to Allah. He then described how the only other witness to the cardinal's treachery had been killed the same night, murdered because of what he knew. 'I can see his face now – the fleeing man. He haunts me in my sleep.'

Marinello blanched as he listened. Then he asked: 'Michelangelo, are there others? Do you have any other names – churchmen who have become Muslims, who, like Battista, are enemies of Mother Church?'

Caravaggio stared hard into the eyes of his confessor. Then he spoke the names of Fra' Luis de Fonseca, of the Knights of Malta, and Battista's secretary, Father Ciro. The Monsignor nodded. 'Is there anyone else, my son?'

'No, Monsignor – none that I know of.'

'And have you spoken of your fears to anyone else? Anyone at all?'

Caravaggio could hardly keep his eyes open. He was finding it hard to concentrate. 'Prince Marzio Colonna,' he said at last.

Marinello's eyes narrowed. 'No one else?' he asked.

'No, Monsignor,' Caravaggio replied. 'After all that happened, I decided that the Holy Father and his emissaries were the only ones I should trust.'

'That was wise,' Marinello said, motioning with his eyes to the hooded monk standing impassively three feet behind. 'But now, my son, you are tired and raging with fever. It is time for you to leave us.'

Leave us? What did he mean? Marinello turned away. Caravaggio, his heart pounding, struggled to get up. His hand went to his belt. Where was his dagger? But he was too late, as he had always known that one day he would be. He struggled onto his knees, sweat pouring down his forehead, and twisted round to identify the danger that he knew was there. The monk had produced a long, two-edged sword from beneath his habit and now advanced on him without a word. His blue, soulless eyes offered no hint of pity.

'You!' said Caravaggio.

The monk smiled and raised the broadsword above his shoulder. Then, with grunt of satisfaction, he brought it down. Caravaggio was reminded in his last moments of the men who had cut wheat in the estate outside his father's house. He had watched in fascination as their scythes swung metrically through the corn, reducing it to stubble.

The blade struck. The artist's severed head, like the head of Beatrice Cenci, like the head of Goliath, like the head of John the Baptist, fell to the floor, teeth bared, eyes staring, while his body slumped sideways.

The Monsignor knelt down and listened. For a second he thought he could hear a sigh emerge from Caravaggio's open mouth. This interested him. Perhaps, as the doctors said, it was a last, involuntary gasp, or the attempt by a dying brain to express in extremis its ultimate despair. But might it not also have been the release of the infidel's soul embarking on the first step of its road to hell? There could be no mercy for the unbeliever. Looking down at the disembodied head with a mixture of satisfaction and distaste, he touched his fingertips to his temples, lips and heart. '*Allahu Akbar!*' he said quietly.

34 *
Conclave minus 2: afternoon

The Prophet (peace be upon him) said: 'There is no prophet between me and him, that is Jesus (peace be upon him). He will descend (to Earth). When you see him, recognize him: a man of medium height, reddish fair, wearing two light yellow garments, looking as if drops were falling down from his head though it will not be wet. He will fight for the cause of Islam. He will break the cross, kill swine and abolish Jizyah. Allah will cause all Faiths except Islam to perish. He will destroy the Antichrist and will live on the earth for forty years and then he will die. The Muslims will pray over him.'

—The Hadith

O'Malley, aware that he was engaged in the most important quest of his life, was in the innermost chamber of the Vatican's Secret Archives. The General Archive, first established in 1610 on the orders of Pope Paul V, was not, in fact, secret, merely restricted. But one room, separated from the rest, deep beneath the museum's central courtyard, was the final storehouse of everything that the Church and the Curia wished to keep hidden from the world. Only his stature as Superior General of the Company of Jesus – in effect the Black Pope – granted him access to this most obscure repository. Here were no computers, no electronic records – only documents, yellow with age. O'Malley blew the dust off boxes whose labels were the stuff of history: Policy and Conduct in Respect of the Knights Templar; the Case of 'Pope' Joan; The Relationships of Cesare and Lucrezia Borgia; The Trial and Execution for Heresy of Bruno Giordano; the Trial and Interrogation of

Galileo; The Trial and Execution of the Cenci family; Pope Pius XI and Mussolini; Relations Between the Holy See and the Nazi Occupiers. Finally, hidden away on a bottom shelf, in a pouch made of leather or vellum: The Investigation of Cardinal Orazio Battista, 1610-1611.

O'Malley pulled the pouch towards him. With fevered fingers, he undid the string holding it shut, then reached inside and slowly drew out the contents. The top sheet, containing a list of those to whom the information was entrusted, came away from the papers beneath with a discernible snap. Battista's early life and career were there: his upbringing in Lucca, his three years as a parish priest in Pisa, his time as a diplomat, taking him to Paris, London and … Constantinople. He had been awarded his red hat by Pope Gregory XIV, Niccolò Sfondrati, at the consistory held on 6 March 1591, as reward for a lengthy, and no doubt stressful, period as a leading prosecutor for the Inquisition. Created a cardinal priest in 1601 (a fact omitted by the Catholic Encyclopedia) he was soon after appointed Camerlengo. And that is where the story ended. What happened to him after that was not recorded – not even the time or place of his death. Whatever documents there may have been relating to the cardinal's later life and career – including the mysterious investigation into his treason and apostasy – were gone.

O'Malley uttered a stifled curse. He couldn't believe that he had got so close, only to fall at the final hurdle. But then he stood back and approached the problem from a new angle. He was a Jesuit after all, trained in logic and lateral thinking, and this was the greatest challenge of his life – the test of his convictions that would redeem his entire career. He turned to the personal archive of Pope Paul V and discovered, in reference to the disappearance of Caravaggio in July 1610, that Cardinal Ferdinando Gonzaga had been asked to conduct an urgent and discreet inquiry into matters raised by the late Prince Marzio Colonna concerning the Camerlengo of the Holy Roman Church. Gonzaga, whose family down the centuries produced innumerable princes of the Church, would later resign his cardinalate after succeeding to the dukedom of Mantua and marrying his cousin, Caterina de Medici. But for several years he had been one of the Pope's most most trusted confidants. Fascinating! O'Malley now turned to the file on Gonzaga himself, whose resignation and marriage had come under papal scrutiny. And there it was, buried in a single sentence. 'In the autumn of 1610, His Eminence led the inquisition and conviction *in camera* of Cardinal Orazio Battista, charged with apostasy, high treason and other crimes against the Catholic Church and the Holy See.'

Mother of God! They were right. A second note, attached at a later date, recorded that on 2 January 1611 Gonzaga witnessed, on behalf of the Holy Father, the execution *intra mures* of Battista and the scattering of his ashes in the Tiber.

No doubt it was said that he had succumbed to a sudden heart attack, or died of the plague while on some foreign mission. At any rate, beyond October 1610, all formal record of his existence in the Church hierarchy simply vanished. No Mass was offered. It was as if he had never been. No details were provided of the nature of the 'apostasy', but the pieces were fitting together. Liam had already determined that it was Bosani, decades before, who removed the files on Battista from the general library. If it could be shown that Bosani had also purged information from the top-secret secret papal archive, the coincidence would be too great for anyone to ignore. But how to prove it?

O'Malley turned next to the lay vice-prefect of the archive, Vittorio Stucci, aged seventy-six, who had presided over the underground vaults since 1975. A tall, thin man, stooped over from years of working in confined spaces, Stucci should have retired eleven years before, but was so much of a Vatican institution that it was decided he should remain 'at God's grace'. Did he remember anyone, years ago, back in the 1970s, taking a particular interest in Battista?

'An awful man,' Stucci began, licking his cracked lips as if to breath life into his dry words. 'He saw evil in everyone. For years, Romans lived in fear of him. Parents would tell their children that if they weren't good, the Camerlengo would come for them.'

The old man looked about him and dropped his voice to a whisper. 'It was even said of him that he was secretly a Muslim, in league with the Sublime Port. Can you believe it?'

'I'm learning to believe something new almost every day,' said O'Malley, whose pulse had begun to race. 'But did anyone from our own time take an unusual interest in him? Someone in the Curia – a bishop perhaps?'

'A *bishop*? Well, I suppose I could check.'

'There's nothing in the record. I've looked.'

Stucci smacked his lips. 'I don't mean those records, Father General, I mean my personal diary. I keep a list, you see, of everybody who steps into this room. Wouldn't be much point in keeping a secret archive if people could just walk in and out willy-nilly. Your name is already on the record.' He walked over to an ancient desk and drew out an old-fashioned ledger from its top drawer. 'There,' he said, opening the latest page. 'Superior General O'Malley, arrived 10.07. Seeking information on Cardinal Orazio Battista, Camerlengo of the Roman Church 1601-1604.'

'Aah! How reassuring. So what about thirty-five or forty years ago?'

Stucci squinted and pushed his thick spectacles back up his nose. 'That's a long time ago, Father General. I still had ambition then. I ...'

'Yes, yes, Signor Stucci. I understand. But I need to know who was inquiring into the life and times of Battista back in the 1970s?'

'A good question,' the old man said. 'I think you'd better go and have a coffee while I consider it. It could take some time.'

'Please, Signor Stucci, it really is very important, and I am, after all' (he drew himself up to his full height, almost knocking his head against the barrel vaulting of the ceiling), 'Superior General of the Society of Jesus.'

Stucci, who sometimes entertained the Pope in his lair, was unimpressed by this uncharacteristic *braggadocio*. 'Come back in half an hour, Father General,' he said. 'That's the best I can do.'

O'Malley bowed to the inevitable and made his way upstairs and outside into the library courtyard. While strolling among the formally organized shrubs and pathways, he telephoned Dempsey. His nephew sounded better, which was a relief.

'Listen closely to me, Liam. I was seriously worried about you. You've done enough. I don't want you to involve yourself in this matter any further. Your father would never forgive me. Concentrate on making a full recovery. That's the best thing you can do for me right now.'

'What about Bosani?'

'Maya was right about him. It's worse that we could ever have imagined.'

'And Hukara? Anything more on him?'

O'Malley paused. 'According to Aprea, there's a real chance he's in Rome. A contact in the Muslim community – a moderate, God help him, who's taking his life in his hands – says he was in the central mosque less than a week ago.'

'And Bosani?'

'He was there, too – to attend an inter-faith meeting.'

'It's all adding up.'

'Yes. But now you must leave Bosani to me and the Ispettore. This is my fight. You've done more than enough already.'

'You and what army?'

'I'm serious, Liam.'

'So am I. I may not be a fully functioning member of the Catholic Church, but I don't want to see Europe plunged into a meaningless war between crusaders and jihadis. And I don't like strangers stabbing me in dark alleys.'

'We'll talk later,' O'Malley said. 'Meanwhile, try and get some rest.'

When he returned to the library and knocked on the door of the Secret Archive, Stucci was waiting for him with a look of triumph on his parchment-like features. 'I've found what you were looking for,' he said. He opened an ancient ledger with a marbled cover. 'January 23, 1977: Bishop Lamberto Bosani – details of the life and career of Cardinal Orazio Battista, Camerlengo of the Holy Roman Church 1591–? Arrived 09.17, left 12.33.'

'Why the question mark?' O'Malley asked.

'Yes, that's odd, isn't it? It turns out there's no official record of what happened to Battista after 1610. He just vanished. I could look into it if you like.'

'No need. But would you be prepared to confirm what you have just told me, in a papal court, if one were to be convened – including the rumours that Battista was a spy for the Ottomans?'

'Of course. My first duty is always to the Holy Father. Only don't leave it too long. I'm afraid I'm not as young as I used to be.'

O'Malley thanked the librarian and turned to go.

'Father General O'Malley,' he heard Stucci say to himself as he inscribed a new entry in his ledger using an old-fashioned fountain pen. 'Left 11.09.'

35*
Conclave minus 2: evening

All but three of the cardinal electors had arrived in Rome. The exceptions, from Mozambique, China and Bolivia, were on their way. A palpable tension filled the air. Ripples from the disturbances outside the Regina Coeli prison were still making themselves felt, adding to the anti-Muslim sentiment whipped up by the death of the papal gardener and the apparent attempted assassination of the judge in Bologna. But in the office of the Camerlengo, a remarkable calm had descended. When Father Visco brought his master's coffee that morning, he discovered, to his considerable relief, that everything was in order. It didn't matter about the Father General and his nephew, Bosani said. They were too late. They were an irritation, nothing more. They could be dealt with later. In two days' time, nothing they could say or do would make any difference. The world would have arrived at a new turning point in its history.

Bosani had waited many years for this moment. As a boy, growing up on his father's vineyard above La Spezia, in the armpit of Italy, his Catholicism was entirely orthodox and wholly unremarkable. It had been learned at his mother's knee and beaten into him at school. Had the local priest, Father Musetti, not taken note of his obvious intelligence and aptitude for learning, it was likely that he would never have entered the Church. More probably he would have become a teacher … or a gangster. In the event, it was by chance, while he was a seminarian in Genoa, that he decided to add spice to an all-too predictable curriculum by taking a course at the Interdepartmental Centre for Islamic Studies, in Bologna. It was three years later, on the basis of that experience, that he had been selected, with three others, to spend a year at Al-Azhar University. The Church, it was reckoned, needed experts in every field, and a sound knowledge of Islam would take him far. In that, at least, his sponsors had been proved correct. What they could never have anticipated, or imagined, was that the truth of Islam would hit him like a thunderbolt, changing his life forever and awakening in him a profound sense of his personal destiny.

He had expected to find Islam both intriguing and challenging. What he had not expected was that he would embrace it quickly and avidly as a natural extension of the Judeo-Christian story. His *aalim*, or teacher, from the Muslim Brotherhood, helped by introducing him to the Gospel of Barnabas, with its confirmation by a recognized Apostle of Muhammad as the true Messenger of God. After that, there had been no turning back. It was as if the Archangel Jebril had taken charge of his life.

Not that it had been easy. He was an old man now and the years since his conversion were made bearable only by his dedication to the cause, renewed each day in prayer, and by an unwavering discipline. In particular, he had had to wean himself off his powerful predilection for good wine. For a long time he had been a sleeper – waiting for the call. Conscious of the tragedy of his legendary predecessor, Cardinal Battista, he had at first tried to work *with* the Church in its dealing with Islam. It was only when John Paul I, just ten days into his office, announced his intention to reinstate the Patriarchate of Constantinople that he had taken drastic action. Such a development, aimed at fostering increased religious freedom in Turkey, could have had the disastrous effect of driving Ankara deeper into the embrace of the West. Battista would have been horrified. Worse, it would not even have been he who was given charge of the experiment. That role would have fallen to a *Jesuit* – the upstart Irishman O'Malley. He would not permit that. Poisoning Luciani, ostensibly in support of the P2 dissidents, had not been easy. The toxin had begun to take effect even before he left the papal apartment. There was time to see the light leave the pontiff's eyes. But the action had strengthened him, purging him of the last vestiges of loyalty he owed to the Vatican and its false doctrines.

Another conclave and another election came and went. At first he had tried to bully and manipulate the Polish Pope, who knew little about the Curia's Byzantine system of government and didn't understand the potential of Islam. But Wojtyla was relentless and implacable, with a mind of his own and a will of iron. For the first ten years of his pontificate, he was obsessed with ending communism – a policy with which, as Fate would have it, the Muslim world concurred, albeit for its own reasons – and by the time the Pole was older and more malleable, ready to kiss the Qu'ran and visit the Umayyad mosque in Damascus, he was already a wasting asset. In terms of Catholicism's relationship with Islam, the impact of his twenty-six years as pontiff was at best cosmetic. The opening of the central mosque in Rome was the highlight, but the faithful of Italy were still made to feel like second-class citizens, tolerated rather than embraced as equals. This had grated. Wojtyla may have been hailed as a 'hero' by moderates in the Muslim world; he was not a hero to Bosani.

Under Ratzinger, a formidable intellectual but also a traditionalist, raised among Nazis, things began promisingly enough. The new Pope, as Benedict XVI, told a French journalist from *Le Monde* that he was against Turkey joining the EU because Europe's roots were fundamentally Christian. Next he downgraded the Pontifical Council for Interreligious Dialogue, renamed by his predecessor, amid fears that the expansion of Islam into Europe could well become unstoppable. Finally, he delivered his notorious speech in Regensberg that caused many in Rome to hope that the days of Christian retreat might at last be at an end. Hiding beneath the sentiments of the fourteenth-century Byzantine emperor, Manuel II Palaiologos, he implied to his audience that what Muhammad had brought into the world was evil and inhuman, delivered at the point of a sword. Bosani remembered the intensity of the pleasure he experienced as Benedict's words hit home. Fatwas were issued by the Markaz-ud-Dawa party in Pakistan, linked to Osama bin Laden, and by the Union of Islamic courts in Somalia. Cairo and Rabat recalled their ambassadors. Demonstrations and protests were held in almost every country in the world. In Iraq, churches were burned. In Somalia, a nun was shot dead. The Muslim Brotherhood said Ratzinger threatened world peace and had ignited the wrath of the entire Islamic world. For twenty-four hours it had felt as if, suddenly, everything was possible. Had the German only had the courage of his convictions, it could have been the turning point of which Bosani had dreamed. As it was, the pontiff retreated beneath a smokescreen of obfuscation. He restored the independence of the Muslim Office and, as a sign of his good faith, agreed to visit the Blue Mosque in Istanbul. From that moment on, if he spoke of Islam at all, it was in exaggerated terms of respect and affection.

The next Pope should have provided the perfect opportunity. An able enough scholar, but a weak man, his election had been secured against the wishes of a majority of cardinals. Bosani had released a series of complex, sometimes contradictory, lies and rumours to secure the victory, setting each faction against all of the others so that the atmosphere in the Sistine Chapel grew poisonous. During one crucial vote, he substituted five false ballot slips – as many as he dared – for five cast in support of two opposing liberal contenders. It was touch and go throughout. Towards the end, when his choice began to acquire the support of older cardinals from Europe and the United States, he had briefly believed that his life's work was about to be achieved, only for the emergence of a last-minute 'agreed' candidate to dash his hopes.

The worst part, looking back, was that the new pontiff, aware of the balancing act that had brought him to power, ended up so reluctant to say yes or no to anything, that he virtually brought the business of the Church to a halt. Bosani believed that in time he would have broken him to his will. His own appointment as Camerlengo was proof enough of that. But the Pope's premature death – apparently accidental, though who ever knew for sure? – had reset the clocks to zero, forcing yet another conclave and one last opportunity for Bosani to act out his destiny.

Recalling the sequence of events, he couldn't help sneering. If the Church was not so contemptible, it would be amusing. Yet he did not spare himself from reproach. Up until now, he had failed in his mission. The forces ranged against him had proved too great. Should he have allowed his own name to go forward for election? Could he have presided over the chaos to come? No. It was impossible. He had too many enemies, had offended too many liberals, who would delight in striking him down. No. His role was to prepare the way – to build up his faction within the Curia and exploit opportunities as they arose. It was not his fate to seize the prize for himself. Like Moses he would view the Promised Land, but could not enter it. Instead, he had prepared three candidates for the conclave, coaching each of them on the evils of Islam and the glory that would accrue to their names when they rescued the Church from disaster. All three men, two Italians and a Dutchman, were aggressively anti-Muslim in their sentiment; all three were distinctly papabile. Crucially, each was ready to support the others, moving behind whichever of them drew the most votes. At the same time, lesser cardinals, like Delacroix and Salgado, tired of the struggle, angling for positions in the Curia, were primed to act on his signal, throwing their weight, and their numbers, behind the most promising contender. Their reward would not be an eternity in paradise but lunch every Friday in the Hostaria dei Pesce. It was, of course, frustrating to have to work through lesser men in this way. But it made sense. The solace was that God was merciful. Everything that had gone before, Bosani now realized, was but a preparation for this moment. With Islam on the march across Europe, sure of its strength, knowing that Western materialism no longer had an answer to Muslims' deeply held religious conviction, the time had come at last for him to stab the Church in its enfeebled heart.

'Think of it, Cesare,' he told his assistant. 'A crusader pope, ready to denounce Islam and all its works. A world shocked by direct action as the faithful, from Andalucia to Bosnia, rise up to throw off their shackles. An intifada spreading like a fire across the continent. Turkey, its faith renewed as foretold in scripture, will join us. The whole Muslim world will be on the march, calling out with one voice that there is no God but Allah and Muhammad is His Prophet. Our Arab brothers, led by Saudi Arabia, will cut off deliveries of oil; Tehran will announce its readiness to use the Islamic bomb, if not against Europe, then certainly against Israel. The EU, fearful and desperate, will demand the creation of a new Fortress Europe. But it will be too late. We will not only be at their gates, we will be within the walls assaulting the keep. In the end, Rome itself will fall and the faithful will applaud us. Has there ever been a prospect more glorious in the eyes of God?'

Visco, though a true believer, converted personally by Bosani, was, like his master, someone who needed daily affirmation of even his most deeply held convictions. 'But how will it end, Your Eminence?' he asked. 'Tell me again how it ends.'

A messianic look suffused Bosani's face as he responded. 'You have read our Holy Qu'ran. You have read the Hadith. As Allah has willed it, so shall it come to pass. It will not be immediate. I will not live to see it, Cesare, but you surely will. Europe is weak. It is like a rotten fruit, ready to fall from the tree under its own weight. It believes in nothing any more. America, the Great Satan, will not intervene. It no longer has a stomach for the fight. The Europeans, led up a blind alley by the baying of the Vatican, will agree to divide the continent into Muslim and Christian spheres. Once more we will stand before Vienna. Only this time, when we knock, they will not dare to refuse us. The Balkans will fall to us, and Venice. And then, when the Catholics and their still more heretical brethren believe themselves at last to be safe in their shrunken world, we will descend on them in their complacency like a wolf on the fold.'

Visco's eyes lit up. He spread his hands in rapture. 'In preparation for the coming of the Dajjal and the return of Eesa, who will curse the wicked and receive the blessed into heaven. Allah be praised!' He paused, dry-mouthed, and looked pleadingly at Bosani. 'And, truly, it all begins in two days' time?'

The Camerlengo bared his teeth. 'Yes, my young friend. They will learn, as Luciani, my first Pope, learned on his deathbed, that it is impossible to build a bridge between truth and lies. There can be no compromise with the will of Allah. They will convert or they will pay the price. The caliphate is nearer than they think. And there is no longer anything that anyone can do to stop it.'

36*
Conclave minus 1: morning

Rome was *en fête*. Nearly a million visitors had poured into the city, conferring, praying, celebrating Mass or simply gossiping. In the Vatican, Bosani, presiding over arrangments for the gathering, underlined his view that justice could only be served if Catholicism reasserted itself in the face of Muslim aggression.

'Let me remind you, Eminences,' he told the cardinal electors as they prepared for the spiritual ordeal ahead, 'Of what we have seen in recent days alone. In Bologna, a judge – a respected member of Opus Dei – barely escaped with his life as he sought to deliver justice in a case of reckless Muslim aggression. There was also the case here in Rome itself of a bomb being thrown into the cloisters of the Lateran Palace – a bomb that killed an innocent gardener, depriving a wife of her husband and children of a loving father. Most recently, the Regina Coeli prison was stormed by a Muslim mob, demanding the release of those held on suspicion of the palace bombing and proclaiming the inevitability of a renewed European caliphate.'

A shudder went around those present.

'A challenge has been issued, Eminences. And there has to be a Christian response. I do not call for the "repatriation" of honest Muslims. I do not call upon the Western powers to bomb Muslim nations. But I do say that we need upon the Throne of Peter a pope who will be a Catholic champion – truly the rock upon which we shall rebuild our faith. Your duty, Eminences, given you by God, is to honour the commitment you gave him when you became priests – to honour, glory in and proclaim the one Holy, Roman and Apostolic Church. In the name of the Father, and of the Son and of the Holy Ghost. Amen.'

Later that morning, Visco left the Camerlengo's office in the Apostolic Palace and made his way out of Vatican City in the direction of his tiny, two-room apartment north of the Via Andrea Doria. He turned left along the Viale Vaticano, overlooked by the massive ramparts, passing a number of large detached villas, until he reached a set of steps that led down to the church of Maria delle Grazie.

The Metro station just beyond the church was one of the city's new demarcation points. The sprawling 1970s estate a few hundred metres farther on had once been lived in preponderantly by working-class Italians. Now, increasingly, it was home to a swelling immigrant population, many of them Muslim.

The priest's mind, as he descended the steps towards the church, was filled with the enormity of what lay ahead. He had no idea that fifty metres behind him, wearing jeans, t-shirt and sneakers, her hair tied up, her green eyes concealed behind a pair of sunglasses, Maya was dogging his footsteps. It was another warm evening. The sun was setting, bringing a blush to the rooftops of the western city stretched out either side of the Via Cipro. Visco was sweating beneath his cassock. Crossing over the Via Andrea Doria, he again turned left until he reached his own street, the Via Venticinque. There were children playing football in the street. He ignored them, even when a stray ball came dribbling in his direction.

'Kick it back to us, Father,' one of the boys shouted. He pretended not to hear. Halting outside a down-at-heel-looking apartment building, he made his way into the front lobby, where he punched a security code into a keypad on the wall. The door buzzed open, admitting him to the main foyer. An ancient lift stood waiting to his left, looking as if it was installed in the 1930s. But it hadn't been working that morning and he chose instead to walk up the three flights of stairs to his apartment.

As soon as he disappeared, Maya entered the building and discovered from the list of residents inscribed on the wall that Visco lived in apartment 4B. Her first instinct was to push any button on the list and pretend to be making a delivery. But there had been a spate of thefts throughout apartment buildings in Rome and she couldn't rule out the possibility that the keyholder, instead of pressing the entry button, would alert the concierge, or even call the police.

Instead, she took a couple of unopened letters from her handbag and stood waiting. After a couple of minutes, an elderly lady came in. Maya jiggled the lock of one of the mail boxes with her own post key and opened a letter, as if she had just extracted it. As she did so, the old lady pressed her code into the key pad with a bony finger. The door again swung open. Maya followed her in, wishing her *buona notte*. Then she took the same stairs as Visco and a minute later found herself standing in the corridor outside his front door.

There was no one about and she was able to listen at the door, hoping, she realized, to hear Visco intoning the words '*Allahu Akbar*'. But she was out of luck.

She wished Liam was with her. But he was recovering from his bad experience and was in no position to assist. It was time for her to step up and provide Father O'Malley with the evidence he desperately needed. Checking that she was still alone in the corridor, she bent down and lifted the metal flap of Visco's old-style letter slot. She had to adjust her eyes to the interior gloom of the hallway, but after a second or two caught sight of the priest moving from what looked to be the living room of his flat towards the bathroom. Another minute passed. She heard the toilet flush, then the sound of a shower. He was obviously going to be some time and Maya released the flap and stood back up. As she did so, the door of the apartment opposite opened and a young man came out. He smiled at her, wondering who she was but at the same time taking in the swell of her breasts, her green eyes and generous mouth. 'You just moved in, have you?' he asked her.

'No,' she said. 'Just visiting a friend.'

'Oh yeah? Anyone I know?'

'I doubt it,' she said, hurrying off.

The young man looked disappointed, but didn't follow her. Three minutes went by. Maya waited patiently in the stairwell until she heard the lift creaking up the shaft, the snap of the concertina doors opening and shutting and the slow descent back to the lobby. Checking there was no one in the corridor, she returned to Visco's door and resumed her crouching stance, gazing down the hallway, hoping for something – anything – that would confirm Visco as a practising Muslim. Then she remembered that as she had entered the building, a clock had struck 11.45. She checked her watch. It was three minutes to twelve, which according to the Father General meant it was time for the *Dhuhr*, or midday prayers.

She listened. For thirty seconds, maybe a minute, there was nothing. Then she heard something. From the living room at the back of the apartment came the muted, but distinctive sound of Arabic. There was a strange, alien beauty to the sound. It must be coming from a recording, she decided.

> *Allahu Akbar*
> *Ash'hadu anna ilaaha illallaah*
> *Ash'hadu anna Muhammadar-resulullaah*

She froze. Even now, she could hardly believe it. Father Visco, a Catholic priest, trained for seven years in a seminary, truly *was* a Muslim. Which meant that Cardinal Bosani must be a Muslim. But what could she see? If only she could see something. Dry-mouthed, she rummaged in her handbag for her digital camera, with its inbuilt microphone and cine-action. Extending the zoom, she poked the lens through the letter slot and pushed the 'on' button. As she crouched, she drew a series of deep breaths. She couldn't stop her hands from shaking. Thirty seconds later, the video mode reached its limit and stopped. She withdrew the lens and released the post flap, which slapped against the woodwork of the door.

Inside, startled by the noise in the hall, Visco jumped up and hurried to the door. At the same time, Maya ran towards the stairs. The priest reached the top of the stairwell just in time to see a young woman disappear from view. She was carrying something, but he couldn't see what it was. Might it have been a camera? He set off in pursuit, then, having descended the first flight of stairs, pulled up, sweating. Even if he caught her, a crowd would gather and someone would call the police. Whoever she was, she must have followed him home and spied on him through the mail slot. He didn't know what to do. All he could think of was to inform His Eminence and put the matter in his hands.

Meanwhile, almost collapsing with nerves, Maya found herself back outside. Rounding the corner of Visco's street, she continued left along the Via Andrea Doria until she found a small café. She went inside and ordered a cognac. The adrenalin that had accompanied her unscripted little adventure was already wearing off and she started when a uniformed police officer sat on the bar stool next to her and ordered an espresso.

'*Scusilo, signora,*' the officer says.

'*Per favore,*' she replies. '*Nessun problema.*'

Later, at home, in her parents' apartment inside the walls of the Vatican, she reviewed her thirty seconds of digital film, transferred it to her laptop and used iMovie software to enhance the quality. The sound was fine. A man was obviously at prayer. But what about the image? Her hands were shaking so much. Was there anything to see? She played the sequence a second time, and a third, until it hit her. There! In the top left of the picture: two arms descending, hands outstretched, to the floor. And, for one split second, a face. She froze the action, adding light and contrast. It was far from a perfect picture. But it was unmistakeably him. It was Visco. It was unbelievable. She rubbed her eyes and sat back in her chair. She had caught him in the act. There was no way he could explain this away. Time, she decided, to call Liam, who could then contact the Father General. But first she must talk to her father. He was bound to believe her now.

37*
Conclave minus 1: afternoon

St Peter's Square was thronged with tourists and pilgrims. Even in a secular age, the ceremony of electing a new pope was one of the greatest spectacles in the Western world and Rome's hotels were heaving with visitors from every nation come to greet the new Vicar of Christ.

Superior General O'Malley, often cited as the Church's second-most powerful individual but excluded from a process that belonged exclusively to the Sacred College, was visiting the gallery of the Palazzo dei Conservatori, behind The Wedding Cake, the hideous memorial to King Victor Emmanuel that he always thought of as The Typewriter.

He had come to the gallery to see Caravaggio's *Deposition From the Cross*, in which, following his crucifixion, Christ is laid in his tomb by Nicodemus, watched over by a grieving Madonna. The veins in Jesus' dangling right arm were clearly visible and the Saviour's body had none of the grace normally accorded by previous masters. Nicodemus struggled to hold his Lord, as if he were truly a dead weight, while Mary looked old and worn, knowing that her destiny, and that of her son, had almost run its course. Only the young woman at the top of the painting – presumably Mary of Cleophas – looked as if she were infused with the love of God rather than grief for the departed.

This artist, O'Malley concluded, told the truth. In spite of his errant nature, he had been a true believer. The offence given to him by Battista's treachery would have been real and must have run deep. There was no evidence that the painter ever spoke out against Islam or was critical of Muslims. More likely he would have wished people, Christian or Muslim, to be true to their faith. Inspired, the Father General said a prayer, then walked briskly from the gallery. As he did so, Father Giovanni called him on his mobile to remind him that he was expected to preside over Mass that evening on the eve of the conclave.

'Honest to God, Giovanni – did you really think that a thing like that might have slipped my mind?'

'Just checking, Father General. Better safe than sorry.'

'Yes, well you can expect me at the Gèsu at 6.30 sharp. Between now and then I'll be working on my sermon.'

'But Father General,' the young priest protested, 'The sermon tonight is to be given by Cardinal von Stiegler, the new head of the German Church.'

'Not any more,' O'Malley retorted. 'Did you not get the note I left this morning on your desk – or was that too low-tech for you?'

An embarrassed silence greeted his inquiry, which O'Malley had to admit, he rather enjoyed.

'I'm sorry, Father General.'

'A bit late for that. So you had better get moving. You will convey my regrets to His Eminence, but the sermon this evening will be given by me and no one else.'

'But Father General …'

'Obey me in this, Giovanni. Tell Cardinal Von Stiegler that I will be delighted to accommodate him on another occasion. But not tonight.'

'Yes, Father General.'

'And let the word go out that in the Gèsu this evening, something very special is planned.'

'Yes, Father General. At once.'

In the Via della Penitenza, Maya was showing Dempsey her video of Father Visco performing the *Salaah*. The Irishman played the thirty-second clip all the way through on his laptop, then sat back for several seconds and stared at the ceiling. 'Well,' he said, 'that clinches it. After this, there's no doubt in my mind that Bosani is a closet Muslim. Well done, Maya. It's brilliant, quite brilliant.'

'Thanks. I nearly died of fright when he heard me and came running to the door. If he'd been just a couple of seconds faster, he'd have caught me. But the big question now is, what do we do with it?'

'This is dynamite. We need to talk to my uncle. That's the first thing.'

'I've already told my father.'

'Really? What did he say?'

'He couldn't speak at first. It was all too much for him. He said he'd think about what to do with the information. Ordinarily, he'd have gone straight to the Pope. But, of course, he can't do that. And he can't go to Bosani either …'

'No. That wouldn't be his wisest course.'

'So he said he'd leave it to you and the Father General to advise him.'

Demspey's eyebrows shot up at this unexpected piece of information. 'That's a turn-up. I thought he didn't trust me.'

'He didn't,' Maya said. 'But he's learning fast.'

As it happened, Colonel Studer was already reassessing his opinion of Dempsey. He thoroughly disapproved of the way the Irishman and his daughter conducted their relationship. But Maya's extraordinary revelation that Father Visco was a Muslim, added to what he had learned earlier from Chief Inspector Aprea, had forced him to change his mind about Dempsey's character, if not his lifestyle. From what Aprea had told him, Dempsey really had been framed by the Vatican, and just last night he had almost been killed by a professional assassin. Studer was a banker by profession and did not change his mind easily. But nor was his thinking set in stone. If Dempsey could convince him that, in addition to not being a criminal, he genuinely loved his daughter and was ready to pursue a career, then he was perfectly willing to welcome him into the family. In the course of the afternoon, before Maya had come to him with her news about Visco, he had spoken at length to the Superior General – a most charming man – who had vouched for the fact that whatever Liam had done, he had done to preserve the honour of the Catholic Church. Studer was greatly relieved to hear this. When O'Malley went on to outline his fears about Bosani – fears since borne out by the images of Visco praying aloud to Allah – the Swiss had agreed to keep a close eye on the Camerlengo, as well as on Visco, and to report anything out of the ordinary. But time was running out fast. From now on, while keeping this latest knowledge in his head, he had to focus his attention on the upcoming ceremony of the conclave and its aftermath, the inauguration of a new pope. Nothing was more important than that.

The Swiss Guard, together with the papal gendarmerie and security service, would work closely with the Rome police, not only to protect the new pontiff and his cardinals, but to ensure order among the vast crowd that was expected to fill St Peter's Square. His own men, wearing their full dress uniforms, would also provide a ceremonial guard of honour. Studer did not expect to serve in Rome for more than another five years and was aware that the conclave would be his greatest test. He would be vigilant, he decided. He would be resolute. But he would not allow treachery and suspicion to mar for him the greatest Christian occasion of his life.

He had already said as much to the Father General. Was it not the case, he asked him, that the Holy Spirit would descend upon the conclave as it met to decide the next occupant of the Throne of St Peter? 'And is it not true that not even the gates of Hell can prevail against the will of God?'

Such a show of faith had brought tears to O'Malley's eyes. For the second time in as many days, he hadn't known what to say.

38*
Conclave minus 1: evening

In their hotel room, Dempsey and Maya made love. Afterwards, they showered together and ended up doing it again.

'Not ready to take your vow of celibacy?' she asked.

'Maybe next year,' he replied.

It was clear to both of them now that they were engaged in something that went far beyond a 'summer fling'. They had discovered qualities in each other that they felt sure would last beyond their present adventure.

After they got dressed, they took a taxi to the Gesù, where Uncle Declan had told them to expect something out of the ordinary. Dempsey hadn't had a chance to talk to his uncle face to face about Visco. There had only been time for a quick two-minute conversation on his mobile. When he had called again later, he was told by Giovanni that the Father General was writing his sermon and had given strict order that he was not to be disturbed. He'd sent him an email instead, warning him that the video of Visco had been sent to *Il Messaggero* and *La Reppublica*, as well as to RaiNews24. Whether or not he'd read it, he had no idea, but he rather thought not. A little after 6.30 the taxi dropped him and Maya in the Via del Plebiscito, from which they made their way on foot to the Piazza del Gesù. Several television units, alerted by the Jesuit communications department, were set up outside the church. Reporters – as yet unaware of the Visco revelation – wanted to know what worshippers expected from tonight's sermon. The Rome police were more concerned with keeping order. Dempsey was impressed. His uncle, he realized, had successfully mobilized the power of the Jesuits and created the sort of buzz normally associated with a corruption trial or the latest 'turning point' in Italian politics.

Inside the church, the atmosphere was electric. In a matter of hours, word had swept the city that the Superior General would deliver a sermon to end all sermons and that the object of his ire would be the government of the Church itself. By 6.45 pm, fifteen minutes before the Mass was due to start, nine cardinals, including Germany's Von Stiegel, seventeen bishops, four abbots and the head of the Dominicans, as well as the president and prime minister of Italy, the mayor of Rome and at least a score of top diplomats, were in their places in front of the altar. Microphones and cameras would relay the sermon to a breathless public that included at least three thousand frustrated worshippers in the Piazza del Gesù.

The High Mass itself, over which O'Malley presided, assisted by three of his senior priests, went on for forty-five minutes, with music provided by the Holy Cross choir from Worcester, Massachusetts. The setting, dating back to the last quarter of the sixteenth century, was spectacular. Designed especially for the Jesuits, the Gesù was one of the most richly decorated churches in Rome and the original model for the Italian Baroque. The enormous, gilded interior, its barrel-vaulted ceiling lit by a soaring cupola, was created to provide the acoustics appropriate to preaching, and O'Malley, the 31st Superior General in a line going back to St Ignatius Loyola, intended to produce a message worthy of the occasion.

As the Mass ended, with the smell of incense still hanging in the air, all eyes turned to O'Malley, who had moved from the high altar to a lectern positioned closer to the congregation. In the old days, sermons were delievered from a special lateral pulpit, set between two side-chapels on the left side of the nave, but the invention of the microphone had made such an acoustic device redundant. O'Malley, dressed, as tradition required, entirely in black, placed his hands on the top rim of the lectern and surveyed the sea of faces gazing expectantly back at him.

There was total silence, broken only by someone's nervous cough that echoed round the walls.

'Tomorrow,' the Father General began, speaking in fluent Italian, 'the Sacred College of the Holy Roman and Apostolic Church withdraws to the Sistine Chapel to elect the 265th successor to St Peter as Bishop of Rome and Supreme Pontiff.

'Some of the cardinals who will discharge this solemn task are with us this evening. Others are engaged in worship elsewhere in Rome, or in private prayer and contemplation. All will wish, with God's help, to elect the man best placed to take the Church forward at a dangerous time in our history.'

O'Malley paused. His eyes passed up and down the rows of pews, hoping to catch sight of Liam and Maya. But it was impossible to make them out. He just hoped they were there, listening.

'Consider the state of the world today. Many years ago, less than a week before his death, His Holiness John Paul I, Pope for just thirty-three days, confessed to me his fear that the next great global conflict would not be between the forces of belief and unbelief, but between a weakened Christianity and a resurgent Islam. The Holy Father warned that this was to be prevented at all costs. But he knew how hard it would be. In more recent times we have learned just how hard. The United States, casting itself as the defender of Christian values, decided in 2003 to invade Iraq. It had already invaded Afghanistan in pursuit of the Taliban. Later, having sustained twin defeats, it sought to isolate and destablize Iran. We all know what happened next. Today, the Islamic world is aflame, united in its hatred of the West, determined to restore its ancient power and honour. At the same time, with the numbers of European Muslims growing every year, a movement has sprung up that demands not merely civil rights and religious freedom for the followers of Muhammad – peace be upon him – but the achievement of a hitherto mythical goal: the establishment of a caliphate ranging from Spain and England in the West to the Balkans and Turkey in the East.

'Is such a development realistic? For Catholics, such a state of affairs would truly be the end of history. It would be the end of certainty – the end of everything. We do not fear the real Islam. We respect the real Islam. We would do nothing – would we? – that would make Muslims feel other than comfortable in the expression of their beliefs and customs. But we, too, are rooted in faith – a faith that has Jesus Christ and the certainty of the Resurrection at its heart. Sadly – I might even say, *tragically* – our belief, centred on the certainty of a life hereafter, has been replaced by belief in an eternal present. We think not of the soul but of the self. So far has our faith shrunk that today in large parts of Europe there are more who worship Allah and venerate the Prophet – peace be upon him – than occupy churches on Sunday that have stood for a thousand years.

'Those of us who cling to the old certainties are particularly vulnerable today. Not only are we beset by our enemies, we must also cope with the enemy within. Our consolation is that a bedrock of faith remains and that, in the general population, there is still a vestigial, one might almost say an *atavistic*, respect for our Christian past. Nothing, we tell ourselves, is beyond recovery. Nothing is impossible. There is still a pope in Rome; there are still bishops and priests; there are still parishes in every corner of every country. Some might even say' – and here O'Malley offered a modest smile – 'that so long as the Jesuits remain, hope cannot die.'

'But what if I tell you tonight that the enemy within is not unbelief, or even indifference, but the growth of a secret Muslim sect?'

At this, a gasp echoed round the church.

O'Malley continued. 'What if I tell you that there is an insidious force at work in the Church today that would pit Christian Europe against the Muslim world not in the hope that the faith of Christ will prevail, but in the belief that the West lacks the strength and the endurance for the struggle and would, in time, embrace the caliphate as the price of its survival?'

'My brothers and sisters,' O'Malley went on, 'tonight I tell you that there is indeed such a faction in the Eternal City, working in the Vatican to elect a pope whose goal will be conflict, whose means will be war and terrorism, whose ambition is a different world, alien to the world we have known all our lives.'

At this, provoked beyond endurance, Cardinal Von Stiegel stood up from the front row and pointed an accusing finger at O'Malley.

'Stop!' he called out. 'Stop this! The Father General has clearly taken leave of his senses. He is seeking to undermine confidence in the cardinal electors and the conclave that begins tomorrow. I urge you all to ignore him and to place your confidence in the princes of the Church whose only concern is the restoration of faith and the peace of Christ.'

The church by now was dangerously restive. The Archbishop of Paris joined Von Stiegel by rising to his feet, shouting in French, followed by the ultra-conservative president of the Polish bishops' conference, who demanded O'Malley's resignation. All three men, dressed for a ceremonial occasion, looked confused and angry. They were not alone in this. Members of the congregation up and down the church were twisting round in their seats, arguing in angry tones. O'Malley realized that if he didn't say something incisive soon, the night would end in chaos.

It was at that moment that the Archbishop of Dublin heaved himself to a standing position. 'Let the Father General speak,' he called out, in English, then Italian. 'If he is wrong, we will know soon enough and he will be forced to bear the consequences of his error. But if speaks the truth, he will have done us a great service. I beg you, sit down and listen.'

A nervous silence greeted the Irishman's intervention. O'Malley seized the opportunity to re-establish control.

'I am grateful to Cardinal McCarthy,' he said. 'And he is right. If what I am saying is a lie, it is a lie that will be quickly exposed. And I will, of course, resign my position with immediate effect. But if it is true, my brothers and sisters, then the conclave that opens tomorrow in the Sistine Chapel faces a conspiracy more iniquitous, more evil in its intent, than anything for a thousand years.'

He raised his hands, then lowered them, fingers extended, in a universal call for calm. When he resumed his sermon, his words came out almost in a whisper. Only the astonishing acoustics of the Gesù bore his message to the hundreds seated below.

'Four hundred years ago, in September 1602, the artist Caravaggio, one of history's greatest and most tortured geniuses, discovered a Muslim faction within the Curia of his day. Cardinal Orazio Battista, then Camerlengo of the Holy Roman Church, had no interest in spreading a greater understanding of the mystery of faith. Instead, with others, he sought to create the conditions that would lead to the conquest of Rome by the Ottomans. Caravaggio stumbled upon the shocking fact that Battista was not a Christian when he chanced upon him and his secretary engaged in the Salaah, the daily obligation of prayer. His life from that moment was a living hell. Two priests who shared his secret were murdered; he himself was almost killed in a duel forced upon him in Rome and obliged to flee south to Naples, branded a killer, subject to a *banda capitale*. Following the intercession on his behalf of the Marchesa di Caravaggio, he sailed to Valletta, hoping to be accepted as a Knight of Malta, dedicating his life to the defence of Catholic Europe. But no sooner had he been accepted into the order than he was again falsely accused by his enemies, this time of assault and blasphemy, and ended up again in prison, facing disgrace and execution. Once more, with the help of a trusted friend – Fabrizio Colonna – he escaped. But the terror continued. Back in Naples, where he was given refuge by Fabrizzio's cousin, Prince Luigi Colonna, he was attacked by an assassin in a tavern, who scarred him horribly. Only the intervention of local people saved his life. Finally, on his way to Rome, intending to regain his honour and put his facts about Battista before the Pope, he died mysteriously, and suddenly, in Porto Ercole. His body was never found, but the record shows that a Monsignor close to Battista, as well as two monks, were in Porto Ercole that day, despatched post haste from Rome. There is no doubt in my mind that Caravaggio was murdered. God rest his soul.'

By now, everyone in the church was hanging on O'Malley's words.

'You may ask, how can I be sure of this? Where is my proof? And what do the events of four hundred years ago have to do with the election of the next pope? For the moment, I ask you to believe that my investigations have led to the uncovering of certain incontrovertible facts, not least that Battista himself was subsequently arrested by the Inquisition, for which he had once, notoriously, been a prosecutor, and made to answer for his crimes. Following his execution, carried out in secret lest it cause alarm and lead to fears of an Ottoman attack, he was expunged from the history of the Church he had betrayed. Even his time as Camerlengo was stricken from the record.

'Which brings me back to the present day. My brothers and sisters, I beg you to believe me when I say that there is a certain, highly placed individual at work in the Vatican today who is steeped in the history of Battista, and aims, like his wicked forebear, to exploit the mistrust that exists in our world between Christians and Muslims. This man is soaked in blood – and it is not the blood of Christ. His crimes are many, his ambition unsated. And he is not alone.'

O'Malley now turned to glare directly at Cardinal Von Stiegel. 'One man at least, who had the courage to stand up against him and would tomorrow have been a voice of reason and tolerance in the conclave, is already dead, taking with him, I fear, the hopes of a generation. I refer, of course, to Cardinal Horst Rüttgers ... *murdered* in his bath, then buried without any post-mortem examination behind the walls of the Teutonic Cemetery.'

Throughout the Gesù, incomprehension and speculation erupted in equal measure. Once again, O'Malley called for silence.

'But that was not all. Two nights ago, my own nephew, who had carried out research in the Vatican Library into the life and times of Cardinal Battista, was attacked by a professional assassin in Rome and was lucky to escape with his life. That crime at least is being investigated by the city police, who believe that an attempt had earlier been made by someone inside the Vatican to cast my nephew as a thief.'

O'Malley sipped from a glass of water set next to his notes, then resumed his sermon.

'Later, I will have more to say on this most dangerous and devious enemy of Christ – a man who, until recently, kept an unlisted portrait of Battista in his private office. He knows who he is. There may well be those, perhaps here tonight, who can guess at his identity. But for now, until the final proof is laid, I implore those cardinals who tomorrow will be locked into the seclusion of the Sistine Chapel to vote not for the end of history, but for an open future, in which freedom is protected and our faith can go forward. I beg them to elect a candidate whose faith in Jesus Christ and all His saints is as sure and certain as that of the Muslims for Allah and the Prophet. Only as equals, worshipping the one God, eschewing all perversion of the divine will, can believers in these two great faiths hope to live in amity and undestanding. Your Eminences ... do not vote for war. Vote for peace and brotherhood and the love of the Lord Jesus Christ. Vote for the best hope of the universal Church.'

As soon as O'Malley turned to move away from the lectern, one of his adjutants general, Father Joaquin Casado y Moncada, from St Ignatius' hometown of Azpeitia in Navarre, rose to lead the congregation in prayer, then raised his right hand to give the cruciform blessing: 'In the name of the Father, and of the Son, and of the Holy Spirit. Amen.' As he spoke, several cardinals and lesser prelates, led by Archbishop Von Stiegel, walked out in protest, followed by their retinues. But as Casado declared the Mass ended and bade worshippers to go in peace, the rest of the congregation burst into wild applause.

39*
Conclave

It was shortly after dawn on the morning of the papal election that a bus driver on his way to work found the body of Father Cesare Visco outside the Church of Santa Maria delle Grazie. Built in 1941, the church was less than half a kilometre from Visco's home on the Via Venticinque. The priest had apparently slit his throat and died with his bloody hands groping up the church steps, indicating to witnesses and the Church communications department his wish to be closer to God.

Cardinal Bosani called an immediate news conference and revealed his shock and horror at his discovery that Visco, his personal secretary, was in fact a closet Muslim. He read out an email, sent to his personal inbox, that he said was Visco's suicide note. In this, the late priest confessed his plan to pervert Bosani's pro-Catholic, pro-European campaign in advance of the conclave into a message of hate that would ultimately benefit the Islamic cause. He was obviously a fanatic, the Camerlengo told journalists, the balance of his mind disturbed by goodness knew what episode in his past.

What Bosani did not reveal to his audience was that he had called Franco, who was about to board a train for Genoa, and asked for one last favour. Visco, he told him, was a traitor to the church and in the pay of the Muslim Brotherhood. He could not be allowed to work against Christ's interests at this critical time. Franco, Bosani said, would be absolved in full and assured of his place in heaven if he now dealt with the problem, then resumed his journey north.

'While I weep for poor Visco and pray for the repose of his soul,' the Camerlengo told journalists, 'I point to his treachery as proof of my contention that there are evil forces at work, directed against us from the East. These forces must be countered by a new pope whose holy mission will be to restore the Catholic Church to its historic pre-eminence in this, its continental homeland.'

Bosani denied all knowledge of Visco's activities and set out systematically to blacken O'Malley's name by suggesting that it was he, the Superior General of the Jesuits, who was determined to divide Catholicism and set brother against brother. He ended the press briefing by confessing his own naivety and accepted responsibility for hiring Visco in the first place. 'But now, ladies and gentlemen, I ask you to defer all further questions until after the cardinal electors have discharged their duty and elected a new pope to the Throne of Peter. I ask you to pray for me, for poor deluded Father Visco and for all those whose task it is to restore peace in the world.'

The entries from the Secret Archive had been kept in Bosani's safe for twenty years. He wasn't sure why he hadn't destroyed them long ago. All he knew was that when he had tried once to burn the two sets of papers, setting light to them with the flame from a candle, he had been unable to do so. Perhaps, he thought, as he once again smoothed out the 400-year-old documents, they served as a necessary corrective, demonstrating how even the best-laid plans could come to grief if one was not eternally vigilant. But there was also his wish that, in the fullness of time, Battista's heroism should at last be recognized. He deserved no less.

The words on the principle document were seared into his head, but he could never resist the Italian text. The author was Cardinal Ferdinando Gonzaga, later Duke of Mantua, appointed to the Sacred College by Pope Paul V at the consistory of 10 December 1607.

21 December 1610

Most Holy Father,

Your Holiness will recall that following the disappearance and likely death of the artist Michelangelo Merisi, known as Caravaggio, you asked me to investigate what truth, if any, might lie behind claims made by the late Prince Marzio Colonna concerning the religious and political allegiance of His Eminence Cardinal Battista, lately Camerlengo of the Roman Church.

It is with the utmost regret that I must inform Your Holiness of my conclusion, that Battista was indeed a Muslim and had been so for many years. It is further my opinion that, in pursuit of his conspiracy with the Ottoman court, by way of the Safiye Sultan, mother of Sultan Mehmed III, he caused to have murdered not only Prince Marzio, but Caravaggio also.

In accordance with Your Holiness's instructions, I put several men on whom I have in the past placed reliance in positions in which they could observe the cardinal's behaviour. Additionally, I travelled myself, with others, to the Prince's palazzo in Zagarola, south of Rome, where I interrogated members of the household of Duke Marzio, as well as to Porto Ercole, where I spoke with the parish priest of the church of Sant'Erasmus, Father Salviati, about the mysterious disappearance of Merisi.

Servants of the late Prince informed me that their master had dined unexpectedly with the Camerlengo days before his death, while on a visit to Rome. They added that the first signs of what was subsequently said to be the plague had appeared two days thereafter, both in the Prince and in his immediate entourage. Yet no others became infected. One servant, whom I had to assure of the Church's protection in this matter, went so far as to say that Don Marzio had blamed Battista for 'poisoning' him.

In Porto Ercole, the priest, Salviati, told me that on a hot afternoon in July of this year of Our Lord he chanced on a stranger, possibly answering to the description of Merisi, lying on the floor of his church, appearing ill and, so he thought, affected with pestilence. Upon leaving San'Erasmus to secure help, he was halted by three riders, one of them a Monsignor, bearing the arms of the papal household, the crossed keys and the triple tiara; the others two brothers of the Order of St John the Beheaded. The Monsignor, said to be of stocky build, aged in his forties, told the priest that they, not he, would take care of the stranger. They then warned him most solemnly to inform no one of their visit. He did not see the three again and when he re-entered the church found only a bloodstain near the front of the church, closest to the altar.

In the meantime, my spies in Rome reported to me that Battista and his secretary, while in the cardinal's quarters in the Sacred College, did on two occasions prostrate themselves in the Muslim fashion, worshipping in what they understood to be Arabic. Prior to these prayers, they washed their faces, hands and feet and touched the tips of their fingers to their foreheads, mouths and hearts.

Knowing of Your Holiness's deep concern in this matter, I took immediate steps to secure the arrest and interrogation of the Camerlengo. I must now report to you that Battista, having been put to the question and tortured for four hours with irons, confessed to his crimes, which he said were committed in the name of Allah, to whom he bore his true allegiance following time spent in Constantinople, now Istanbul, in service of the Church.

Your Holiness commanded that should I find Battista guilty as charged, I should first ascertain which accomplices, if any, he had retained in this affair and then have him put to death both quickly and secretly lest his crimes become known to the wider community to the detriment of Your Holiness and the Universal Church.

Three names were revealed under torture: that of a senior Knight of the Order of St John, Fra'Luis de Fonseca; also that of Battista's intimate secretary, Father Scaglia; and that of the Monsignor seen in Porto Ercole, Father Domenico Bellarmino, employed in the office of the Camerlengo. It is my hope that I shall secure the names of the Brothers assisting Bellarmino by the end of this week, at which time I will inform Your Holiness further. Each of these men will be dealt with by your order – secretly. Fonseca will die, by your instruction, at the hands of Fabrizio Colonna, whose uncle, Don Marzio, was a victim of this conspiracy and who most nobly rescued Caravaggio from his unjust incarceration in Valletta. None of those who die shall know of the stain they leave.

You will wish to know that Battista was beheaded in a dungeon of the Castel Sant'Angelo. His body, by your express wish, was burned, without ceremony, in the adjacent grounds and his dust scattered in the Tiber. His last words, I must regretfully report to Your Holiness, as the axe fell, were 'Allahu Akbar'.

I pray to Jesus and His Holy Mother that this matter is now concluded.

I have the honour to profess myself with the utmost respect, Your Holiness's most obedient and humble servant.

Gonzaga

Bosani gazed at the familiar letter for several long seconds. Even after all this time, he could feel the sense of injustice burning within him. Battista was a hero of Islam, a martyr in the cause of Muhammad – peace be upon Him. A fragment of his ashes, recovered from a charnel house in Trastevere, had been deposited in the foundations of the mosque of al-Malika Safiyya, in Cairo, on the orders of Safiye Sultan herself. It was his only memorial. But his death would not go unavenged. More than four hundred years had passed since that terrible day in the confines of Castel Sant'Angelo. Bosani, though, did not forget, and neither would the world. Offering a short prayer, he flicked open his mobile phone and pressed the now familiar numbers.

Watching Bosani's press conference on the television, O'Malley recognized a masterful performance. 'The fellow could have been a Jesuit,' he told his nephew. 'But now we need to find out what impact all this business may have on the conclave. After Mass, the cardinals go into purdah and we will have no further chance of reaching them. Let's see what we can do in the few hours remaining.'

O'Malley called a news conference of his own, in which he repeated, in modest terms, the accusation he had made in his sermon in the Gesù. He asked journalists not simply to assume that Visco killed himself. 'Instead, ask yourselves who benefits from his death. Not Visco, obviously. Not me, I submit. The man whom I suggest most gains from the poor wretch's demise is in fact Camerlengo of the Holy Roman Church, who as he vanishes into the conclave would have us believe he is in mourning – a visionary, cruelly duped by a traitor, whose stern, even heroic, warning against the coming predations of the Islamic world rings truer today than ever.'

The Italian press had splashed that morning with O'Malley's doom-laden sermon. Now, following the two news conferences, the internet was awash with sensational claims and fresh 'revelations'. Television stations, geared up for the spectacle of a papal election, not realizing that the vote could be rigged, began to explore every aspect of the bitter quarrel between the Camerlengo and the Superior General of the Society of Jesus.

Dempsey turned to his uncle. 'Why did Visco do it?' he wanted to know.

'Don't be stupid, Liam. Visco didn't kill himself. He was murdered.'

The younger man looked shocked. 'But why? He couldn't be sure that Maya had pictures of him praying. All he knew was that someone had been spying at his door. It could easily have been a child.'

'Quite possibly,' said O'Malley. 'But by telling Bosani of his fears, he was signing his own death warrant. Bosani already knew his plot had been exposed. Any properly organized investigation was bound to lead to his door. Even though I didn't mention his name, it was plain as day that I was on to him. He needed a scapegoat – someone against whom there was genuine evidence – who would make it look as if I had fingered the wrong man. Visco fitted the bill perfectly. He had also failed his master and deserved his fate. Maya's film footage, once handed to the media, would have shown to the world that he was a practising Muslim. From that moment on, it was a question of damage limitation, and fair play to Bosani, he almost succeeded in turning Visco's death to his advantage. I'm not saying the Camerlengo wielded the knife personally. That wouldn't be his style. But he will certainly have given the order.'

'Jesus Christ!' said Dempsey. 'No wonder I gave up religion.'

High Mass on the morning of the papal election was celebrated in St Peter's Basilica. To indicate the global nature of the occasion, the officiating priests were drawn from Uganda, Hong Kong, the United States and Peru. The dean of the College of Cardinals, Cardinal Urbano della Chiesa, who would later preside over the conclave, next to the Camerlengo, then gave an address. Della Chiesa was as straightforward a cleric as Bosani was scheming. Due to pressure of business, he had been unable to attend the previous night's Mass at the Gèsu, but had watched it afterwards on television. O'Malley's comments had caused him grave concern. Never in his lifetime had a Superior General of the Jesuits intervened in such a fashion in the matter of a papal election. But the dean had worked with the Camerlengo for several years and had long sensed that something was not quite right about him. In his address – intended less as a sermon than a speech of welcome to the cardinal electors – he urged his 121 voting colleagues not to be swayed by rumour but to focus on the need to proclaim a new pastor for a troubled Church.

'You will have read and heard much in the last day about conspiracies and clandestine plots to subvert the will of God. But I tell you, those who seek to divert the Almighty from His divine purpose are surely doomed to fail. Our duty in the conclave that will shortly begin is to elect from the ranks of the Sacred College a priest of God to sit on the Throne of Peter. Our new pope, whoever he may be, will face grave challenges. He must therefore be both strong and humble, able to resist the impulses that at times affect us all and proclaim the mystery of faith and the certainty of Christ's return. On Earth, he must be a pastor – the Good Shepherd. Within the Church, he should be a leader, but also the Servant of the Servants of God. Let us pray that today and in the days ahead we shall each of us do our duty and find a pope who will so light the path ahead that all of us in this world can find our way. I ask this in the name of Jesus and His Holy Mother. Amen.'

Halfway down the aisle, with Dempsey and Maya sitting next to him, O'Malley said a silent prayer.

As the choir of St Peter's began a soaring anthem, Della Chiesa and Bosani – who as Camerlengo was the sole member of the hierarchy still in office – then led cardinals in procession from the Basilica to the nearby Domus Sanctae Marthae, built on the orders of John Paul II to house cardinals in civilized conditions during conclaves. By tradition and canon law, the electors would not re-emerge until a new pope was elected, notice of which would be conveyed by white smoke issuing from the chimney of the Sistine Chapel.

Along with the cardinals, into the hostel went the secretary of the College of Cardinals; the papal master of ceremonies and his three assistants (who would prepare the new pontiff for his investiture); the former dean's secretary; confessors; two doctors and a selection of cooks and housekeepers, most of them nuns. No televison, radio or newspapers were permitted. Mobile phones and Blackberrys were confiscated. There would be no communication of any kind with the outside world. Security was provided by the Swiss Guard, commanded personally by Colonel Studer.

Outside, the crowds in St Peter's Square continued to grow. By lunchtime, police estimated that as many as 300,000 people had arrived from every corner of the globe. There were nuns from Ethiopia and Uganda; priests from France and Paraguay; worshippers from Wisconsin and the Ukraine. There were even parties of Japanese tourists and punks from London – well-wishers of every religion and none. No other international event, with the possible exception of the World Cup, could have produced such a multitude.

Dempsey, granted a special security pass by Colonel Studer, pushed his way through the heaving throng with Maya. Unknown to anyone, Franco Lucchese was also there. For he, too, was on a special mission.

The first black smoke, indicating a failed ballot, emerged from the chapel chimney after two hours. A groan of disappointment rose up from onlookers. Most of those present, including a majority of Italians, were in good humour, soaking up the carnival atmosphere and not wanting it to end too quickly. But others were dour and intense, like compulsive gamblers, rooting for their preferred candidates. The fervour shown reminded Dempsey of passionate meetings in town squares at which Shiite clergy would stir up renewed hatred of the Kurds. He sensed unease as well as expectation among sections of the faithful and couldn't help becoming wary himself. He tried to imagine how Bosani would play it. He wanted his man elected and had done everything in his power to influence the cardinals' choice. But he left nothing to chance and was sure to have one final trick up his sleeve. Dempsey did his best to keep his wits about him. The Swiss Guard, armed with more than medieval halberds, were on duty outside all entrances, backed by the papal gendarmerie. The security services of the Vatican and Italy had men patrolling St Peter's Square and its environs. More than a thousand officers from the Rome city police were on duty, with hundreds more in reserve. Closed-circuit cameras surveyed the crowd. A helicopter flew overhead.

Another puff of black smoke curled up from the chimney. This meant that another vote had failed to produce a result. Voting, ideally, was by 'inspiration'.

The mood of the gathering would be judged by the dean and Camerlengo and a name put out for approval by acclamation. Inspiration, however, was extremely rare. The standard practice, when no obvious candidate emerged, was an elaborate process of secret balloting, known as 'scrutiny', aimed at finding someone who had the support of two-thirds of the electors. This could take days, sometimes weeks. Another groan rose from the crowd. Whatever was going to happen, it was clear it wasn't going to happen quickly. As the mid-summer temperature continued to soar, an unstoppable lethargy overtook the multitude, which slowly spread to the police and security services. It was as if the world and everything in it had stopped for the afternoon.

Shortly after four, Dempsey took a call from his uncle on his mobile. 'I wish I could be there with you, Liam. What was it the O'Rahilly said as he set out for the GPO in 1916? "I've helped to wind the clock, now I've come to hear it strike." But the truth is, I'd only provoke a riot. Best if I stay out of sight for a while. After all, there's nothing more anyone can do.'

'Isn't there, though?' Dempsey replied.

'What do you mean?'

'Bosani's in there. I don't doubt that Plan A is unfolding as we speak. He will have prepared the ground and mustered his troops. But there has to be something more – something we haven't thought of. From what you tell me, there are few enough liberals left in the College of Cardinals, which is as old school as they come. But that doesn't mean he's going to have everything his own way. What about the pragmatists, or the ones who simply want the Church to continue on its own terms? They won't want to vote for someone who could end up leading Europe into an unwinnable war with Islam. There has to be something else – a Plan B – that will drive the waverers over the edge and persuade them of the rightness of his cause.'

'What are you suggesting?'

'I don't know. But I'm trying to put myself in his position. I've lived among madmen, don't forget. Iraq was full of them. They don't stop at half-measures. If he can't change things from the inside, it'll have to be from the outside.'

'Oh, dear Lord!' his uncle said.

'What?'

'A suicide bomber!'

For a moment, neither man spoke. Then Demspey said, 'That's what I was thinking. But he wouldn't dare ... would he?'

'He might. He just might. The man is demonic – a monster. He's already killed one of his own, as well as Cardinal Rüttgers. Why not 500 Catholic pilgrims? The way he sees it, he'd be doing God's work.'

'It would also explain why Yilmaz Hakura is in town.'

'Exactly. Bosani is like an army general calling in special forces.'

'... who can be counted on to perform the actions that others would baulk at.' Dempsey thought hard for a moment. He could feel his heart begin to pound in his chest. 'Call Colonel Studer,' he said. 'He's the only one we know with the clearance to make something of this.'

'I'll get onto it right away. And I'll speak to Aprea ... he'll know who to contact to get things moving. Meanwhile, keep your eyes skinned – and get Maya the hell out of there.'

Maya had been talking to two tourists from Lyon while Demspey was on the phone. Now she looked alarmed. 'You've turned pale,' she said. 'What did your uncle just say to you?'

'I want you to go home,' Demspey said. 'Seriously. Get inside and stay there. Bosani has only one card left to play and I don't want you around for it.' He dropped his voice to a whisper. 'If you see your father, tell him there could be a suicide bomber in St Peter's Square, dressed as a priest, or a nun, or just an ordinary tourist. It could be anybody.'

Maya's face turned pale. 'Good God! What are you going to do?'

'My uncle's contacting police headquarters. In the meantime, I'm going to keep my eyes open, see if there's anyone acting suspiciously. Other than that, I swear to God, I don't know.'

Less than a hundred metres away, also in St Peter's Square, Franco was engaged in his own search for the bomber. Renzo Giacconi, his Genovese capo, had been shocked to learn from him that Father Visco, far from being an opponent of Islam, was actually a Muslim himself, trying to foment a war with Christian Europe.

'But Visco was only a puppet,' he had said. 'The question is, who is pulling the strings?'

Franco had thought about this. When the truth hit him, it was with a sense of shock. Yes. Bosani was the puppet master. Who else could it possibly be? The truth had been staring him in the face for years. Visco had always done the Camerlengo's bidding. He was no more than his master's voice, desperate to please through every word and action. The assassin had been raised in a culture of hierarchy – Church, Mafia and the army – and could not imagine how someone of Visco's essentially empty nature could simply have drifted into such a dangerous conspiracy. His conversion could only have come about at the behest of a powerful personality, and there was no more powerful personality in Rome than Cardinal Lamberto Bosani.

The Camerlengo had always been careful to sound like he was the most Catholic of high Catholics when Franco was around. But how else could he play it? He could hardly have confessed all to a mere hitman. The justification he gave for the actions he ordered (followed invariably by five minutes in the confessional with Father Visco) was that, in setting the Church and Islam at each other's throats, he was doing God's work, helping prepare the way for the ultimate triumph of Christ. Though dismayed by the murder of priests, even a prince of the Church, Franco had comforted himself that Bosani knew what he was doing and that he, for his part, was only following orders. But now, after talking with his capo, he felt that he had been used and, worse than that, betrayed. And who was to say that when Bosani's final purpose was achieved, he wouldn't find some reason to extinguish the faithful Franco? That would be a sensible move. It would tie up a dangerous loose end and reduce the circle of those who understood his true purpose. There was also his mother to consider. Mama would be horrified to learn that her son, however unwittingly, had acted against Jesus and His Holy Mother, and Franco was not one to offend his mother, even after she was dead.

Giacconi was following the news from Rome with great care and attention and believed he had worked out Bosani's likely strategy. Once you accepted, he said, that the cardinal was not who he said he was, but a Muslim agent set on bringing down the Church, the suicide-bomber ploy followed as night followed day. Franco had been despatched on the overnight train from Genoa, and told to keep a close watch in St Peter's Square for any signs of trouble. He was then under orders to do whatever was necessary to stop it. From a payphone in the terminus in Rome, he had called the security services and left an anonymous warning of a threat to pilgrims, which he assumed would be ignored. Other than that, he reasoned, there was nothing more he could do.

It was therefore a fact that by 4.30 in the afternoon, both Dempsey and Franco were actively looking for a bomber. DIGOS, aware of the possible presence in Rome of Yilmaz Hakura, was aware that anything could happen and had circulated details of the Hizb ut-Tahrir operative. But the Vatican's position was that there was no reason to fear a terrorist attack. They were on high alert because the election of the Pope was that kind of an occasion, but in their hearts they did not expect to have to deal with more than medical alerts, occasional rowdies and the inevitable upsurge of joy that would greet the first puff of white smoke.

O'Malley had tried and failed to contact Colonel Studer, who was not using his normal mobile phone. He left a message with the front desk and on his voice-mail. Maya hadn't reached her father either. Not even her mother had any hope of speaking with the colonel until the new Pope was announced and the crowds had dispersed. Frustrated, she had then called the Rome police and told a duty officer of Dempsey's fears of a suicide bomber in St Peter's Square. The young woman duly took a note and promised to pass it on. It later turned out that Maya's call was the 147th that day with essentially the same message.

Equally frustrated, not knowing how best to be useful in a situation that had escalated far beyond his control, O'Malley called Chief Inspector Aprea, and agreed to meet him in the control room of the Vatican Security Corps, part of the gendarmerie, based on an upper floor of the Governate. The control room was the hub of the surveillance operation. Scores of high-resolution LCD screens were arranged in banks along one side of the room, monitored by trained officers able to zoom in on groups and individuals gathered in the square.

Aprea had already spoken to the inspector in charge, asking him to direct his officers to look out for anyone, including religious and clergy, carrying too much bulk or seeming to have another purpose in mind than celebration of a new pope.

Below, standing on the pedestal of the Egyptian obelisk in the centre of the square, Dempsey was beginning to think that he must have got it all wrong. There was no bomber and Bosani's cause was lost. He started to think about Maya and wondered how soon they could meet up again once all this was over.

Fifty metres away, Franco was coming to the same conclusion. The Camerlengo was a ruthless man and his behaviour in recent months had been increasingly bizarre. But was it honestly possible that he could be a Muslim? It was crazy stuff. The capo was deluding himself. He was so used to people who lied to him about everything, just to save their skins, that he couldn't recognize truth any longer. And even if he was right and the Camerlengo had switched faiths, not even he, for God's sake, would set off a bomb among a crowded throng of pilgrims come to greet their new Pope.

Dempsey and Franco, without knowing it, were less than fifty metres apart. The Italian had dyed his newly shorn hair and was again wearing dark glasses. The last thing he wanted was to be picked up by the police. He was watching for any kind of supicious movement, especially from anyone who might be an Arab or an Iranian, or any kind of Muslim ... but also for shifty-looking priests, or nuns carrying a bit too much weight.

Dempsey, having seen the results of two suicide bombs in Iraq, was equally vigilant, but here, out of the Middle-East context, was less sure what a potential bomber would look like. He was also curious to learn what was going on in the conclave, which had failed twice now to produce a result and ought to be gearing up for the final ballot of the day. Bosani was clearly a man possessed and would be working to set up someone he could control – a small-minded bigot with a martyr complex. But there were no guarantees. What if the conclave chose a technocrat like Ratzinger, who became Benedict XVI, or a saint like Roncalli – John XXIII – or a bore like Montini, who as Paul VI presided over twenty-five years of stasis? Who among the crowd of pensioners he had watched shuffling into the Sistine Chapel, worried about their prostates, their bad hearts and their flatulence, was really capable of turning the world upside down and leading the West towards an early date with Armageddon?

The press of people around him was suffocating. He had never seen a crowd like this. Three hundred and fifty thousand – that was like the combined population of Cork, Limerick and Galway. And the temperature was a sweaty thirty-five degrees! A cold beer – that's what he'd like right now. And a cool bath, and Maya to share it with him.

That was when the phone in his pocket rang. He didn't hear it at first and when he snapped it open the connection was broken, leaving the message on-screen, *Missed Call Jesuit 1.* Uncle Declan. Seconds later, O'Malley's voice came on the line. He sounded excited.

'Listen to me, Liam. I'm in the Governate with Aprea. One of the surveillance cameras has picked up a monk behaving suspiciously. He's obviously tense. He keeps looking round him, and he keeps one of his hands permanently inside the fold of his habit, as if he's got got something hidden there. But more to the point, I think I recognize him. The other day, when I went to visit Bosani, this same fellow – a Benedictine – was talking to Visco. He's tall – six-four at least – aged about thirty. And he's got a tonsure. At the moment, he's about thirty or forty feet from where you're standing, in the direction of the Sistine Chapel. The head of the gendarmerie has ordered two of his men to make their way towards him, but they're in uniform and Aprea is worried they may startle him.'

'Don't worry, Uncle. I'm on it.'

'Please be careful,' O'Malley said. But Dempsey had already rung off.

A tall man. Six-feet-four. Wearing a monk's habit and with a tonsure. At least he shouldn't be hard to spot. He fixed his eyes on the Sistine Chapel, a hundred metres or so to his right, and began to press his way through the throng.

'Excuse me. Please let me through. This is important. *Mi scusi. Excusez moi. Entschuldigung.*'

His progress was plainfully slow. One person in ten in the square must have been a priest or member of a religious order. At least the priests would mostly be in their everyday suits, while most of the religious were nuns. Even so. It was like looking for your cousin in a football crowd.

He took a deep breath and pushed ahead. That was when he smelled it. Drifting into his nostrils: the sweet smell of marzipan or almonds. He sniffed again. The bomb that nearly killed him four years ago had given off an aroma of marzipan just before it went off in the sickly summer heat of that September afternoon. He remembered it like it was yesterday. He was leading his platoon on a routine patrol on high ground about ten kilometres northeast of Kirkuk. A device fashioned from decaying plastic explosive had been concealed beneath a water trough. It detonated less than four feet from one of his troopers ten paces behind, killing the young man and two comrades and, in his own case, stripping the skin off the right side of his back from his shoulder down as far as his buttocks.

That was the day his old life had ended.

He stopped. There it was again. That smell … like marzipan in a low oven.

He looked around cautiously. There were at least a dozen people within six feet of him: a middle-aged couple, Spanish by the sound of them; a group of overweight Romans; two Germans in their twenties; a pregnant woman; an elderly nun wearing a Carmelite habit; a student-type drinking from a bottle of Evian water … and a tall monk with a Benedictine tonsure. He swallowed hard. Was this the man who would start the next world war? He inched towards him, trying not to appear in any way interested. The smell grew stronger as he drew closer. The explosives must be sweating in this heat. He brushed past him, looking straight ahead, while allowing his trailing left hand to touch lightly against the man's cassock. There was no doubt about it. He was wearing something solid around his middle.

He didn't know what to do. There were officers on the way, but with 300,000 people in the square focused on what they regarded as a sacred event, no simple order to clear the area could be given. In any case, action by the police might very well have the effect of ensuring the disaster it was intended to prevent. The bomber could almost certainly trigger his device with one flick of his thumb – assuming, that is, that he had activated it. But maybe he hadn't got to that point yet. As Dempsey struggled to keep up with him, the suspect edged his way through the crowd in the direction of the Sistine Chapel. Maybe he wanted to get closer to the conclave before he pressed the switch, for maximum impact. It was even possible that he planned to damage the chapel itself, thus adding to the sense of outrage that would sweep the world. Dempsey halted for a second and looked around him, hoping against hope to see a policeman or a gendarme nearby. But there was no one. What should he do? If he kept on following him, the suspect was sure to realize that he had been spotted. And then what? He swallowed hard. There was nothing for it. He would just have to tackle him and hope for the best. If he could just knock him over, then hold firm to his arms until help came …

He got ready to charge. *Holy Mother of God!* he said to himself. *Here goes!*

He leapt forward, pushing two Japanese tourists out of his path, and jumped the man from behind, encircling his waist, hoisting his arms upwards, shouting out at the same time, 'Move away! Everybody back!'

A woman sreamed. Then everyone was screaming. The crowd shrank back like a single frightened creature. 'It's a bomb!' somebody shouted. 'He's got a bomb!'

He could hear commands being shouted through a megaphone, too far off to be of any use. Then a police whistle. Maybe Uncle Declan had actually persuaded someone to *do* something. But they were too late. All the while, he and the bomber were grappling. '*Lascilo andare!* – Let go of me!' the man shrieked. 'I am here to do God's work! Allah is with me!'

He wasn't just tall, he was exceptionally strong, his power boosted by the adrenalin charge of knowing that these were his final seconds on earth. Dempsey, with his injured left arm, could barely constrain him. Amid further desperate struggle, their legs gave way together and they fell over, rolling over and over on the cobbles. During one twist, Dempsey managed to hook his feet round the man's ankles, so that he now held him from both ends. But it was obvious he wasn't going to give up. Once more calling on Allah, he gave a mighty heave and broke the Irishman's grip. Wriggling to his right before he could be ensnared again, he groped with one hand around his middle until he found what he was looking for. A red light came on. Too late, too late. For Dempsey, the world now stood still. All he could focus on was the man, screaming out 'Allahu Akbar!' while his left thumb trembled over the simple pressure switch that would set off the bomb. Dempsey felt fear – fear and regret, and shame. He closed his eyes.

The next thing he heard was the dull thwack of a silenced automatic, then another, and another. He opened his eyes again. The smell of marzipan had been replaced by the stench of cordite. The bomber's brains and skull were spread out over the cobbles, which were thickly stained with blood. His left foot twitched for a second, then lay still.

The screams from the crowd had reached a crescendo. Dempsey could feel the intensity of the excitement among the onlookers pressing in on him. Whoever had shot the monk had saved his life and the lives of hundreds of pilgrims. He sat up, noticing for the first time that his hands were shaking. Standing straight ahead, gripping an automatic in his right hand, was the assassin who had attacked him with a switchblade two days before. It wasn't so much his face that he recognized. It was his bulk and the way he held himself – like a professional. The man was nodding down at him as if in acknowledgement of something. Then, twisting the silencer off the muzzle of his pistol, he turned away and disappeared into the crowd. No one tried to stop him. They were too stunned, too scared, and too grateful.

Seconds later, Sergeant Weibel of the Swiss Guard turned up, his P226 handgun out of his holster. He looked disappointed that he had arrived too late to shoot anybody. After that, it was the turn of the paramedics. O'Malley and Aprea were not far behind. Dempsey was immediately proclaimed by the crowd as a hero – or one half of a team of heroes. So where was the second man? Sergeant Weibel wanted to know. But no one knew, and Dempsey was saying nothing.

Meanwhile, in a hotel room in Nicosia, Yilmaz Hakura switched off his television set. The news from St Peter's Square was a setback, but not a defeat. With Bosani at the new Pope's elbow, there would be other times and other opportunities. The crusaders had to win every time; jihadis only once. From the minaret of a nearby mosque, the voice of the muezzin could be heard calling the faithful to prayer. Hakura did not ignore the call.

It was another two hours before the white smoke rose from the chimney of the Sistine Chapel. Colonel Studer, it turned out, had broken the iron rule of the conclave and entered the building to talk to the dean. To do so, he required not only his own key, but those of the prefect of the Pontifical House and of the official delegate of the Holy See. The prefect acquiesced as soon as he learned what had happened. The delegate, however, had to be pressured into giving his consent. 'Listen to me,' Studer said. 'If you say no to me, first I shall take the key anyway. Second, I shall tell the world that you refused to inform Their Eminences of an unprecedented attack on the sovereignty of the universal Church.' At this, the delegate, a retired banker, caved in completely.

Studer was not exaggerating. 'Please forgive me, Your Eminence,' he began. 'I greatly regret this intrusion. But something terrible has happened.'

'Yes,' the dean replied. 'Cardinal Bosani told us.'

Studer had suspected as much. That's why he had broken a rule established centuries before. 'But how did he know?' he asked. 'Aren't you supposed to be *incommunicado*?'

The dean looked uneasy. 'The Camerlengo had apparently kept hold of his mobile phone ... in case of an emergency. We live in a new age, Colonel.'

'More's the pity. And did he tell you what happened?'

'He said an Islamist from somewhere in the Arab world had tried to kill himself and hundreds of pilgrims in the square. He said it was the work of those from outside Europe who wished to restore the caliphate.'

The colonel absorbed the significance of the dean's comment. 'Well, Eminence,' he said. 'I'm sorry to have to tell you this, but the Camerlengo has deceived you.'

Studer went on to explain to the 75-year-old prelate that a suicide bomber had been about to detonate the plastic explosive strapped around his middle when two young men, one the nephew of the Father General of the Jesuits, the other as yet unknown, had tackled him with conspicuous bravery and foiled the attack, killing the bomber in the process. What he most wished the dean and his fellow cardinals to know was that the terrorist was not an Arab, or an Iranian or any kind of cradle Muslim. He was, in fact, as the battered ID card found in a pocket of his habit revealed, a monk, born in Padua, who had converted two years before while spending time in a monastic community in the Sinai. 'Our civilization may indeed be under threat, Your Eminence, but not all of our enemies are to be found on the outside.'

While Studer and the dean were talking, no one noticed that the Camerlengo had left the Sistine Chapel by a rear door to which only he held the key. Bosani was in a quiet fury. He could not understand how all his planning had come to nothing. It was a crime against God that the bomber had not succeeded in his holy task. It was a further insult to Islam that the cardinals should now turn away from the candidate around which he had built a consensus and select instead a pope from among the Church's so-called moderates.

Worst of all was the certainty that he himself, after thirty years in the Curia, would now be exposed as a spy and a 'traitor'. He was not a traitor, he was a martyr – a hero of the One True Faith who, like his heroic forebear, Orazio Battista, would be traduced and expelled from history.

They would make up stories about him. They would say he was a madman. They would plant lies in the media. And then, after he had been humiliated in the courts, he would be sentenced to life imprisonment in a Western jail, alongside the scum of the earth – men of all religions and none.

His throat was dry. His failure was too much to bear. It was literally unendurable. He knew that he should flee, melt into the city and make his way east, where he would be received as an honoured guest, free to spend his last days in open worship of his God. It was not enough. Such an end, after his decades of power, was unacceptable. There had to be a way out consistent with his honour. He shut his eyes. Then it came to him. There was one last card to play – if only he dared to play it. He took a deep breath. Strapped to his left forearm, hidden beneath the sleeve of his soutane, was a curved dagger that had once belonged to Battista, given to him by the Safiye Sultan herself. Battista had died at the hands of the papal executioner still proclaiming that God was great. He would go one better. With this sacred dagger, he would kill the Father General of the Jesuits. O'Malley had prevented him from initiating the last great war – the war that would result in the establishment of a caliphate stretching from Pakistan and Afghanistan in the east to Spain and Portugal in the west, with its capital in Rome, as foretold by the Prophet. For that audacity, the Irishman would die and, in response, Muslims throughout Europe would come under attack. They would call on the Arab world, and Iran with its Islamic bomb, to rise in their defence – and this time their call would not go unanswered.

He stifled a laugh. Oh, the irony! O'Malley would turn out to have been the instrument of Allah's divine plan. He would play his part in history after all. Yes!

All was not yet lost. He looked around him, wiping a fleck of spittle from his lips. It was beautiful. Alone, in spite of everything the Christians could throw against him and without the help of the fool Hukura, he would rescue God's plan from the wreckage imposed by the infidels.

O'Malley at this time was in the middle of St Peter's Square talking to Aprea, Studer and the divisional commander of the Roman police. The crowds had been pushed back and urged to get as far from the square as possible. The body of the suicide bomber had been taken away, to a chorus of jeers from onlookers. Franco had melted away. Dempsey was being treated for delayed shock by paramedics.

Maya, finding her path out of the Swiss Guard barracks blocked by police, had found a back way into the square that ran between the Apostolic Palace and the Sistine Chapel. She knew better than to approach the conclave, but hurried along to a side gate that she knew would be guarded by one of her father's halbardiers.

The young man recognized her at once. He was from the same canton.

'I need to speak with my father,' she told him through the grill. 'Please let me through.'

The soldier, in his blue, everyday uniform, shook his head. 'This is a closed area. But in any case, the colonel isn't here. He's over there.' He pointed to a huddle in the middle of the square.

Maya thanked him and hurried on. What she failed to see was a figure in scarlet arriving at the gate she had just left.

Bosani waved a hand at the young pikeman. 'Let me pass,' he said.

Recognizing the Camerlengo, the soldier hesitated, then reluctantly barred his path. 'I am sorry, Your Eminence,' he began, 'but Colonel Studer has given us strict orders to admit no one and to allow no one to leave until a new pope is elected.'

'Get out of my way!'

'It is the law. You must return to the conclave.'

For a moment, Bosani simply stared. Then, without warning, he shoved the young guardsman out of his path and sped past him into the square.

Maya, desperate to find out what had happened to Liam, had almost reached the huddle in the square when her father, alerted by a sixth sense, or perhaps a flash of scarlet, spun round.

'Maya!' he shouted in Schwitzerdeutsch. 'Behind you!'

The warning came too late. Bosani had caught up with her, and as she turned she was astonished to see the grinning cardinal, his teeth bared, encircling her neck with a silk-clad arm.

It was an ecastatic moment for Bosani. Maya Studer, the daughter of the commandant of the Swiss Guard … the little whore who had thrown in her lot with O'Malley and his accursed nephew. Yes. She would do. She would do very well. In some ways, her death would be even more symbolic than that of the Father General. A good Swiss Catholic girl, of high rank, whose father had dared to thwart his plans and was sworn to protect the Pope. The entire Christian world would be outraged.

On the edge of the square, news cameras were running. The international media was all around. Without intermediaries, with himself as the messenger, he would proclaim the coming triumph of Islam. Having delivered his message, he would kill the girl, slitting her throat with Battista's dagger. They would shoot him. Oh yes. He would die at her side. But while her soul went to hell, his would soar to heaven, where Muhammad – peace be upon Him – would be waiting.

Days before, reasoning that if everything went wrong he would not end up entirely defenceless in the face of his enemies, Bosani had concealed his predecessor's richly decorated knife beneath a ledge in his place in the Sistine Chapel. Now he pressed the edge of the curved blade, inscribed with lines from the Qu'ran, against Maya's throat. She tried to scream, but couldn't. His arm was too tight about her neck. Her eyes pleaded with him, begging him for mercy. But none would come and she knew it. She waited for death, praying that it would be quick.

'Allahu Akhbar!' Bosani cried out, addressing his words to the cameras. 'God is great! Europe has lived too long in sin. Soon the unstoppable forces of Islam will be loosed upon you and you will have the choice either to live as Muslims or die as slaves. No pope can save you. No army can rescue you from your fate.' He glared at O'Malley. 'The death of this Christian whore will only the first of many. I go now to glory. The triumph of Is …'

At that moment, a single shot rang out and Bosani, a look of shock and disbelief in his eyes, fell backwards. From the side of his head, just above his left ear, a wound had opened up that spewed blood all down his robes and onto the flagstones. The dagger fell onto the cobbles, its point hitting the ground so that the blade shattered into two pieces. This was not … *fair*. He cursed his fate. He looked to the heavens for some sign that the gates of paradise were opening, but saw nothing. A final, despairing gurgle emerged from his mouth as his brain died, and then he lay still.

From the edge of the huddle, next to the ambulance where he had been receiving treatment, Dempsey began to walk forward, a police pistol held rigid between his two outstretched hands.

No one tried to stop him. Only when Maya, shaking with fear, managed to turn towards him, raising her arms, did he drop the gun. Then the two of them began to run. They didn't stop until they arrived in each other's arms. As they embraced, with tears running down their cheeks, white smoke rose from the chimney of the Sistine Chapel.

Epilogue*
Habemus Papam –
We Have a Pope

The new Pope, the 267th successor of St Peter, had just announced his regnal name, to the joy of the anxious crowd still gathered in St Peter's Square. An experienced administrator and diplomat, doctrinally conservative but socially progressive, he promised in his *Urbi et Orbi* address to engage the Muslim world in 'constructive dialogue'. There was no talk of war or revenge. For a start, he said, on whom would Christians be revenging themselves? No 'outsider' was party to the plot; all involved had been born and raised as Catholics. Instead, the new pontiff vowed to tackle the central issue of faith in the Church and the 'absolute imperative to live in harmony with our fellow citizens of all faiths and none'.

Most Muslim leaders, bar the usual suspects, welcomed the choice and deplored the attempted bomb attack, which they insisted was a sin against Islam, having no connection with anyone beyond the Vatican. They called on the Church to renew its dialogue with Islam and to speak out in favour of greater integration by Muslims into the greater European society. Putting their best face on a bad business, they looked forward to a new era, though not one without its tribulations.

Only four days after the conclave did it emerge from an anonymous article in *Il Messaggero* that the front runner at the time of Studer's intervention was Cardinal Pietro Albonetti, a hardliner, born near the airport at Fiumicino, who was close to both Bosani and Von Stiegel, and was an acknowledged anti-Muslim bigot. Few at the outset considered Albonetti papabile, let alone the favourite, but after three failed ballots, each engineered by Bosani and his cohorts, his candidacy was gathering momentum. Only after the dramatic events in St Peter's Square, followed by the personal intervention of Colonel Studer, did a new search begin, with the nomination of the successful candidate by Cardinal McCarthy, the Archbishop of Dublin.

O'Malley and his nephew were sitting in the Jesuit's office in the Borgo Santo Spirito. 'You realize, of course,' Dempsey said, 'that Albonetti was Peter the Roman.'

'I suppose so,' O'Malley conceded, reluctantly.

'The Antichrist.'

'If that's what you believe.'

'You still don't give the idea any credence, then? Even after all that's happened?'

O'Malley clasped his hands in front of him. 'I'll give you this much. Years ago, when John Paul I died – or was murdered – it was noted that his pontificate corresponded almost exactly with the moon's monthly cycle. Believers in the prophecies of Malachy insisted this was why he was described as *de medietate lunae* – the crescent moon. But I always saw it another way. The crescent moon is the symbol of Islam ...'

'... and Luciani was one of the first to foresee the crisis that was building between Christians and Muslims.'

'Exactly.'

Dempsey looked lost in thought. He twisted round in his chair and stared out the window towards the dome of St Peter's. 'When you come down to it,' he said at last, 'the Antichrist and the Dajjal are pretty much one and the same.'

'I don't deny it.'

'Mirror images of the same grotesque prophecy.'

The older man nodded.

'And from what you tell me, both of them have their origins in scripture and neither has been repudiated by scholars.'

'That's about the size of it.'

'It's scary.'

'Very.'

O'Malley swallowed hard. He looked troubled. Then he brightened. 'But that doesn't mean everything has been decided in advance. Let's not forget, Malachy didn't say anything about Peter the Roman coming close, only to lose out to a surprise choice out of nowhere.'

'He could hardly be expected to forsee every contingency.'

'Oh, come on now. Isn't that exactly what astrologers are for?'

'I suppose. But tell me this. You're not comfortable with the idea of a monster, in the form of the Antichrist, stalking the earth, only to be defeated and sent to hell by a vengeful Messiah. And I don't blame you. It's more like *The Lord of the Rings* than the Lord Above. Yet, in *The Betrayal of Christ* – leaving out Caravaggio's unusual take on events – poor old Judas was only acting out the script that had been written for him.'

'Exactly right,' the priest said.

'If he'd exercised free will and not betrayed his master, he would in fact have been acting contrary to the will of God.'

'That's true ... and also impossible.'

'It's a mess.'

'It's a mystery.'

There seemed nothing left to say, and the two men stared at each other.

'So what happens now?' Dempsey asked. Before his uncle could respond, there was a polite knock on the door and Father Giovanni came in, smiling beatifically at Dempsey. He distributed coffee and biscotti, then turned to leave, still smiling.

Dempsey smiled back. '*Grazie*, Giovanni.'

'*Prego*.' The young priest retreated, closing the door after him.

O'Malley picked up his coffee and took a sip, glad of the chance to break the mood. 'Father Giovanni seems to have taken a bit of a shine to you since you prevented a massacre in St Peter's Square.'

'I'd noticed.'

'You'll need to get used to that. But to answer your question, what happens now is that the Pope confers on you the Grand Cross of the Order of Pius IX.'

Dempsey squirmed. 'Is there no way out of that?'

'None that I know of. But sure don't knock it. As a papal Knight, you'll have every head waiter in Dublin falling over himself to give you a decent table.'

'That would be nice if the Pope was settling the bill.'

'A St Peter's credit card, you mean?'

'From the old Bank of the Holy Spirit. Something like that. I'll let you know how it goes. The main thing is, though, I have to be back in Galway at the end of the month. I've a PhD to prepare for, remember, and I'm months behind in my research.'

'After all that's happened, take it from me, you'll waltz it. More importantly, what about Maya?'

Dempsey grinned. 'Well, now, that's the good part. She's got a job with UBS in Dublin. So we can see each other at weekends. And I'd guess we'll be out here for the holidays.'

'I look forward to it.'

'If she should ever agree to marry me ...'

'Make an honest man of you, you mean?'

'Exactly … I hope you'd do the honours.'

'In Rome, in the Gesù? If course. A pleasure and a privilege, my boy. Your father would be proud of you.'

They both sat back and sipped at their coffees. O'Malley said, 'You'll come to the special Mass, of course?'

'I wouldn't miss it.'

High Mass in the Gesù for the repose of the souls of Caravaggio and the two murdered priests, Pope John Paul I and Cardinal Horst Rüttgers, was to be held the following Sunday. It would be celebrated jointly by the Pope and Superior General O'Malley. Attendance would include artists from around the world, surviving members of the family of Albino Luciani and representatives of the German Church, led by Cardinal Georg Sterzinsky, the retiring Archbishop of Berlin and new acting head of the German hierarchy. Media interest was enormous. Al-Jazeera had requested, and been granted, facilities to record the occasion. Security would be provided by the Swiss Guard, under the command of Colonel Studer, while mounted above the altar, by permission of the Society of Jesus and the National Gallery of Ireland, would be *The Betrayal of Christ*, with its startling, telltale image of the fleeing man.

'Of course, all this still leaves one loose end,' Dempsey said.

'The mysterious stranger, you mean?'

'I looked into his eyes – twice. I could describe him. I could narrow it down for them.'

'Is that what you want?'

Dempsey thought for a second. It was something he and Maya had talked about without coming to any firm conclusion. 'No,' he said finally. 'He's obviously a hard bastard. But he saved my life and maybe even saved the Christian world. The Muslim world, too. He deserves a break.'

'So let's give him one. If he wants to confess his sins, he knows where to come.'

'Fair enough. Let's leave it at that, then.'

O'Malley took a deep breath and stretched his hand across the space between them. 'There's one more thing,' he said. 'I want to talk to you about your father.'